Don't Hate Me

Eden Emory

BEFORE YOU CONTINUE

This is not an accurate portrayal of the BDSM community, if you are curious and what to learn more please conduct your own research and do not rely on what you find in this book as accurate knowledge of the BDSM community, their etiquette, and their ways. Things in this book have been dramatized and are not an accurate reflection of reality or my personal thoughts and opinions on these matters.

ALSO BY EDEN EMORY

EDEN EMORY

The Ties That Bind Us

Don't Stop me

Don't Leave Me

Don't Forget Me

Don't Hate Me

Two of a Kind

Hide n' Seek

Queer Meet Cute Anthology

ELLE MAE

Blood Bound Series:

Contract Bound: A Lesbian Vampire Romance

Lost Clause

Other World Series:

An Imposter in Warriors Clothing

A Coward In A Kings Crown

Winterfell Academy Series:

The Price of Silence: Winterfell Academy Book 1

The Price of Silence: Winterfell Academy Book 2

The Price of Silence: Winterfell Academy Book 3

The Price of Silence: Winterfell Academy Book 4

The Price Of Silence: Winterfell Academy Book 5

Winterfell Series Box Set

Short and Smutty:

The Sweetest Sacrifice: An Erotic Demon Romance

Nevermore: A Deal with a Demon

Patreon Only

Wicked corruption: An FF Mafia Romance

Watch Me

Tales of the Stolen Demon Brides

For those who wanted to see Corky in Bound blush while being railed in front of a crowd.
You're welcome.

PROLOGUE

The cold barrel of the gun pushed against the back of my head, causing me to freeze.

I hadn't heard her move.

The fact that she snuck up on me caused a powerful heat to run through me.

Looks like the little agent still has some surprises to show me.

I took a deep, steadying breath, trying to calm down the excitement that was bubbling up inside of me.

A normal human would have been scared to find themselves with a gun pointed at their head, but I had been dreaming about this day. Dreaming about when she would finally shed that innocent mask of hers and show me the bloodthirsty, violent person she was below the surface.

I paused my rummaging through the nightstand to turn around and look at her.

Her face was hard. Lips smooshed into a thin line, eyebrows pushed together. She was angry. So angry that the hand that had once been so steady when pointing a gun to someone's face now shook.

Those brilliant green eyes showed the betrayal she didn't allow to be shown on her face.

I shouldn't have felt the thrill go through me like it did. Or allow myself to take her in like I did. But I couldn't help myself. From the moment I saw her on stage, I had been sucked so deep into the pools that there was no way possible to pull myself out.

Even now.

My training told me to disarm her and turn the gun on her instead.

Grab.

Twist.

Turn.

Shoot.

It was a motion I had done hundreds of times before. I could do it right then and end the entire job. But the anger in Blake's eyes, *god,* I needed to feel it.

She cocked the gun, though her finger was not resting on the trigger like it should have been when she found someone riffling through her stuff. Stuff that was obviously very incriminating. Stuff that she shouldn't want anyone to find.

She didn't want to kill me, but she would if I gave her no choice. It was clear in her face.

It caused me to shiver.

"You manipulated me," she whispered. Her voice did not betray the hurt I knew was lingering under her skin. A part of me felt bad that I was the cause of her hurt, but my excitement far outweighed it.

"What are you talking about, Blake?" I asked, feigning innocence. "Why are you pointing a gun at me?"

Her jaw clenched.

"Is this why you followed me?" she asked. "How much do you know? Did *he* send you? Tell you to fuck with my emotions like this?"

"I don't know—"

She pushed the gun straight into my forehead. The cool metal sent a violent bolt of electricity up my spine.

"Cut the bullshit, Quinn," she growled. "Tell me, or I swear to God I'll blow—"

I grabbed the gun and forced it upward to allow me to lunge at her. Blake was quick in her movements because of her training, but not quick enough.

I tangled a hand in her short locks while the other gripped her throat. I squeezed the sides letting her know exactly who was in charge. Her eyes widened, and for the first time, I saw fear flash across them.

I used to love seeing the fear in my target's face... *so why did it cause me to stall?*

It was enough of a mistake that she used her body weight to push us to the ground. She straddled my hips and brought the gun under my chin, tilting it up.

My hands flew to her hips. Heat flared through me when I realized that Blake had only put on a sleep shirt with nothing else underneath after our time together.

I was so turned on it was ridiculous.

"I'll ask you again," she said, though this time she was breathless. "Who the *fuck* are you?"

I held my breath as my hand trailed from her hip to her thigh.

Her breath hitched, and she pushed the gun harder against me.

"Maybe I should be asking you that," I said with a chuckle. "What have you been hiding from me, little agent?"

"Who sent you?" she asked again, though her tone was more of a plea than a demand.

"Does it make you feel powerful?" I asked, squeezing her thigh, my voice dropping low. "To have me immobilized here while you straddle me?"

She didn't stop my hand as it traveled up and brushed across the tuft of curls between her legs. Nor when I traveled the path from her clit into her wet cunt.

Her eyes narrowed at me.

"I could kill you."

I couldn't help the moan that spilled from my lips.

She could. She could pull the trigger right now, and my miserable existence would be over. At least it would mean that I wouldn't have to finish this job.

Something that should have been easy for me, but it turned complicated once I tasted her on my lips.

"Do it," I dared.

Her wetness dripped onto my fingers, and I used it to massage her clit.

Even in the darkness, I could see the familiar blush spread across her face.

"Are you not scared?" she asked. "One wrong move, and I could blow your brains out."

She let out a strangled moan when I forced two fingers inside her.

"This is the most turned-on I've been in my life," I admitted. "Keep the gun there while I fuck you. Better yet, force me to keep going until you can't come anymore."

I expected her to pull away, but yet again, Blake surprised me.

She lifted herself up just enough to allow my fingers better access. She leaned forward, putting a hand right beside my head. Her eyes were level with mine, and the grip of her gun stayed steady.

"I won't forget about this," she warned.

A wicked smile spread across my face.

"I hope not," I said in a teasing tone.

QUINN

Immobilize.
Swipe across the throat.
Drop.
Steal valuables.

Simple. It always has been. After so many years, my body moved on its own.

My steps were silent against the plush carpet as I stalked into the dim study. The curtains were closed save for a small opening that gave me a sneak peek at the shimmering night sky. It was just enough light for me to make out the room.

Luxurious imported furniture, lush carpets that perfectly conceal my approach. Shelves on either side of me shone with medals and awards, my masked reflecting catching off of a few of them.

And right in the middle, sat the target in his chair, his back toward me and his front facing the closed, dark red curtains. The only thing separating us was the mahogany desk between us.

The sounds of him fucking his secretary's throat rang through the room. He grunted and whispered something to her under his breath, but I couldn't quite make it out.

The rest of the room was dark—no doubt he wanted to keep

what was happening in here his dirty little secret all while his wife and kids were downstairs, none the wiser that his cock was being warmed by a person who had spent Christmas holidays with them. Her husband hadn't shown up tonight, and I didn't have to wonder why.

I hated people like them the most. Hated how little they manipulated the people around them just so they could get five minutes of pleasure. They thought they could do whatever. They thought no one would think twice, even as they destroyed their families.

But they were wrong. And I was here as Karma's messenger.

I had only caught a glimpse of her on their way in. I almost pitied him for being in the wrong place at such an awful time. He was a twisted, disgusting man, but he wasn't the reason I was here. If they hadn't snuck away, he may have had a chance to live.

But that pity only lasted a second. *I had a job to do.* Plus, her seeing this would only make that much more of an impact.

Light music filtered in from the hallway, a constant reminder that I had but ten minutes before our next interruption. Guards, not just from the man, but many of the other important businessmen lying in wait for any hint of danger. Voices and laughter from below floated up the stairs, only to be muffled by the doors and drowned out by their noises.

I fixed the mask on the lower half of my face and readied the heavy knife in my hand.

The party downstairs provided the perfect cover for me to sneak in. My name for the night was Tara Knight, but no one even bothered to check my ID as I walked in with the confidence of everyone else there that night.

But in all honesty, if they had, it wouldn't have stopped me anyway.

The shrill ringing of his phone caused him to jump in his chair. I paused in my steps as he scrambled to dig his phone from his pocket.

"Foster?" he asked with a slightly out-of-breath tone. I caught sight of him pushing down the girl's head.

Her gagging filled the air. His hips bucked in the chair, causing the seat to squeak.

A muffled voice filtered through the phone.

"What?" he asked. "I hadn't seen anyone come up here besides me."

Alarm bells went off in my head. *Had I been careless?* I had already managed to lose the eyes of his main men, but did he have plain-clothed ones that I hadn't managed to see?

That would be a first. I may have just come back from an international stint, but I wasn't *careless*.

"Okay, I'll leave in just a moment. Just let me—hurry up, sweetheart. We have to get out of here."

Disgust filled me. *Well, better now than never.*

"That's right—*ah*. Take it like a good girl, and I'll get you that purse you wanted."

As soon as he placed the phone back in his pocket, I lunged over the desk and sliced my knife across his throat with the same precision I kept with all my kills. Blood splattered all over the woman in front of him and on my clothing and mask. His body jerked against me as he fought the inevitable.

It only took a few seconds before his body went limp, the woman was too shocked at what she had seen to process what she should do next. She froze, her hand still on his cock and her mouth just centimeters away from his head.

It happened so fast that she didn't even have the time to realize she was now holding a dead man's cock.

"Scream, and I'll kill you," I warned as I met her widened hazel eyes.

She scrambled backward, the understanding of what just happened finally dawning on her. Her mouth flopped open in horror, a scream building. I gave her a look.

"Quiet," I reminded her, holding a single finger to my clothed lips.

Her hand was shaky as she brought it up to her mouth. All the color left her face, and she looked like she was about to—her body convulsed as the vomit all but launched from her mouth.

She had just enough time to turn to the side before it got all over that sparkly dress of hers that no doubt cost whatever this old bastard was paying her a good chunk of money.

With quick movements, I placed my hands on the hard surface, then swung myself over the desk and landed right in front of her. This time, she jumped away and didn't try to stop the bloodcurdling scream that fell from her lips.

My free hand shot forward to grab her by the throat and manually stop her scream.

"Ah, ah, *ah*," I whispered, unable to clamp down the small burst of excitement building in my chest. "What did I say about screaming?"

Tears fell from her eyes and a voiceless "please" fell from her lips. I had the urge to pull my hand away so I could hear her begging, but wouldn't risk her scream.

"Things don't look good for you," I whispered. "First you fuck this low life, then you ruin my plans. You couldn't have just gone for some fresh air, hm? Or maybe taken some time to yourself in the bathroom? Now I'm gonna have to jump out a fucking window because you thought sucking his cock would be better."

She made a noise in the back of her throat that sounded a lot like a "please," but it came out more like a gurgle.

"Don't you feel bad about what you did to his family?" I asked, tilting my head. "He has kids, a wife, could you really look at them while sitting at the dinner table all while knowing had his cock in your mouth just moments prior?"

She was panicking. I could see it in her eyes. How they widened. How they darted from me to the dead man behind me. She was trying to think of a way to save herself.

"No," I murmured, my eyes searching her face. Her eyes gave no indication that she felt bad about what she was doing. "I don't think you care that his kids will grow up without a father and that all the debt he had accrued because of you is now the responsibility of his widow, do you?"

I shot a look back at the man who was currently slumped over in the chair. He was a corrupt state treasurer who got a bit too handsy, not my usual target. But *her*...

I sent the girl a smile, though I'm sure it looked more sinister with the blood splattered across my mask.

I brought my bloodied knife to her cheek causing her to let out a fearful squeak.

"You had it all and threw it away for someone who wouldn't even buy you the Mercedes you wanted," I mused. "Your kids? Your husband? Forget any career in government after this. Men may be able to get away with affairs without imploding their careers, but you got the short end of the stick, my dear." I ended my sentence with a light chuckle.

I couldn't help myself. The excitement from the kill was already setting in, and I could easily imagine just how beautiful the woman in front of me would look with her own blood staining her skin.

And those eyes... they were calling to me.

I let the edge of my knife trail her lower lashes. *Just one slip, and they would be mine.*

Heavy footsteps sounded from the hallway beyond.

Damn.

"Your husband says hi," I told her. "How about you stay in his bed next time, hm?"

Without another word, I threw the sobbing woman to the ground and headed for the windows. I pushed it open without hesitation, only pausing when the cold night air hit my face. A sigh escaped my lips.

Beautiful night.

The stars twinkled in the light as if to let me know that even though the curtains were drawn, they all saw what I had done in there.

I swung my legs over the sill with a smile and jumped.

The door being broken down and the scream from the bloodied woman muffled my fall from the third-story window.

I had worn extra-padded shoes just in case, but they did nothing for me.

With a grunt, I pushed myself off the ground and made an exit for the parked cars in the back. I took deep breaths, letting the cool night air sing my throat and lungs. It helped me keep focused though the pain.

I was limping by the time I got to the parking lot, but I didn't let it slow me down.

There's a car waiting for me. By the time they start searching the place, I will be long gone.

That had been the third job I'd had since coming back to the States. Previously, I had been in France, Tokyo, and Germany for the last two years completing jobs.

I enjoyed the time spent traveling, but as I looked up at the night sky, I couldn't help but feel relieved that I had finally made it back home after so long.

The limp became less of an issue as I crossed the grounds. I made sure to stay in the shadows as people rushed around the perimeter of the property. The thuds of their booted footsteps filling the night air.

No one had sounded the alarm yet. He may have been found, along with his mistress, but my guess was that they didn't want to alarm the over three hundred guests that were packed in the house.

That would be just a bad PR move.

The car was parked inconspicuously by the exit of the lot, giving me a perfect getaway. I looked around at the various other vehicles, making sure none of them had any witnesses. I caught one on the other side rocking as two people inside got it on, but they were far too busy with themselves to bother with me.

I let out a chuckle under my breath as I slipped into the car. *A job well done.* In and out without so much as a double take. The jobs in the States seemed to be much easier than what I had been handling in other countries.

Or so I thought until the cold barrel of a gun was pushed to the back of my head. My entire body froze, thinking of all the ways I could disarm the person. My eyes shot to the rearview mirror, but all I saw was a shadow.

"Getting sloppy." The gruff voice of my handler came from the back.

Instead of relief, violent anger filled me.

Without responding to him, I checked for the keys, opening the visors and the small compartment between the seats.

"Looking for these?" he asked, his gloved hand reaching from the back seat and into my line of vision. The car keys sparkled in his hand.

Finally, I turned to look at him.

Rolf, last name unknown even after all the years I had worked with him.

His face was wrinkled but his eyes were sharp. He was dressed in all black and melted into the darkness of the back seat. His blue eyes dug into mine, the emotion in them clear.

He was enjoying one-upping me. He always did. Liked to remind me that no matter how good I was at my job, he was better.

Sirens echoed around the place, cutting whatever time we had left in half.

I reached for the keys, but he jerked his hand away at the last moment.

"What do you want?" I spat.

His laugh filled the small space.

If there wasn't a gun to my head, I would have finally made good on my promise to kill him after all these years. He thought that I had come to care for him in the years we were together and that it saved him from my wrath.

But he was wrong.

I could care for someone and still kill them. One day, he would be my proof.

"I have a job for you."

"I have to finish this one first," I reminded him. "Now give me the keys."

He slapped the keys into my hand but pushed the gun against my head as a reminder to not fuck this up.

"Then you better hurry," he said. "'Cause this one starts tonight."

How the fuck did I get roped into a job in a sex club?

There were many other agents who could do something like this. Someone who specialized in seduction and not high-profile murders.

So what gives?

"I sent in your profile a few months ago, and it took them some time, but you got approved. I would have sent you in right away, but well, Germany was more important at the time," he said. "They take this kind of thing very seriously, so we are being more cautious this time around. I've heard that their owners are no strangers to breaking the law and got out of prison a few years back."

Strange, but not totally surprising.

"So stay away from them," I said, letting my gaze travel over the club.

It was a multi-story mansion with large gates surrounding the entire property. The front yard alone was probably about an acre, and from our vantage point, I caught a glimpse into the back. There weren't many people out at that time. My guess was that they were still prepping the back for some type of outdoor concert.

"This is their newest club," Rolf said from behind me. "They're still working on it but have just started to allow more guests in to visit. It's also less... jarring than the other. This one has stricter rules and a recommended dress code. Which you will be expected to follow."

His footsteps were silent as he came closer. I didn't let myself jerk away from him even though I wanted to.

Could an assassin just have a single night off? Was that too much to ask for?

I let out a small huff and leaned into the tree next to me. We had taken cover in the small forest a few blocks away from the house-turned-club. The wooded area was up on the hill, which gave us an unobstructed view of the club. I used my binoculars to take a closer look at the security.

Exhaustion from the job before weighed on me. I could still feel the blood drying underneath my clothes and itching my skin.

Not only was the outside packed, but for at least another two blocks, I caught suspicious-looking men stationed out on various street corners. Some even hid in their cars.

That's a lot of men for a sex club.

"There's someone important in there," I noted.

"Multiple someone's," Rolf said, his voice coming from right beside me. I knew better than to react to it.

I lowered my binoculars to give him a look. I was still pissed about his stunt in the car.

It was a valuable reminder to be vigilant, but that didn't mean I had to forgive him just yet.

"There has to be someone better for this."

He shrugged and fished a phone from his pocket. I took it from him and entered my agent ID, not surprised that it is unlocked.

In minutes, hundreds of case files were at my fingertips. I scrolled through them, trying to glean as much information as I could in the short amount of time he allowed me to procrastinate up on the hill.

Something went off in my mind when I saw the application Rolf submitted on my behalf. It was an old picture of me when my hair was much shorter. I remember taking this picture for a separate mission, but that wasn't what threw me off.

It was the fact that they used my real name. Sharp stabs of betrayal hit my chest. It took more effort than I'd like to admit to keep my face straight.

"Tiffany Yates," he said in a low voice. "At the age of twenty, she was one of the youngest to be hired as a secret service agent. She had been recently reassigned to Senator Bennett, an unforeseen problem you will have to work around. Before this, she was on former President Grant's wife—"

"I can get that from the file," I said. His stare caused my skin to burn. "Why her? Who put the hit out?"

Rolf stayed silent for a few moments before his blue gaze ran over me.

When I was younger, the sharpness of his gaze would scare me. It had taken years of being his ward to realize that no matter how dangerous Rolf was, he would never hurt me.

At least not enough to kill me.

He too was alone in this world, and I would like to think that he thought of me as family. Or at least an extension of himself.

Someone worth protecting.

"Someone who needs information," he finally said. "Page seventy-two."

I looked back at the phone to find what he was referencing.

My eyes widened when I saw the name on the screen.

Alec Crowe.

There wasn't much that spooked me in this world. But that man... I had made it my goal to never cross paths with that psychopath again.

He started out as a low-level gangster, but over the span of just three years, he had annihilated two bigger gangs in the area and consumed them. He was something more akin to a small warlord than a gang leader.

His men were now in the thousands, and they specialized in the trafficking of nuclear weapons. Many of which had made it across borders. This person wasn't one to fuck with. If he were involved, it would automatically make this one of the most dangerous missions I have been on.

Sure, I had killed heirs and heiresses, upcoming world leaders at times, but they all worked in the light and paid people to do the dirty work. Alec was darkness himself. And someone who was so accustomed to it would let nothing get in his way.

"He's the client?" I asked.

When he didn't respond, a sinking feeling filled my gut. If I had a choice, I'd want to be on the man's side, doing some type of dirty work for him instead of going against him.

"What does a secret service agent know about him?" I asked.

Again, no answer.

"Why does she have so much attention on her?" I asked. "I thought the agents were supposed to be the ones with the entourage. Isn't it strange how many people are watching her? Regardless of who she's watching?"

"She's important, that's all you need to know," he said, his tone warning me that I was on the verge of pissing him off. "She frequents this club, gives her team the slip. Many think she's going to the gym or is out drinking. She hadn't reported that she has a longer-term sexual partner, so the assumption *was* that she has many one-night stands, but if my intel is correct, she is actually seeing someone right now. Has been for some time but is rarely seen out with them."

"And where does this intel come from?" I asked. "Someone in the club? Maybe they can do this instead."

This was far out of the norm for me. Enough to make me slightly uncomfortable.

"Are you ungrateful for this opportunity, agent?" The lowering of his voice caused something inside me to shift.

"No, sir," I spat out.

"Good," he said, his voice notably lighter. "Because she has someone at her side, it will be hard to get to her. I expect you to figure something out."

"So you want me to kill the partner and seduce the agent. Got it."

Rolf let out a sigh and shook his head.

"If you must, but this is one of the only places she frequents that isn't crawling with agents," he said. "There is a rumor about her having access to a USB drive that contains some... *harmful* information. If you can find it and bring it back, all the better. If not, force the information from her and put a bullet in her head. When you're done, leave her body someplace visible. For her partner, on the other hand, just try not to make it too obvious. A disappearance would be easier to work around than a murder."

I gritted my teeth and sped through a couple of the documents. I paused when I caught sight of her.

She had the most brilliant green eyes. Ones that looked so expressive, even in the professional headshot they had attached.

I made the mistake of letting my finger brush across them. The other woman's eyes had tempted me, but Tiffany's were much more than a simple temptation. I *needed* them. More than I needed this job. More than I needed the security of it.

Hell, I would shoot Rolf right now if it meant that I could have them.

"You can take them," Rolf said, causing a flurry of heat to run through me. "The client doesn't care much about the state she ends up in, just that it's done."

His permission to take those beautiful orbs was enough to send a bolt of excitement through me. Maybe he did it on purpose. To somehow make it more enticing to put myself in this situation.

Well, it fucking worked.

"Should I get her fired?" I asked. "Maybe even kill off the senator?"

"Don't touch him," Rolf barked out. My head snapped toward him, the sudden change in his voice putting me on edge.

Something passed through his features. Something I had learned to recognize as fear... but that couldn't be right. Rolf didn't "fear" on my behalf.

He was probably worried I would fuck this up and cause too much attention to our organization.

"Work *around* him, agent," he ordered. "If I find you meddling in his affairs, there will be hell to pay."

I gritted my teeth to stop myself from saying what I really wanted to.

"You got it, *sir.*"

Rolf kicked the duffel bag on the ground toward me.

"Get dressed, and don't forget the mask," he said. "We expect this to be a longer-term job, so get comfortable and expect more work to come your way."

I couldn't keep the snort inside. *We* meaning the invisible organization behind Rolf. The organization I could have no contact with. Something the others dubbed "*the* guild". Now *they* wanted me to take on this shitty job while also reaping the benefits of my being back in the States.

"I thought this was important. Shouldn't I give it all my attention instead of splitting it with other jobs?"

Rolf shook his head and let out a laugh.

"You and I both know you'll get bored," he said. "You should be thanking me."

"I'll be thanking you when you let me add to my collection."

He paused for a moment before sighing.

"*Fine.*"

Giddiness burst through my chest.

"You're being rather nice to me, Rolf," I said with a smile. "Should I be worried about what awaits me in there?"

He shook his head. "Nothing you can't handle. But truly, no one else is suited for this job. Both the client and I have full faith that you—and only you—will be able to complete this. Don't let us down."

I bent down in an exaggerated bow before grabbing the duffel bag.

"You won't regret this," I said, snapping back up and throwing the bag over my shoulder.

"That's not a thank you—"

"Thank you!" I called back as I turned on my heels and headed straight to the club that was lighting up the dark night.

Maybe this would turn out well for me.

BLAKE

Something unexpected twisted in my stomach when I saw the message come in.

The phone was on the floor, lighting up the darkness of the room, but it was close enough to make out the messages that were coming in.

I miss you, Blake.

I didn't have time to grab for my phone before the next one came in.

Meet me in our room later? I'll even schedule a match if you want.

Rough hands grabbed my hips, forcing me back onto the fake cock. I let out a cry and pushed my face into the soft comforter below us. A mix of pain and pleasure spread throughout my body.

My pussy was swollen and aching from being abused, but it made each and every orgasm after that so much more powerful.

"When you're with me, I expect your full attention, baby girl," Payton cooed from behind me.

I arched into her, needing her to fuck me harder. My skin was on fire. My pussy clenching around the fake cock. But still, it wasn't enough to push me over the edge again.

I didn't need to tell her what to do. Payton shifted behind me and used my hips as leverage to drive into me. The cock she picked was oddly shaped, with ribbing on all sides. One I had never tried before, but I made a note to add it to my personal arsenal.

The ribbing rubbed against my G-spot, causing my toes to curl and my legs to stiffen. My body was turning into soft molten lava as the heat from her movement swirled inside me.

Fuck I needed this. I didn't realize how badly I needed to get fucked until I was almost at Payton's feet, begging for it. I was so desperate, it was embarrassing. Normally I would have liked a bit of degradation, but not being able to get off when it was something I was known for, was just downright pitiful.

Payton was an odd choice for me. Usually I would stick with the other performers if I needed to get off or, in a desperate moment, call Bailey. But it had been weeks since I had a good fucking, and it's not like Bailey would do it for me.

I regretted slowing down my performances for Bailey. I regretted a lot about getting involved with her. I wanted so badly to make it work. I thought I was ready. Thought I could handle all that came with having a relationship again... but I was wrong.

At first, I was enamored by her. I remember telling Sloan, my closest friend in the club, once just how much I wanted her. I had never let a single person to derail me so completely from my normal schedule, and now I was paying the price.

To Bailey, we were in an open relationship. One with limitations around my performances and who I fucked. She didn't want anyone outside of the club because, at least then, she could know who I was fucking.

To me, she was a disappointing and controlling fuck who didn't know when to end things. I had tried hinting at it so many times. Tried to *gently* let her know that performing and having sex were two big parts of me that I didn't want to give up.

But she was... unhappy whenever I mentioned it. And whenever she was unhappy, the entire club would know about it.

That was what sucked about being here so often, I couldn't get away from her even if I tried. What was once my safe space was starting to turn into something else entirely.

I don't know when her captivating brown eyes and easy smile turned into narrowed eyes and a scowl. Or when her easy-going personality started to turn controlling. It had happened slowly over the last few months, changing until I didn't even recognize her anymore.

What was even worse was how *boring* the sex had gotten. She was good with her fingers, but that was about it. She never liked using toys or trying anything new.

At first, I didn't think it was an issue. As long as I got off, I was happy. But the longer I was with her, the more it started to bother me.

I didn't pretend like I was a good person. I knew I wasn't. I knew I was only making it worse by not being able to put my foot down.

I was going to have to break it off soon. And if I couldn't entice her to leave, I would have to force her hand.

Hence, Payton.

I forced myself to look back at her, taking in her wild smile and hooded hazel eyes. Even in the darkness, I could make out the tattoos that littered her skin. Her hair was damp and sticking to her face after our many rounds.

Unlike me, she had torn her mask off long ago. She didn't follow the rules much, but it wasn't like Ax and Sloan would kick her out. She was somewhat of a celebrity.

A sort of performer, but of the musical kind.

It wasn't often that she came here, looking for a lay, but I just happened to be in the right place at the right time. And *god,* was I grateful for it.

At the first hint of my orgasm on the horizon, I froze. Payton noticed right away, of course, and instead of keeping her pace, she slowed, chasing away my orgasm in a painful fashion.

"Please, Payton," I whined.

"Please what?" she asked with a throaty chuckle. "Gotta be more specific, or I may just think you're asking me to stop altogether."

I fisted the comforter under, arching for her.

"Please let me come," I begged.

Payton's mouth opened as if she were going to speak, but then her eyes were torn from me and to the phone on the floor.

"Someone missing you, baby girl?" she asked. The seriousness in her tone caused me to snap my attention to the phone as well.

I was ready to see Bailey's face flash across the screen, but instead it was the one person I *really* didn't want to hear about in that moment.

I cursed under my breath and crawled forward. The strap-on was pulled out of me painfully, but I couldn't even give it a reaction. Not when *he* was calling me.

What did I fucking do to deserve this?

I reached forward, grabbing the phone, and took a deep breath.

"Don't you fucking speak," I warned Payton.

She let out a laugh behind me as if she wasn't at all bothered about my order. I wouldn't be surprised if she wasn't. I envied how much she just didn't care about anything.

"Hello? Sir, is there something—"

"Tomorrow, my office. Nine a.m. sharp, agent." The familiar voice of my boss broke through the speaker.

Shit. I hit my closed fist against my head. *Shit. Shit. Shit. Shit.*

"Sir, whatever it is, I can explain—"

"You can explain tomorrow," he growled. "You better be in my office before I am, or you can kiss your badge goodbye."

He hung up on me without a warning. I looked at the phone with a sigh. There were also three new messages from Bailey.

What's this I hear about you with Payton?

Blake, answer me.

We talked about this.

Hands gripped my legs and flipped me over. I let out a gasp, and Payton lowered herself between my legs.

"Sounds like someone's in trouble," she sang, her breath hot on my swollen pussy. Sharp zaps of pleasure worked themselves through my core, expanding out into my belly and thighs.

"What did you hear?" I asked.

"Hear?" she asked, sending me a grin. "I don't know what you're talking about. I didn't hear anything."

"Keep it that way." I tangled my hand in her hair. "I have to go soon."

She dragged her tongue up the length of my slit, causing a powerful shudder to work itself through me.

"Let's forget about the world outside tonight, Blake," she said before pulling my clit into her mouth.

I shouldn't have let my head fall back. Shouldn't have ridden her mouth until I came so hard I was sure people in the room overheard my cries. And I sure as hell shouldn't have ignored Bailey while I did the same exact thing to Payton.

The slamming of files down caused me to jump.

Breathe in.

Breathe out.

Try not to let the urge to shoot this fucker in the head take over.

At first, I had been worried about being called into the corporate head office, but now I was just annoyed.

DC was beautiful, but it had been three hours since I sat my sore ass down on those stupid plastic chairs they had in the waiting room. Apparently, because of this meeting, I wasn't able to wander around like how I normally would and was instead forced to sit outside and wait to be called on like a kid being punished by their principal.

Though this didn't feel that much different.

Ross, my boss, was a man past his prime who still held onto his position with an iron grip. I didn't hate the dude, not in the slightest. What I felt toward him was more like... an annoyed indifference.

Especially when he was treating *me*, one of his best agents, like a child.

It was no secret that I was good at my job. Even in the less important jobs that I had been in, I always found myself with glowing performance reviews from both colleagues and clients.

And it wasn't like that just because I had a natural affinity for this job.

I worked my ass off. Every morning, if I wasn't hitting the gym, I was going for a run. I kept myself in peak physical condition while also making sure to hone my skills.

So being called in like I was in trouble for something didn't sit right with me.

"It's been all but two weeks since you started with Senator Bennett," my boss growled. "Why am I hearing about late-night excursions?"

My ears burned. *Shit.*

And here I thought he had called me for something unnecessary. *This is a hundred times worse than what I thought it was.* I had tried my best to be careful about being unseen, especially when I wanted to go out to the club. My job and life depended on it.

It had been easier when I was working with the former president's wife. More relaxed. They were both in their eighties, and no one cared too much about them anymore. But with Senator Bennett's bid for president, I guess the surveillance was doubled, and not just for the man and his family.

I could easily lie it off. Tell them some made-up story... but honestly, some version of the truth may be the safest bet. As long as I didn't spill about Bailey, I would be fine.

Because of my *situation* and my role in the agency, each long-term partner I had was required to go through a background check and their name would forever be next to mine on some file.

And it's not that I hadn't been having fun with Bailey, especially when it first started out, but I just wasn't ready to take that step. It was a serious one that needed serious consideration. Something that didn't seem worth it with Bailey.

Jesus, can you sound any more like an asshole?

"Honestly, sir... I go out to get laid," I said after a moment.

My boss's entire face pinched before he let out a loud sigh and fell back into his chair. He face had a brush or red on his cheeks and tips of his ears. He looked out of the window, obviously trying to collect himself. It had been six years since I joined the Secret Service. Four of those years had been under this boss, and never once had we had an issue.

But that was because I had never been surveilled in such a way before, so now he was about to know things about me that he wished he never had.

Everything besides this, I had been painfully honest with him about. My situation. My home life. My fears. All of it helped me convince him to keep me out of sight and on the less important projects.

Until now. He turned back to me with a bunched facial expression.

"Can you at least be more discreet?" he asked, his voice exasperated. "I'm no fool, and neither is the team. I get that agents have... needs, but just do so quietly, got it?"

I nodded. "Yes, sir."

Though what I really wanted to say was, *"I thought I was."*

When I didn't move, he looked up at me with a raised brow.

I shifted on my feet. I had been planning to bring this up to him for a while now, and I guess now was as good a time as any, though I wished it was under a less humiliating circumstance.

"I don't want to seem ungrateful for this opportunity..."

"Not a great way to start off the conversation, then."

I winced. *God, this is already embarrassing enough.*

"You and I are both aware of my... *situation*," I said, lowering my voice. "Working with the senator is a great opportunity, but just...why did you—"

"Put you in a place so visible?" he finished for me.

I nodded. *Not just visible. There's a fucking spotlight on me.* If I didn't know any better, I would say he was trying to sabotage me. Even the house speaker was pushing it, but this fucker was going to be televised soon, meaning there was a chance I would be too.

He let out a sigh, his eyes trailing to the window. I followed his gaze. It wasn't often I made the trip to DC, but every time I found myself falling more and more in love with the city.

The cherry blossoms, the environment, and people.

I wondered if one day I too could be in an office like this. To lean back in my chair and look at the cherry blossoms falling in the wind outside instead of constantly being on edge with one hand on the trigger.

But it was a fool's dream, and more than once I had to bring myself back to the reality of the situation I was in. There would never be a time when I would be anything more than an invisible foot soldier. It was safer that way.

"You're good at your job," he said after a moment. "I thought it would be good for your career."

I swallowed thickly, waiting for him to finish. When he didn't, I said, "But you know I can't have one. Not with my past. Being here is more than I could have ever asked for. And to Senator Bennett of all people?"

Senator Bennett was known to love the spotlight. In just the few weeks I had been with him, there had been five manufactured situations that caused reporters to flock to his door. More than once, I had to sneak in the back.

"He won't win," he said, and he looked at me with a small smile. The wrinkles near his eyes deepened and caused me to relax enough to give him a smile back. "It's temporary. Do this well, and you have a bright future ahead of you. You'll be out of sight for anything televised and with his family most of the time. I didn't put you here without thinking of the risk, trust me. I wouldn't harm you like that."

I nodded. There was nothing else I could say. If he said he thought it all through, then I had to believe him... *right?*

He had never once put me in harm's way before, *so why would it start now?*

But after a lifetime surrounded by liars and letdowns, I couldn't help the feeling that this was all a setup. That the only reason they wanted me in the spotlight was not because of how good I was at my job but because they had grown tired of me and wanted to get rid of me once and for all.

I gritted my teeth and pushed those thoughts into the recesses of my mind. *Take a step back and realize that for once, someone is just looking out for you.*

I took a deep breath and held it for a moment.

"Thank you," I said, releasing the breath I had been holding. "You know, just after so many years, I can't help but feel anxious about it all."

He nodded, though if I was being honest, even after the breath, the anxiety still had a chokehold on me.

"Unfortunately, it's also what makes you good at your job," he reminded me. He sat up straight, his eyes shooting toward the door behind me and then back to my face. "Just be more secretive when you go out, okay? Shift changes are usually around seven thirty and one forty-five—*don't* tell anyone I told you that."

I took a step back and sent him a smile. Even with all of the awful feelings that put me on edge, this was a small kindness I couldn't look over. The club and the people there meant more to me than anything.

It was my place. My home. Somewhere that I could finally be *me* without having to worry about any of my past following me.

"Thank you again, sir," I said, this time with a sincerity I hope he felt.

He huffed but didn't say anything else as he waved me off.

I took a moment to dismiss myself before leaving and shutting the door softly behind me. Only then did I let out a relieved sigh.

"Thank *God*."

My eyes caught a man who was sitting on the chair I once occupied, and quickly I schooled my expression. Heat traveled up my ears and face, causing the embarrassment that was flooding me to only intensify under the man's gaze.

Well, at least I had the club to look forward to tonight. Whether Bailey liked it or not, I was going to perform.

QUINN

O ver twenty years in my role with more kills than I could count, and the thing that would do me in was the stifling suit I was forced to wear to the damned sex club.

Not from any of the hundreds of missions I've been on. Or a poetic ending at the hands of someone out for revenge.

No.

A fucking suit that made me look like an idiot. Whatever Rolf had in mind for this job, it all hung on whether or not the target would even look twice at me, and I had serious doubts that *the fucking suit* would get the job done.

Stop being so salty about the job and just get it done, my inner voice hissed at me.

There was more than one reason why I wasn't happy about this job. Not just that I had just come from a job, but I was still mad that Rolf had to one-up me in the car.

I had a sneaking suspicion that this job was his way of reeling me back in. To remind me that I couldn't just go off and steal the eyeballs of my targets or go off and cause mass political scandals.

At least he sweetened the deal for you, I reminded myself. Not all handlers treated their assassins as well as he had with me. If any other assassin had given their handler even an ounce of the sass I had, they would most definitely be shipped back to the guild's headquarters for *"retraining"*. I had been lucky to only have to endure that punishment once in my life, but it was enough so that I'd never want to go through it again.

With a clenched jaw, I pulled at the fabric and walked toward the entrance. The men at the doors didn't even bother to check my ID as I strolled in. They saw what I was wearing, paired with the mask, and that was all the answer they needed.

Gullible, just like most of the "guards" I've seen in these types of places. Maybe this would be over faster than I thought.

Club Pétale, to those who had the privilege of knowing it, was a haven for all those looking to get in touch with the dark, depraved versions of themselves. It was made to be a high-class version of a sex club that invited all non-men, including but not limited to: women, genderqueer, transgender, and non-binary people only.

On top of that, all the patrons had to go through an extensive application process before being accepted. Even after the application process, there was no guarantee that you would be accepted.

Getting in here was short of a miracle, especially with the shitty application they submitted on my behalf.

I wanted to say I got lucky, but I never believed in luck.

Karma on the other hand was a constant in my life. I had not wanted to believe it, but time and time again, for my targets *and* myself, karma always decided to show its ugly little face as a reminder of its existence.

Like forcing me into a sex club.

It was like all the recklessness I had shown aboard came back to bite me right in the ass.

The first thing that hit me when I walked through the clubs' large double doors was the light floral scent wafting through the house. It mingled with the stench of arousal that was so strong in the air it caused my throat to tighten.

I had seen the blueprints of the place on the way over, but nothing prepared me for what it looked like filled with people.

The large, elegant house had been decorated with blacks, whites, and even some gold here and there. A huge glittering chandelier hung from the ceiling, and there were blown-up pictures hung up on almost every free space showcasing all different types of erotic acts.

My eyes lingered on one with a girl's tongue lapping up the other's pussy.

"Welcome, name please."

My gaze was brought to the little woman that stood before me smiling brightly with an iPad in her hand. She wore a floor-length deep-red gown with nothing underneath.

"Reilly," I said with a light smile, though the use of my real last name felt wrong.

Applicants had their choice of names, and not only did Rolf put my government-given name on the fucking application, but the fake name that was *supposed* to protect my identity while in the clubs' walls was actually my real last name.

For years, I was forced to use my agent number to identify myself, or on the occasion I was going undercover, I would use something like Alex or River. Something that had nothing to do with who I was.

It was easier that way. *Safer.*

This felt like they were throwing me to the wolves. Even after everything I had done for them.

It was hard not to feel even the least bit betrayed.

Karma. You decided to push their boundaries the last two years and this is what you get. It was hard not to huff and puff and stomp my feet like an upset toddler.

The girl didn't bat an eyelash as she took in the information. I was probably one of three hundred that night. Just another faceless person in the crowd. She typed a few things into her iPad, and without another word, she stepped to the side and waved me in.

"If you need a tour guide, let me know," she said with a wink.

"There is an open bar to your right, a coat closet to your left, and farther in are the showrooms. Feel free to enter any one of them, though rooms need to be reserved. If you would like to match with someone for the night, please make sure to fill it out on the website or app before coming in as we cannot guarantee a same day match. Also if you have a phone, please leave it here."

"I didn't bring it," I said before stepping into the main room. My eyes lingered on the bar. As much as I hated being even the slightest bit off my game for a job, the urge to down some vodka was getting stronger by the second.

There were fewer people than I thought, though having them all in a concentrated area drinking, laughing, and leaning into each other caused my mind to go into overdrive. The instinct was to catalog all of them. To take in their expressions, what they were wearing, who they were with. But I couldn't make out any of that.

Not with most of them wearing masks. Even with my mask on, I felt so exposed. I didn't belong here, and there was someone —probably more than one—that had seen what I truly looked like *and* knew my name.

But everyone else in here was awarded a luxury, even though I wasn't. They could mingle, get fucked, ruin their lives, all while under the protection of the mask and fake name. To them, that was enough.

To me, this was suicide.

It made it worse when many turned to look at me as I walked in. My mind told me to be on guard. That maybe they were looking at me because they knew who I truly was... but realistically, I knew that wasn't the case.

This is the anxiety of being in an unknown place, logic told me. I was all too aware of *why* I was feeling what I was, but knowing the emotions and where they came from didn't stop me from feeling them.

Focus on the mission.

I had been in there less than a minute, but the longer I stood, the more attention was drawn to me.

I forced my gaze to wander. I caught a few people not wearing masks—workers I assumed based on the file—but none of them were who I was looking for.

Stage six. Main performer.

I was shocked to hear that someone like her was willing to get up on stage, but there was little description of what went on in these rooms, so maybe it wasn't all that bad. Tiffany Yates seemed like a well-adjusted woman who grew up in an affluent family. She stayed at home all throughout college before graduating early and joining the Secret Service. That was what the files told me, at least.

Maybe this was her way of getting out of her comfort zone. A way of rebelling against her parents after all those years of being the *perfect* daughter.

I braced myself to see her in a revealing outfit, maybe dancing on stage. Something that would give her just enough of a thrill to make that stuffy secret service job seem not so bad. A way to let out all the pent-up feelings she had.

It took me a moment to collect myself, but that moment was enough to cause even more people to stare. To them, they saw a random person hanging by the entrance, looking like they didn't know why they were here.

And to be truthful, they would be right, but I didn't want the extra attention.

I pushed into the house, nodding at the people who continued to stare, though most looked away when they realized I wasn't there to mingle. It gave me great comfort to know that even in a place like this, people would shy away from me.

Humans could feel the darkness inside me. They may not be aware of it, but it was almost instinctual. Like the part of them that was trying to keep them safe was setting off the alarm bells when they caught on to what I was hiding.

Which was why it would have been much better to get someone in who was better at seduction than I was. They would fit right in, move through the crowd with ease. They would flirt, party, and then finish the job.

But there I was, sticking out like a sore thumb and hoping desperately that I wouldn't scare away the target.

Soft music flitted through the air, hiding the light conversations of the people around us. It wasn't hard to get past the main crowd and to the back rooms. The entire hall on both sides had darkened rooms that patrons could duck in and out of. The music was softer there, and it allowed the moans to filter out of the rooms.

Loud moans. I had the strangest urge to peek my head into one to see what all the fuss was about. Especially when I heard a loud scream.

"Fuck it," I hissed under my breath and peeked into the first room.

My breath caught in my throat, and my heart hammered against my ribs when I saw a woman suspended upside down and two people on either side of her. She was mostly clothed, though the big wet spot on her underwear showed exactly what had happened to cause her to scream like she did.

*I thought this was supposed to be **less** intense than the main house. If this was what they did here, what the hell did they do there?*

I shook my head and left the room quickly, needing to get my head back in the game.

Every thought I had about this being a normal performance left my mind as I walked into her room.

It was dark save for the light on their small stage. Comfy-looking chairs were spaced out in front of it with quite a few occupied.

She's quite popular, it looks like.

On the stage was a girl with short brown hair and a black mask. She was hogtied and writhing on the ground in tight latex bra and underwear. The stage was slightly higher than the chairs and gave the people watching a perfect view, but even if they somehow missed it, there were screens on either side of the stage. One showed her pleasure-ridden face, the other her swollen and wet cunt. The latex was so tight, you could make out the folds of her pussy. Wetness leaked from the sides of her tight underwear and fell to the ground.

There was a woman off to the side, but I ignored her completely, too focused on the girl on the floor.

Her legs were bound behind her and forced wide open, showing the bulbous vibrator that had been tied to her inner thigh with rope and lying directly on her clit. There was a puddle beneath her, and by the looks of how she writhed, she had already had more than a few orgasms in front of these people.

If it wasn't for the job, I would have left as soon as I saw her.

Or at least that's what I told myself as I took a seat near the middle. I didn't quite understand how she did it, but with each moan from her mouth, I became even further and further entranced.

She wasn't just up there dancing for people. She was exposing herself in ways I never even dared to. Having them watch as she came over and over again. Having them watch her as she made a complete and utter mess of herself.

Yet she still somehow lies on the ground begging for more.

"Oh fuck!" tumbled out of her mouth as she arched into the feeling. She was begging under her breath for something... but what was it? The more I watched her, the more I longed to know.

But not just what she was begging for... I wanted to know everything that file had kept from me. Wanted to know why she would do *this*. Why she took the job she did. Why she felt so comfortable exposing herself like this.

I felt an emotion expanding in my chest... it tasted a bit like awe.

Then, when I saw those green eyes pop open and look at the crowd, I froze.

They were just as expressive as I thought. Maybe even more so.

They told me everything I needed to know. How she was about to come again. How she loved the way people looked at her as she was forced to come over and over again. She was meeting everyone's eyes, making sure they got a good look at what she was feeling.

"Please, please, I can't come any more."

The girl off to the side laughed and walked over to her, heels clacking on the floor. She leaned down and ran her fingers through her folds. While I couldn't see her up the speed from here, it became apparent when her cries stopped abruptly.

"You're done when I say you are."

Her entire body stiffened, and the loudest, shakiest moan spilled from her lips, along with a gush of fluid spilling from her and dripping down to the ground below. Her eyes searched the crowd until they landed on me.

Her flushed face and pained moans sent a burst of heat up my spine.

I gritted my teeth and let my blunt fingernails dig into my thighs.

Tiffany Yates... no Blake, had caused me to feel something I hadn't in years.

Pure, burning desire coursed through me.

I wanted to watch her more. I wanted to see her spread those legs, baring that pretty pussy to me while she came all over me. I didn't want to hear her beg to stop, I wanted to hear her beg for *more*. I wanted my name to fall from her lips as I—

I stood as quietly as I could and snuck out of the room.

No, *no*. Maybe I couldn't do this job after all. I don't like to think of myself as a coward, but it would be another few weeks before I came back for fear that the next time I saw her on stage, that I might be unable to control myself.

BLAKE

As it turned out, my boss wasn't lying. The same night he let it spill, I waited until the clock struck seven thirty, then climbed into my beat-up carriage, hoping that my night wouldn't end up like Cinderella's. I tied my laces extra tight just to be safe, and over two months later, I hadn't been caught.

Paranoia kicked in, at first causing me to search for the blacked-out vehicles from my employer, but just like he promised, there were none. Though if they were, I would have lost them just like last time.

I had perfected my drive there, making sure to go the long way around the club and through a few residential neighborhoods to be safe. I even made sure to park my car over two blocks away on the off chance they still found me.

I guess I'd do crazy things to get off. I mean, Club Pétale has been a godsend for me.

I liked performing. I liked the people. Well... most of them.

Most importantly, it was a safe space that allowed me to explore the sexuality that I thought at one point didn't exist. My whole life, sex and love had just been viewed as something used to keep your husband happy. I remember vividly listening to my mom and her friends when they were over. How they viewed their "duties" to their husbands.

Back then, I never thought of how deep a scar it left on me. Or how it molded my expectations of the act and changed them into something undesirable.

Until the club.

The club was the place that taught me just how good sex felt. And how erotic it was in front of others. That I was allowed to do things for myself. To make myself feel as dirty and unhinged as I wanted without feeling guilt afterward.

Sometimes the guilt would hit me out of nowhere, like a shadow pain of my old way of thinking, but that was few and far between.

I hadn't felt it... *well, until someone stormed out of my performance.* That night marked the second month since then. I remember her well. The way her eyes drilled into me, I thought there was something there—a connection, maybe—but then she left.

She had tried to be quiet about it, even polite, I guess. But I saw it.

And it shouldn't have bothered me... but it did.

Something else that had only been worsening my anxiety. A part of me wanted to know why she had left. Though it wasn't the first time. The rooms had allowed people to come and go as they pleased, and it wasn't uncommon for people to leave, but her...

I had dreams about her eyes. About the striking blue with broken pupils. In my dreams, they watched, just like that night. But in those dreams, they never faltered. They watched and watched and watched until I was begging for someone to touch me... but they never did.

Maybe that was why I had been so careless in the last few performances. She showed up a few times periodically in the last few months, but she never lingered long. It had been two weeks since I saw her last, and maybe that was what caused me to take up more performances. Riskier ones than what was typically allowed at the club. Maybe it was the need to prove myself that caused me to go out more than usual. To cause me to not watch my surroundings. Something that hadn't happened since before the incident.

But that carelessness had almost cost me this place.

I had been asked to perform here because of the type of clientele. Apparently, many of them came from backgrounds like mine, and Ax and Sloan, the owner and head of cyber security, wanted this place to be a bit high-class for them. They wanted the performances behind the curtains and in dark rooms to make them feel safer. There were halls with both two-way and one-way mirrors that could be booked by people looking for something a bit more adventurous, but they were out of the way.

I knew what they wanted with this place, so how had I fucked up so badly that it caused someone to storm out?

I hadn't been thinking when I walked into the club. My mind had been buzzing with thoughts of the performance and hopes that certain blue eyes would be watching me. It had been some time, but my hope never wavered.

A part of me felt bad for how easily she had caught my attention while I had still been ignoring Bailey. She had been trying nonstop to get in contact with me, and each time I came here, I ran the risk that I would see her. I tried not to dwell on it or *her* too much, but even as I walked through the club, I couldn't ignore the buzzing of my phone.

I shook the thoughts out of my head and beelined for the dressing room, and before I knew it, I was being bent over and flogged for the crowd.

I jolted as the heavy leather flog came in contact with the meaty part of my thigh. It was a dull ache that would stick around for days after, reminding me just how good it had felt to be fucked in front of the crowds. I would hide them under my suit pants, but every time I sat down or my clothing would burst across it, I would get a burst of a delicious achy pain.

The crowds' murmurs and whispers caused a buzz to run

through me, and their eyes left trails of heat on my skin. I caught a few of them having fun on their own, only making it that much hotter.

They're like that because of you, I reminded myself. *You still have the ability to enrapture them.*

My partner tonight, Gale, forced me across the bench they had set up for us, but instead of letting me look up at the ceiling as she drove into me, she had forced me to look at the crowd. To watch their reactions to me exposing myself to them in such a dirty, disturbed fashion.

They loved to see it, and I loved to show them. There was a power in it. One that was enough to remind me of the person I used to be.

Bailey hadn't shown up since I started performing again. *Thank God.* There was a fight waiting to happen, but I pushed it far out of my mind.

What was important was that I was enjoying myself. That I was able to explore what my body liked in a safe and empowering environment. Bailey had been what I needed then. A taste of what a real relationship was like, but she couldn't give me what I needed anymore. We weren't compatible.

In the first half of the performance, I had lost count of how many times I had already come and just let Gale do whatever she wanted to do to me. It was better this way. Just to give into the pain and pleasure and take whatever came. I didn't have to worry about anything, my partner would take care of it all and make sure I would leave this place feeling better than I had in days.

She switched from a vibrator to my clit for something a bit more *creative*. Which so happened to be forcing a tentacle-shaped dildo inside my sopping pussy.

Today wasn't nearly as painful as some of the other nights. This time, we just focused on getting me off as many times and in as many different ways as possible, only using small bits of pain to heighten the experience. And with it only being fifteen minutes in, I had to hand it to Gale, she really brought her A game tonight.

The notches on the underside of it caused it to rub so sweetly against my G-spot that I couldn't even form the words to tell her to slow down. Not that I wanted her to. My mind was beginning to swim, and the warmth from all the orgasms started to relax my muscles in a way I desperately needed.

The anxiety of it all had been building and building until it left my muscles tense. Gale knew just how to fix it. I just needed to trust her.

I couldn't help but look out into the crowd. Seeing what I did to people was a different type of intoxication. I took in their looks greedily, letting it feed the ego I kept locked inside during the day. I let my eyes roam over the people in the crowd until my gaze landed on *her*.

I recognized her from that night. Her hair was in a long, light mullet style and fell messily over her face. Her black mask hid her face from view, but I could just make out those piercing blue eyes. Her pupils were different than others, they looked like they had been ripped from the bottom and left to leak out.

She was always well put together in the suit, but in combination with her eyes, it caused her entire vibe to change. She went from refined to dangerous. There was something off-putting about the way her eyes narrowed in on me, in the way the aura around her seemed to scare off even the most distracted patrons.

*So she **had** come back.*

Maybe my dreams had been warning me about the moment she finally decided to come back. Preparing me for the onslaught of heat her gaze rose in me. People from all walks of life had sat in the chairs in front of me, staring at me, but none of them had caused such a reaction from me before.

I wanted more. I wanted her. At least just to try. To see her come in, to look at me with such a gaze, but not be able to try? It was pure torture.

I didn't care what I had to do, but I *needed* to try and talk to her.

"Tell them how it feels, lovely."

"So good," I forced out while keeping her gaze. "Please fuck me harder, ma'am. Make me come again."

"This is what, the seventh time already?" she asked from behind me. "You get fucked here almost every night and your greedy pussy still wants more?"

Not every night, but I didn't correct her.

"*Yes*," I groaned. At this point, it wasn't a want, it was a need. I needed to come just as badly as I needed to breathe. My entire body was shaking, and when her hands looped around me to rub circles on my clit, I couldn't hold back the whimpers.

I was so overstimulated by that point that it was bordering on painful. I wanted to scream. Wanted to cry and beg for her to stop. But I kept it inside because what I wanted more than anything was for her to continue.

She pumped the dildo inside me lazily while keeping up the firm pressure on my clit. She knew I was going to come without much work and she wasn't rushing it. But soon, her presence fell by the wayside, leaving just the bursts of pleasure she was sending through me and those piercing blue eyes.

I almost felt bad about how enraptured the stranger from across the room had made me.

Since our gazes met, I couldn't pull my eyes from hers.

She gave no indication that she was loving, or hating, what was happening on stage. It's as if she was watching paint dry rather than me getting fucked.

The only slightest hint that I got was when I came and moans spilled loudly from my mouth, her own mouth opened just slightly. My pussy spasmed violently on the fake cock, and when her pink tongue darted out to lick her lips, I all but lost it right then and there.

I should have been paying attention to my partner. Hell, I should have at least looked out at the crowd more.

But no. I couldn't pull my eyes from the corner. Images of her walking right up to the stage and dipping her hands between my legs before bringing them up to her mouth to taste flashed through my mind.

Was she imagining being in Gale's place? Or she just liked watching as I turned into a moaning writhing mess, and that's why she wouldn't come up?

I couldn't help but wonder what it felt like for her hands to roam my body. For her hot tongue to trail my skin. Thousands of thoughts flew through my mind so quickly that I couldn't even prepare myself for when the vibrator was forced back to my clit.

My back bowed, and my eyes were forced shut. Gale held me still as I begged for her to stop.

I knew the safe word, but I wouldn't use it. I liked this part too. There was something cathartic about being forced to come over and over again. Being forced to sit still while your body fell apart from the inside out.

It was about the control. The control I willingly gave up to my partner, who in turn assured me that I would be safe and protected while I was allowed to fully lose myself in the feeling.

It was another few painful minutes before my eyes opened again, though this time she was still there in the corner, staring at me.

It was in that moment that I vowed to get her into my bed. If I had to stop performing just to catch her, I would. If it meant crawling to her on my hands and knees, I would.

The curiosity of her was far too enticing to get out of my mind. And in a word, I became obsessed.

The only thing that pulled me from her was when she turned her head toward the entrance.

My breath caught in my throat, and lead filled my stomach.

Familiar long auburn hair, brown eyes, and a disapproving scowl met me. Bailey had decided to make her entrance.

"Since when did you start performing again?" Bailey said, the scowl on her face seemingly permanent.

Her comment made me bristle. My hands gripped the vanity behind me. I didn't want to be mean to her or hurt her feelings. I knew I would regret that far more than just hanging on for a bit longer.

Right after the show, she cornered me in the dressing room. Something that was a big no and went against many of their performers' boundaries. *Even my own.*

No one else was here just yet, all of them were doing their aftercare. For some people, that consisted of a wind-down in a room alone or with their chosen partner. For Gale, she usually took an extended shower, had a snack, and then we'd usually talk about the performance. Go over what we liked and what we didn't. I just hoped she would come back soon and put me out of my misery.

"Our deal never stated that I *couldn't,* just that—"

"You get it okayed with me first," she said with a pointed stare.

"You keep saying no," I pointed out. "When was the last time you actually *let* me perform? Did you forget that's how you met me in the first place? You *knew* this was what I did going into it."

She let out a gasp. "Then shouldn't you respect that I don't want you doing it? Not only that, but you also haven't been giving me a heads up before you spread your legs for someone. *Payton,* really? You know she's slept with every willing pussy out there, don't you?"

I stood straight up, closing the space between us. I could handle a lot, but I wouldn't let her talk down to me like that.

"I won't let you shame me," I spat at her. I wouldn't let anyone do that. It had taken me years to come to terms with what

I liked and had been shamed enough by—I didn't even let my thoughts wander there. I was already getting too worked up, going down memory lane would only ensure that I'd do something I'd regret.

She let out a huff and rolled her eyes as if what I said was an annoyance to her.

"I thought we had something good going for us? What happened? You were so eager before, but now it feels like you want to find anyone *but* me."

Well, at least you hit the nail right on the head.

It was my own cowardice that didn't want to end this. As much of an asshole as she could be at times, I still didn't want to hurt her. She wasn't a bad person, just... we weren't on the same wavelength.

She had been a trial for me. A look at what a normal relationship should look like. What it was *supposed* to feel like. After years of not allowing myself to get close to anyone, this was supposed to be an introduction back into dating.

I'd like to think we both failed spectacularly.

She was the one who sought me out. At first, I thought she was shy, and that's why she waited so long to come up to me.

Later, I would come to learn that she was in a relationship before this, and when it ended, she propositioned me into what we had now.

"I miss performing," I admitted with a sigh. "I need it. It gets me excited. It lets me try new things. At the end of the day, it's something *I* enjoy, and that should be enough for you to support me in doing it."

She let out a huff and crossed her arms over her chest. Just like an overgrown toddler having a tantrum.

Some parts I got. I could have done better with communication. I could have gotten her permission beforehand. But the rest was getting too much for me.

"I'm not enough for you? Too boring, then?"

I winced at her accusation. *What the fuck am I supposed to say to that?* That I had to seek out other people because every single time I left our room I was unsatisfied? I opened my mouth to speak, but I was saved by Sloan ducking into the changing room.

Thank God.

Her eyes widened when she saw the two of us. "Hey, I was here to talk to you about the performance schedule, but maybe I'll—"

"I'll text you," I said quickly, sending Bailey a smile. "Better yet, let's meet? Tomorrow in our room?"

Her eyes lingered on mine before she nodded. I knew there was so much she wanted to say, but that would be tomorrow's problem. Tonight, at least she could sleep it off, and *hopefully* she wouldn't be as mad.

"See you," she muttered under her breath and stormed past Sloan, who just barely had enough time to jerk out of her way.

Sloan sent her a shocked look before looking back at me. "What crawled up her ass?" She jutted out her thumb, pointing down the hallway Bailey stormed down.

"The usual," I said with a forced smile. "Though, to be honest, it's mostly my fault."

Sloan shook her head and crossed the room. I had the urge to pull her into a hug, but she must have seen it on my face and took the initiative to do it herself.

The warmth of her body was familiar, along with the cologne she wore. I couldn't help but sigh into it. Sometimes a person just needed a hug, and Sloan was exactly the person I wanted one from.

"Long day?" she asked.

"The longest," I said, though my voice was muffled by her shirt.

"I know you don't want to hurt her feelings, but maybe it's time to break it off, Blake." The tone she used caused my chest to twist and guilt to sit heavy in my chest. She pulled me away so she could give me that smile she was known for, but it lost all its playfulness in the moment and just felt pitying.

"I know," I said with a sigh. "I just—I think it's my fault. Like I shouldn't need to perform and sleep with other people to make it work—"

"Imma stop you right there," Sloan said, squeezing my shoulders. "You want different things, that's it. And obviously she can't compromise in a way that keeps you satisfied. Move on. Life is too short to be in an unhappy situationship."

I raised a brow at her.

"Weren't you the one that literally spent years pining after your *step-sister—*"

"*Shh,*" she said with a laugh. "Different scenario. Lillian was my end goal. This girl, she..."

Is definitely not.

"Fun for some time and good to get me back into the swing of things," I said, giving her a forced smile. "I'll talk to her. Don't worry."

She patted me on the shoulder and gave me a smile.

"Good girl, now let's talk performance. Does e-stim or tattooing sound interesting to you?"

Fuck it.

"Both," I said, crossing my arms.

Sloan's eyes twinkled in the dim light. "I knew you still had it in you."

QUINN

I was an assassin. A cold-blooded, ruthless killer... so why the fuck had I lowered myself to hiding in a closet?

I tried not to shift as Tiffany and that pierced girl got closer. Their voices were slightly more hushed now as they looked over the taller girl's iPad.

Sloan. My mind supplied for me.

I had seen her in the files, and if my memory serves me right, she had been one of the ones to allow me into this club.

Her mistake.

If I had seen the profile that Rolf submitted on my behalf, I would have denied it right away.

There was barely any history. No life stories or quirky anecdotes about why I *deserved* to be in the club. They were asking for it to get rejected.

It was even more sparse than the file on Blake, and even *that* was suspicious.

"Ax says the members miss you at the Oakheart location," Sloan said as she pulled the iPad away and held it against her chest. "Maybe you could go there for a bit? Get away from Bailey?" She leaned against the counter, her long legs stretching out in front of her. Even in this position, Blake was still slightly shorter than her.

"I think I saw you in her performance room. The *illustrious* Blake."

Damn. Here I thought, after all the times I came here, that I was hiding in the darkness pretty well.

"I have," I said with a hum.

"Of course you have," she said. "*Everyone* has. Everyone is just so in love with her and she just *eats* it up, forgetting about everyone else she leaves behind."

Everyone meaning you, I wanted to spit out.

"So while she's up there getting fucked, you're out here getting drunk?" I asked. "Doesn't seem like a fair trade."

"It's not!" she said a bit too loudly.

I put my drink down, giving a strained smile to the bartender before letting my hand rest on her elbow.

"Walk with me," I said in a low voice. "So we can continue without too many *prying* eyes."

She looked around as if she just now realized where she was.

She let me help her off the stool and out into the lobby. "It just gets me so angry," she muttered. "I thought we had something."

"Sometimes the flame just dies quicker in some relationships than others," I said, leading her to the back of the club, opposite the performance rooms.

She continued complaining about Blake. Each word was just more fuel added to the fire, slowly eating me alive. She didn't care who overheard her talking shit about the person she was supposed to have her heart. It seemed like at times she even *wanted* them to hear.

Just like her words were building up the need to murder inside me, they seemed to just make her angrier and angrier as she spoke. I was half concerned that she may even explode with it.

I pushed us out into the almost-finished backyard. It was much quieter than the inside, and there was not a soul in sight. In front of us was a half-finished stage that was marked off with thin black tarps. Just beyond there was a small back house concealed in the trees and shrubbery.

Darkness cascaded over the area, but the security camera's small red dots broke through the night. I made note of each and every one, making sure they matched the map I had in my head.

"Fresh air is nice," she commented. "You know, even *you* are treating me better than she does, and I don't even know you."

I let out a laugh and led her around the side of the house, trying to hide from the security cameras that were pointing straight at us.

There was a large tree right by the gate, and on the other side were large bushes that hid us from view. *If I could just get her over there...*

"Should I be scared you're taking me to a secluded, dark place?" she asked with a laugh. All the anger subsided from her face, now just replaced with the giddiness of a person who was about to get fucked.

The empty martini glass was in her hand and she waved it about, motioning to the darkness around her.

"Actually," I said as we reached the blind spot and grabbed her by the front of her shirt, pulling her closer. "You should be."

I grabbed the martini glass, hitting the top of it against the tree, causing it to shatter. Her gasp was cut short as I forced the broken stem into her neck. She struggled against me. Her eyes turned wide and filled with tears as her mouth opened to beg me to let her go.

But she couldn't speak.

"Has anyone told you how *fucking* annoying you are?" I asked, driving the stem further into her. "Maybe if you had a shred of decency, Blake would actually want to fuck you, you bitter *bitch*."

I cursed as her eyes rolled into the back of her head and she slumped onto me.

I hadn't planned to lose my temper so easily, but the sound of her voice was still grating on my nerves, even after she lay there actively dying.

The blood started to seep into my suit, and no doubt the evidence of my crime would be left on the floor for the workers to find in the morning.

"Goddamn it," I growled.

Now I have to figure out how to get rid of this damn thing.

Brown eyes with light flecks of black stared back at me through the glass.

The container was heavy in my hand, grounding me to my spot.

I ran the microfiber cloth over it with care, chasing away every speck of dust that had the chance to accumulate.

This was my favorite part. After all the blood. After all the noise that came with it.

The after, when I could settle in the serene. In the silence. In the comfort that I was alone.

My whole life was filled with chaos. I was constantly running. Constantly using my hands to end lives.

But in the dark hole I called my home, I could relish in the tiniest bit of freedom I had.

It was a small place. A single bedroom that I had turned into my work-slash-possession area.

There was a single pull-out couch in the living room, and nothing was stocking the random fridge I had bought for the kitchen.

I didn't decorate or leave anything personal. *Nothing except these.*

I turned the container to the side, looking at the brown orbs from all angles.

The once-so-expressive eyes had gone unfocused, and the pupils that were once wide with lust had shrunken when she realized what was about to happen to her.

After death, the pupils often dilate, chasing away the emotions stored in them. Sometimes I got lucky and they stayed relatively small, especially when I could treat them right away. Those were the ones I found myself drawn to the most.

It was shortly after I began my training that I started to develop this... *thing* when it came to eyes.

Before I could fight, they taught me everything they knew about body language, including what the eyes could tell an assassin.

"You see that, agent?" Rolf said, his voice coming close to my right ear. I hadn't gotten used to him touching me yet and flinched away from the sound.

"Look," he said in a harsher tone.

My eyes traveled to the couple a table away from us. They were in a heated discussion, trying to keep their tones hushed but failing miserably.

"Do you see the hatred she has for him?" he asked. "Look at her eyes. Whenever she looks at him, all she sees is incompetence. There is hate, resentment there. You can see it all."

I tried to see what he was seeing, but I failed. All I saw was the girl, eyes wide and brows pushed together. Sure, her expression told me she was angry, but I couldn't make it out from her eyes alone.

"I can't see it," I muttered under my breath. "Isn't it good enough to just see the expression on her face?"

Rolf let out a laugh and patted my shoulder.

*"When I kill her later, I want you to watch her eyes," he said, his tone menacing. "**Then** tell me you see nothing in those eyes."*

He took me on his missions, making me watch over and over again as he killed countless targets.

And then one day, maybe the seventeenth or so kill... I got it.

The eyes that once seemed dull, changed. It was small—so small that if you looked away for just a second, you would miss it

—but it was there. Hiding behind the shadows and divots of the iris, the emotions would pour out for the world to see.

Carefully, I placed the eyes back on the shelf, making sure to line them up with the light so that the eyes were clear in the dimness of the room. There were twelve more just like it sitting on the shelf.

Rolf didn't let me indulge often, so I made sure to keep them well.

I walked backward, lowering myself back into my chair while holding my breath.

Perfect. Seeing them all lined up in a row caused a low roll of satisfaction to inflate in my chest.

The incessant buzzing of a phone snapped me out of my haze.

Turning toward my desk, the blood-covered phone I had taken from the body lit up the dark corner.

BLAKE read legibly on the screen.

I grabbed it with a smile. *Had the little agent finally found her heart?*

My actions were reckless, but I couldn't find the will to stop myself. I accepted the call and waited silently.

"Bailey?" Blake's voice ran through the silent room. "It's really late, but I wanted to see if we could talk. You didn't show up today, are you still mad?"

I leaned back in the seat, closing my eyes as I listened to the girl. It hadn't taken long for the clean-up crew to arrive, though they had been pissed about how secretive they had to be. They weren't able to bring all their normal tools because of the cameras. They were lucky to get a few down so they could carry on with their job, but we couldn't keep them down for long before suspicion would arise. They hated it even more that I invited them, so they let me take out the eyes. But before long, I went back home, treated the eyes, and let them sit while I took a quick nap.

I hadn't realized it had been twenty-four hours since the kill and almost totally forgot about the reason I did it in the first place.

That happened often when I got my next pair of eyes. I had lost countless hours treating them, cleaning their containers, and just looking at them in all their beauty that sometimes I just let the world fall away around me.

"Bailey?" Blake's voice snapped me out of my daydream. I couldn't help but imagine her in the club, looking for Bailey but finding no one. Or maybe she had waited this long because she too forgot about her presence and only remembered when she hadn't shown up for their scheduled time.

The thought made me unreasonably giddy.

The background was quiet, save for the low music. It was already past twelve in the morning, and according to Blake's schedule, she should be leaving soon. Most of the club was probably leaving as well, trying to keep up the mask they put on for the real world. Many had jobs that required their presence, so most of the time they left around midnight, giving Blake the quiet she needed to call her girlfriend.

Or was it fuck buddy?

"Are you doing this on purpose?" she asked. "I know you're mad and you don't like that I'm performing, but maybe we can talk more about this? Bailey? Are you there?"

She stayed on for a few more moments before sighing and hanging up.

I threw the phone to the ground, making a mental note to dispose of it the next time I was on a job.

One roadblock down, one more to go.

"Oh little agent, I can't wait until you find out what happened to her," I said, a giggle rising in my chest.

QUINN

"Are you saying this job is too much for you?" Rolf's gruff voice came from the other line.

I placed the phone between my ear and shoulder so I could hoist up the sniper rifle and peer through the scope. My body was aching from a few nights ago, when I had cornered Blake's plaything. She fought back hard. Harder than I imagined she would.

But just like always, I listened to my training and with the help of the clean-up crew, I was out of there without a soul even noticing.

The wind was light that night, but it caused a slight chill to go through me. I had to ditch my normal all-black uniform for something a little less suspicious. Though a hoodie, ball cap, and jeans were great for a late walk at night, the gun in my hands said something entirely different.

From my vantage point, I could just make out the small corner of Blake's small living room, but not much else. The warm glow of the light in her apartment shone in the darkness and acted like a beacon for all those currently watching her.

She had been walking back and forth from her bedroom to the living room in different outfits for about forty minutes.

Some of them I had seen before. A tight-fitting tank top with leather pants. A loose blouse with jeans. All of them looked perfectly fine, but each time she would stand in front of the mirror, she would frown, twist around, then go straight back to her room.

Blake was getting ready for something.

My guess is that it was the club. It was the only place she went at this time of night. All while not knowing that her plaything's body was currently decomposing in a forest not far from the club.

At the thirty-minute mark, I called Rolf, only for him to turn it into some type of lecture.

"I'm *saying* that it's suspicious," I growled. "The guards she has on her are insane. She's *supposed* to be the calvary, but somehow she seems to have more people around her than the senator himself."

There was a noise to my right. Alarm bells rang in my head, and I whipped the gun over toward the sound. The rest of the rooftop was empty but the one just across from me suddenly had two birds on it. Their squawks caused a dull headache to start behind my eyes.

How long was I supposed to wear myself so thin? How long would I force myself to take job after job?

More importantly, *how much longer would I let Rolf push me?*

"She's a target for a reason, 7739." I cringed at the use of my agent code. I didn't like it when he used it after all these years. He did it when he wanted to remind me of my place in the organization, and I would be lying if I said it didn't hurt.

It put a wedge between us that was hard to shake, and I would be lying if I said my first instinct wasn't to try and smooth over whatever caused the gap in the first place.

"I haven't been able to get close outside of the club," I said, scanning the area where I knew the agents were hiding.

Many stayed within a few blocks of her apartment but there was one that was further from the rest. Instead of watching his back, he never once let Blake out of his sight.

back over a week's time, two weeks' time? By the sixth visit, I realized that she had looked for me in the crowd.

Now on my twelfth time to the club, I went to the normal room only to see a different performer take the stage. My fingers dug into the cool glass.

I had seen her leave. I knew she had to be here... right? Where else would she have gone at this time of night?

Confusion filled me along with annoyance.

Where the fuck was she?

I took a deep breath, held it, then let it out.

Track.

Assess.

Engage.

Terminate.

I was still between assess and engage even after months of tracking her. Way behind schedule compared to how my jobs usually go. It only added to the frustration that had been boiling under my skin.

I repeated the words over and over again in my head. *Track. Assess. Engage. Terminate. Track. Assess. Engage. Terminate. Track. Assess. Engage. Termina—*

Cursing under my breath, I threw the drink back. The alcohol burned as it went down, but it was the thing I needed to get my mind straight.

With a lingering look at the newest performer on stage, I turned to leave the room. Heat prickled at my skin, and a muted shock burned my chest. *She's here.*

The woman of the hour may not have been performing that night, but she sure as well was ready and waiting for me. Blake leaned against the wall of the hallway, dressed up in tight-fitting slacks and a blazer with nothing underneath. I had watched through her window as she tried on that same outfit multiple times.

Despite my annoyance, light amusement tickled at my senses at her choice of clothing.

She was waiting for me, which means... She was going to corner me finally. The bait had worked.

She dressed up for... me? The thought caused my lips to twist, and I wondered if she would look at me the same if she realized what I had done.

She tilted her head when she saw me, a light pink coated the tips of her ears. *Cute.* Even after everything, the target is nervous.

She's going to come up and talk to you. You knew this was coming. You knew this was the only way.

Be charming.

She pushed off the wall and walked toward me, but even when she came to a standstill, she didn't speak.

"You aren't performing," I noted.

A smile pulled at her lips, and her eyes lit up. This was the closest I had gotten to her in person. My eyes roamed her face, cataloging every freckle, every hair out of place. The way she looked at me from under her lashes. The way her pink lips looked to be freshly moisturized.

Something stirred inside me. Something I didn't like.

"No, but I had a feeling you'd show up," she said. Her tone was attempting to be light, but there was a light shake to it. *Nervousness? Her?*

"Did you now?" I asked, my lips curved, and there was a slight teasing to my tone, though I meant it to come out flat. I leaned forward and dropped my voice. "Do I have a stalker now? Should I be concerned?"

Pink dusted her cheeks, and her mouth popped open. It took all my strength to stop the light chuckle from escaping my lips.

I had assumed the target was charismatic, seductive even... but I hadn't been prepared for her shyness. *How is it that she pulled people in like she did?*

A part of me didn't understand it, but as she shifted nervously under my gaze... another part of me began to see exactly why people were falling over themselves for her.

"No-o," she stammered, her eyes leaving mine to look at the

floor. "I just noticed you watching me, and I just—I don't know. I—"

Feeling emboldened, I allowed my free hand to brush her cheek. The action caused her gaze to shoot back up to mine.

"Who knew someone like you could so easily get flustered." The pink on her face traveled down her neck. Her facial expression changed to something akin to shame. "I like seeing this side of you. So different from the one on stage... but yes, I was watching. I quite enjoy seeing you up there."

She swallowed thickly, the shame slowly melted away and was replaced with a teasing smile of her own.

"There's a reason I'm not performing tonight," she said. *Here it goes. My chance.* "I was wondering—"

"Would you look at who *finally* showed up?"

My skin raised, and I couldn't help but stiffen as an arm slid across my shoulders. I knew that voice.

I didn't have to turn to know that Avery Maddox was right next to me. Out of all of the people that I could have met here, she was the least desirable.

"Weren't you kicked out of this place?" I growled under my breath.

She *was* kicked out if my research was correct. And last I checked, she was hiding out in Princeton. Seeing her only meant one thing: *trouble.*

"Someone's been digging into things they shouldn't, *Quinn,*" Avery teased. The use of my real name caused me to freeze. But not in fear. It was anger. I wanted nothing more than to bash her head into the wall, but I knew it would fuck over whatever chance I had with the agent in front of me, so I forced myself not to move.

Blake took a hesitant step back. I was thankful she did. I didn't trust Avery with her. With one wrong word she would ruin this all for me.

I turned to look at her. Her light blue eyes dug into mine, and a teasing smile spread across her lips. She hadn't changed much since I saw her last. Dirty blonde hair fanned out in waves and framed her face. She didn't bother to wear a mask, like she didn't care that anything she did here would be traced back to her. With her reputation and her father now in jail, I doubt there is much she could do here that would prove sufficient enough for blackmail.

I met Avery back when I was just getting into my career. I fucked up and didn't check to make sure the coast was clear after a job.

It wasn't, and she took full advantage of that.

She would do anything to get the upper hand, both back then and sure as hell now. I wouldn't put it past her to even try to ruin this job.

I turned to see if the small professor she had her eyes on was with her, but her side was empty. It gave me some relief that there wouldn't be too much of an audience. Avery may have been one of the few people who knew what I did for work, and I wanted to keep it that way.

I dropped my voice low enough for Blake not to hear. "Interfere, and I'll kill you."

Avery threw her head back and let out a booming laugh. I looked around the all but empty hallway to check if she drew any attention to us, but luckily the only people there with us were too far away to take notice.

"Oh, you're too funny," she said, and when she finally got ahold of herself, she narrowed her eyes at me. "As if you could."

Red flashed across my vision. My hands itched to circle around her throat.

"Just kidding," she said, shaking her head. "I have one more thing for you to do. Then we will call all debts paid off."

Now? She was calling in her favor right fucking now?

I cast a glance toward my target. All the time I spent preparing for this was about to be ruined by this slimy fox. She knew for a fact that I would *always* repay my debts, so bringing it up right here and now all but guaranteed that my night would be wasted.

"Blake, Avery?"

Goddamn it. How hard was it to be alone with my target?

We all turned down the hall to catch three people walking down the hallway. Sloan, cyber security for the club, who has a track record of money laundering and fraud. Her partner and stepsister, Lillian, was at her side, and next to her was Avery's partner, Willow.

Sloan had straight silver hair, light skin, and piercings all over her face. Her stepsister, Lillian, was the exact opposite, with curly hair, taupe skin, and no visible piercings besides the ones in her ears. Sloan's mom had married Lillian's father before his death.

Sloan and Blake were close. Before she got together with her partner, Sloan and Blake often performed together on stage. Or at least that's what the file said. What they didn't tell me was how the pierced girl would look at me.

Sloan's gray eyes narrowed when she saw Avery's arm around my shoulder.

"I didn't know you knew Reilly, Avery." At least *someone* could use the fake name. She led the group to us, her eyes assessing Avery and me. There was a smile on her face, but just like most humans, her eyes gave away everything. She suspected something she shouldn't have. "You should have said something."

I gritted my teeth. *This is karma coming to bite me in the ass.*

"We go way back," she said. "It was like high school or something?"

"Something like that," I muttered. I may have played a high-schooler during the job we met on, but never went to high school and she fucking knew it.

Sloan looked toward Avery, and her face told me she wanted to say something, but didn't.

"Well, Blake," Avery said with a sugary-sweet tone. "I hope you don't mind if I take this one for a moment. I promise I'll have her back within the hour."

Blake gave her a forced smile before I was pulled away by Avery.

"I swear I will slit your throat as soon—"

"Oh, be quiet," Avery moaned as she pulled me into one of the empty performance areas. The room was dim with just enough light for me to read her expression. "Think of this as something for the both of us."

I didn't want to cave so easily, but if Avery had something for me, it was a once-in-a-lifetime chance. Intrigued, I raised a brow at her.

"Avery Maddox doing something for someone other than herself?"

"Wanna talk about the woman you murdered instead?" she asked, grabbing my attention immediately.

"You'll have to be more specific," I spit out through clenched teeth.

Avery let out a chuckle while shaking her head. "Man, I really think we could be friends one day."

I let out a huff. *Not a chance.*

"Don't worry, I won't tell little *Tiff,*" she said with a smile. "Bailey was annoying anyway. Tried to get me and Sloan to spill about her personal life more than once."

I let out a noise but otherwise didn't respond. The way Avery was able to *see* everything was unnerving. She would be a better assassin than I was. Information was never my thing, but boy, was it powerful.

Avery chose to remind me of that multiple times.

She pulled out something wrapped in clothes from her pocket. It was bulky and made me wonder how I hadn't seen it before. *Probably too busy imagining killing her.*

"You know that FBI agent I had you get in touch with a few months ago?" she asked. "Jonson?"

Of course I fucking remembered. As payback, she had me sneak into the fucking FBI agent's office and leave a note. It was so stupid and almost cost me more than her debt was worth.

But somehow, back then, she had gotten her hands on the knowledge of my newest target, *Tiffany.*

Slimy fox.

It had been shortly after I started the job, so how she got her hands on that information was beyond me.

"Yes," I grunted out.

She nodded, then pushed the object into my stomach. I grabbed it from her and pulled apart the cloth, my curiosity getting the better of me. A brilliant green emerald shone in the dim light.

My breath caught in my throat. This was worth a hefty fine.

"So you were the one that stole it?" I breathed, remembering the headline about a *very* expensive jewel being stolen from a traveling arts dealer. Something about it being gouged out of a scepter.

I couldn't help but be at least a little impressed.

"Oh, not me," she said, waving me off with a laugh. "But anyway, I need you to deliver that to Jonson. He helped me get Father behind bars."

My eyes narrowed on her.

"I'm not going to be your fucking mail lad—"

"You *owe* me," she reminded me. A smirk spread across her face. "*And* I think you'll find that if you play your cards right, you can get rid of a little problem of yours."

"What do you know about my problems?"

She rolled her eyes.

"Suit yourself," she said with a shrug. "All I am saying is that two days from now, the senator that Blake is watching will have an unannounced visit from a few special agents. He been seen *fraternizing* with some unsavory people and rumor has it, accepted some bribes for his campaign."

Her words packed a punch. *Damn it.* If what she was saying was true, this may be my only chance to get Blake reassigned.

Rolf wouldn't like what I was doing, not one bit. But that's only if he finds out.

"And Jonson will plant it for us?" I asked.

She gave me an almost disbelieving stare.

"He will if he's reminded about how good it will look for him. The choice is yours."

I clutched the jewel in my hand and looked up at the dark ceiling.

Avery may have been another level of crazy, but goddamn was she useful.

"Consider it done."

She stood up straight and sent me a smile. Her hand reached out and was about to land on my shoulder, but I pushed it off.

"After this," I warned in a low tone. "Leave Blake and I alone."

She pulled her hand back, though the smirk never left her face.

"Your wish is my command," she all but sang as she passed me. "But if I were you, I'd hurry, or else she might find someone else to warm her bed tonight."

With a clenched jaw, I walked out of the room with her, only to see that the hallway where my target once was, was now empty.

"Aw, too bad," Avery said with mock pity.

Grumbling under my breath, I shoved the gem into my pocket and stalked out of the club.

Just this one thing, and I will come back for you, Blake.

I was uniquely positioned in this place to get exactly what I needed at all times, but there I was, fucking myself under the covers like some horny teenager.

"You better not get me in trouble for this."

I perked up instantly. My heart pounded in my chest, and a burst of excitement ran up my spine. *Really?*

I peeked at her through my fingers, allowing my gaze to trail her face, but there was no sign that she was anything but serious.

"I won't, I swear," I breathed. Hope burst in my chest so painfully I thought I might swoon right then and there.

"I won't get you her number..." Her words caused me to deflate. She noticed and let out a laugh. "*But* I will set you two up as a match."

"Really?" I asked, unable to keep the excitement out of my voice.

A match with Quinn. It was perfect. The club was a safe middle ground. And it would save me from having to chase after her.

Sloan reached out to ruffle my hair with another low chuckle.

"Of course I would," she said. "We're friends, right? Plus you helped me once, and I would like to return the favor."

I gave her a meek smile. *Friends.* That sounded really nice.

And it was true. I did help her once before when she was on the rocks with Lillian. I didn't ask much about what was going on, but I just lent an ear. It was all that I could do, but it seemed to help Sloan when nothing else would.

"And friends help friends get laid?" I teased.

"Damn right, we do," she said with a laugh, but it slowly faded and a concerned look passed her face.

"Something wrong?" I asked.

She gave me a forced smile. I had seen this look only once before on her, and it caused my hackles to rise.

"Just... be careful with her, okay?"

I tilted my head to the side.

"What do you mean, be careful?" I asked, worry coating my being. "Do you know something I don't?"

"Reilly is..." She pushed her lips into a thin line. Kinda like she didn't want to have this conversation at all. Like she was fighting herself over what she should tell me.

Not Reilly...Quinn. The name fit her too well. But the way she reacted to Avery spilling her name was something I hadn't expected. She was angry, looking like she would start a fight right in the middle of the club.

Avery, on the other hand, looked like a cat playing with their food. She wanted a reaction... and she sure as hell got it.

She said they went to high school together... so who the fuck is Quinn really?

After all the years of being on guard, I found myself hesitating to reach out to Quinn... no matter how much those eyes drew me in.

"From the beginning, we were worried about her," she said after a while. "Her application was sparse, and knowing how many important people come here—including you—we were worried she would put everyone at risk."

When she saw the look on my face, her hand reached out to squeeze my shoulder.

"But she hasn't shown us anything to be concerned about." *Yet* was unspoken, but the weight of the word hung between us.

"I can't risk myself, Sloan, you know—"

"Your job, I know. Trust me. I just want to warn you. Again, she hasn't shown me anything to be worried about yet, but..."

"Avery knows her, shouldn't that mean something?" I asked. She worked here previously, after all, so whoever she scooted with shouldn't be too bad, *right*?

The wince that Sloan gave me made me think that maybe Avery knowing her was a bad sign.

"She didn't tell me she knew her," she said in a whisper. "*That's* what's giving me pause on this. Look, if you want me to set you up still, I will. I won't stop you. But I recommend doing everything under the safety of the club's roof. At least then we could somewhat protect you."

Protect me. The words were bitter as they ran through my head. *As much as I trusted Sloan and Ax, it was me who was protecting myself. Always.*

But even as she told me her concerns, I couldn't get those piercing eyes out of my mind. She would haunt me until I got her out of my system, this much I knew.

If I valued self-preservation though, I may just call off this whole thing right now. A few months ago, I would have before this. As soon as there was any bit of doubt, I would drop the person right away.

All she did was watch me. Brush her hand against my cheek. I had been fucked and defiled in so many numbers of ways in front of the crowds. *How on earth was this what drew me in?*

Maybe it was the game of it all. How she dangled herself right out of reach. How she teased me in just the right way to keep me reeled in.

It would be a lie if I said I hated it.

How long had it been since someone had controlled me so thoroughly before? Forced themselves so deeply into my mind that the only thing I could think of was them?

And still I wanted more. *Needed* it.

"Let's do it," I said, my voice filled with a conviction I hadn't had a few minutes before. "I get your concern. If anything is fishy, I will pull out immediately. Just please help me set it up. I need to—"

"Get fucked?" she said with a laugh. "If the performers are lacking, I can talk to Lil about starting something between the three of us. You know Lil and I are always open to play, Blake."

Her words caused heat to flare in my belly.

I knew far too well the promise that lay within her words. One she would wholeheartedly deliver on, but...

"If this doesn't work, I may take you up on that offer," I said with a light laugh to dispel the tension growing inside me.

It had been different since Sloan pulled away from the performances. But the performers were still good. It wasn't an issue about getting off. It was slowly about wanting something that was just out of my grasp.

But not any longer. I was sure that once the match was set up and we finally fucked, that I would be over her.

If not, I had... things to consider.

"You got it," she said, motioning for me to follow her outside. "In the meantime, let's go pick out a room for you, hm?"

Blush crawled up my neck and to my cheeks, pulling another laugh from Sloan.

"And I thought I was pussywhipped."

"How can I be pussywhipped when I haven't even had a chance to talk to her?" I muttered under my breath.

"When you know, you know," Sloan said with a wink. "I fully expect an invite to the wedding."

All the warm feelings inside me chose that moment to shrivel up and die. I couldn't even respond to her with anything other than a forced smile.

A wedding. Something that could never happen. *Ever.* No matter how obsessed I was with any one person, there would be no wedding in my future. It was something I had come to terms with a long time ago.

Sex. That's all it would be, and I didn't let myself imagine anything else.

QUINN

As it turned out, the little secret agent had something up her sleeve as well.

When I sat down in the café near her post, I was angry. Angry that I had been interrupted. Angry that Avery Maddox had destroyed my plan. And angry that I would need to figure out a way to get in touch with that FBI agent before the raid went down.

I had ordered a cappuccino topped with cinnamon and sat down near the window where I would have a view of the restaurant the senator was visiting. I even brought a book just for an extra cover, but I knew that I wouldn't be reading it.

It was a nice day. The sun was out, there weren't many people out, the café itself has soft music spilling through its speaker and the chatter was enough to drown out the noise outside, but not enough to overwhelm. The coffee was a perfect mix of bitterness and frothy milk. Even the padded chairs were comfortable. If I was in any better of a mood, I would have thought it'd be the perfect way to spend a day off.

Then I got a notification on my phone.

You've been matched!

Confusion washed through me when I saw the message, but as soon as I clicked into the email, I couldn't hide my smile.

Right in the body were two blurred-out profiles, one of myself that I could make out and the other of someone I had come to know too well. Even with her picture blurred out, I could make out Blake's facial structure.

Below it was a big "You're Matched!" in bright gold letters.

The rest of the message told me where and when we would be meeting, along with some of her more notable kinks.

Exhibitionism.

Bondage.

Overstimulation.

Estim.

The list went on and on, but it was nothing I hadn't seen before. I had read her entire file previous to this, so it wasn't the thing that surprised me. What surprised me was that she somehow went around the system to get us matched.

I had never opted into their matching services, nor did I want to.

Amusement tickled my senses.

Blake really wanted to fuck, didn't she? I guess she was missing her plaything more than I thought.

But it still led her right where I needed her to be.

It was obvious, but I hadn't realized how cunning the little secret agent could be. But it seems like there was no shortage of surprises with Blake. Her job led me to believe that she was a straitlaced control freak, but what she did in the darkness was the complete opposite of that.

It caused the demon inside me to purr. It whispered to me whenever I watched over her, begging me to push her further into the darkness and see exactly what she was capable of.

And what she was hiding.

I had been curious about targets before. Wanting to know what made them tick. Wanting to know what made them fuck up their lives so badly.

Blake was no exception.

But the more I learned about her, the more interesting she got. This whole job felt like one big test. Like Rolf and the organization behind him wanted to know just how far I would go to get something done.

And just how tempted I could be before I decided to take a forbidden taste.

After years of being their puppet, they had to know me better than I even knew myself. That's why they gave me this job, is it not?

A way to keep me doing their bidding.

Had they sensed the tiredness that ran through me and caused my soul to ache? Or maybe they realized that the assassin they sent after politicians and secret royal babies wasn't as sharp as she once was.

I didn't pretend to know what was going on in their minds. I could guess, but the answers I was seeking would never come to me. They hadn't in the twenty years I had been working for them, and I didn't expect them to come anytime soon.

When I was younger, I pushed for more information from them.

More about my parents. More about the life I once lived. More about what my future held.

Each time Rolf would give me a stern look and add on to my training regimen, distracting me until I forgot all about the questions racing through my mind.

After a while, I stopped asking and acted like the puppet they expected me to. Only recently with Blake did I let my mind wander to the more... explicit fantasies.

Fantasies I never once allowed myself to indulge in. But instead of being able to escape into them, they haunted me day and night, demanding I give them the attention they deserved.

I was shackled by them, and even though I knew very well what I had to do, it didn't stop me from wondering what I could get away with.

I looked back down at the phone, allowing my gaze to run over Blake's. I could imagine it. Blake sitting in the assigned room. Blush would coat her face, but as soon as I got close, she would stand. I had seen her walk on stage a hundred or so times. She would have a hypnotizing sway in her hips. And when she got close enough, her hands would rest on my chest before she—

A flurry of gasps and shuffling pulled my attention from my phone to the window. Sure enough, the senator had arrived, though there was far less press than I expected.

The SUV was parked right in front of the restaurant, and only two men were on either side.

I almost laughed aloud at the pitiful sight.

He had more secret service agents than press surrounding him.

From the information I gleaned about the senator, he wasn't very popular among the voters. His voice was one of the loudest, though, so he sure did cause a stir on social media at times. But none of that translated into votes.

He had money—a shit-ton of it—from his father's side. While his father never got into politics directly, he was a very prominent donor to some of his son's colleagues.

It caused his ego to soar. It was obvious in the way he greeted people when he got out of his car. Even if the crowd was small, he acted like it was hundreds of people. He raised his hand, waving at the passersby and film crew. His gleaming smile shone in the light.

I wonder if people noticed the distance between him and his wife. Or how it was a secret service agent who had to help her out of the car. Did they notice how his smile dropped when one of the workers got just a bit too close?

He was a vile human being disguised in a perfectly polished flesh suit that was more similar to a reality star than the demon he truly was. I yearned to run my knife across his throat just to see if the demon would show.

Why Blake was assigned to him was beyond me. According to her file, she was a good agent with no prior record. Assigning her to him was a bit of an insult.

But after tonight, she would say goodbye to him for good. I did exactly what Avery suggested and gave it to the FBI agent. Now it was up to him to do the dirty work. All I had to do was wait until she got reassigned, and then I would swoop in and take care of the rest.

I caught sight of my little brunette getting out of the car right behind the senator's wife.

I had seen her without her mask multiple times before this, but seeing her in the daylight, with the sun shining on her face, showcasing her freckles and glittering eyes... it was like seeing a totally different side of her.

She was focused on the wife. Her eyes scanned the area like anyone else trained in her position would do. There was not even a hint of a smile on her face until the wife met her eyes, and then the smallest one appeared. It was like a ghost of a shadow. Her lips curved, but the rest of her expression stayed neutral.

This wasn't the girl who got on that stage and allowed strangers to fuck her.

This wasn't the girl who was stammering and blushing in front of me as she asked me to share her bed with her.

No, this was Tiffany, and she was in control of everything.

She pushed the press away that dared to get close and safely led the wife into the restaurant. When they disappeared, I let my eyes wander back to my phone.

Tiffany wants to be in control now, doesn't she?

Apparently she didn't like our interruption either and decided to take things into her own hands, but that wasn't how we were going to play this game. I was the one in control here, and she would come to learn that sooner or later.

I scrolled to the bottom of the email, and there were two options for me.

"Accept" or *"Reject."*

My finger hovered over the buttons. Just as I was about to press one, a scream broke out.

My gaze snapped toward the restaurant. My breathing was

calm as I watched a man stumble out of the place, but my heart skipped a beat when Blake's messy brown hair and disheveled clothing made an entrance.

I sucked in a sharp breath and ground my molars together. *Had he hurt my target?*

The people still lingering on the sidewalk jumped out of the way of the man, allowing him to get away. Blake was close behind and took off running after him and winked out of sight in seconds.

Cursing under my breath, I stood as calmly as possible to not draw attention to myself before grabbing my stuff and walking out the back.

As soon as the door slammed behind me, I took off jogging in the direction that they went in. No one was following her, leading me to believe the others were controlling whatever mess he had left back in the restaurant.

I picked up my pace, determined to get a glance at my target. It wouldn't do me any good if she was disposed of before I could get my hands on the information the client wanted.

It wasn't long before I found them in an alleyway only a few blocks from where we were. Blake had tackled the man to the ground and started punching him in the face.

I froze in my steps when her fist crashed into his face. Again, and again, and again. Blood splattered out from him, painting Blake's face and clothing. The sprinkles of blood swelled in with the freckles seamlessly and looked more like a work of art than the horrific sight it should have been.

Her eyes were wild, and her movements were erratic, but her breathing was almost silent. Her eyes were wide and fixed on the man below her without blinking. Even as blood continued to splatter on her face.

She beat him with an anger I had never seen from her before. An anger I didn't think she possessed.

When she pulled away, the air around us stilled. The breath

was stolen from my lungs. The hair on the back of my neck stood straight up.

Her eyes told me she wasn't done. Not by a long shot.

Show me what you're hiding, little agent.

With smooth movements, she reached behind her and pulled her gun from her holster.

"I'm sorry!" the man below her cried. "Please! I wasn't trying to hurt them. I just wanted to send a message!"

She pointed the gun at his forehead. *Pull the trigger,* my demon ordered her. It was bloodthirsty, just like they created it to be.

She had one too, I realized in that moment. A demon of her own. It was controlling her movements. Pushing the gun against the sweaty skin of his forehead.

I took a step forward, unable to stop myself.

"I know who you are," she said, her voice so low I could barely make it out. "You've been stalking them for weeks. Leaving comments on their social media profiles. *You* wanted to send a message?" She let out a laugh. "You're no better than the so-called *monsters* you're trying to save us from."

Icy coldness trickled down my spine and mixed with the shock swirling within me. But there was something else deep inside me that was just coming to the surface. Something warm. Something that caused tingles to run through my body and curl in my stomach.

They created the demon inside me, but they sure as hell never meant for it to react like this.

"Please, *please*, let me go! I have a family!"

She shook her head. "They wouldn't miss you," she spat. "I've seen the disgusting comments you leave about his wife. The rape threats. Maybe I would be doing the world a favor."

It was arousal and excitement that filled me. Seeing her mask finally snap in two and give me a glimpse of what lies hidden below was a fantasy I didn't understand just how much I yearned for until it was right in front of me.

The darkness that was exuding from her was something I had never seen before and reminded me—well, it reminded me of myself.

I saw the way I looked at my targets reflected back at me in those green pools. I saw the slight twist of my lips gracing her own face.

I couldn't pull my eyes away from the image. I was getting lost in her. Counting the blood splatters on her cheeks. Letting myself swim in the anger brimming her eyes.

This is personal.

She was taking something out on this man that had nothing to do with the family she was protecting.

Then I heard it. Footsteps closing in. And they weren't too far away.

But Blake didn't notice. She was glaring at the man. Her finger was brushing against the trigger.

I turned back the way I came, my eyes searching the dingy back alleyway until they rested on some tin trash cans. *Perfect.* Acting fast, I jogged over and delivered a kick right to the side of one, causing both to tumble over in a loud crash.

Silence filled the air. Blake's movements had stopped. I heard her sharp intake of breath before the shuffling.

"Hands behind your back," Blake ordered.

I looked back toward the mouth of the alleyway but I was too far away to see her. As much as I wanted to go back and see her, I instead pulled out my phone and opened the email I received earlier.

With a small chuckle, I pressed "*Reject*" and stuffed the phone back into my pocket.

I'll find you soon, little agent. Wait for me.

BLAKE

"She rejected?" I echoed as Sloan's message came through on my phone.

When the voices around me quieted, I realized just how loud I had been. My face heated, and I sent an embarrassed smile to the people surrounding me, though no one was looking at me. The person next to me was face down, attention solely focused on the game, fingers tapping rapidly on the worn-down buttons of the machine.

Get a hold of yourself, Blake.

It was dark in the arcade with only the overhead neon lights and the screens from the games lighting the space. Cheers broke out across the room causing me to jump. I leaned against my machine and let out a deep sigh.

The whole day had been a bust. First, I found out I was on duty with the senator, *in public,* after I had specifically requested not to be put in the spotlight. Then that disgusting stalker showed up at the restaurant for the third time in a four-month period.

Last I heard, he was thrown in jail for his dangerous stalking tendencies and threats, but apparently no one cared much about the man since he hadn't actually hurt anyone *yet.*

Yet being the key word. He grabbed at the senator's wife, attempting to pull her into the back with him. An idiot to think the gaggle of secret service agents wouldn't see what he was doing.

I didn't know what had happened to me. I was off and chasing him down like any other good secret service agent would do, then a sort of haze covered my eyes, and I only snapped out of it by the time my fists were bloodied and I had a gun to his forehead.

So now I was here, letting off steam in the only way I knew how.

That's a lie, actually. My favorite way to let out steam was to get railed, but I couldn't really go to the club after someone fucking rejected me.

Like seriously? *She* rejected *me?* As if she hadn't been coming onto me the entire time. Had been waiting until I was untied to get with me. Who the fuck went to every single one of my performances and then flirted with me like she had if she *didn't* want to fuck?

Maybe I was getting rusty.

I slipped a few coins into the machine while grumbling under my breath.

The soundtrack and series of gunfire from *Zombie Revival 5* blasted through the speakers.

I grabbed a hold of the familiar plastic gun with a frown and pointed it toward the screen.

It was lighter than the gun I had been assigned, but it reminded me too much of it. I was hit with not just images of the man I had chased but also of another man long ago who had been in the same position.

Red flashed across my vision, and my body moved on autopilot.

It had been three years since I discovered this dirty, run-down arcade. Two and a half since I found this game collecting dust. And two since I had reached the highest score.

I don't know what it was about blowing zombie brains out,

Or at least I thought she was leaving... until the door to our right opened and she walked right in.

Fire shot through me, licking up my spine and causing my breath to catch. The person below me had fused her lips back to my clit.

A hand tangled in my hair and jerked my head back, so I was forced to look at the stranger as she entered.

Fuck. I forgot how tall she was.

I was short, but she was a fucking giant compared to my small form. She crossed the room, her dress shoes muffled by the carpet below. When she stopped at the edge of the bed, all of the air left my lungs.

From afar she was captivating, but up close? Up close she was goddamn addicting. Her musky scent surrounded me, and those piercing blue eyes with broken pupils seemed like they were staring right into my soul.

Her fingers slipped into my collar, the warmth of them causing tingles to spread throughout my body.

Heat expanded in my belly, and before I could prepare myself, I was coming again. This time they were muffled by her mouth covering mine. I gripped her shirt with urgency. Pulling her closer to me as her hot tongue skillfully brushed across mine.

Kissing her was different than I imagined.

I imagined a pent-up lust spilling out into our kiss. I imagined rough hands and breathless moans.

Instead, I got controlled, yet heated. Calculated but messy. She took the lead with the kiss, exploring my mouth as if it were just her and me and not like I had a person licking up the cum that had leaked from my cunt.

The heat from her kiss caused another zap of pleasure to shoot up my spine, but she needed it far too soon.

When she pulled back, I hung onto her shirt.

"You rejected my match." I was panting from the kiss and breathless because of the multiple orgasms, but the words came out strong.

There was that quirk of her lips again. I don't know what it was about my words that caused her to give me *that* face, but I wanted to see more of it. I wanted her to look down on me like she was just then, acting as if she wasn't affected, but inside, both of us knew just how much she wanted this.

The kiss made me more sure than ever before.

"I did," she said.

"But you want me," I said, gripping her shirt tighter. The action seemed to amuse her.

Her fingers brushed against the heated skin of my cheek. "I more than want you. I want to devour you. And when I do, I want you to be mine and mine only."

I was getting desperate. She could tell me to do just about anything, and I would say yes.

A part of me wanted to mess with her for her rejection, but the other part wanted me to submit even more.

"Was that why you didn't come to me?" I asked. "She won't bother us anymore. I can fuck whoever I want."

The quirk in her lips caused my entire body to shudder. *Oh I know,* was what her gaze told me.

"Stay," I forced out through a moan. The person below me hadn't yet stopped their assault on my clit even as their own groans filled the room. "Play awhile. I'll be yours."

She gently untangled my hands from her shirt and stood to her full height.

"I don't play with a crowd, little one," she said and brought my hand to her lips. She paused when she caught sight of the scabs that littered them. Then when her eyes met mine again, my breath was stolen from me. "Next time."

Then she turned and left the room.

"Not everything you'd thought she'd be, huh?" the person said from behind me.

Her words spurred my actions, and suddenly I was pushing myself out of the bed and diving for my clothes.

"Blake, leave her. We got you," the one that was between my legs whined.

"It was fun, friends," I said as I hastily buttoned my pants and slipped on my shoes. I grabbed my shirt and put it on, skipping the bra for now. I sent them a smile. "I appreciate your help, but until next time!"

I didn't let their whines stop me as I left the room in search of the stranger.

No—Quinn.

There was no sign of her in the hallway, but that didn't sway me in the slightest. If she wanted a chase, then I would allow it.

Then, as if the gods were against this union, a pinging vibration went off in my pocket and caused me to freeze.

Of course it had to happen right now.

I pulled out the phone from my pocket. Ax had allowed me to keep it on me given the nature of my job, but it had only gone off once before. My heart stopped, and blood rushed through my ears.

The burrow is flooding. Report immediately.

BLAKE

I didn't even have time to wash the stench of sex off of me before speeding to my assigned position.

Luckily I kept a spare suit in my trunk, but I prayed to God that no one looked twice at me.

As soon as I pulled up to the expensive upstate town house, I knew there was no one that would even look in my direction. Not with all *that* going on.

Police cars, both marked and unmarked, lined the streets. Red and blue lights were flashing. I had to squint my eyes to see through them. Men in suits and badges were all over the place, many of them murmuring to themselves. What was most surprising were the men and women in their jackets with a big "FBI" plastered on their backs.

What the hell?

The news cars weren't here yet, but it was only a matter of time. I caught only a few people with the all-black Secret Service uniform on, guns at their sides. I parked haphazardly in the middle of the street and bound up the stairs.

Inside was chaos. The small entrance that led to the foyer, connected living room, and kitchen were packed with bodies. Even the staircase to the right of the entrance had cops bustling up and down it, pushing past everyone who got in the way. People were yelling, and the Bennett family was all huddled in their living room.

I didn't recognize many of the faces and paused when I realized just how lost I was. Then, as I pushed through the crowd, I saw a familiar figure standing near the foyer. The squad leader was there, his arms crossed over his chest and a scowl on his face. When he saw me, he visibly relaxed. Ryan had been in the business for over twenty years. His black hair was speckled with gray, and his cold gaze seemed even harder than it usually did.

I hadn't known him for long as I had only been on the senator's team for a short while, and while he and I were friendly, I also knew that he was a no-business kind of man, and if he was there in person... there was something really wrong.

"Thank fucking god at least one of you showed," he said, his voice carrying over the crowd. Some people even turned to look at me.

I pushed past the sea of uniforms, glaring at whoever tried to stop me. The town house was filled with more bodies than it could hold making it hotter than hell. As I got further in, I recognized a few of the cops and uniformed officers, but none of them were people dirty enough to trust.

As soon as I got close to Ryan, I looked up at him with a questioning gaze.

"Where are the other—"

I had my answer before the question was even out of my mouth. A few shouts rang throughout the room. I peered behind him to see something I never thought I'd see in my lifetime. Before my very eyes, three secret service agents were being arrested. The cops wrangled them, ignoring their curses as they forced their hands behind their backs and pushed them toward the exit.

My blood ran cold at the sight. This wasn't supposed to happen.

Since when did the cops get to direct us? If anything, I thought they would be here—

"Where the *hell* is Mr. Bennett?" I asked, noting that my charge, and a presidential candidate, was missing. "This doesn't seem right, Ryan."

Ryan sighed and ran a hand over his tired face.

"In the back of a goddamn cop car," he said. "Tonight you are in charge of the family. I have five other guys on their way. Direct them how you see fit, but I need to figure out why the fuck my men are in handcuffs."

I swallowed thickly. *Me? In charge?*

Ryan stepped to the side and motioned behind him. I was too busy watching my teammates being cuffed and dragged outside to notice the family had been sitting behind him in the small foyer the entire time.

The two children were visibly upset, with tear stains marking their faces. The older girl was clutching the small boy in her arms while leaning on her mother's side. I had worked with Mrs. Bennett many times, but my interaction with the children had been limited at best.

"I'll take care of it," I whispered to Ryan. "When the agents come, I'll keep one with me and the rest will guard the perimeter. With this many people in and out, we can't chance any unauthorized people getting in here."

Ryan gave me a sharp nod before clapping me on the shoulder and disappearing into the sea of bodies.

Steeling myself, I looked over at Mrs. Bennett and the children with a small smile.

As much as you would rather be anywhere else, these people need you right now. You know what it's like to need someone. Be nice.

"I'll be looking after you for the time being. I work with Senator Bennett often. My name's Tiffany." I said it softly so as not to alarm the youngest. He was only five and his eyes were already bloodshot. No doubt the flood of people scared him half to death.

The older one, who I knew was about twelve years old, looked me over with a sharp eye. I could see she was trying to put on a tough facade, but the red that rimmed her eyes told me she too was scared.

"Thank you, Tiffany," Mrs. Bennett said with a forced smile. "For this and... earlier. Sorry I didn't have time to talk to you about it sooner. I know now is not the time with—"

Her voice cut off, and her cool mask fell. The emotion was thick in her voice and clogged her throat. She cleared her throat before whispering a "sorry" to me.

"Don't worry about it, ma'am," I said. "I am here to protect. Can you tell me what happened? Only if you are comfortable, that is."

Her eyes shifted back to the children at her side before she let out a shaky breath.

"We were cleaning up dinner," she said. "The children were in here, watching TV, when we heard a bang, and immediately I thought it was another one of those heinous men from the internet. I screamed for the agents, but before we knew it, policemen and FBI agents were storming the place. They forced us to this couch before taking him."

I nodded and reached out to pat her shoulder as her eyes turned glassy.

"And the agents?" I asked. "Were they interfering?"

She shook her head.

"They complied for the most part, so I'm not entirely sure why they are being taken in," she said.

Someone cleared their throat behind me. I turned to them with a scowl, but the weight on my shoulders lifted when I saw not one but three secret service agents waiting for my command. The other two looked relatively new, both looking toward one off to the side who looked like he hit the gym daily.

"Ryan sent us here," the one in front said. "Ready for orders."

I straightened my shoulders and pointed to the quiet one off to the side who looked like he knew more than the other two. "You stay with me and the family, guard the back. You take the back, near the kitchen. You take the front door. Cops and FBI agents are crawling around the place. If anyone wanted to sneak in, now would be the chance."

The other two nodded and excused themselves without any fight.

I turned to the other secret service agent to ask exactly what the hell he saw out there, but the shuffling of feet and the low murmuring of voices caused me to look at the intruders.

My breath caught in my throat, and my heart pounded in my chest. Panic seized my entire body, and as soon as I met those familiar brown eyes and scowl, I forced my eyes to the ground.

FBI... What the fuck was he doing here? Our paths shouldn't have crossed ever again. He was supposed to make sure of that.

For one of the first times in my new life, I froze. Froze because seeing someone associated with the life I left was too jarring to keep me rooted to this charter. Frozen because the man that was in front of me was someone I had wanted to see for years but knew it would never be possible.

But if he was here, it meant that something was going on with this family. Something that should scare me. Because Jonson never got involved in something that wasn't filthy. He was somehow the most and least trustworthy FBI agent I had ever met... but he sure did stick up for those he believed in.

Unlike the cops at his sides, the ones glaring at us and whispering God knows what under their breaths, he had a moral code. One that was a bit twisted, but one that existed nonetheless.

I snapped out of it quickly, remembering exactly why the fuck I was here.

Look at him. Because if you don't, people will notice. Ryan put you in charge, so act like it.

"We don't need any more FBI agents here," I said to them in a low voice. Finally, my eyes met those brown ones. I couldn't help but notice how the years apart had aged him. How the stress from the job had worn on his face and grayed his hair.

The man behind him scowled, but Agent Jonson's face stayed still.

"I have some questions for Mrs. Bennett about her husband," Agent Jonson said, venom seeping into his tone. He nodded toward the agent at my side. "Take the kids. This isn't for them to hear."

When the agent began to move, my grip shot out to hold on to his wrist.

"We don't report to the FBI," I reminded. "Whatever this is, needs to—"

"Are you infringing upon our investigation, agent?" Jonson said with a raised brow. "I want to remind you that I have the power to throw you in jail with the rest of your team."

"I am just saying—"

"You should be assisting with the investigation, and it is perfectly legal and in no way harming Mr. Bennett's family," he said, as if scolding me. His tone was not missed by the people around us.

I hated when he used that tone on me. I almost forgot what it felt like to be around him. I had to suppress my pout.

"Take the kids to the kitchen, make them some warm milk or something," I said to the agent next to me, letting go of his wrist.

"I'm not a babysitter," he huffed under his breath.

"Care to repeat that?" Ryan's voice caused us both to jump. I hadn't heard him approach. He stood taller than Jonson, but the FBI agent didn't seem to be bothered by it. He just looked up at him with a small smile.

"Oh, Ryan, nice to see you again," he said with mock politeness.

The agent at my side used that as his cue to escape with the children. I maneuvered myself closer to Mrs. Bennett, acting as a sort of shield for her. She gave me a grateful smile, but it only caused my suspicion to grow.

What did she do?

"I wish I could say the same, but your cop buddies have my men arrested for aiding and abetting? Care to tell me what that's about?"

Jonson smiled and turned to Mrs. Bennett.

"Maybe Mrs. Bennett would be able to help? Want to share what you know about the jewel we found in your husband's office? The story in the news was that it was stolen, but it looks more like a bribe to me."

Her eyes widened.

"I have no idea what you're talking about," she said in a scandalized gasp.

Jonson fished out a bag from his pocket, one that contained the brightest emerald I had ever seen.

"It was placed really prettily in his safe," he said. "Along with a few others. And loads of cash. We received intel that your husband and his entourage were seen leaving the same hotel as Julian Otero with a suspiciously heavy bag. The arts dealer reported the emerald missing the same night. But why have this and so many others in his safe? My guess is Otero wasn't happy with the cards your husband dealt."

What is he going on about?

I wouldn't put it against the senator to do something like accept a bribe, but this all seemed too convoluted and circumstantial at best, unless...

My eyes traveled Jonson's face. He seemed so *sure*. *Was there some actual bribery going on that he can attest to once he has the senator in custody?*

"Hotel?" Mrs. Bennett asked with her eyebrows pulled together. "What hotel? He has been at home. I can attest to that."

"Ah," Jonson said as he exhaled. "Don't act like you haven't benefited from it as well. I could have sworn I saw a brand-new Mercedes parked outside. One which isn't on your or your husbands bank statement."

"What are you on about? It was a *gift*." Mrs. Bennett said, standing. I moved to her side, placing my hands on her shoulders. She sent me a pleading look.

"Sit," I whispered. "You don't want to make this worse than it is."

"But they are insinuating—"

"There is no insinuation here. Just a completely normal, non-suspicious meeting between your husband and a few people who have a deep pockets and something to gain by bribing your husband," Jonson said. "So *Ryan*, that is why your agents are under arrest. Even if it is *stolen,* as the dealer says. They saw him take it, and one already confessed to seeing him order another agent to commit the crime while he watched. No whether that crime is bribery or robbery, we can see find that out in trial, hm?"

Ryan straightened his suit, then nodded. It was obvious on his face how much he didn't like this. The whole situation didn't sit right with me.

"Understood," he said. "We hope to have eyes on your report in the morning."

Shock ran through me at how easily he accepted it. *That was it?* He was just going to accept that they had taken them and let them go?

"Mrs. Bennett, we will probably call you down for questioning," Jonson warned and motioned for the man behind him to leave. "We have a few more pieces of evidence to collect here, but we should be out of here soon."

My eyes were trained on Ryan, as there was something he wasn't saying. *What had he seen out there?*

Jonson nodded toward him before turning on his heels and leaving. Ryan didn't come to my side until he was fully out of view.

"We can't do anything about the agents," he said, keeping his voice low. "They fucked up, and that's on them. Per Mr. Bennett, he has no idea why those jewels were there and blames it on the agents. Saying that they probably targeted the arts dealer and planted it on him. But I know for a *fact* he won't sit in that interrogation room for more than five minutes."

My gaze shifted to his.

"He won't?" I asked, trying to keep my voice low. "Even if all the agents point to him?"

The muscles in Ryan's jaw clenched. He was obviously just as unhappy with the idea as I was.

"You know by now how this works," he said. "Just be cautious out there, okay? You were lucky you were off duty that day. Going forward, if you see anything suspicious, let me know, okay?"

I nodded, unable to find any other words to describe what I was feeling.

I knew the senator was powerful... but even putting the crimes on his own secret service agents?

My entire body froze when I saw the man of the hour sauntering through the house as if he wasn't just forced into the back of a cop car.

He had a cocky grin on his face, and his eyes traveled over the various law enforcement officers in the room before they came to rest on mine. His smile fell just slightly before it was plastered back on his face.

The light in his eyes was gone, and behind that smile, I had no doubt that inside he was fuming.

God fucking dammit, why couldn't I stay anywhere less noticeable?

QUINN

I t didn't fucking work.

"What do you mean he's not getting charged?" I growled into the phone.

"I mean what I said," Avery said from the other line. There was a bit of annoyance in her tone as well.

"You said he would handle this," I reminded her. "I *needed* him to handle this."

"Jonson had planted it perfectly," she said, her voice dropping to a whisper. "Even went so far as bribing the secret service agents to conspire against him, but still—"

I let out a frustrated sigh and leaned back in my chair to look up at my dark ceiling.

"We can't control the outcome of everything," Avery reminded me. "The senator has to have his hands in something. Otherwise this should have worked. I even dug up some low-level tax fraud and bribery evidence as a backup but it was swept under the rug."

Damn it. I should have known better than to let that *murderous* nepo baby take care of something so important.

"Thanks for the update," I said and hung up before she could say anything else.

Anger boiled underneath my skin. The need to destroy was something I couldn't keep contained inside me. Not for long.

Letting out a frustrated sound, I slammed my hands down on the desk, careful not to push off any of the files. I would just get even angrier if I had to clean up a mess I made afterward.

I should have known better than to expect that a super-rich politician wouldn't let himself get framed so easily.

I trusted Avery far more than I should have. She sounded so sure that this would work. And with her track record, it was hard not to believe that she could make even the most impossible things happen.

At the end of the day, I blame myself. This was my job, and it was my responsibility to get this done.

With a heavy sigh, I flicked the mouse on my computer. The screen lit up showing me pictures of Blake, her apartment, and various other documents.

Whoever was watching her was probably after the same thing as me, because I highly doubt that the Secret Service would go *so* far to keep one of their members safe.

Unless they also suspected her, a voice in my head whispered. Suspect her of what though? Her record with the Secret Service had been perfect. There had never once been any documentation of her ever receiving a reprimand or getting in trouble.

There was no doubt that she was hiding something.

Images of her beating down that man in the small alleyway flashed through my mind. The anger and darkness that she showed wasn't a new thing. It had been sitting there, festering underneath her skin until she couldn't hold it back anymore.

My anger turned into something else entirely at the memory.

Curiosity. Blake had piqued my curiosity.

Even through the tiredness and frustration of everything going on, I still found it in me to want to know more about my target.

I pulled up her location on my computer. An all-black map with a slow-blinking red light filled my vision. I took special note of the streets, realizing that she wasn't where she normally was at this time of night.

A smile spread across my face.

Well, if I couldn't get rid of the senator and the people that guarded her so I could sneak into her apartment, I would have no choice but to force her to bring me in.

I had no more time to waste.

I'd already spent enough time dealing with her plaything and watching her. If I didn't get the information soon, it would be a stain on my record.

Standing, I turned toward the wall of my collections. All of them staring at me.

I imagined the moment when I could place the two emerald eyes of Blake's on the shelf.

It caused a shiver to run up my spine.

But before that, I needed to end this.

I didn't want to admit that I was panicking... but I was. I needed to try to salvage the relationship as soon as possible.

Whatever that may look like.

At this point, my desperation was clawing at me night and day. I couldn't sleep. Every moment became about *Blake.*

Blake this Blake that. What was Blake doing right now? Would she like it is I unbuttoned my suit? If I sat closer to her performance?

Everything was about her. More than it should have been.

Normally I was able to turn my brain off for rest times, not matter the meeting, but whenever I closed my eyes I saw her plea- sure contorted face as she looked at me while riding that person's face. How her eyes widened when I slipped my fingers into her collar.

I was a fucking mess.

I sighed as I looked around the corner as Blake ducked into the arcade for the second time this week.

For a girl who led such a crazy double life, I would have expected her to go out more. But between this and the club, there was nothing else going on in Tiffany Yates's life.

She would go to work. Go home. Go to the club. And sometimes play the run-down zombie game until the place closed. Then rinse and repeat. She never brought anyone home, nor did she go over to anyone's house.

Until now.

I had to intervene. There was no other option. If I just sat around and acted as bait any longer, this whole operation may take years.

I set it up perfectly. At night between the fantasies of touching Blake in ways I shouldn't be allowed to, I planned. I needed to enter her life. And if the plan worked how I imagined it would, soon, I would be waltzing right into Blake's apartment whenever I pleased. There was nothing or no one that was going to stop me.

Nausea swirled in my stomach, reminding me of what was to come. Images of her lifeless eyes looking at me while I stood over her, hands bloodied.

Why did this feel so sickening?

I gave her a few minutes, mostly centering myself, before I entered. In my mind, my excuse was that it allowed her some type of fun before I swooped in to ruin it all. But in reality, it was I couldn't get over the mix of nervousness and excitement that was broiling in me.

I gritted my teeth as I was hit with the loud noises. As soon as the door shut behind me, it felt like the small, darkened arcade caged me in with all the chaos.

The sound of the machines rang out all around. Loud, thumping music filtered through the speakers. Patrons screamed in triumph while others wailed at their defeat. The musky smell of smoke and stale food was thick in the air, causing my nose to itch and my throat to tighten.

This wasn't at all where I thought someone like her would spend her time. It was almost repulsive.

But I had been in far worse places than a sweaty, hormone filled enclosure.

I lingered a few machines away as I watched her, sending a glare to those who dared look my way.

Most of them were younger boys who flinched when they met my gaze. I expected some jeers from the more reckless of the group, but luckily enough for them they read my aura well enough to understand that I wasn't to be approached.

Blake was enraptured by the game. She stood with her feet wide and two hands on the gun. Her eyes were trained on the screen while her finger pulled the trigger in quick succession. I let my eyes follow the bead of sweat that travel down her jaw line, her taunt neck, and the light bit of collar bone that showed through clothes.

She was just like that day when she took down the man and pummeled his face. Cold. Focused. And slightly excited.

It seemed silly to think she was dangerous in this situation, but I knew what those steady hands could do if they were put to use.

And fuck did it do something to me.

Nervousness clawed at me, causing my stomach to roll and my palms to sweat. If I wasn't the least bit attracted to her, this whole thing would have been easier. I was so far out of my comfort zone that, while I knew exactly what I had to do, I was afraid that I would mess it all up due to my... inexperience.

I had to stifle my groan.

I could do this. Maybe I wasn't a specialist in seduction, but I knew how to do my job. And at the end of the day, that's what it was. As... *personal* as this may get, I would have to separate myself.

It was time to act as a professional and if that meant fucking the little secret service agent, then that is what I would do.

And it's not like I wouldn't enjoy myself.

I had seen Blake get off countless times, and more than once I had imagined that it was *me* causing her to fall apart. *But now I had to put it to the test.*

She didn't notice me as I stalked forward or as I leaned against the side of her machine. Even when the game ended, she mechanically reached into her pocket to pull out some change, all while not even sending a glance my way.

"So *violent*," I commented in a teasing tone. "And zombies? I never took you for the type."

Her head finally whipped toward me, and there was a moment of confusion before recognition splashed across her face.

Then panic.

Her eyes widened, and her mouth popped open, showcasing the pink tongue just beyond. Pushing past the anxiety, I let myself feel the pang of arousal she sent through me.

Soon I would get to taste her again. The thought caused my mouth to water.

"Quinn?" she asked in a low voice. "How did you—I mean, we probably shouldn't—"

I motioned for her to be quiet by putting a finger to my lips. Her eyes shot around to the dark arcade around us. No one was looking at us, but the weight of the people who lingered just outside was heavy in the air.

"It's nice to meet you," I said, holding my hand out for her. "Blake, right? Or do you prefer...?"

I let the question linger between us. *Tiffany* was right on the tip of my tongue, especially since she decided to use my real name. The petty part of me wanted to level the playing field but I needed to make her trust me first.

She looked at my hand for far longer than she needed to.

"I won't attack you in public if that's what you're worried about," I said with a light laugh. Her eyes shot to mine.

"In private then?" she asked, her brow raising.

My smile widened. "I guess you'll just have to see, won't you?"

She looked again behind her, as if she expected the agents to storm the place. The noises from the machines would hide our conversation from anyone around us, even the agents outside. I doubt they noticed that I had removed the bug they stuck on her game and moved it to one not far away.

They were all out back in one of the minivans, half of them bored out of their minds and messing around on their phones. They didn't give two shits about what she did in here.

So it was perfect for what I needed.

Slowly, her smaller hand slipped into mine. I had the strongest urge to yank her closer, so I gave into it. Something I learned with Blake is that if I waited too long, someone was bound to interrupt, so I needed to take the initiative when it hit.

She let out a small gasp when I leaned forward and brushed my lips against the shell of her ear. Her reactions only fed my ego.

"I meant what I said about the crowd," I murmured. "And about you."

The sound of her swallowing could just be heard over the noise around us. I inhaled deeply, savoring her scent. It was musky from her sweetness, mixed with a sweet rainforest smell that caused my mouth to water.

"Are you following me?" she asked with a slight tremor in her voice. *Was she scared? Already?*

"Yes," I admitted. Blake didn't seem like a person who would get over my lies easily. So for this at least, coming clean was necessary. "I wanted you alone."

She pulled away and looked up at me from under her lashes. Her cheeks were dusted with a light pink. *So she's not scared...but something else?*

I didn't like just how much I was willing to fold for the agent as soon as she showed even the slightest reaction to me.

"You can call me Blake here too," she said. "I prefer it."

I nodded and reached down to take the fake gun she was still clutching in her hand. I let my fingers brush across hers as I took it, an electric-like heat bursting through me.

"Well, *Blake*," I said, letting a smirk spread across my lips. "Let's make a deal, hm? If I beat you in a game, you take me to your place."

The blush left her face almost immediately, and she leaned back.

"How do you know I still want you after you rejected me?" she asked, raising her brow. There was a teasing smile playing on her lips. "Maybe you lost your chance."

I couldn't help the light chuckle that escaped my lips. For the first time since I took this job, my chest started to loosen, and a light feeling filled me.

"Then if you win, I leave," I said with a shrug. "Since you're so good at the game, that shouldn't be hard, right?"

She pulled her bottom lip between her teeth before looking at the scoreboard. She was number two right now, so the chances of her winning were very high.

"I don't usually take people home," she murmured, her voice not as strong as it once was. She was thinking about it. I could see the thoughts of the two of us dance behind her eyes.

"I don't usually try to win video games to try and get laid." My comment caused her lips to twitch.

"Deal," she said and leaned down to place two more coins in the machine. "But I doubt you'll get higher. I've been playing this for years."

I gave her a smile. "We will see about that, won't we?"

She kept that confident face until I pushed her aside and readied my stance. She probably expected me to give some half-assed attempt, thinking that this was easy. But I knew it wasn't. I also knew how important it was to her.

"Hit start for me, would you, babe?"

Her face flamed red and caused my stomach to heat. I learned quickly that I loved riling the little secret agent up.

Reaching forward, she slammed her hand down on the start

button. I sent her an amused smirk before turning my attention to the game. I shot the first few zombies in the head, missing one on purpose. She froze next to me, her breathing stopping entirely.

How does it feel for someone to beat you at your own game, little agent?

BLAKE

No, she couldn't—in less time than I ever had, she had gotten multiple combo shots and a streak. *If she kept this up... she would win... and I would have to take her into my apartment.*

The apartment that was being monitored by the Secret Service nonetheless.

If they saw me bring her in, they would expect a report on my relationship with her and would probably run a background check.

It would be troublesome, but—

I watched in awe as she ruthlessly killed the zombies. This was something I had never been able to share with anyone, yet here she was—*and* threatening to beat me. Anger and frustration started to build inside me.

I didn't want anyone to be better than me at this, *especially* the girl who had rejected my match.

It was childish, I knew that, but that didn't stop the anger from boiling under my skin. But not just anger. Anger and fear that I may actually have to watch someone beat me at a game that was supposed to be *mine*.

I couldn't take my eyes off her. She stood there, both hands gripping the gun as she shot it. Her face was concentrated on the screen, the light bouncing off her fair skin.

It was odd seeing her without the mask. Her eyes had been captivating enough behind it, but seeing her without the mask was even worse.

After some time, I wasn't even paying attention to how she was playing the game and instead just focused on her. Memorizing the planes of her face. Her high cheekbones and plump lips. I wanted to trace them. Wanted to run my hand through her hair.

I had imagined what she looked like under the mask. It was always hard to make out the face behind it, but now that I could see all of her unobstructed and out in the open, I couldn't help but replace all the images in my fantasies with her real face.

"You're good," I said with a dry mouth.

She didn't respond. She didn't have to. We both knew I was stating the obvious.

And then, in the last few minutes, she somehow missed the opportunity to get double points for her kills. I opened my mouth to mention it to her but quickly slammed it closed.

You could still win.

I would have to be almost perfect, but I could do it. I gritted my teeth as her score flashed across the screen. It was five points more than my last game. *Just* five.

She pushed the gun into my hand with a smirk.

"Show me what you got." Her chuckle caused heat to flash across my skin.

I grabbed the gun from her with a frown and put two more coins into the machine.

"You think you can beat me?" she asked, her voice suddenly too close.

Fuck.

This was the least sexy situation, but my body was already responding to her like it did at the club. I was warm all over and even the heat of her body seeping into mine was enough to cause my stomach to clench with need.

"I know I can," I all but spat back. She laughed again. I hated the way it made my skin tingle. Hated that out of all of the people that could have found me here, it had to be her.

But she didn't find you here, she followed you. Something that should have scared me... but it didn't. Bailey had tried for months to get me to take her home, and every time she tried to find out something about me, I panicked... but Quinn?

I was getting excited. She came here for me. Tried to get on my level. She didn't think this was stupid, or at least it didn't look like it.

For the first time, someone I was interested in was actually showing up in my real life. Giving me an excuse to take this further than I ever had before.

What was happening to me?

I slammed my hand down on the start button and readied my gun. The normal chunk of plastic I used so often suddenly felt alien in my hands.

Win this, or she comes home with you.

Her hand brushed across my back and down the side of my hip. Her breath was hot on my neck. The smell of her musky cologne filled my senses. I wanted to lean into her. Wanted to stretch my neck to the side so she could run her lips down my sensitive skin.

She was so close I could barely breathe.

"It's cute how into this you are," she whispered. Anger and embarrassment fought each other inside me. "You really *don't* want me to come home with you?"

I gritted my teeth. I spoke the truth before. Since joining the Secret Service, I haven't brought a single person to my house. Friend or lover.

She would be the first, and that meant something more than just a casual one-night stand. It was her seeing into my *life*. Seeing something I had kept hidden for my entire time in the Secret Service.

But it's been years... Isn't it time to allow yourself to let your guard down just a bit?

She would be seeing a part of *me*. A me that no one else knew existed.

Why was that so exciting?

I let out a loud moan as she pushed me against the cool wall of the elevator. Her lips were on mine in seconds, and her hands gripped my hips hard enough that I knew there would be bruises the next morning.

I loved it. This was the first time other than that night at the club that she had touched me, and it took her seconds to understand exactly what would make me melt against her.

Maybe all that watching was worth it.

The entire walk, the tension had been unbearable, and it was a wonder that we even made it this far without tearing each other's clothes off.

"You think you're being sneaky?" she asked with a chuckle, pulling away. "You lost on purpose."

My entire body was already on fire, but her words fanned the flames.

"I actually tried," I spat, and wrapped my arms around her, pulling her closer. She pushed her body against mine and let her hand wander down my thigh before forcing it around her waist.

There was already a dull ache between my legs. My body was begging for her touch. Heat pooled in my core, and I unashamedly ground against her front.

I didn't care what the other agents saw anymore. I was too enthralled by the person who had shown up in front of me. I had only gotten a glimpse of her like this at the club, and I was already addicted. I needed to see what else she was hiding behind that cold gaze of hers.

Her other hand grabbed my ass and pulled me closer before helping me grind against her body. *Fuck.* Delicious, *delicious* low bursts of pleasure shot through me from the friction.

"*Liar,*" she said with a chuckle. She refused to kiss me now. Instead, those piercing blue eyes were watching me turn into a puddle before her. Her mouth was slightly open, mimicking the way mine had fallen as moans spilled out of me.

The worst and most embarrassing thing was that I *did* try. I had been trying at the very beginning, trying to save face, but as soon as I got toward the end... I—I just couldn't bring myself to up her score.

She could reject me a hundred times over, and somehow I think that I would still lose that game for just a chance at getting her to touch me again.

I reached down to unbutton my slacks.

"Safe word," I whispered.

Her eyes searched my face.

"*Zombie,*" she said, her lips quirking.

Fuck why was that so hot?

"Please," I breathed, pushing down my slacks just enough to show her how ready I was. "We can talk more about what this means later but I want you. *Now.*"

The ding of the elevator caused us to freeze. When I realized it was my floor, I wasted no time pulling her along with me and walking down the hallway to my door.

My hands shook as I tried to open the door, but I somehow managed it in record time. I turned around and pulled her in by her shirt.

A wicked yet somewhat forced smile spread across her face. Any other time it would have caused warning bells to go off in my head, but instead I kicked the door closed behind us and brought her lips back to mine.

I was vaguely aware of her locking the door behind us before her arms wrapped around me.

"Please. I don't think I can wait anymore," I confessed against her lips. "I have never been so ready to fuck someone in my life."

She didn't laugh at that. She turned us around and pushed me against the wall. She pulled away, her eyes staring into mine, as one hand fastened around my neck and the other slipped into my pants.

Even just the lightest brush of her fingers against my swollen and aching clit caused a moan to spill from my lips. Her touches were so gentle and hesitant that it only made me buck against her harder.

"Is this where you want me?" she asked. There was a teasing smile on her lips, but her tone was serious.

"Harder." I gasped when her two fingers came to rub hard but slow circles in my clit.

I spread my legs for her, needing her to go faster, to fuck me more. But she didn't. She just watched me as I shuddered against her.

I let out a whine as my hips bucked against her movements.

"Please, it won't take long," I whined. "Just a little faster."

"What if I wanted to take my time with you, little one?" she said, her voice low and seductive. "What if I wanted to play with this greedy pussy until you're writhing and begging for a release that will never come?"

Yes, please was on the tip of my lips, but then the tingling heat of my release played at my senses, warning me of its arrival. I didn't speak for fear that she would pull away. She realized it all on her own, though.

Her eyes widened as the first wave of my orgasm rolled through me and caused a low groan to spill from my lips. This orgasm, unlike the ones I had been chasing at the club, was softer. It wasn't a violent onslaught of pleasure that had me screaming at the top of my lungs.

It rolled gently through me, causing my sopping wet cunt to

squeeze around nothing. I relaxed into it. Letting myself experience the orgasm that caused my body to relax more than it had in months.

It was addicting. The way it lit my entire body up while simultaneously feeling like I was dunked in a bath of warm water.

"I'm surprised you didn't know after watching me for so long," I teased breathlessly. "If you're not careful, I'll come without you even knowing it."

She paused for a moment, her nostrils flaring. There was a renewed hunger in her eyes that caused me to shiver.

"So easy," she murmured while continuing to play with my clit. "I need to see it again."

"Just go a little faster—"

"No," she growled. "On my time. I want to explore."

"Explore what?" I said with a laugh. "You've seen me naked and in all positions you could imagine. There isn't anything—"

She silenced me with a kiss. Her hand left my clit to hoist me up and start carrying me across the apartment. She walked around the furniture in my living room, finding my room without any trouble, and deposited me softly on the edge of the bed.

I should of asked how she seemed to be able to walk through my apartment without so much as a glance, but my lust clouded my senses.

"Take off everything," she said, looking down at me with a famished expression. Her tongue darted out to lick her lips.

I did as she said, taking off my top first, then my bra. Her eyes narrowed in on my pierced nipples. I kicked off my shoes and pushed down my pants and underwear in one go.

"Is this suitable for you?" I asked and spread my legs for her, giving her a perfect view of my wet folds. She gave me a quick nod and fell to her knees. Her face was at the perfect level for my tits.

One of her hands reached out to brush against my nipple. Her hand was shaking.

"I've seen people be so rough with these," she murmured. "Does it hurt?"

I shook my head and pushed my chest out toward her. I was going to go crazy if she planned on teasing me like that.

"I like it," I whispered. "You can be rough too."

She swallowed thickly. Both hands were at my chest now, lightly rolling my nipples between her fingers. My light gasp filled the room.

"Does it feel good?" she asked.

I nodded and pulled my lower lip between my teeth. It felt *really* good. Even better when she leaned forward and sucked one into her mouth.

I moaned in encouragement and leaned into her.

"You've seen me on stage," I said with a laugh. "Don't be nervous about breaking me."

Her eyes met mine, and I shuddered when she pulled away just enough for me to catch sight of her tongue circling my nipple.

The image went straight to my core.

"That's not what I'm... nervous about," she said as she pulled away. Her eyes fell to my now-erect and swollen nipples.

"Then what?" I asked, my own nervousness filling me.

Did she have second thoughts? Maybe she didn't want to be with me after all?

"You're so experienced," she said. "Constantly getting fucked by people who know what they're doing."

I swallowed thickly. Shame tickled the recesses of my mind, but I pushed it away.

"Worried you won't be up to par?" I teased. It was a joke meant to lighten the situation, but her expression was serious.

"Yes," she admitted after a moment. "I don't have as much experience as you. But I want you. *Badly.* I've been yearning to taste you ever since I first saw you bent over that goddamn bench, and now that you're here, cunt soaked and waiting, I can't help but think how much more enjoyable it would be for you if—"

I cut her off by tangling my hand in her hair and forcing her lips to mine. She met me with an enthusiastic kiss, moaning in my mouth as I showed her just how much I wanted her as well.

When I pulled away, we were both panting. I kept my hand tangled in her hair, forcing her to look at me.

"I want you too," I said. "If you've fucked a hundred people or none. I want *you*."

Her gaze darkened.

"Then teach me, Blake," she said. "Teach me how to fuck you."

QUINN

There was no taking it back now.

There was a reason I had waited so long on the sidelines. A reason why I had wanted to turn down this job for the first time in my career.

And it all came to this.

I was going to fuck her, and the little experience I had would be no match for hers.

Her flushed face was inches from mine. Her breathing was heavy. And her eyes... god, they were so expressive. She wasn't lying.

She watched my face for a moment before leaning back with a smirk.

"And to think you had me so flustered," she joked.

She tangled her hand in my hair and pushed my mouth toward her pierced nipple. I brought it into my mouth and started teasing it with my tongue. She let out a light groan.

"I like this," she whispered. "My nipples are sensitive."

I pulled away, a line of spit following me. I gripped her thigh and spread her legs further. The hair between her legs was short, giving me a perfect view of her puffy pussy. She was dripping onto the comforter already. The sight made my mouth water.

"And here?" I asked, trailing my hand up her thigh. "How do you like it here?"

I trailed my fingers down her folds, brushing against her clit before teasing her entrance.

"Fuck," she whispered under her breath.

"Too much?" I asked, looking back up at her.

Her hand was covering her mouth, as if hiding her embarrassment. She shook her head. "I don't know why, but this is driving me even crazier than if you just fucked me."

I watched her face as I sank two fingers into her. Her mouth opened, but no sound came out.

"Here is also sensitive," I said, using my other hand to rub slow circles on her clit. The piercing gave me pause at first, but when she didn't say anything I took it as a good sign. "Am I doing good?"

She shook her head, her face flaming. I clicked my tongue.

"Come on, Blake," I teased, pumping my fingers in and out of her. The squelch of her wetness filled the air and caused my own cunt to clench. "Tell me how good I'm doing."

I put more pressure on her clit, but didn't up the pace just yet. Her expression was intoxicating, and she started making this light mewling sound that made my head spin.

"So good," she moaned. Her hips jerked against my hands. I could tell she was trying to keep herself still, letting me take my time to explore her body, but it was getting harder for her to control herself.

"My clit," she gasped out. "Faster, *please*."

"Begging me now?" I asked with a chuckle but obliged her anyway. *How could I not when she cried out for me like that?* I had killed more than I could count. Held the lives of men between my fingertips. But never had I felt more powerful than when Blake was begging *me* to bring her pleasure.

Power that I could easily get drunk off of.

She didn't answer me and just moaned against me. I leaned

forward and took her nipple into my mouth, sucking it hard. She cried out, her pussy clenching my fingers.

"More," she panted against me. "Add a—*fuck*—add another finger."

I pushed another one in with ease. She was sopping wet. So ready for *me*. The knowledge made me impossibly feral for her.

"*Faster.*"

"No," I said around her nipple before biting down on it lightly. "I want this to last."

"It will. I just need to come, *please*, Quinn."

God. Her begging did something sinful to me. She may have been begging me for an orgasm, but if I didn't get my own soon, I don't know how much longer I would be able to go on.

"Maybe if you encourage me a bit more, I'll think about it," I said. "Are you forgetting I'm new to this?"

She threw her head back and let out a moan.

"Fuck, so good. You're doing so good. Please—*ah*—yes, yes, just like that—"

Her mouth cut off into a cry when I brought her other nipple into my mouth. My hand worked between her legs, pushing her further and further toward the orgasm her body was begging me for.

I couldn't get enough of the way she was gripping me. Of the way her cries filled the apartment. Of the way she was begging *me* to fuck her.

It became strikingly clear why she went to the club. Why anyone went to the club.

Up until now, I had seen sex as a transaction.

For money.

As a way to get a job done.

But this... if *this* was what sex was supposed to be like, I would have no problem fucking Blake for nothing in return at all. All I wanted was to hear those sweet cries over and over again. I wanted to make her come so many times that the back of my head started to ache from how hard she was pulling on my hair.

"*Ah*—I'm coming, don't stop, just keep it going just like that. *Oh fuck*—"

She came with a cry, her pussy fluttering around my fingers. Wet heat slashed over my fingers, and I was vaguely aware of her cursing between her moans. Her thighs shook so hard I was worried that I may have done too much.

But then her hand was there, forcing me away from her chest, only to crash her lips against mine.

I launched us back onto the bed, pushing her down so I was on top of her.

I ravished her mouth, moaning against the taste of her. Whoever the person I was before I stepped into this apartment was not the person who was shaking with need for Blake. Nor would I be the same when I left.

"I need to taste," I murmured against her before trailing kisses down her body. She leaned into them, writhing under me as if each kiss sent a bolt of pleasure through her body. Her reactions were dangerously feeding my ego, but I didn't want it to stop.

When I settled between her legs, I heard a sound of protest coming from her mouth, but as soon as my tongue dragged across the length of her folds, she quieted.

"Yes," she moaned breathlessly. "Flat tongue. Drag up until— *yes,* like that."

I did as she said, licking up all of her release.

If I thought her moans were intoxicating, the taste of her cunt was pure heroin.

I could feast on her all day. It was totally selfish and had nothing to do with the sweet noises she was making. *Well, almost nothing.*

When I got to her clit, I applied harder pressure, but it wasn't having the effect I wanted, so instead I sucked the swollen nub into my mouth.

Her back bowed. Her hands were in my hair again. Her hips were grinding against my face.

I was the one between her legs, eating her pussy like it was my last meal, but she was the one taking control. She forced me to stay in my position as she shook and bucked her hips against me.

She's coming again. Already. I knew women could come multiple times in one go. I knew *she* could as well. But still, experiencing it firsthand was amazing.

She was so sensitive. So perfect. So... right. I had never seen a more beautiful picture than her coming while I fucked her with my tongue.

After she came on my tongue, I climbed back on top of her to pull her back into a kiss.

It's a pity she has to die. If she didn't, I would be tempted to keep her.

The thought caused me to jerk away from her. She met me with a hooded gaze and a sleepy smile. Those eyes that called to me so much were shining brightly under the lighting overhead, but like all other clients, I didn't have the urge to keep them. Even the thought of art caused a pit to form in my stomach.

She's a job. You're here for information.

But as she pulled me into another kiss, this one sweeter, I found myself unable to focus on the task at hand.

It was two a.m. by the time I found myself sneaking out of her bed.

At this point, the people watching her would be back, but that didn't matter much. They saw me come in, and I would now be on their radar.

My eyes glanced around her room. It was simple. A bed and two end tables. The closet was to my right, behind a closed door and the bathroom next to it.

Not many places to hide things.

I glanced back at Blake's sleeping form. She was bundled up in her deep purple bedspread, her hair stuck out messily from the top. Her deep breaths were barely audible over the sounds of the night right outside her window.

I peered out of it, trying not to be too obvious about my intentions. Just on the right, there was something small and shiny on a rooftop two buildings away. Because she was on the sixth floor and the building across was eight, it was hard to see the people watching, but the small shine of what I assumed was their weapon gave it away.

Instead of dropping to my knees and searching the drawer like I wanted to, I made a note to get some curtains for her.

I ducked into the bathroom, shutting the door softly. Light purples and blues decorated the space, but just like her room, she had the bare essentials.

Toothbrush, toothpaste, mouthwash, face soap, an organic bottle of—*ah.*

I grabbed the bottle, my eyes widening when I realized that Tiffany Yates had a prescription for Xanax.

That wasn't in the file.

Tilting it, I made note that she hadn't taken many.

So if she didn't use them, why were they here anyway?

Spurred by the discovery, I placed it back where I found it and dug through the medicine cabinet.

I frowned when only floss and an extra toothbrush greeted me.

"What, you don't like pink?" I jumped, grabbing the first thing I saw and using it to face the intruder.

Act first, ask questions later. To the neck or eye, whichever is most—

I stopped in my tracks when Blake's smiling face met mine. The pounding of my heart forces blood to my ears, muting the world around me. It took more than a few seconds to remember what my mission was.

How the fuck did she get up without me hearing her? Or even open the door?

Alarm bells went off in my head. Years of the training I went through told me one thing and one thing only: *she's dangerous.*

"Sorry," I said quickly, clearing my throat. I looked down, realizing that I had grabbed the pink toothbrush as my weapon, and gave it a bitter smile. "I don't mind pink, you just caught me off guard."

When I looked back up at her, her smile didn't waver. She lightly grabbed the toothbrush out of my hand and placed it back on the counter before pulling me back into the room with her.

"I thought you were trying to leave," she said, shooting me a smile.

"I was considering it," I admitted. She let out a hum, her eyes searching my face.

Blake had this whole flustered persona about her, but more than once I was surprised by how easily she could read me. *I needed to move with caution.*

"I know," she said. "But I would prefer you stay. I liked our time together, and I want to do it again."

Heat crawled up my neck. I hadn't expected to like it as much as I did. To lose myself so easily.

"I would too," I said softly.

She pulled me back into bed, and I let her pull the covers over us once more. How long has it been since I let myself get so close to someone? Since I let them wrap their arms around me?

"Sorry I didn't have much else," she said. "I'm kinda clueless when it comes to clothes."

I laid back on the pillow, looking at her. I brought the t-shirt up to my nose, inhaling deeply.

"I don't mind," I said. "I like that it smells like you. The shorts are a bit short, though."

More than a bit short. They rode up my ass even while just lying in bed. At least her sleep shirts were oversized.

Even in the darkness, I could see the blush that coated her cheeks.

A silence fell over us.

"I'll tell you one thing if you do," she proposed.

No, was on the tip of my tongue, but I swallowed it.

"You first."

She let out a light laugh and turned to look up at the ceiling. When I did the same, only then did I realize that there were faded yet still glowing stars on the ceiling.

"I think a single mother and child lived here before me," she whispered. "I couldn't bring myself to bring the stars down."

They were worn, and barley glowing, but their presence was unmistakable. It caused something to twist in my chest. We were never allowed something like this back in the guild. Especially if it's something that could give away our existence in the night.

Our bunks were bare. Every single one the same drab grey colors. No posters or tack marks allowed to be left behind.

Erasing us completely.

"A bit of a sign that someone came before you," I murmured, knowing the feeling all too well.

Since starting under Rolf, I have yet to stay in one place for longer than a few months, with the exception of the house I occupy now. Every time I did my sweeps of the place for bugs, I would take special note of the wear and tear of the house. I couldn't leave any signs of my existence, but that didn't stop me from taking not of others'.

I imagined what the people before me did. How they lived. If the apartment smelled clean and flowery. I would imagine the plants they must have kept in there. Scratches on the wall? Maybe a pup got too excited when the owner came home.

It reminded me that people had actual lives to live, even when mine felt like a never-ending job.

"And that maybe someone will remember that I came before as well."

Her words caused an ache in my chest that I couldn't identify. No one could know that I had come before. My apartment was completely redone each time, leaving no trace of who I was.

No one would be left to remember me.

"Is that your thing?" I asked, swallowing the knot in my throat.

Another light laugh followed.

"My thing is that you probably noticed my medication in the bathroom," she said. "I used to suffer from anxiety attacks, and whenever I would feel one coming on, I would take a pill."

"But it's full," I noted, and I wished I hadn't.

"I hadn't had one in a while," she said. "But before I say anything else, it's your turn."

My turn? I never expected to be in this situation, so I didn't have anything prepared. My backstory for this job wasn't well thought out because I was being forced to use my real name, so it would cause problems if I tried to make it up as I went.

"I lost my virginity later than most," I said after a while. Embarrassment creeping up on me.

"Never met the right person?" she asked.

"More like..." *I was too busy murdering random people for money.* "No chance to form a connection deep enough to even try."

"So what did you do?" Her hand found mine under the blankets and threaded our fingers together. Such a small gesture... but it made the tightness in my chest grow. I had to pause to adjust to the feeling.

"I knew I couldn't put it off any longer, so I asked my coworker to help me... experience it," I admitted. Shame and embarrassment washed through me. I remember the encounter so vividly it caused my chest to tighten.

It was another assassin in the seduction unit. She was perfect. Taught me the basics and made me come a few times, but it was no longer than a quick forty-five-minute session, and I never saw her again. We had planned to practice again a few times after, but she had been decommissioned.

Even so many years later, I felt a bitterness fill me. I was upset back then. She hadn't been the first person to die that I knew, but she had... meant something to me.

But that was just how the job was.

Besides that, I often had to kiss or touch targets to get them to a secluded place, but once I was there I could end the job quickly.

I never had to probe them for information like this before.

"Where are they now?" she asked.

Dead. "We don't work at the same job anymore," I said with a strained smile.

"There's no shame in any of that," she said, reading me all too well again. "My first time was... well, let's just say that person may have unknowingly set off the reason why I have anxiety attacks now."

I latched onto the information.

Was this how she knew Alec Crowe?

"I'm sorry to hear that," I said and squeezed her hand. I don't know why I did it, just that it seemed right in the moment. "I am glad to hear you don't have them often anymore."

She let out a hum before turning back toward me.

"Let's go back to bed, yeah?" she asked. "If you stay until morning, I can guarantee you a hot coffee on the house."

A smile pulled at my lips. "Sounds like a deal."

I had never slept in the same bed as someone else. Especially one that I was going to kill. But that night I found myself falling asleep faster than I ever had before, with the sound of Blake's steady breathing following through my dreams.

BLAKE

"Is this a... date?" I asked with a light laugh.

Quinn's gaze, which had been locked on the windows to our right, met mine. Her hair was slightly disheveled from sleep, and there were small dark circles under her eyes. I wondered if sleeping in a stranger's bed had any effect on her. I stayed up quite late, listening to the sound of her breathing, but not once did she stir.

She wore the prior day's clothing and held a hot cinnamon cappuccino in her hands.

Unlike me, who had gulped down their hot coffee in a matter of minutes, she seemed to want to savor the drink.

No matter, after the night before, I needed the coffee. Quinn may have been able to sleep soundly, but my nerves kept me up. I didn't trust Quinn. She was a stranger who found her way into my apartment. No matter what kept drawing me to her, there was a bigger part reminding me that I knew virtually nothing about her.

That thought alone kept me up most of the night.

She shifted in her seat, crossing her legs and leaning back into the car with a sly smile.

"Do you want it to be?" she asked.

I leaned forward, placing my chin on my hands.

"Maybe it's more like a continuation of our arcade date," I said. "After all, I assume one has to go home to actually end the date before the next one starts."

The twitch of her lips caused a bolt of satisfaction to go through me. During those twenty-four hours, I had a first-hand look at the real person Quinn was. The stoic mask she had on at the club was slowly starting to drop.

It gave me hope.

Hope that my anxiety was just that—an incessant worry that means nothing. Hope that I could have something, as little as this may be, to myself without fear of what would happen to me or that the rug would be pulled out from under me.

"So..." she trailed. "Going out for coffee at eight a.m. on a weekday... Shouldn't you be heading to work soon, or is the club...?"

The panic must have been obvious on my face because she trailed off toward the end.

"Actually, I think we should probably talk about that," I said nervously, looking around. The morning rush hadn't started yet, so now would be the perfect time to drop any bombs I had. The café itself was large enough that the customers wouldn't overhear each other, but it didn't stop my anxiety.

I looked out the windows, trying to search for the familiar black sedans that followed me almost everywhere I went.

There was no sign of them.

But that didn't mean that they *weren't* around, it just meant that they didn't want to be found.

"Do you want to go someplace more secluded?" she asked.

I shook my head. This was as safe as it would get, for the both of us. Public with no one around to eavesdrop. "You should probably know that I have a job in the government."

If the news shocked her, she didn't show it on her face.

"A job in the government, huh?" she asked, her eyes trailing down my figure.

If she were anyone else, I would have assumed that she was assessing my form. Trying to figure out exactly what I did there.

"Yes," I said, watching her expression.

"Is that what's causing you to look over your shoulder every time I'm near? Is there someone watching us that I should know about?"

Her observation caused ice to replace the blood in my veins.

"Yes and no," I said after a moment. "They are probably keeping tabs on me, but it's nothing you need to worry about. The only thing you should know is that this job in particular requires the people I bring home to have background checks done on them."

"You mean me?" she asked, her tone teasing. I averted my gaze to the table.

God. I hated how her teasing, no matter how slight it was, caused my skin to heat.

There was another hope lingering in the back of my mind. One that thought that maybe we could keep this up. Maybe she could not only accept what I do but actively seek out my company even after she found out what a shitshow my life was.

It was the whole reason I brought her here in the first place. Somehow the café seemed like a safe, neutral space. If she wanted to leave she could. If she decided that the baggage was too much for her, she could turn around and walk right out of my life, never to be seen again.

I hope she won't.

She was the first ever that I brought to my apartment. First ever to meet outside of the club, save for a few run-ins with random people in the real world.

I couldn't help but feel like after so many years of hiding, meeting her was a sign of... well, *something.* What that something was, I didn't quite know yet.

This was the difference between her and Bailey. I had never once felt comfortable introducing Bailey into my life this way.

Bailey was a good introduction to a relationship. It was messy, and we weren't exclusive, but it was *something*. The perfect something that prepared me for this. She was but a steppingstone. One that decided to fall away at exactly the right moment to prepare me for this.

Maybe the world was finally repaying me for the shit it put me through. Karma and all that, right?

"I didn't know I let someone famous pop my cherry," she said with a light laugh.

My gaze snapped to her, my mirth falling over in shock.

"I thought you said I wasn't your first!" I exclaimed in a harsh whisper.

Only when I caught sight of the small smirk on her lips did the tension in my shoulders dissipate.

With a breathy chuckle, I sat back in the chair and sent her a relieved smile. I couldn't even pinpoint a time when I felt so comfortable in someone's presence. *Maybe Sloan*, but even then I couldn't talk to her like this.

"I'm not famous," I said after a moment.

She just shrugged and brought the cup back to her lips.

She took a sip before setting it down and leaning forward. My eyes lingered on her throat, I had the strangest need to sink my teeth into the taunt column just to see her reaction to it.

"I don't mind," she said. "And I have nothing to hide."

I blinked rapidly, trying to get my head in the game. *Nothing to hide.* I nodded, though I didn't quite believe her. Everyone had something to hide.

"So... it's probably a good time to ask what you do?"

"Or ask what skeletons I'm hiding in my closet," Quinn suggested. Her tone was dark, her eyes slightly narrowed. Outwardly, nothing really changed, but there was a shift in the air.

One that excited me when it shouldn't have.

"I just hope they are well hidden. I can handle almost anything but jobs that hurt or take advantage of people." I said. My response seemed to stun her. She blinked before leaning back in her chair.

"What about jobs that hurt *bad* people for a cause?" she asked.

"I—um—"

"*Kidding*," Quinn said, lifting the tension that had fallen over us. "I am but a lowly contractor for a construction company owned by a family member. Though becoming a vigilante *would* make for an interesting story, wouldn't it?"

"It would," I said with a nervous chuckle.

It didn't feel right. There was nothing wrong with the way she said it or the type of job... but it didn't fit her at all. Not that she wouldn't be able to oversee construction projects and the like... but that was just so *boring*.

Boring and just... *wrong*.

This is your paranoia talking. Just like your paranoia talked you into following her into the bathroom last night.

But if she was just a normal person... *what would she think if she knew what I did?* I couldn't help but think of my job in comparison. Or how it felt to pummel that man into the ground. I hurt people. All the time for the sake of my job.

He wasn't the first, nor was he the last. Men like him—men who *hurt* people—brought out something dark in me. Something I had no control over. But she... she would never find that out.

I waited for her to ask me about my job, but she stayed silent.

"Are you going to ask about mine?" I asked hesitantly.

"Nope," she said, popping the "p." "You'll tell me when you're ready."

I shifted in my chair. Sweat coated my palms, and my mouth went dry.

I could tell her. It would be easy... *then why couldn't I? Why couldn't I just open my mouth and say it?*

"And if I *hurt* bad people to protect others?" I finally asked.

"Then I would call you a hypocrite."

Her words caused me to freeze. They shot straight through my chest like a knife, stopping my heart.

"Because why are you allowed to but others are not?"

"My job makes it complicated," I explained, all of a sudden feeling like I needed to defend myself.

She let out a hum.

"So it's the job that's the hypocrite?" she asked. When I opened my mouth to spill everything, she raised her hand. "I'm not trying to give you a hard time, sorry. I was just curious."

"Hypothetically..." I trailed. "I believe some of those acts can be... forgiven depending on the who. Though my job might say otherwise."

Quinn's eyes lingered on me for another moment longer. *Was that too much? Does she think I'm some sort of monster now?*

But her eyes gave no indication of it. Instead, there was a sort of... intrigue in her face that caused my chest to swell.

"Good to know," she said, then rose from her seat. She handed me the discarded napkin she left on the table. I hadn't noticed when she wrote her number on it. "Text me sometime. If the background check comes back clean, that is."

My face heated, and I took the napkin from her, careful not to crumple it up.

"If you don't hear from me, it didn't," I said and sent her a smile. "Though I really hope it comes back clean. I want to see you again."

The smile that spread across her face caused my heart to stop. She swooped down, not just to brush her lips against mine but to give me a deep, knee-quivering kiss.

I couldn't help but return it.

When she pulled away, we were both breathless, and her lips shone in the light.

"I want to see you again too," she said in a low voice. "But in all honesty, the background check won't stop me from finding you again."

Before I could respond, she stood and left the café.

"Hey if anyone asks, the senator never got arrested, okay?"

I paused, unpacking the light lunch I had brought myself and looked up at Ryan with a bewildered expression.

The room was quiet, the light sounds of the children playing outside muffled by the windows. I looked over my shoulder out into the backyard.

Mrs. Bennett and her kids were out with two other secret service agents. The children had decided to play with bubble wands. One of the agents scowled when the bubbles popped on his suit, the other afforded the children a genuine smile and said something to them I couldn't make out.

"I don't talk about my work outside if that is what you're worried about," I said, turning back to him with a strained smile. "Besides my contractual obligations, it's not like I have friends."

"But you do have a partner," he said, his eyes flitting back to the windows. "In all the time you've been here, you've never reported one."

"It's new." *Less than twenty-four hours since I put in the paperwork.* "I didn't know you were so interested in my personal life."

"Well, it's not just the senator that we need to keep safe, right?" he asked. "Ross told me about your *situation.*"

Why would he do that? All the hair raised on the back of my neck, and my mouth went dry. *What the actual fuck? Did no one know what confidential meant?*

I tried not to panic, but it was hard when we both knew what my *situation* meant.

"We're not supposed to talk about it," I said, looking down at my sandwich. I wasn't all that hungry anymore.

"Not supposed to talk about what?"

We both jumped, our heads snapping over to the entrance

where the senator leaned against the doorframe, seemingly unbothered.

Ryan let out a sigh and relaxed against the counter.

"Nothing, sir," I said, turning around with my sandwich in hand. I took a bite just so I wouldn't have to talk but regretted it as soon as the bland food hit my tastebuds. My anxiety was raging inside me and causing my stomach to ache.

I wasn't safe anymore. Not if they were giving my secrets away like candy.

The excuse was that my superiors needed to know just in case anything happened. But someone on Ryan's level never should have counted. He shouldn't have clearance for those files.

"What are you not supposed to talk about, agent?" the senator asked again.

The command in his voice was clear. *I hated when he did that.* It wasn't often he used that tone with us. I had seen him use it on his kids and subordinates, but rarely on the agents.

Because at the end of the day, we were there to protect him, not bow down to him.

I chewed my food before swallowing it with a grimace.

"The fact that you got arrested," I said, giving him the sweetest smile I could muster. "Ryan here was just making *extra sure* that I wouldn't go running my mouth about you stealing those jewels. But don't worry, I abide by the documents I sign. And anyway, they let you go, no? Must have *all* been a misunderstanding."

I don't know what felt better. Getting back at Ryan for his obvious and inappropriate digging into my life or the look on the senator's face as he realized the weight of what I just said.

"You have time to gossip?" he growled toward Ryan.

"It's my lunch break," I said, waving my sandwich, though neither looked at me.

"Just covering my bases, sir," Ryan said.

His tone was surprisingly meek, his eyes lowered to the floor, and his posture looked like he was trying to shrink in on itself.

I understood how terrifying it could be on the other end of that stare. How the sliminess of his gaze made your skin feel. The senator had a nice mask, but inside you could tell his soul was just as corrupt as the people we protected him from.

But there was no reason for Ryan to act like the senator had any kind of power over him.

"Dad, look!" the older daughter called from outside. And just like that, the deadly tension that had been rising around us broke. The senator's face changed in the blink of an eye, turning him into a completely different person.

I have got to stop working with politicians.

He left us without so much as a nod. When he was out of hearing range, Ryan let out a heavy sigh.

"I thought we were on good terms," he muttered.

"Would be if you didn't pry," I said, taking another bite of my sandwich. It hadn't been the first time someone had tried to pry into my past, but it still stung nonetheless.

One thing this whole situation taught me was that the only person I could trust was myself.

Quinn

*Y*ou work fast, little agent.

    I couldn't stop the curve of my lips as the first, then second, message came in. I hadn't expected her to message me so soon, but I wasn't complaining. I had been thinking of her since I left her apartment, and as much as I didn't want to admit it to myself, I couldn't wait to get back into her bed again.

> It's Blake.
>
> From the arcade.

So we are sticking with the cover story now, are we?

Before I could respond, a sound not too far in front of me sounded in the night. Steeling myself, I put the phone into one of the pockets of my vest before grabbing the gun from my thigh holster.

In front of me was a looming building that resembled more of a warehouse than the hideout it was supposed to be. It was also surprisingly hard to find, as it had been nestled between two ship-yards, but I guessed it was good for whatever legal business they ran.

"Alright! *Fuck*, don't get your panties in a tw—"

He didn't have time to finish his sentence before I swiftly shot him straight between the eyeballs. There was a silence as his body fell to the ground, but then chaos rang out. I barley registered the blood splattering across the exposed part of my face.

Men inside started yelling. The shuffling of their feet and click of their guns caused spikes of adrenaline to run through me.

Instead of running into the open warehouse, I jerked to the side, letting another man run out into the night. My uniform helped me blend into the shadows, so he too was unaware that he was about to die until I grabbed him and used him as a shield to enter the warehouse.

Gunshots rang throughout, many of them embedding in the chest cavity of the poor man I was holding.

"Gather reinforcements—"

I used the automatic at the man's side to shoot one of the supposed leaders off to the side, mostly because his yelling was grating on my nerves.

There were only two more people in the main room, both of them running toward me. With ease, I shot both of them multiple times in the head before they fell to the ground with a thud. Only then did I push the dead man I had used as a shield away from me with a noise of disgust.

The silence that filled the air was a bad sign because none of the men I had just killed were my target, meaning the man in question may be using this as a means of escape.

I took an automatic from another dead body before heading down the hallway that connected this building to another. In my mind, I brought up the image of the blueprint, following the red dotted line to where I knew the man would be stationed.

Not his office, though. There were probably men waiting for me there.

As soon as the gunshots rang out, the coward would run to his safe room.

It was hard not to hear the thundering of the footsteps coming down the hallway as they followed me.

I could have stopped and killed them all in minutes, but I wanted this over as soon as possible.

Especially when my fingers itched to reply to my little agent.

Imagining Blake on her couch, staring at her phone, and waiting for me to respond caused me to move even faster, and before I knew it, I was flying down the stairs and kicking the door to the boss's safe room open.

"Get her!" the boss yelled as I came into view. The room was small but decked out like his personal man cave. A leather couch was placed straight in the middle, with him cowering behind it while his two bodyguards struggled to ready their guns. Both of them had been sitting on a set of recliners, not at all expecting me to be here so soon.

The smell of beer, sweat, and smoke caused my nose to twitch.

I dodged to the right, narrowly missing one of their shots, but when I did, the other seemed to finally get his shit together and fire his own gun.

White-hot pain shot up my leg as the bullet grazed me. Normally I took pleasure in the fight, but this time it only made me angry.

Not only did I have things to do after this, but I had been so ready to end it all that I had somehow gotten myself injured.

Rookie fucking mistake.

I lunged for him, getting close enough to wrap my hand around his neck and hold him close to me before switching to my handgun and firing multiple rounds into his chest.

I swung us around as the other fired at me, but he was too slow. With a single shot, he was down.

Then I turned to the man, and only then did a single ounce of excitement run up my spine.

I caught sight of him trying to scurry up the walls and to the small window that lined the ceiling. It was pitiful to watch him try to jump up high enough to get his hands on the sill before dropping to the floor.

I stalked toward him, pulling out my knife.

Make his death painful, the note had said.

Easy said, easy done.

I grabbed the small tuft of hair the man had left, forcing his head to tilt back. I should have had something to say. Maybe taunt him a little, make fun of how disgusting he was... but instead I just sunk the knife right in between his ribs. I could feel the blade puncture his left lung with ease.

He would drown in his own blood as he gasped for air. All I had to do was wait.

Just to be safe, I punctured the right one as well. It was probably quicker than the client wanted, but it wouldn't allow him the chance to escape.

Not that he would get very far.

The sound of the rest of his men running down the stairs caused me to let out a noise of frustration. I turned to them as they flooded in, showing them what I had done to their boss before throwing his body to the ground.

"Come on," I said, and I readied the second gun I had strapped to my left thigh. "Let's get this over with, hmm? I have places to be."

Their cries filled the room as they charged. I stretched out my neck, loosening up the muscles that had tightened in the time it took me to storm the place.

Two minutes. Two minutes, and I can give into the urge to text her back.

Two minutes and thirty-four seconds. Not bad.

I sat back on the bloodied leather couch with a heavy sigh.

The world around me had gone silent.

Off to the side, there was the sound of water droplets falling onto the concrete floors of the hideout.

No, not water. My eyes turned to look at the destruction I left.

Bodies lay sprawled on the floors. Some bleeding out from multiple stabbings to the stomach and chest, while others are long dead from bullet wounds to the head.

My target was lying at my feet, each breath getting shallower than the last. The sound of fluid filling his lungs was disgusting. I almost regret letting him live this long.

The vibration of my phone caused a burst of excitement to go through me.

I fished it out of my vest, not caring about the blood smearing over it and the screen.

> If you gave me a fake number, I'll kill you the next time I see you.

I let out a laugh. *God,* this little agent was something else. Death threats over a government-monitored phone? *Ballsy.*

> People have lives, baby. Trust me when I say I have been itching to respond to you. I was just... preoccupied.

The bubble that told me she was typing popped up and then disappeared again. I wished to be back on the rooftop, looking into her window as I watched how she responded to my messages. Did she blush? Was she excited to hear from me?

But instead of responding, the agent took it one step further. My screen lit up, showing her on caller ID and a picture that I took of her the first night when she was sleeping. In the picture, her face looked so serene, so innocent. Her hair was a wild mess around her head, and she was holding onto her blanket for dear life.

Warmth readied in my chest, and I answered the call.

"Did you miss me?" I asked, shifting on the couch to a more comfortable position. One that allowed me to lean my head back against the cushion and spread my legs. My body pulsed with pain, reminding me of the battle I had just won.

I should probably leave. No doubt someone heard the commotion and called the cops. But I couldn't bring myself to. Not when Blake's voice filtered through the speaker.

"Should I be worried that my girlfriend is *preoccupied* in the middle of the night?" Blake asked. Her tone was hard, but I could tell that she was more teasing than anything.

I let out a breathy chuckle. The sounds of her intake of breath caused a burst of heat to run through me and travel south.

"Is this your way of asking me out, baby?"

"I kinda guessed that it was clear when you agreed to a background check," she said, the pout obvious in her tone. "I thought if you didn't want anything serious, you would have backed out."

I hummed and wiped the blood from my hands off on my uniform.

"What about Bailey?" I asked. "Do I have to worry about someone stabbing me in my sleep?"

There was silence. It was reckless of me to ask, but I wanted to know what Blake thought. She obviously was okay with moving on, but once she found out... would she be upset? Would she regret what was happening with us?

I shouldn't have been excited about her finding out, but I was.

"I didn't know you knew her name," she muttered.

Shit. Should I not have spilled that?

"Everyone in *that place* knows," I said, then paused. "Maybe we shouldn't talk about it on the phone."

"She's not a problem anymore," she said. "It wasn't serious, and she ghosted me a while back after a fight. It's just me and you now."

I left out a sound of disbelief. "I dunno," I said, letting my voice trail. "Maybe you can give me something to sweeten the deal?"

"I'm not sweet enough for you?" she asked with a laugh that caused my heart to skip a beat.

Reel it the fuck in, agent.

"I may need a reminder of just how sweet you are," I said, dropping my voice low. "Touch yourself for me, baby, remind me how you felt."

"I thought you said you'd never done this before," she said, her voice breathless. Like she had already started the party without even fucking inviting me.

"Those perfect nipples first, baby," I said. "Pluck on them for me. Pretend it's me. Don't you dare try and get yourself off yet."

She let out a whine, but I heard a shifting of her clothes and a light moan not long after that.

"If I were there, I would take my time with you," I said, letting my own hand wander down my front. "I would kiss every part of your body before circling my tongue over your nipples. You would be writhing, grinding against me while you begged me to touch you, but I wouldn't. Not until your head swam and your body felt so hot you might explode."

I didn't need to do this. I could continue this relationship without having phone sex with Blake while my last target died at my feet. He was still breathing, his blood still staining my hands and face, all while I was getting hot and heavy with Blake.

She had no idea. No idea what I had done. *I wanted her to know.* I wanted her to imagine me covered in blood, shuddering at the idea of me fucking her with my still bloodied fingers.

"I want you to touch yourself," she gasped. "*Please* let me hear you."

I didn't want to comply. I froze before I forced my clumsy fingers to unbutton my pants and slip into them. I inhaled sharply when my fingers came into contact with wetness.

"I would let you touch me," I said in a low tone. "I would guide your hand right to my pussy and let you get me off all while you watched, yet unable to reach your own release."

I let out a low moan as my fingers came to rub circles in my clit over my underwear. I imagine they were her fingers. That she was here, kneeling in between my legs, a bloodied and naked mess.

She would look up at me with those green eyes while her fingers worked my wet cunt.

"Please," she whispered. "I can't hold it back anymore."

"Trail your hand down your stomach. You can *lightly* run two fingers down your cunt. But don't come yet."

I picked up the pace of my fingers. I closed my eyes and let my head fall back fully. I was lost in the fantasy of Blake. Of how I couldn't wait to see her drenched in blood. How I couldn't wait to make her come over and over again until she was so lost in her own pleasure that she didn't care about the mountains of bodies surrounding her.

"I want to hear you come first," she said. "I'm so wet. My cunt is begging for you, but I'll be good for you. I'll make you feel good."

"*Fuck*," I groaned as a bolt of pleasure licked my spine. "So good. You make me feel so good, baby."

"You're going to come for me, aren't you?" she asked, her voice dropping into a purr. "So fast, and I've barely even touched you?"

Goddammit, I was. My cunt was pulsing. So close to coming that my entire body started to tense in preparation.

"I am," I whined. "I am. So close."

I didn't even recognize myself in that moment. I was needy

and far too embarrassing. Was I really going to get myself off to Blake's moans?

I totally fucking was.

"Come with me," I ordered. "Fuck yourself. Bring the phone closer so I can hear the sound of your wet cunt."

She let out a sound but did as I said. The sound of her hand hitting her wet pussy filtered through the phones. Her moans were audible, but not as loud as before.

"Ah fuck, I can't wait to taste you again," I moaned. I opened my mouth to tell her how good she was being, but no words came out as my orgasm burst through me. Wet, hot pleasure gripped my entire being, forcing me to succumb to it as my pussy convulsed. I couldn't move. I couldn't think. All I could do was ride the waves as the sound of Blake reaching her own orgasm flitted through the speaker.

"Again," Blake commanded breathlessly. "Come again, Quinn—"

"For you, not me. One more time for *you*, let me hear." I ordered, standing and fixing my pants. I gritted my teeth when my eyes caught sight of my target.

How long was it going to take this fucker to die?

Instead of waiting, I walked right over to him and placed my booted foot on his throat.

"Fuck, Quinn, I need more," Blake whined. "I can't help but imagine you between my legs again. Lapping up my pussy."

"Keep going," I ordered and put more pressure on the target's neck. His eyes widened impossibly, but there was nothing he could do. "Come for me again, baby. I can't get enough of how you sound."

Her moans were muffled, the sound of her fucking herself taking over. My pussy clenched again. I wouldn't be able to make it. I needed to see her.

Just as Blake came with a cry, I slammed my heel down on the man's throat. He died even before Blake had come down.

"Meet me at the place," I ordered and hung up. I would rather fuck her anywhere but the club, but I couldn't show up to her house like this, not with everyone watching.

Sirens filled the air. A warning. With quick steps, I walked through the warehouse, exiting out the back and slipping into the night, leaving my target—and his eyes—behind.

BLAKE

"Someone will see, you're not worried?" I asked as Quinn fell to her knees before me.

"I don't care," she growled.

I rushed over here after my call, needing to feel her. I was going crazy without her.

It had been a week since I gathered the courage to text her, but I never expected for it to lead where it had.

She helped me pull off my pants, though only on one leg, so I wouldn't be left completely naked in the hallway.

Not that I would fucking care.

The club was lively tonight, with a band playing in the newly finished back garden area. The sound of people laughing and talking was just around the corner.

I couldn't stop myself from shivering under her touch. My breathing deepened as I thought of people rounding the corner and seeing Quinn's face shoved into my cunt.

She placed my leg over her shoulder, kissing my thigh while her eyes were narrowed on me.

I threaded my hands through her damp hair and pulled her closer to my pussy.

"I've been touching myself to the memory of your mouth on

me." I moaned when she placed an open-mouth kiss right on my clit.

"Invite me over more so you won't have to do it yourself," she mumbled against my clit.

My gasp echoed throughout the hallway.

"The more you come over, the more interested *they* will be in you," I said and threw my head back, not caring about the pain that it caused as my skull hit the wall.

She was barely touching me, but I was already becoming a writhing mess in front of her. No one had ever made me feel this way before. Like even just the slightest brush of her hand against my skin would cause my head to spin and my heart to race.

There was something in the way she looked at me. Something unrestrained inside her that she was desperately trying to reel in. It came out in the times she touched me.

Like then, as her hands wrapped around my thighs and her teeth scraped against my sensitive clit. She was inducing whatever it was inside her that she desperately didn't want to see the light of day.

She was harsher than usual. Her hands were gripping me hard enough to leave bruises. Her movements were wild. Her goal obvious.

She wanted me to come, and fast.

"Quinn," I breathed. "More please. I'm going crazy."

She looked up at me, the bottom half of her face glistening with my wetness. Her mask was slightly askew, giving me a hint at the woman I saw when she was outside of this club.

"I shouldn't want you like this," she said, breathless. "I shouldn't be tripping over my feet just to get a taste of you."

She trailed her fingers up and down my folds until my hips were bucking against her. Only then did she push two of them inside me. She teasingly pumped them inside of me, her eyes never leaving mine as she slowly finger-fucked me.

The voices were getting louder now, and if they kept walking down the hallway, they would be privy to exactly what Quinn was doing to me.

"You think I haven't done the same?" I asked, my voice raising an octave as she fit a third finger in me. I was so impossibly wet that her fingers slid through me with ease. "I risked everything to come here tonight."

A smile spread across her face. *Damn it, I shouldn't have fucking said anything.*

"Did you now, little one?" she asked with a light laugh. "Does it have something to do with that fancy job of yours?"

She pushed a fourth finger inside of me. The stretch caused my head to spin and my breath to catch. She curled her fingers inside of me, causing me to let out an embarrassingly loud moan.

When I didn't answer, she leaned forward to nip at my thigh. I let out a yelp that quickly dissolved as her tongue lapped at my clit.

"I wonder what else you're hiding?"

"Now that you've made me come a few times, you sure are full of yourself, huh?" I hissed.

Instead of punishing me for the remark, she sucked my clit into her mouth with a type of pulsating effect that shot bursts of pleasure through me. I was trying to pull back my orgasm, maybe as a type of punishment for her arrogance, but I couldn't.

She pulled out her fingers before slamming them back into me harder than before. I gritted my teeth, trying to think of anything other than how good it felt, of how the voices had gotten progressively louder. I tried not to think of what they would stumble on. Tried not to think of how it would feel with their eyes running across my body.

I was mostly dressed, something that caused me to feel too covered. I wanted them to see more of me. Wanted them to see just how much I was enjoying what Quinn was doing to me. The evidence was dripping down my legs, but still I shoved my shirt up, bringing my fingers up to my aching nipples and pinching them.

Quinn let go of my clit only to rake it with her teeth again.

"I wonder how many more fingers this greedy pussy can take, hmm?" Her laugh was cruel, but it only made my reaction to her words to be that much stronger. "Do you feel that? Do you feel how your cunt is gripping me? How it's sucking me in and begging for more?"

I opened my mouth to respond, but I found myself unable to reply, especially as she pushed her hand further into me. I could feel myself stretch as her knuckles brushed across my opening.

My back arched painfully. The stretch from her was beginning to be too much. We hadn't even used lube, but with a few thrusts, it became less of a worry.

She was right. My pussy was greedily taking everything she was giving it. This hadn't been the first time that I had been stretched like this, and definitely not the biggest I had taken. But it was still just as intoxicating as the other times, if not more so.

I was addicted to the way her eyes watched me. Addicted to how it felt to be fully consumed by her until I couldn't breathe.

"God, you're making such a mess," she said, though her voice changed. It was no longer teasingly cruel, instead, it held something akin to wonder. "Is this all for me, Blake?"

"Always," I breathed. I couldn't hold it back. My orgasm hit me like a tidal wave. White hot pleasure coursed through me, causing my legs to shake and wetness to spurt from me. My pussy was convulsing around her fingers as she continued to fuck me, helping me ride out the waves.

I felt the stretch before I registered what was happening. I assumed it was because of my pussy clenching around her that it had felt so tight, but then she twisted her hands and—

"I knew you could do it, baby." The sultriness of her voice caused my eyes to flutter open. I hadn't realized I had closed them until she called to me.

I felt so full. So much so it was hard to breathe. And then, as she slowly moved, helping me get used to the feeling of her fist inside of me, I found the tension easing just slightly to be replaced with something else entirely.

"You lied about your experience," I whispered to her. For the first time, her gaze was not locked into mine. It was watching as I sucked in her fist. She pulled it out slightly, looking at the way we were connected, before pushing it back in just as slowly.

"I'm a quick learner," she said. "Especially when it comes to you." She leaned forward, wrapping her lips around my clit and sucking once more.

"Ah fuck," I whined. I couldn't take it anymore. I was a convulsing, drenched mess. I should have had more dignity than to act like this in a random club hallway, but I couldn't stop myself, or her.

I knew the moment I opened my mouth and told her to stop she would, but I couldn't bring myself to.

My gaze fluttered to the end of the hallway. Heat burst through me when I saw just how many people had gathered at the end of it, all of them watching.

I caught eyes with a glance to the side. The masc was bent over slightly, with a hand around her neck, while a femme was pounding into her from behind. Some of the people around them were watching, their hands lingering on their tits and clits, but no one dared approach us.

Ax and Sloan are going to be so mad.

This was a sex club, and more often than not, sex was on display, but because of the types of clientele here, they keep everything to rooms and shows, with little actual fucking like this in the common areas. You may see some people with their hands wandering or in a heavy make-out session, but this was going to get out of hand.

And I fucking loved it. Knowing that *we* had caused such a reaction. Knowing that we had caused them to break such rules in the first place. That *we* had broken those rules.

It made the whole thing that much hotter.

"Oh *damn*, look at Riley go," Avery's voice filtered up the hallway and caused Quinn's head to snap in that direction. Avery *and* Sloan appeared from the crowd, both of them taking in exactly what was happening.

"Oh wow," Sloan said with a smirk crossing her face. She turned to the crowd and ushered them away. Many of them looked embarrassed to be caught. "Okay guys, remember, if you want to fuck like that, there are many rooms available, or you could go join one of the exhibition rooms. While we love to see our guests have fun, let's keep the hallways clear, yes? Fire hazard and all."

Quinn cast a glance at Avery before taking my clit into her mouth again. I let out a surprised gasp and tried to hold back my moans.

"Maybe you *are* in the right field," Avery said, and she walked up to us. I didn't like the way she looked at Quinn, especially when her face was in my pussy. "Better make your target come soon. I doubt Sloan will let you stay here forever. Especially with the scene you caused."

Her target? I was tempted to ask what she meant by that, but my breath was stolen from me as she kept pounding into me.

It wouldn't take long. Especially not when Avery's eyes glanced toward me.

I hadn't had much experience with her or found myself attracted to her in that way, but damn did I love it when people watched me.

I gripped Quinn's hair and rode her face as she fucked me. I was unashamed, and by the way Quinn acted, I was guessing she was coming around to fucking in front of others.

As my second orgasm hit me, Quinn pulled away to look up at me. Her blue eyes were alight with something I hadn't seen before.

"Shut your mouth, or I'll shut it for you," Quinn growled. It took me a moment in my haze to realize that she *wasn't* talking to me. Avery threw her head back, her laugh echoing throughout the hallway.

She pulled her hand from me, the action filling me with an aching hollowness that I absolutely hated.

Quinn stood and helped me dress as both Avery and Sloan watched. An oddly caring gesture that I hadn't expected from her. Sloan's expression was wary and not at all like the easy-going version of her I knew.

From the beginning, we were worried about her...but she hasn't shown us anything to be concerned about.

Was she still so worried about her?

"I blame myself for not giving you the tour and explaining how we work here," Sloan said, giving Quinn a smile. "Why don't we fix that? And don't worry, I'm not kicking you out. Just let's keep scenes like these to where people are *supposed* to watch them."

Quinn gave me a look before leaning in and giving me a quick kiss on my lips before joining Sloan.

Her actions caused me to still, and I couldn't get my limbs to cooperate even as they walked away. My hand ghosted my lips, the shock of the entire situation still not fully sinking in.

"Ah, Quinn, always so careless," Avery said.

I thought she meant the hallway incident, but then her hand shot forward and grabbed my wrist.

My eyes widened when I saw the blood staining my palm.

"What the—"

Avery used the fabric of her shirt to swipe it clean before moving to the next which was just as bloody.

"From the moment I figured out what she was doing here, I just knew she wouldn't be able to distance herself," she said with a tsk. "What did she do? Come here from a job?"

"What are you talking about?" I asked, my voice low.

Avery sent me a sickly-sweet smile that caused goose bumps to break out across my skin.

"Oops, did I say something I shouldn't have?" she asked with a laugh. "My bad."

She dropped my hands before stepping away and motioning

for me to follow them. They were almost at the end of the hallway now, and I knew for a fact I didn't want to be left alone with Avery.

"You've known her since high school," I noted. "Does she often have blood in her hair?"

Avery sent me a shrug. "I guess that's something you'll have to ask her. Though I'm sure she won't open up until you spill something as well. My suggestion is to tell her the truth about why you have people following you."

Her words caused the blood in my veins to freeze.

"What did you just say?"

But she didn't answer. Instead, she turned on her heels and bounded down after them.

Who the fuck is Avery?

QUINN

This is where I die.

Not in a shootout. Not while I slit some bastards' throats. *Here.* Sitting in a comfy room where the couch squeaked when I sat on it and the carpet smelled like something died on it.

'Cause it probably had. Most likely multiple someone's. People who were just like me. People who Rolf had groomed from a young age to be the perfect monsters for him.

I'd like to think that I was unlike them because Rolf had saved me. *Raised* me from when I was but a child until I was ready to go out on my own. That he had done this because he saw a poor and struggling family willing to sell their child to the highest bidder.

It could have been much worse, and I should have been grateful that he had saved me from whoever else wanted to do me harm.

So why was I feeling so angry? I should understand that this was his job. Understand that he would do this to any one of his projects. But instead, I feel betrayed.

I had conflicting feelings about Rolf. The child inside me looked at him as a father. Saw him as someone that I should have been close to. Someone who protected me.

But the adult in me knew he was just as flawed as the rest of us. That he was just looking out for himself. And no matter what, I shouldn't trust him as much as the child inside me wanted to.

Rolf was across from me, not sitting at his desk but standing right in front of it. It made it so he was towering over me. Something he had done on occasion to remind me exactly who was in charge here.

I had only been invited to his office a few times before this. All of them were when he was reprimanding me for something I did. Though this time, I couldn't tell what I had done. Which made me all the more angry.

I had been getting close to Blake like they had asked. It was taking a long time, but for a job like this, I needed to move with caution. Rolf should understand that.

But this felt more serious than all those other times. He hadn't once opened his mouth to speak since telling me to sit down.

Which meant he was waiting for something. *Or someone.*

My phone vibrated in my pocket, the loud, harsh sound cutting through the quiet.

Rolf's gaze shot to mine, watching my reaction. I kept it as cool as possible.

"Are you going to get that?" he asked.

"Nope," I said and leaned back into the couch. "I can reply later."

"Is it the target?"

I pursed my lips, unable to help the uncomfortableness that spread throughout my body. "Yes."

"Let me see—"

"No," I said far too quickly. There was a silence between us. Rolf shifted, causing me to tense up and get ready for a fight. "I have it handled. Don't interfere."

Rolf let out a bitter laugh.

"If you had it handled, you wouldn't fucking be here," he said, shaking his head.

Now *that* got my attention.

"What do you mean?" I asked. "I have been doing my job. Getting close to her. What am I missing?"

"It will be five months since you've successfully infiltrated the club and made contact," he said. "Even longer since you've had the job. The rate this is going is unacceptable."

"And you should remember that this job came with not one but *two* complications. Not only did I have to murder her obsessive *fuck toy*, but she is assigned to a fucking presidential candidate. You even told me this would be a longer job, so I am not sure why I am here." I growled. "I *just* got invited to her apartment after cleaning up the mess you forced me into. How do you expect me to get all the information in such a short amount of time?"

Rolf shook his head and let out a bitter laugh.

"Short amount of time? Agent, this is the longest job you have ever been on. I knew I should have sent someone who was better at seduction."

Anger boiled under my skin. What the fuck happened within the few months that I had taken this job? Did someone say something? Was there a change of plans from the client? Sure, this was longer than usual, but I thought we were all on the same page.

"Seduction isn't the issue," I hissed. "You have to be kidding me, Rolf. What the fuck is this about? We both knew it would take a long time, which is why I am also taking small side jobs. Did you forget about that?"

His jaw twitched, and he let out a huff.

"I didn't forget," he said.

"So what changed?" I pushed, leaning forward. "This isn't about me, is it?"

His eyes searched mine. *Finally.* I was getting somewhere. The child inside me rejoiced. I *knew* he wasn't going to call me in here for any of this bullshit.

Maybe he too was under pressure from the client. That's the only reason I could think as to why Rolf would act like this.

A ping from his phone pulled both of our attention to it. It was face up on the desk and lit up when the message came in. From my spot I couldn't make out the message, but Rolf's body language told me it was someone important.

Rolf's entire demeanor changed to that of my stern handler once more. *One step forward, two fucking steps back.*

"It's the client," he said as he picked up his phone. "He wanted to speak with you."

My heart seized in my chest. Directly? The client wanted to speak to *me*?

Was this Alec Crowe? It had been bothering me since I saw the name in the files.

I had done my best to try and research exactly how they could be connected, but I came up with nothing.

He put the phone on speaker as it dialed the number. It took a few rings to pick up, but when he did, it was silent.

"I have the agent here with me," Rolf said, placing the phone down. "Feel free to speak your mind."

Rolf's gaze pinned me to my spot. It was his warning that I better act right or I would join the others that had been decommissioned on this very couch.

"I'm disappointed," the man on the other line said. His voice was low, a bit husky, but overall calm and not at all as angry-sounding as I thought he would be. I tried to commit the voice to memory, the only clue I had about him. "I pay you good money, and yet she still isn't taken care of."

"It's been difficult to gain her trust," I said. "But I am working on it. As soon as she spills the information she has, I will gladly put a knife in her chest."

My stomach clenched at the thought of Blake's blood all over my hands. I had fantasized about others' blood on her, but when it came to her own? I didn't like thinking about it one bit.

Seconds ticked by with no response.

"What have you learned so far?" he asked.

"Only the basics," I replied. "She's been hiding from some-thing. She's been scared. She has to take anxiety medicine to curb panic attacks. Though from what, I am not sure. She has yet to divulge that information. My guess is that it has something to do with Alec—"

"Is this a fucking joke?" he asked. "I told you I needed to know what she knew as soon as possible, and *this* is what you give me?"

Rolf crossed his arms over his chest. *Fuck.* I was fucking this up badly.

"She's had eyes on her the entire time. We need to move with caution, or else there's no chance at me getting the information you need. If this were any other person, I would torture them until they spilled, but you and I both know whoever is following her would catch me. Maybe even before I was able to get the infor-mation you desire."

The man didn't speak, and I didn't expect a man like him to enjoy getting talked back to by me.

"But if your motives have changed, let me know, and I'll just kill her instead," I said. "Though if you'd like to stay the course, you could always tell me why you are so interested in this agent, and maybe it would help me navigate her."

Rolf gave me a warning look and stepped forward as if he was about to teach me with his fists not to speak back.

"The information she has is about the inner workings of Alec Crowe and his close associates," he said. "Some of whom are connected to me in ways I would rather have them not be. Knowing what she does would help with... damage control and who knows what. If she leaks any names, maybe you'll get more business from me."

Relief caused my shoulders to sink. *He's not Alec Crowe at least... but someone who can't be associated with his gang.* That should have been the best-case scenario, but something sank to the pit of my stomach at the knowledge. My gut instincts had never been wrong before, and this time they were telling me that whoever was on the other side of the phone may be even more dangerous than the gang leader.

"Anything else, sir?" Rolf asked.

"Two months," the voice said. "Finish this in two months, or I will have Rolf decommission you." There was a sound on the other line that I couldn't quite make out. It sounded like a soft voice and maybe the sound of footsteps, but I couldn't be sure, he hung up too quickly.

My shocked gaze shot to Rolf, but his eyes were on his phone. The hot pain of the betrayal burned my insides.

"Rolf, what did h—" I moved to get up but was forced back by his hand connecting with my face.

Normally, I would have been able to see it coming. To at least block it before it made contact. But the shock of what the client said combined with the action caught me completely off guard.

Rolf was no stranger to physical punishment... but I had thought we got through that conversation pretty well. *Why would he—*

"I'm starting to regret ever taking you in," he spat at me. "If I had just an inkling of how much trouble you would have been, I would have had your parents cut your price in half."

The whiplash from his violent change in emotions caused my head to swim. His words were like salt to an already gaping wound. A wound that had been open and festering since I learned the truth about how I came into his possession.

I was young when it happened, maybe six or seven, and since then, my memories have grown blurry. I didn't remember my parents' faces, or what they sounded like, or the horrible stories of my life that Rolf told me.

I only remembered the seaside where I grew up. I remembered the black sand beaches and rocky shores. I remember the chill it left in my tiny body.

Then my memories pick up when I first started training. It

wasn't long after I was taken in that they started my training, but it would be a good few years before they even considered sending me on a job. One that I fucked up so badly that I just recently began to pay back the blackmail that was hanging over my head.

I understood Rolf to an extent. This job was his life, just like it had been mine. Any chance of fucking it up would mean the end of our lives, literally.

But I thought he cared more than that. Or at least my inner child foolishly hoped he did.

"I would argue to say that you got far more money out of me than they ever did," I said and rubbed my stinging cheek. "I don't need to tally up the jobs to know I've been the best investment you've ever made."

"If you don't finish this up real quick, I will lose all of it. *We* will lose all of it. So you better get your ass back to her before you ruin this for the both of us," he threatened.

I gritted my teeth.

I wanted to say so much more to him. I wanted to yell at him. Throw shit. Hit him like he hit me.

Most of all, I wanted to make him take back those cruel words.

I hated him at times and thought about ending his life more times than I could count, but I always thought that there was at least some part of me that he still cared for.

Maybe it was finally time for me to realize that the man who had saved me from whatever fate had in store for me saw me as nothing more than a cash cow.

I turned my back toward him, hiding the grimace on my face.

"I'll end this soon," I vowed.

"Before the clients' deadline," he ordered. "Two weeks, and I want you back here with her blood staining your clothes."

I didn't answer him. I couldn't. Whatever strength I had left had been used to fuse my mouth shut. There was a sickening feeling in my stomach that threatened to cause bile to rise in my mouth.

I couldn't put an emotion to it. I had never felt something like this before. Through all my kills. Through all the times I carved the eyes out of my targets. Through all the bloodshed. I had never felt this way.

But here it was. So strong that it threatened to choke me. I almost wished it would.

BLAKE

"Sir, I have a call on the line for—"

I paused in my tracks when I opened the door to the senator's office.

All the lights in the office were off save for the computer on his desk which glowed softly. He was standing at his desk, slightly bent over the table, and staring down at his phone. His head snapped in my direction. His eyes were narrowed, and his mouth was set in a grimace.

I had never seen him look so angry before.

"Sorry, I didn't mean—"

I turned to walk right back out the door.

"No, it's okay, Tiffany," he said and took a deep breath. He ran his hand over the back of his neck and rolled his shoulder. "Sorry, you said there was a call for me?"

"Yes, sir," I said, handing him the secure phone we used for communication between him and various government officials. We had strict rules to keep it on one of us at all times and it changed shifts with us. "It's the treasurer. He has something urgent to speak with you about."

"Got it," he said and reached out to take the phone from me. I walked toward him, meeting him halfway. "Thank you."

"Of course," I said with a strained smile. I was about to leave when he spoke again.

"How are you liking your new position?" he asked.

Was he just going to ignore whoever was on the phone?

I looked toward him, remembering what he looked like when he came back into the house after being arrested. He was angry then too, but hid it behind the same exact mask.

It caused a shiver to go through me, and suddenly I felt all too confined in the space. A voice in the back of my head told me to turn back and run in the opposite direction.

"Definitely a change from before," I said with a smile. "But I think I'm fitting in quite well. I'll leave you and Mr.—"

"Oh, he can wait," he said, hanging up the phone and slipped the phone into his pocket. "After all, I think it's in my best interests to learn about the person who's protecting my family, right? You were doing some events before this and then moved on to former President Grant's wife?"

I let out a forced laugh and shifted on my heels. *This is beyond uncomfortable.* The memories of his harsh words when he caught Ryan and I ran through my mind.

He hadn't acted bothered about it since then, but that didn't mean I wanted to be in a dark room with him.

"Do you do this much research on all of your secret service agents?" I really didn't know what I expected him to answer, but it wasn't for him to give me that slimy smile of his before—

"No," he said all too cheerfully. "Only to the special ones."

I don't want your fucking attention. Inside I was torn between being creeped out and anger.

I knew this was a bad fucking job, so why did my boss do this to me?

"The events were mostly around New York, with the rare visit to DC before my assignment," I said. "Though it was nothing exciting."

Please just stop talking. Please just stop talking. Please just—

"Did you want it to be more exciting?" he asked, his eyes

never wavering from my face. "I mean, you're young. Heard you entered this career even younger. I would expect someone like you to want the more exciting role, yet you only just took one after all your years with the Secret Service."

I swallowed thickly. I don't know what it was about him that tipped me off, but I got some serious bad vibes from the man. I mostly hung around his wife and kids while he was holed up in the office or doing other things, so I didn't get to interact with him like this.

I was glad I didn't fully shut the door behind me.

I tried to stop my eyes from looking back at it so as not to let him know just how uncomfortable I was. But by the gleam in his eye, maybe he was excited about the possibility of me being stuck in here against my will.

"Is this a bribe?"

His face cracked, and he let out a laugh.

"No, just making conversation," he said. "Is it wrong to try and get to know people in my service?"

Not your service, but the government's, I wanted to say, but I didn't let it slip past my lips.

Even if everyone else wasn't sure he would win the presidency, he sure as hell was.

"It seems your research was pretty thorough," I mused. "Maybe this conversation isn't needed."

Something passed through his eyes before a smile spread across his lips.

"Maybe it's not," he agreed and took a step back. "You can go now. Thank you."

I nodded and left the way I came, feeling his eyes on me the entire time.

> Will you come over tonight?

I stared at the unanswered text message on my phone with a frown. The silence in my apartment seemed that much more prominent now that Quinn wasn't messaging me back. It had been over five hours since I sent it, a new record for her.

Besides the first time I ever sent a message, she usually responded right away, and her lag caused a new anxiety to sprout within me.

Did Sloan say something to scare her off? Sloan didn't seem like the type of person who would intentionally scare off someone I was interested... but she did seem rather worried about her.

The image of Avery wiping the blood that had come from Quinn's hair off my hands caused me to shudder.

What kind of person would come to the club drenched in blood? It was obvious that she had tried to shower it off beforehand given her damp hair, but had she really been in such a rush that she would miss it so completely?

That didn't seem like Quinn.

From what I could tell so far, she was meticulous in everything she did. In the way she dressed, her suit was always without a wrinkle. In the way she interacted with me. She always knew what to say, like she had thought it out well before I said anything.

The only time I seemed to catch her off guard was when we had sex.

Or maybe... she finally got bored of you?

Was our time enough for her? Based on her words, I would have assumed she was just as interested in me as I was in her....

For the first time, I wasn't afraid to admit it.

I liked Quinn. *A lot.* I wanted to see her all the time and have her sleep over every night if I could.

I didn't care that she never invited me over to her place. Or that whatever "contractor job" she had seemed to give her far more free time than I had.

Maybe she was just busy?

That would be logical. People had lives, including her. My situation was an anomaly, and I had to remember that there were people out there with family, friends, and people outside of the relationship other than just me.

Did Quinn have a family? Avery was obviously a friend... or something like that? But I hadn't heard her talk about her family at all...

She could be doing whatever caused her to get blood in her hair in the first place. Maybe she was a serial killer, and I was her next victim—

"Oh my god, shut up," I murmured to my racing thoughts.

But they just kept coming. I thought about texting her again. Maybe even calling her. Anything would be better than just sitting here with these crazy thoughts going through my head.

It was pathetic and almost scary that I was so crazy about her.

When my thumb hovered over her contact, a knock came at the door.

My heart skipped a beat, and my mouth went dry. Excitement burst through me, and before I knew it, I was bounding toward the door.

It had to be her. There was only one person who would show up at my door at this hour.

And true to my thoughts, when I flung the door open, she was there. But my smile dropped when I saw the look on her face.

Something was wrong. That cold mask she had on at the club was firmly back in place. Those piercing blue eyes of hers seemed to dull in the dim light of the hallway. There was an aura about her, one that warned me to stay away.

She took one step in, closing the door behind her. The sound of the lock clicking into place echoed throughout the room.

She closed the space between us in two large strides before grabbing the hair on the back of my neck and yanking my head back so that I was forced to look her in the eyes.

"Are you okay?" I asked, my voice just above a whisper.

She didn't answer. Her eyes searched my face for... *something*, but from the look on her face, it was safe to say she didn't find it.

"Are you okay?" I asked again, gripping the front of her shirt.

"Don't ask me that." Her words came out like a plea.

I brought my hand up to her cheek and pulled her lips to mine ever so gently. She lunged forward, meeting my kiss with a ferocity that made me gasp.

Her hands were at my waist, hoisting me up and wrapping my legs around her in seconds. Her hot tongue slid across mine, covering every inch of my mouth.

Her kiss burned. Caused my stomach to flip. She was speaking to me in a way she couldn't with her words.

Pay attention to me, it told me. *Take away whatever it is that is making me feel this way.*

Of course, I obliged. There was nothing more in that moment that I wanted to do besides make her forget everything outside of this apartment.

We didn't make it into my room. We made it as far as the couch before she deposited me on it, and we started shedding our clothing.

Once my pants were off, she gripped my thighs and pulled me to her. I let out a yelp, and the suddenness of it quickly turned into a moan when her lips found my clit.

"I want to touch you," I whined as I bucked against her mouth. Two of her fingers pushed into my entrance. Neither of us were surprised that I was already wet. It was a given. As long as she was around, my body would react in ways even I didn't comprehend.

"Me first," she all but growled between my legs.

She pumped her fingers into me at an animalistic pace. At times her movements were still clumsy and needed guidance, but *goddamn* did this girl love to eat pussy. *And* she learned fast. Over the few times we had been together, she learned exactly what to do to make me come.

It wasn't hard, and it never has been, but somehow it was

different with her. Like she made it her mission to watch me fall apart.

I readied my legs for her and grinned against her mouth. She was causing a delicious heat to build up in me that was already threatening to burst. My stomach quivered as the orgasm neared, and my thighs shook. Wetness was trailing down my thighs and to the couch, but I didn't care.

Neither did she. Like her kiss, Quinn was saying something with her touches. She was reminding me of what she could do to me. Reminding me who made me feel this way.

I came with a scream.

It hadn't been too long since my last orgasm, but the one she forced from me ripped through me like none other. It seized my entire body and made my pussy clench around her fingers with no remorse.

Sweat broke out over my body as I rode wave after wave of it.

It was so addicting that I didn't want it to stop. I greedily rode her face even after my orgasm subsided.

"Let me touch you," I panted. "Please, I need to make you come."

She chuckled against my wet cunt.

"So eager to taste, huh?" she asked, lifting her face to show me how much of my release was coated on her lips.

"Please," I begged and brought my fingers down to play with my clit. "Sit on my face. Ride me until you can't take it anymore."

She paused before cursing under her breath.

"If it were anyone else, I would say no," she said, then lifted herself. I watched as she unbuttoned her pants and pulled them down with her underwear. The tuft of hair between her legs caused my mouth to water.

"But you trust me," I finished for her.

Her answer was crawling over me until her pussy sat right above me. She was so wet she began dripping on my mouth. I licked my lips, moaning at the taste of her.

"I don't know how it happened," she said, lowering herself. "But ye—*oh fuck.*"

The curse that fell from her lips as I wrapped an arm around her waist and pulled her down to me was sinful. I couldn't wait to hear more of it.

I ate Quinn's cunt like I was starved. I made sure to show her how good she was to have trusted me. I sucked on her clit hard enough to make her back bow before teasing her entrance with my tongue.

When her hips jerked, I tried to pull her back down so she could do it on my face, but she was barely putting any weight on me.

"*Sit* on me," I commanded. "Fuck my face like you want to. I can feel you holding back."

She leaned forward, putting her hands on the arm of the sofa behind me. I looked up to catch her gaze.

"I don't want to..." She frowned.

"Hurt me?" I supplied for her. She gave me a tense nod. I laughed and turned my head to the side to bite into her thigh. Her gasp went straight to my core. "You won't. But if you're so worried, three taps means pull back, okay?"

She nodded before lowering herself onto me.

This time I hooked her, though, and threaded my hands together in front of her waist making it damn near impossible for her to move away from me.

"Blake be—*ah.*"

Her complaints died when I brought her clit back into my mouth. She stayed still, letting me do the work on her clit. But when I faltered my tongue and teased it from her sopping entrance to her clit, she began to buck against me.

I hummed against her, and she took it as a sign to go even harder.

If I hadn't been falling for the woman before then, I certainly had been after.

For the first time, I saw her truly unrestrained. Her head was thrown back, showing off her strong, elongated neck. The buckles in it tightened as her hands gripped onto the arms of the couch for dear life.

Her small tits bounced with her movements, and her stomach contracted as the pleasure she was chasing finally came to a head.

Beautiful. She was beautiful in the most unrelenting and cruel ways. The image of her riding my face until she came with the most enchanting cry was something I would never forget.

"Okay, okay," she panted above me. "I came. My turn, now let me—"

She let out a groan when I tightened my hold on her and fused my mouth back to her clit.

Just like her, I couldn't get enough. I loved pussy. I loved eating it. Loved fucking it. But most of all, I was starting to realize it was her that I loved the most.

How someone so cold and mysterious sunk their claws into me was beyond me, but for the first time I couldn't help but feel happy she found me in the arcade when she did.

I wanted to learn more about her. Learn what made her tick. Learn where she came from. Learn who she wanted to be.

It was small, but it was a start. A start that, for the longest time, I never thought I would have.

Quinn

Something changed.

I don't know when it happened, or why, but something between Blake and me changed.

I should have realized it sooner because every time I thought about her, I had this sinking feeling in my gut that threatened to poison me. Every time I was around her, that same feeling filled the air, invading my lungs like a toxic fume.

But it was that same toxic fume that made me feel so warm on the inside. The same fume that made me pull Blake into my arms as she slept and inhale her scent like I may never smell it again.

I sighed against her, letting the warmth of her body take over me.

I had never felt a warmth like I did when I was with her. The world has always been so cold. So unforgiving. But her warmth somehow sank past the harsh walls I had erected during my life.

Even if it was just for a few moments, I wanted to relish in what we had.

Even if it was fake.

And it was going to end soon. Even just the thought caused my stomach to twist and bile to rise in my throat.

Two weeks. That was the timeline Rolf had forced on me. He knew what it would force me to do.

He didn't want me to linger any longer. What would have been an easy, humane way to pry information and end the target was starting to turn ugly.

He wanted to force my move.

But I didn't want to hurt her. That much was true. I couldn't finish saying it then because it felt like a lie. But deep down, we both knew it wasn't.

I didn't want to hurt her. Even if Rolf was forcing my hand. I wanted to do this my way.

It was that thought that spurred me.

I gently unwrapped myself from Blake before slipping out of bed. I wasn't sure the next time I would be able to sneak into her place with all the eyes watching, so I had to take whatever chance I could.

She didn't stir as I left her room.

Most of the house was bare, save for a few decorations. The bookshelf was the first place I searched, pulling out book after book and checking to see if anything was hiding inside.

I came across a few books about the arcade game she seemed to love so much. A bitter smile spread across my face that I forced down.

I didn't like that my first thought after seeing those books was to visit again with her one day.

Because that one day won't happen. Something I needed to keep reminding myself of.

With a frustrated sigh, I put the books back and moved on to my next area.

But there was nothing. After searching the kitchen, living room, and guest bathroom, I was left with no other place to look than the bedroom.

I tiptoed inside, checking to see if Blake was still asleep. I could just make out the heap of blankets she had covered herself with in my absence. The sound of her deep breathing filled the room.

Every time I slept over, I was always on the left side. There was nothing in that nightstand, I had already checked, so the last place to look was hers.

I was silent as I walked across the room. When I kneeled down, the boards creaked beneath my feet and caused me to freeze. I listened to see if the sound startled the little agent, but she didn't so much as stir.

I didn't want to find anything in the nightstand. I was praying that I wouldn't.

I pulled it open slowly, noticing the all-black notebook at the front. I pulled that out first, flipping through the pages.

It's a diary.

For some reason, I wasn't surprised that someone like Blake had a diary. What I was surprised to find was just how long it had been going on for.

It dated back about eight years. So even before she went into the Secret Service.

I shouldn't have been wasting time going through it, but the urge was too strong to ignore.

I never thought I'd be writing my last will and testament, but it's becoming clearer and clearer that I may not make it here any longer.

He's getting angrier. The times between are becoming shorter and shorter.

Mom, I'm sorry I'm leaving you so soon.

Burn my body. Leave no trace of me on this earth. If anyone wanted to do just a single thing nice for me please listen to this: when I die, erase my pitiful existence from this earth.

Her words caused my chest to squeeze painfully. They were so raw, so hopeless... and almost word for word what I had filled out for my contract with Rolf. There was a certain way they disposed of our bodies in order to keep their secrets intact, but many times the assassin would say what they wanted and it was up to the agency to decide whether it should be granted or not.

I too wanted to be burned. I wanted the entire world to forget about what I had done. I wanted my ashes to float up into the sky and, for once, give my soul a taste of the freedom I would never get.

But then, the quieter, sadder part of me always hated the idea of being burned. The same part was crying and screaming at Rolf to save me. At *me* to save myself.

My mind went back to the conversation we had in her bed while we looked up at the stars.

The secret we whispered. One that we knew would never come true.

A bit of a sign that someone came before you.

And that maybe someone will remember that I came before as well.

The memory hurt more now that I realized that it was *I* who would be taking her from this earth. Was her inner child also crying out with their arms wide open, their face covered in tears, their voice hoarse from screaming for too long as well? Or had it quieted over the years when she realized no one was coming to save her?

I flipped through a few pages. Each entry was longer than the last.

He brought me to a party last night but it was... different from before.

His friends were looking at me in that *way. A way that only he has looked at me.*

When his hands trailed my thighs when they were looking, I didn't know how to react.

He got mad when I pushed him away.

I still was unable to discern who *he* was in this scenario, but maybe the friends were a part of Alec's crew?

I flipped forward a few.

I did it. I ran. I'm sitting on a bus on the way across the country to meet J.

He saved me.

I owe him my life. He will come after me until I'm dead. I know too much.

But I couldn't stand it. I'd rather be on the run for the rest of my life than have them—

The words were crossed out as if she couldn't bear to look at them written on the page.

I closed the diary with a sinking feeling in my stomach. My mind was painting a picture. A disgusting one that I didn't want to think about. One that made my blood boil.

I slipped the diary back in before shifting through the papers in the drawer. Many were newspaper clippings. I pulled out a few, my eyes lingering on the headlines.

Missing Women Still Not Found.

Mother and Father Plead for Their Daughter's Safe Return.

Unease twisted my stomach, especially when I caught sight of a teary-eyed older couple, holding each other and speaking to an audience.

I put them back. There was nothing else in there save for a few empty paper bags. Then, at the very back, my fingers brushed across something small. A rectangular object that was mostly plastic save for a square at the top.

The USB. My stomach filled with lead. *No.* My thoughts were loud in my head. Screaming at me to forget my mission entirely and just put the USB back where I had found it.

It was here the entire time. Unguarded and all but thrown away in the bedside table.

A part of me wanted to take it out only to smash it on the ground, but the bigger part of me knew I should take it and report back to Rolf immediately.

But then... this would be over, wouldn't it? I would have to dispose of Blake and move on to the next target.

This is your job, I reminded myself. *You got far too involved, and now it was your chance to pull back.*

Gripping the USB, I pulled it out. My heart stopped in my chest when I finally caught sight of it.

What was on here that made someone as powerful as my client come down on someone as harshly as they did Blake?

The cold barrel of the gun pushed against the back of my head, causing me to freeze.

I hadn't heard her move. Hadn't even heard the hitch of her breath as she woke up.

How long had she been watching me?

The fact that she snuck up on me caused a powerful heat to run through me.

Looks like the little agent still has some surprises to show me.

I took a deep, steadying breath, trying to calm down the excitement that was bubbling up inside of me.

A normal human would have been scared to find themselves with a gun pointed at their head, but I had been dreaming about this day. Dreaming about when she would finally shed that innocent mask of hers and show me the bloodthirsty, violent person she was below the surface.

I paused, dropping the USB back into the drawer, to turn around and look at her.

Her face was hard. Lips smooshed into a thin line, eyebrows pushed together. She was angry. So angry that the hand that had once been so steady when pointing a gun to someone's face now shook.

Those brilliant green eyes showed the betrayal she didn't allow to show on her face.

I shouldn't have felt the thrill go through me like it did. Or allow myself to take her in like I did. But I couldn't help myself. From the moment I saw her on stage, I had been sucked so deeply into the pools that there was no way possible to pull myself out.

Even now.

My training told me to disarm her and turn the gun on her instead.

Grab.

Twist.

Turn.

Shoot.

It was a motion I had done hundreds of times before. I could do it right then and end the entire job. But the anger in Blake's eyes, *god* I needed to feel it.

She cocked the gun, though her finger was not resting on the trigger like it should have been when she found someone rifling through her stuff. Stuff that was obviously very incriminating. Stuff that she shouldn't want anyone to find.

She didn't want to kill me, but she would if I gave her no choice. It was clear in her face.

It caused me to shiver.

"You manipulated me," she whispered. Her voice did not betray the hurt I knew was lingering under her skin. A part of me felt bad that I was the cause of her hurt, but my excitement far outweighed it.

"What are you talking about, Blake?" I asked, feigning innocence. "Why are you pointing a gun at me?"

Her jaw clenched.

"Is this why you followed me?" she asked. "How much do you know? Did *he* send you? Tell you to fuck with my emotions like this?"

"I don't know—"

She pushed the gun straight to my forehead. The cool metal sent a violent bolt of electricity up my spine.

"Cut the bullshit, Quinn," she growled. "Tell me, or I swear to God I'll blow—"

I grabbed the gun and forced it upward to allow me to lunge at her. Blake was quick in her movements because of her training, but not quick enough.

I tangled a hand in her short locks while the other gripped her throat. I squeezed the sides letting her know exactly who was in charge. Her eyes widened, and for the first time, I saw fear flash across them.

I used to love seeing the fear in my target's face... *so why did it cause me to stall?*

It was enough of a mistake that she used her body weight to push us to the ground. She straddled my hips and brought the gun under my chin, tilting it up.

My hands flew to her hips. Heat flared through me when I realized that Blake had only put on a sleep shirt with nothing else underneath after our time together.

I was so turned on it was ridiculous.

"I'll ask you again," she said, though this time she was breathless. "Who the *fuck* are you?"

I held my breath as my hand trailed from her hip to her muscular thigh.

Her breath hitched, and she pushed the gun harder against me. *Fuck. She's so fucking perfect.*

"Maybe I should be asking you that," I said with a chuckle. "What have you been hiding from me, little agent?"

"Who sent you?" she asked again, though her tone was more of a plea than a demand.

"Does it make you feel powerful?" I asked, squeezing her thigh, my voice dropping low. "To have me immobilized here while you straddle me?"

She didn't stop my hand as it traveled up and brushed across the tuft of curls between her legs. Nor when I traveled the path from her clit into her wet cunt.

Her eyes narrowed at me.

"I could kill you."

I couldn't help the moan that spilled from my lips.

She could. She could pull the trigger right now and my miserable existence would be over. At least it would mean that I wouldn't have to finish this job.

Something that should have been easy for me, but it turned complicated once I tasted her on my lips.

"Do it," I dared.

Her wetness dripped onto my fingers, and I used it to massage her clit.

Even in the darkness, I could see the familiar blush spread across her face.

"Are you not scared?" she asked. "One wrong move, and I could blow your brains out."

She let out a strangled moan when I forced two fingers inside of her.

"This is the most turned-on I've been in my life," I admitted. "Keep the gun there while I fuck you. Better yet, force me to keep going until you can't come anymore."

I expected her to pull away, but yet again, Blake surprised me.

She lifted herself up just enough to allow my fingers better access. She leaned forward, putting a hand right beside my head. Her eyes were level with mine, and the grip of her gun stayed steady.

"I won't forget about this," she warned.

A wicked smile spread across my face.

"I hope not," I said in a teasing tone. Satisfaction exploded through me when she ground her hips against my hand.

"You think an orgasm will make me forget about this?" she growled.

"No," I said hurtfully, and I fit a finger into her. I fucked her slowly, savoring the look on her face, and I brought her close to an orgasm. The sound of my fingers fucking her wet cunt filled the air, causing my own pussy to clench. "Maybe it's time we were both a little more honest, huh?"

I picked up my pace, letting my heel slam into her clit with each thrust.

Her mouth dropped open, moans spilling out.

"I don't owe you answers," she spat. "But you owe me a lot, considering."

I paused in my motions, only for her to push the gun harder into me. Something flashed across her eyes. A recognition, or maybe an idea. Whatever it was caused her to force the gun past my lips.

"Maybe I should make better use of your mouth since all it does is lie."

Before I could stop her, she lifted herself from me and turned around. In my mind, I cursed her for putting her guard down but quickly swallowed my complaints when she lowered her pussy onto my face.

I grabbed her hips, pulling her to my mouth like she had done mine.

I was vaguely aware of her pulling my shorts down.

I gasped into her when I felt the cool metal of the gun push against my clit.

"Keep going," she ordered. "God, you have such a pretty pussy. It's a shame."

"I've never been called pretty in my life," I mumbled into her folds.

"So pretty," she cooed. "And so wet." As if to prove her point, she trailed the gun from my clit to my entrance.

"Think I could fuck you with this?" she asked.

This was a new side of her I'd never seen before. In control, insidious, sadistic even. It had me spreading my legs for her.

"Oh, you're even a bigger slut than I am." She laughed, but it quickly turned to a moan when I brought her clit into my mouth and gave it a sharp suck.

"The safety is o—"

"Don't tell me that," I hissed against her before going back to devouring her.

She let out a breathy chuckle before pushing the hard metal into me. I wanted to squirm against her, but I stayed deadly still.

The way she pulled it out of me only to push it back in, further this time, was obscene.

It was dirty. Depraved. Everything I had been missing.

"Keep going, pretty," she said, leaning down to lick my clit as she thrust the gun into me.

I trembled against her but obeyed.

All thoughts of the hit left my mind, and I was left trembling at her touch.

I was going to come. Even faster than she was, which was a first for me.

"You're shaking. Don't tell me you're about to come?" The way she said it with a laugh caused my skin to flame.

I didn't answer her, but instead tried to make her come faster.

But it was no use. She pulled my clit into her mouth, and I was exploding around the gun, my pussy clamping onto the hard metal, the moans stuck in my throat.

I couldn't move. I couldn't breathe. I couldn't make a single sound.

She fucked me with the gun as the orgasm destroyed my body, rendering me completely useless. White spots bloomed across my vision. I screwed my eyes shut, unable to believe Blake pulled such a mind-blowing orgasm out of me while fucking my pussy with a goddamn loaded gun.

When she pulled it out of me, I pushed her off of me so I could climb on top of her.

The gun was forgotten as our lips crashed together. Her hands tangled through my hair, pulling painfully.

Fine if she wanted it to hurt, she'll have her way tonight.

I bit her lip hard enough to break the skin. She gasped against me before digging her blunt nails into my back.

My hand was between her legs in seconds, forcing three fingers back into her as I fucked her without remorse. She writhed against me each time the heel of my palm hit her clit.

"You're fucking terrible," she groaned against me.

"Just who do you think I am, little agent?" I asked, pulling away from her.

The conflicted feelings that crossed her face caused my head to spin. She didn't want to like this, but she did. She didn't want to come on my fingers, but she was going to.

"You're not a contractor," she said with a moan.

I shook my head.

"Are you one of *them*?" she asked.

"Say it," I growled. "Who's them?"

I knew this was what I needed, but inside I was screaming at her not to say it.

Her hand fastened around my neck.

"If you're one of Russell's men, I won't hesitate to put a bullet in your brain," she warned. "I'm not going back."

Russell. Not Alec. The violent relief that spread throughout me was obvious by the crazed smile that spread across my face.

"Whoever you think I am, Blake." I leaned forward, brushing my lips against hers. "I promise you I'm *much* worse."

Her pussy clamped around me so tightly that I wondered briefly if I had done everything wrong from the beginning.

"No, *fuck*."

"That's right," I purred. "Come on my hand. Your mouth may say no, but your body has *always* known who it belongs to."

She came with a cry. I couldn't help but lean down and take her mouth with mine. I swallowed her moans until she was pushing me away for air.

Breathing heavily, we met each other's gaze. Now that the high was coming down, we both had a choice to make, and there was only one gun.

I allowed Blake to flip us around, ready for whatever choice she made. There was only a moment of hesitation before her lips were back on mine and her hands were between my legs.

BLAKE

I should have listened to my instincts when they told me there was something Quinn wasn't telling me.

But there was also a relief in the fact that she wasn't connected to the ghost that was haunting my past.

Whoever you think I am, Blake, I promise you I'm much worse.

But there was also comfort in knowing that, because if she was worse than *them*, maybe there was a chance that I would never again be subject to what they threatened.

That didn't mean I was any less mad at her. But being mad at her didn't stop the weird, explosive chemistry between us.

She was *supposed* to leave, yet when she came from behind me as I was peering at the gun on the dining room table, her hands slipped into my shirt and spread across my stomach, my skin still heated. My pussy ached with need. My fingers itched to grab her hair and force her to her knees.

So that's exactly what I did.

I turned around, shivering when her heated gaze met mine. When I threaded my hands through her hair and tugged it back, she said nothing.

"On your knees," I ordered.

"Has the little agent found her claws?" she asked but fell to her knees anyway. Her hands trailed my bare thighs, pushing up my oversized shirt as they traveled up.

"I don't know why I can't stop myself," I admitted, hooking my leg over her shoulders. I placed a hand behind me, using it as leverage as I threaded a hand through her hair. "I should report you. Or end it all. But I can't."

"Because you're too much like me," she said, leaving a burning kiss on my inner thigh. Her tongue darted out to lick the sensitive skin before sinking her teeth into it.

I let out a strangled moan.

"Stupid?" I supplied.

She let out a laugh before placing another kiss on the place she bit.

"You want something you shouldn't have," she said. "Someone who, like you, is begging for the world to take note. Yet the powers that be awaited to bury her."

"Are you going to kill me?" I asked.

She didn't answer. Instead, she lunged forward and did what she was best at: eating pussy.

"If you do," I said breathlessly. "Burn my body. Make sure no one finds it."

She growled against my folds.

"Don't fucking talk like that."

I let out a bitter laugh but bucked my hips against her mouth regardless of the emotions the topic was making me feel.

"You are going to, aren't you?" I asked. "At least you can answer that."

She jerked up, pulling my shirt up with her.

"Shut up," she murmured and swooped down to bring my nipple into her mouth. She did that thing where she pulled away enough for me to watch as her tongue curled around it, then sucked it fully into her mouth, her teeth grazing against the piercings.

Her hand pushed its way between my legs, circling my clit as I writhed against her.

I couldn't hold in my moans anymore. I let them fill the silent apartment, taking advantage of perhaps the last time she would touch me.

"I hate you," I whispered.

She chuckled against my nipple before slipping two fingers into me. Her other hand wrapped around my throat and pulled me to her. All thoughts left me when her broken pupils zeroed in on me. There was a cruel smile spreading across her face.

"We both know that's a bold-faced fucking lie, especially when your sopping cunt has my fingers in a death grip."

I let out a strangled moan.

"That's right, Blake." Her cruel tone only turned me on that much more. "You're going to come apart on them even though the both of us know I could end you right here and now."

"They're stained with blood, aren't they?" I asked.

"Oh, they're fucking filthy with it," she said with a laugh. "But I have a feeling that turned you on even more, doesn't it?"

"No," I spat.

"Such a horrible liar," she said, hooking her fingers inside me. "Let's try not to lie to me when you're coming on my fingers, hm?"

I couldn't hold it back any longer. The orgasm crashed through me like a tidal wave.

"I fucking despise you—*fuck.*"

"Uh-huh, sure you do," she said with a chuckle. Her thumb found my clit, rubbing hard circles on it as I came down. "I'll give you another chance. Just say—"

"Oh *wow,* sorry to interrupt."

Quinn whipped around before I could even register what happened. I reached for the gun behind me, but she already had it in front of her, pointing at the stranger.

I leaned over to look over her shoulder. My heart dropped to the floor because the man walking into my apartment in a clean-pressed suit was my worst nightmare.

Russell Crowe, my husband, has finally come to take back what he was owed. I gripped her shirt, hiding myself behind her. He slammed the door behind him with an anger I had seen far too many times before then.

"You," I breathed. He took a few steps forward, his eyes on Quinn.

Russell's mouth twitched. "Me," he agreed. "I also hear you have something of mine. Go get it. We're going home."

I couldn't breathe, couldn't move. Every moment from the years we had been together passed through my mind in a flurry. *How had he found me?* I should have been hidden away, locked so tight that no one would ever know who I once was.

Did he see me with the senator?

"This can't happen," I said with a gasp. My mind swirled, and my throat began to close.

"Well, it is," he said, letting out a sigh. "I'm done playing this fucking game, Tiffany. Get your sorry ass over here—"

"Quinn, *please.*" I don't know what I was begging her for, but she seemed to understand.

A shot rang out. Russell fell to his knees, blood blooming from his pants leg.

"Goddamn it," Russell said with a laugh. The strain in his laugh was the only thing giving away that he had been shot. How many times had he come home covered in blood? How many times had I helped him clean up his wounds? This was nothing to him. "Not only is my *wife* cheating on me, but to have them shoot me as well? The lawyers are going to have a field day."

If Quinn was surprised about the news that I was married, she didn't show it.

"I'm not your wife anymore," I reminded, my fingernails biting into Quinn.

"I didn't sign no goddamn divorce papers, *bitch.*"

I had to physically hold Quinn back from taking another shot at him.

But what Russell didn't say is that he wasn't here for me alone. Quinn had seen it last night. Not only did I leave him passed out on the floor as I cracked for the first and last time, I also took something from him. Something he would kill to keep a secret.

His sharp eyes narrowing at me told me that he was here for exactly that. If Quinn hadn't been here, he wouldn't have hesitated to kill me.

Panic seized my throat, and my breathing became erratic. The world swam around me, and my grip on Quinn shook.

Fuck, not now.

"You broke into the house of a government agent," she said, her tone deadly. "People are no doubt swarming the place now."

You know it too, a voice inside my head reminded me. *Get your fucking shit together, or the next time Russell comes to get you, Quinn won't be able to protect you.*

I quickly grabbed the gun from her, wiping the fingerprints off with the back of her shirt. They were going to come and take everything, especially if Russell was involved. His ties to dangerous gangs would make this difficult.

Quinn stayed intently on me, glaring daggers at Russell, and I pulled my shirt on. My phone vibrated loudly off to the side. Quinn grabbed it without looking away from the man bleeding out on my carpet.

When she handed it to me, her hand lingered. It caused a soothing shift in my tightening chest.

"Hello?" I asked shakily.

"My men heard the gunshot. Agents are on standby. Are you okay?" My boss's voice came through the phone, startling me. I knew his department and Agent Jonson had come together for a deal, but I never expected him to actually care for me like his voice told me he did.

It caused my eyes to tear.

"My... girlfriend is acting as my shield," I explained. "We are ready for them."

I heard something on the other line, and not a moment later, the door was broken down. Three agents tackled Russell to the ground before two more lingered by the door.

Quinn froze against me.

"It's okay," I whispered to her. "They will escort him out."

She leaned back, her eyes shifting to mine. The seriousness in them caused my body to go on high alert.

"These aren't the ones watching the place. Something is off."

Her words were like a bucket of ice water being thrown at me. My eyes shifted to the agents in the room. They looked legit, even had their badges on them. So what was she going on about?

"Blake?" my boss asked from the other line.

"I'm here," I said after clearing my throat. It was tightening by the second. If I didn't get out of here soon, all these people would see me fall apart.

"Good. I will meet you at your house in a few hours. Debrief with the agents. But in the meantime, you will need to leave the place while we do a thorough investigation."

"Leave the place?" I asked, my fingers digging into Quinn's back. "But I don't have anywhere to—"

"You'll stay with me," Quinn cut in. "Tell him I have property we can stay at."

I didn't need to repeat it. She said it loud enough for him to hear.

"Great, get me the address for the file," he said. "Take care of yourself and wait for me."

He hung up before I could say anything.

Two agents came up to us, but Quinn didn't dare move. Even went as far as staring them down as they got closer.

"Agent Yates," one of them, whom I recognized, said with a smile. "You may want to put some clothes on for this conversation."

Jesus Christ. I couldn't do it. I need air, but no matter how much I gasped, I couldn't get it to my lungs.

Quinn said something to them, and before I knew it, I was being lifted and carried to my room. I grabbed on to her for dear life, screwing my eyes shut as the tears started to come.

I was pried off of Quinn. My eyes shot open only to see her kneeling in front of me.

One of her hands pushed itself against my chest, the other against my back.

"*Breathe,* Blake," she commanded. I tried to do as she said, but my body wouldn't cooperate. All I got were short bursts of air that caused my head to spin.

"He won't hurt you, Blake," she vowed. "I am here, and I won't let him hurt you. Okay? Nod if you understand me."

I gave her a shaking nod. My hands found the one she placed on my chest and pushed it harder into me. I needed the weight. All of the panic from seeing him again caused my entire body to feel so light that it threatened to fly off into space.

"Do you want medicine?" she asked.

I shook my head. And motioned for the same bedside table she had been rummaging through. Her eyes widened, and she dove for it before pulling out the paper bags I kept in there for exactly something like this.

They were mostly reserved for the nightmares that still plagued me every once in a while, but we were lucky to have them for this moment.

She helped me open it before letting me grab it with a shaky hand and place it to my mouth.

I took a few breaths in and out before my head stopped swimming. I don't know how much time had passed or how long she had stayed there while I breathed into the bag, but she never left my side throughout it all.

When I finally got myself calmed down enough to take the bag off, her face remained impassive.

"You said you didn't have attacks often," she noted.

It wasn't the words that triggered me, it was a combination of things. It was seeing Russell again. It was waking up to her getting so close to the one secret I had keeping me alive.

It was more her *betrayal* than her sudden hero complex.

My hand stung as it came into contact with her cheek. Her head snapped to the side, a feral smile slowly spreading across it.

"I lied. I have nightmares," I said. What I didn't tell her was that the attacks had stopped since the night she stayed over. That the nightmares hadn't come back and woken me up in the middle of the night causing me to dive for a bag and get my breathing under control since then either.

"I deserve it," she said, running her hand through her hair. I hadn't realized how much the weight comforted me until it was gone.

"Tell me something," I demanded.

She raised a brow at me.

"You should get dressed and talk to your coworkers," she said, her head jerking back toward the closed door. "We can talk at the safe house—"

"Just *something*," I pleaded, hating how vulnerable my voice sounded. "I'm going crazy, just anything, please. I need something to focus on that's *not* him."

Her facial expression sobered before her eyes fell to my lap.

"I used to have nightmares sometimes when I was a child," she admitted, her voice low.

"About?" I asked.

She pushed her lips into a thin line. We were reaching territory she didn't want to talk about.

"Death. Blood. But most of all, I had nightmares about what would happen if I wasn't sold to the person I was sold to."

All the thoughts about everyone else disappeared in that moment, and I looked at Quinn with wide eyes, horror filling my body so strongly that I couldn't stop myself from grabbing her shoulder.

"What do you mean you were *sold*?" I asked in a whisper.

Her eyes searched mine.

"You're recovered now," she said and stood. "Get dressed. I'll guard your door."

I couldn't call out to her as she walked away, I was too shell-shocked about what I had just learned.

What happened to her?

QUINN

"You didn't tell me she had a fucking husband," I hissed into my phone. "Is he the client? Was he so worried I wouldn't get it done in time that he decided to take matters into his own hands?"

I was fuming. My blood was boiling so hot that it threatened to overtake me. One wrong move, and I would explode all over everything and everyone in that goddamn place.

I had barely managed to keep a straight face when the agents pulled the man out of the room, but hearing Rolf's voice?

The same voice that used to bring me some sense of security was now grating on my nerves.

How could he let me go into this without knowing? Why the fuck wasn't any of this in her file?

I had killed significant others for less than the crimes we had been committing.

But knowing that she was married brought up a whole other slew of questions.

He staked his claim on her, but she seemed adamant that she wasn't his wife. What was the truth?

Why was she with him in the first place?

"You know I can't confirm any of that, agent." His tone was just as annoyed as mine was.

I growled and almost threw my phone across the room, but that would definitely alert Blake. I was already pissed about the situation, but even more so that I let myself be overcome by the weakness I was feeling toward her and caused me to spill something I never should have.

Goddammit, Quinn, can you be any stupider?

"Well because of that, I need you to get me a safe house," I said. "Blake needs to leave, and I offered her to stay with me."

"That was stupid," he said with a huff. "I don't have anything for you—"

"You want her to see my trophies?" I asked, though it was more of a threat. I would take her home, we both knew it. It was up to him if he wanted to see this job through at this point.

There was too much happening which caused me to rethink everything about Blake. *A husband? The USB? What the fuck was going on?*

Rolf was silent on the other line before I heard him curse.

"You don't keep them in like a freezer or something?" he asked.

I scoffed aloud. Now Rolf was acting like the dumbass? I was at my limit for the day.

"No," I hissed. "You have to preserve them. You think I'd go through such trouble to just let them rot in there?"

In reality, preserving the eyes has proven to be a difficult yet rewarding hobby. I had lost quite a few in the beginning, but over the last few years I had perfected my craft, and now my office had an entire shelf filled with them.

But if Blake saw those... I actually had no idea how she would react, and a part of me wanted to keep it hidden as long as possible. Even if she had an inkling about what I did, it would be nothing compared to what seeing it would do to her.

I wasn't ashamed of what I did. Even if I wished I didn't have to do it to her.

But some part of me felt scared to show her. Like I knew, she would run screaming and crying in the other direction.

"Damn it, fine," he hissed. "I'll send you the coordinates, but this *will* be coming out of your pay."

He hung up on me, and I let out a sigh and ran my hand through my hair. *It was all so fucked. Definitely Karma biting me in the ass.*

"Did you get done what you needed to?" Blake's voice caused me to jump.

I twirled around, sending her a glare.

Yet again, I hadn't heard her come into the room, but there she was, leaning against the doorframe with an almost blank expression. Her eyes were the ones that gave it away. They glimmered with curiosity.

"Yes." I nodded. "How are you so quiet all the time?"

"When it's life or death, people learn how to conceal their footsteps," she said.

"Was it because of him? Did he hurt you?" I asked, remembering the way his eyes narrowed on Blake. If there weren't multiple teams of government agents watching, I would have killed him.

I didn't like him one bit, and there was only one conclusion I came to based on what their body language told me.

I just needed *her* to say it.

"I haven't seen him in years," she said with a shrug. "Were you surprised?"

Yes. Because it wasn't in your file. But instead, I asked, "Did you run away from him because he was hurting you?"

She squared her shoulders and held her chin high like she needed to compensate for what she was about to say.

"And if I say yes?" she asked.

"Then I put a bullet in his head," I growled, unable to help myself. My vision was already turning red. I wanted to do more than just put a bullet in his head. I wanted to slam his face into the concrete. I wanted to puncture his internal organs, leaving him to die a slow and painful death. I wanted to tie him upside down with a small puncture wound in his neck, letting him bleed out while all the blood rushed to his head, and—

This whole situation is bullshit.

How had she changed me so much? How had I gotten so *weak* that just the sight of him caused me to want to kill him for my own vengeance? I *never* killed anyone outside of a job. Yet for Blake, I was willing to kill just about anyone who threatened to put their hands on her.

She deflated slightly, a small smile spreading across her face.

"You wouldn't be able to," she said. "Not while he's expecting it anyway. He's dangerous, Quinn. Even now, I'm debating whether I should keep this identity or flee."

"What's stopping you?" I asked, knowing that if she so much as attempted to flee, I would be right there behind her.

Her face heated at this, and her eyes fell to the floor.

"The need to be remembered," she said. "This life I built here... it's nothing to brag about, but it's *something*. I have people who mean a lot to me here. A life I never thought possible before."

I swallowed thickly. It was going to be destroyed. Everything she had built here. Whether it was because of me or him. Either way, the life she lived here would cease to exist.

Why did the knowledge of that feel like a punch to the gut?

"What did he do to you?" I asked, needing to think of anything other than her inevitable death.

"Everything, anything," she said. "I was young, right out of high school, and he took advantage of that. I only left because I knew whatever he had done, his friends would do worse."

Rage simmered under my skin. But was in that moment that I vowed to do something I would have never even entertained.

No matter what happened or what she said, there was no changing the future.

I was going to kill that bastard. A slow and painful death.

Imagining how someone could hurt a person like her was too much for me to handle.

I was messed up, willing to kill just about anyone for money... but even I had hard limits.

"I have a safe house for us," I said. "I'll protect you for the time being."

"Until you finish your job?" she asked, her voice turning bitter.

"You don't know what my job is," I said, sourness filling my mouth.

"I hate you," she said, her voice holding the power to silence the room.

It was a lie. We both knew it. But I let her have it. I let her feel the weight of the words, and I let myself feel the hurt of them.

"Let's go," I ordered and passed her without so much as a backward glance.

New Haven was not where I had originally thought to keep a safe house, but by the time we got there after a silent two-hour drive, I was about ready to take anything. They had questioned us for hours, and by the time we were on the road, it was already dark.

What made it even worse was the fact that it started raining.

The house was a quaint two-bed, two-bath house, but it was old and creaked under the weight of the rain. The upside was that it allowed just enough space for us to sleep separately but close enough that if anything happened, I would be able to get to her if she was in trouble.

I had thought she was sound asleep in her room, but when her bedroom door opened, I was met with a wide-awake Blake. She frowned when she saw me sitting on the couch.

"Where were you going?" I asked, turning to look at her.

This time she chose to cover up for bed, wearing a hoodie and sweats, though I doubt she was actually sleeping. Instead, I imagined her sitting on the bed, her eyes glancing from the door to the window as she stressed about what to do.

She probably debated coming out of her room for over an hour before actually taking the plunge.

"To your room," she said with a huff, and she walked to the other side of the living room, plopping down on the love seat. She was oddly relaxed in my company.

"Did you want to talk?" I asked. "Scared of something?"

She let out a huff that caused amusement to tickle my spine.

"I wanted to fuck," she mumbled. "Though now I'm starting to regret it."

I opened my mouth to tell her that I would gladly dive between those legs of hers for a chance to taste her cunt when a loud rumbling sound broke through the air.

Her ears turned a bright red.

"I damn near thought it was beginning to storm," I said, unable to keep the laughter out of my voice.

Her head snapped toward me, anger and embarrassment obvious on her face.

"Shut up," she growled. "You know I'm still pissed at you for —what are you doing?"

I was already halfway to the kitchen when she turned to watch me.

"The place should be stocked," I said and yanked open the twenty-year-old refrigerator. There wasn't much in there besides lunch meat, some chicken breasts, mushrooms, and some cream, so I moved onto the cabinet. Just as disappointing, but I found some chicken stock and spices.

That would work.

"Are you going to..."

"Cook something?" I gathered the ingredients in my arms, placing them haphazardly on the kitchen counter. "*Something* for sure. It'll be cream of chicken and mushroom since that's all we have, but I assume you're not picky."

More like I *knew* she wasn't, but that didn't stop the worry I had that she would hate what I was cooking.

"My mother loved it," she said, her voice close to me. *Again,* I hadn't heard her as I was too busy in my own feelings. "I, on the other hand, thought it was bland. Though most of what my mother cooked was bland."

I turned to her with a smile.

"Come from a family that doesn't like salt?"

She was about a foot away from me, and already my body craved to pull her closer. She sent me a forced smile. I realized this was the first time she talked about her parents since I met her, and maybe this was territory she didn't want to explore at the moment.

"I don't remember much about my mom," I admitted. "But I did remember that she made *really* good clam chowder."

I could still taste it in my memories. Still smelled it as it filled the house that stayed forever blurred in my memories.

All I could remember was the feeling of the house. The comfort and warmth it brought. Of the softness of my sheets.

I couldn't remember my mother's face or voice. Those fell away long ago. But at least this much I could remember. I tried not to let what happened to me ruin those feelings. Maybe it was a delusion or a hope that my parents weren't as bad as Rolf told me.

"Was she the one that taught you?" she asked. "Before everything?"

I couldn't look at her anymore for fear of what she would see on my face. For fear that the hurt, anger, and betrayal would be far too obvious. I had told her too much already. How long until she puts the pieces together?

"No," I said as I turned to the refrigerator and pulled out the rest of what I needed. "I took... survival-like classes, though they really only teach you how to live on what you have. Nothing fancy."

"Pity," she said with a sigh. I looked back to see her leaning against the counter. "I would have really enjoyed a clam chowder right now."

"Me too," I muttered under my breath. It was such a small truth, but it felt so vulnerable spilling from my lips.

She was silent as I prepared the food, looking deep in thought. I didn't want to intrude and just let us linger in the moment without forcing anything.

It was hard to admit to myself just how much I liked having the company.

"How much do you remember about them?" she asked. "Do you have a dad? Siblings."

Don't answer. This isn't vital to the mission.

What I should be doing is going through her stuff to find the USB I knew she brought. I tried to find it when she was talking to her coworkers, but it was nowhere to be found.

She was steps ahead of me already.

"Dad, yes. Siblings, not from what I can remember. Though maybe once I was gone, they could have expanded their family. I only remember some things from them, including the smell and taste of soup and..." My throat threatened to close. "The ocean. It was cold, and I hated it."

But the same child who screamed and cried not to go in the water was now screaming at me to return one day.

I didn't understand it.

The ocean was cold and unforgiving. I remembered how scared I had been of it, and later, when Rolf realized my weakness, how he would force me into it as a child, kicking and screaming.

It didn't scare me much anymore. The depths of it sure, but it was more the memories of it that haunted me. The memories of how it felt to be held down, unable to breathe, saltwater burning my eyes and throat.

"They gave me to him," she admitted after a while.

I tried not to pause as I stirred the soup. *A story for a story.*

"They grew up in the type of environment that enjoyed the

idea of a *wholesome* nuclear family. They were religious and used it as an excuse to hand me over."

At that point, the anger I had been feeling never left and just continued to rise as her admissions stroked the flames.

"What do you mean they handed you over?" I asked. "Were they in some type of trouble?"

"Maybe handed me over is the wrong word," she said. "Though it felt like it. I was young. Seventeen at the time, and he was thirty-five. My family grew up telling me that I was meant to get married and have a bunch of babies. It was a miracle I was even able to get a degree online with him or my freaking parents."

"They set you up with him, and being the good girl you were, you married him."

"Your turn," she said. I couldn't help but frown.

"I have traveled to thirty-seven countries," I shared. When she was silent, I knew I had to dig deeper. "I... worked with Alistar Lockridge once."

Maybe that was too much. Giving her the name of your target? But I don't want to reveal anything about Rolf or any other childhood trauma.

"Wasn't that the royal who got his throat slit?" she asked.

I couldn't stop the smile from spreading across my face.

"The very same," I said. "Pity. He had the prettiest golden eyes."

Rolf didn't let me take them because of how visible the crime was. My gaze shot toward Blake, but she gave no indication that she pieced it together or that if she did... she didn't care.

A bubble of hope filled me.

"I wanted to fight back, but I was so... scared," she whispered. "So I went. We had a small wedding in a church down the street from my house with only a few people in attendance. I thought that would be the end of it, but..."

"Why you?" I asked. "How did he even pick you?"

I divided up the soup, ready to hand her a bowl, but the look on her face stopped me.

"He was living in that area doing... business. He said he saw me one morning going to school and then approached my parents. I think he knew I was vulnerable and unable to fight for myself."

"But you learned," I said and walked to the small, round dining table to place the bowls down.

She didn't follow me.

"You're not his," she said. It wasn't spoken as a question. Just a cold, hard fact. I turned to look at her.

I wanted to tell her I wasn't, but even I couldn't say for sure. *I fucking shot him and still wasn't sure if he was the one who was going to pay me.*

Either way, I wouldn't have changed what I did.

"Do you know what he does?" she asked. "What he helps transport? You can't, because if you knew, there is no way you would even be here. You think we are safe here? We will never be safe."

I didn't speak yet. Giving her the space to talk. When I was sure she was done, I motioned for her to come to the table.

"It's not great, but it's something. Come eat, Bl—"

"Do I need to spell it out?" she seethed. It looked like anger on the surface, but her eyes showed me it was fear. "He's not some white-collar criminal. Do you know who he works for? His name is literally Russell Cro—"

"Don't tell me," I pleaded. "Do *not* tell me who he is connected to. *Please.*"

"Because you already know? Is that why you're here, because of who he works for?" Her voice was rising with each syllable. All the fear and anger she had been holding back since the night she forced a gun to my head was coming to the surface. "That's why this started, right? It's fake? It's the least you can tell me. This isn't your house. Your job is *obviously* not a contractor. Now what? Is Quinn even your real name?"

"It's real," I said, my eyes burning into hers. "I didn't want to use it at first, but it's real... what we do is real. Even if the way we met wasn't. And don't forget, I know Tiffany Yates isn't your name but unlike you, I don't care about the past you. All I care is about the you right now and the you of the future. Whatever happened in the past... that shouldn't exist as a barrier between us. "

Her face softened just slightly.

I did care about the past. I cared a whole fucking lot about it. I wanted to know everything that fucker did to her. I wanted to know where she grew up, what she dreamed of being as a child. The file that they had given me was filled with the story she gave everyone else, but I yearned to know just how much of it was real and how much of it was to help cover up her identity.

But I didn't yearn to know because of the job... I yearned to know because of *her*. Because of the little agent who, above all odds, seemed to make me feel things for her that I *really* shouldn't.

"Who knew you could get so romantic?" she said with a small smile. My face heated. *Was it romantic or cowardly?*

"Sit the fuck down, *please*. If your stomach growls again, I'm afraid the whole house will crumble from the ferocity of it."

She walked to the table with a newfound skip in her step. I didn't have to force her to eat, and I was irrationally happy when she moaned after taking a spoonful. *Thank God.* When I took a sip of my own, I couldn't help but grimace. It certainly wasn't awful, but I could do a hell of a lot better if the fridge was stocked.

"Better than your mom's?" I asked hesitantly.

"*Way* better," she said, then paused. "I'm sorry that I said I hated you."

Her words caused me to freeze. I hadn't really thought twice about them since she said it. Her apology hurt even more than the original words.

"You should hate me," I muttered. "It would be easier for the both of us."

Hate me. Yell at me. Throw me out and never speak to me

again. At least then I would be forced to leave or make a quick decision. If it continues on like this, I won't be able to pull myself away from her.

"It hurt your feelings," she said. "I saw it."

I pursed my lips, not at all wanting to have this conversation.

"I knew you were lying," I admitted after a moment. Did it hurt? Did it hurt for her to look at me with so much hatred and pain that I couldn't think of anything other than falling to my knees and begging for her forgiveness?

"Doesn't stop it from hurting," she said. "I just... I don't know what to do with you."

Hell, I didn't know what to do with her.

"Enjoy the time we have together," I said with a shrug. "Regardless of everything, I don't think I can stay away from you. Nor do I want to."

The rising blush on her face caused warmth to spread across my chest.

"Yet you still don't want to know more about me," she muttered.

"I *do*," I said with a force I hadn't meant. "I didn't mean to insinuate that I didn't."

"At least let me tell you my real name?" she asked, her eyes brightening. "Then when you remember me, you can know the *real* me and not this... cover."

I shrugged. I would remember her as the emerald-eyed, shy little agent that changed what I thought I knew about myself, her real name didn't matter.

"Only if you want."

She sat back with a smile.

"Yates is my grandmother's," she said. "Hughes was my father's, but before I changed my identity, I was officially Tiffany Crowe. Honestly, I'm glad for the name change. They all just sound so—Quinn?"

No. No. No. No. No.

I froze as soon as I heard that name. I knew Russell was

connected, but never did I think they would share the last name. *No. Please can the world just go back in time, even for a few seconds?*

I cursed the universe for dropping this on me. Cursed Rolf for putting me in this situation.

But most of all I was cursing myself because even after everything, I opened my mouth and asked, "What do you know about Alec Crowe?"

BLAKE

She knew more than she was letting on.

There I was, worried that after her *job* was complete, she wouldn't know who I truly was. She would just forever see me as Blake, the sex club performer-slash-secret agent. I wanted to know more about her, but at the same time, I longed to tell someone about what happened to me.

Keeping all those secrets inside me had caused my insides to blacken and rot. Had caused my life there, as happy as it was for me at the time, to dampen.

If I knew Alec's name would cause her to react this way, I would have never opened my mouth.

"Russell works for him," I explained, taking in her expression. She didn't so much as blink. "When we were together, he brought me to work often. Threw me to the wolves more than once. They thought I was stupid, thought I was weak."

"So they continued on their business like you weren't even there," she finished for me.

I nodded.

More than once, I had heard some of the awful things they had done. They didn't care about anyone's life, all they wanted was money. They could destroy families, cities, fuck they even jokes about whole countries. They didn't give two shits about anything other than power and money.

"Alec has this... thing," I explained. "If you're high enough, you get initiated into his family. That's how you get the Crowe last name."

"And Russell?" she asked. "What's his rank?"

"When I left, he was vying for second in command," I said. She let out a curse.

I remember the day like it was yesterday. I had slipped drugs into his alcohol, hoping for a night of peace, but they didn't kick in fast enough.

I had been planning to leave for a while, but he pounced and I—

My small, shaking fists pounded into his face. One after another. Blood splattered around us, and I couldn't stop. Not until he stopped fighting.

I leaned back, realizing what I had done, but instead of horror filling me, I was... happy.

Happy that it was finally over.

I ran out of that room and packed only what I could carry, including the USB I was going to use to secure my freedom.

I passed by the bathroom mirror, my eyes lingering on my long hair. It had been years since I cut it, and before I knew what I was doing, I grabbed a spare kitchen knife, cutting my hair as I began my escape.

By the time I was safely out of the city, I was unrecognizable.

"The initiation is to share something of yours," I whispered. I had seen the women after their husband's initiation. Bruises and wounds covered their skins. Some of them would be in bed for days before they were able to hobble out. The men were sick and twisted in their own right, but together? They were monsters. "That's why I left."

I straightened my shoulders and looked at her head-on. There was no shame in this. *No shame* in getting myself to a safe place.

"What did you put on the USB?" she asked. "What does he know?"

I shrugged. "You heard what he said. I have something of his. I don't know why it took him so long to come looking for it. Though I doubt he gives two shits about me aside from healing his own wounded pride."

"What's on there, Blake?" she asked again.

I gritted my teeth. I couldn't share, especially not knowing exactly who Quinn worked for.

What if she had just been playing me the entire time? Just trying to get all the information from me so she could report to them?

But if so, she wouldn't be trying so hard to get me away from him.

It wasn't even a question of whether I trusted her or not, I couldn't help it. Ever since I saw her watching me in the sea full of people, I was drawn to her. My body and soul knew that Quinn wouldn't hurt me.

She had had her chance. Many times in fact. I had slept by her. I had been fucked by her until I couldn't move. At any moment, she could have taken advantage of that fact and ended me right then and there.

But she didn't. And as much as I kept pushing her for an answer on what she was going to do with me, I had faith she wouldn't.

"Enough information to guarantee me a new life," I said pointedly. "I gave it to someone I trusted, and in return, he helped me build a new life."

"So the one you have is a copy, then. Any reason you think your contact won't follow through?"

I averted my gaze from her. I trusted Jonson. He was the only person to see what was happening to me and offer a way out. But just the trust in him alone would not guarantee my safety.

"I learned quickly not to have all my eggs in one basket," I explained.

When I looked back at her, her gaze was locked on her hands. They were tightly threaded together, her knuckles turning white from the force.

What was going on inside that head of hers?

"This information," she said. "If it got out, is there anyone you think it would adversely affect? Someone that is *not* on Alec's side?"

I cocked my head to the side.

"Of course. Alec has millions of clients that would have to cut ties with him," I said. "Is that who your boss is?"

It was coming together now, and as much as it hurt, I couldn't find it in me to distance myself from the woman in front of me.

She was here for that information all along, and once she got it... I had a good idea what was supposed to happen, but the hope that she wouldn't was hard to ignore.

"I don't know," she whispered. The way she said it sounded so hollow it caused my heart to break for her.

"I just request that *nothing* is left behind of me. I can understand why—"

"Stop saying that shit," she growled, her hands slamming down on the table.

"Why?" I urged, leaning forward. "We both know why you're here, even if you won't say it. You really think me that dense, after everything?"

Please say it. Say that you don't want to do it. Say that you couldn't bear life without me.

She meant something to me, but *god* did I want to mean something to her so badly.

Her breathing was heavy now, her eyes lit up with unbridled anger.

"Eat your dinner," she ordered, getting up from the table.

I wasn't feeling very hungry.

She's been... different. It had been a few days since we came to the safe house. A few days since I spilled to her exactly what my husband had done.

It would have been easier to distance ourselves. Easier to ignore each other and pretend whatever was happening between us *wasn't*.

But just like me, she was unable to keep her hands to herself.

Paired with the lack of sleep, Quinn had become far more... *intense* than usual.

"Let me feel you, little agent. Your cunt is already wet for me, isn't it?"

A whine escaped my lips as her hand sneaked into my sweats. Our bodies were pressed together, her spooning me with one hand holding my throat and the other between my legs, her fingers pinching my clit.

Whatever she had been holding back due to inexperience before was long gone. The woman next to me knew my body better than anyone had in my life, even all of the partners I had at Club Pétale.

It was the emotional connection.

The raw, tender, electrifying current that ran between us. The constant need to be touching each other, near each other, even though we both knew that whatever the fuck was going on between us would never be.

There was a promise in her touches. Unspoken words in her burning kisses.

I knew what she wanted to say because I wanted it too.

Somehow, through it all, I wanted her to stay. Wanted to see through whatever end it was we were sprinting to.

I wanted to play games with her. Wanted to wake up in the middle of the night to her sleeping form.

"You need to rest," I gasped out as her teeth dug into my neck. Her left hand glided down my body to my legs, forcing them open so she could fit three fingers inside me. I flailed to push down my sweats for her.

"In a bit," she murmured against my skin before dragging her tongue along the length of my neck. "I want to feel you come first."

I slipped my hands under my shirt, pinching and rolling my nipples between my fingers.

"But it's been two days since you've—"

"Enough," she growled and unwound herself from me so she could hover over me. In that position, the heel of her palm hit my clit with renewed vigor, causing my mouth to fall open.

Her blue eyes were wild. They were watching my every move —*no*—it was more like she was committing it to memory in case she wouldn't be able to see it again.

I did the same, taking in how her mouth fell open and a moan pulled out from my lips. Watching as her skin dampened with sweat. How her panting breaths changed to match mine.

When she curled her fingers inside me, I started to close my eyes, but her hand was around my throat before they could flutter shut.

"Look at me, Blake," she commanded. "Let me see those pretty eyes of yours as you come apart."

I forced them open, arching into her. I wanted more. Wanted her to fuck me faster. *Harder.*

As if she were in my mind, she obliged. Her pace picked up between my legs, the heel of her palm slamming into my clit so hard it would be sore for hours after.

Delicious heat mixed with the pain, and when her hand closed around my neck, I—"Mesmerizing. Your eyes," she purred. "So vibrant. So *expressive*. They say the eyes are the windows to the soul. Yours are no exception, and I find myself captivated by what you're showing me right now."

I tried to speak, but the pressure of her hand on my neck stopped me.

"They are what did me in," she said. "I had a plan. I am good at my job. But these *eyes*. They showed me exactly what you refused to tell me. And it's something I never thought possible."

My cunt clenched around her fingers.

"What do they tell you?" I choked out.

A devious smirk spread across her face.

"They tell me that it's possible for someone to see the monster I am and still want me. Though I'm not sure it will stay that way when you know what I was sent to do."

My heart pounded in my chest.

"To kill me?" I asked, almost not wanting to hear the answer. As long as we played this game, I could pretend like we still had a life to live together.

"I don't want to hurt you," she said almost angrily. "Even if my mind tells me to. I want to worship you. I want to care for you. I want to—"

I came apart with a cry, keeping her gaze the entire time.

Yes. Yes. Yes. Please. I wanted to hear her say it over and over again. To confirm that it wasn't just I who had fallen head over heels for someone I wasn't supposed to.

When my body came down from the violent onslaught of my orgasm, I said, "I want to hate you."

"It would be easier than *this,* wouldn't it?" she said with a chuckle. "Does it hurt?" Her hand left my neck to rest right over my heart.

"Less than I thought," I admitted softly.

"Because you don't believe I will?" she asked.

"Because it's becoming increasingly more obvious that you won't."

Something flashed across her eyes, and before I could prepare myself, her lips were forced to mine.

How many hours had it been since our bodies met in this sleepless haze?

How many times had I been pulled from sleep because of her wandering hands?

That time when I awoke, it was something different.

For the first time, Quinn was beside me, fast asleep. I didn't expect her to sleep for long, maybe an hour at most.

Her diligence in watching over me only made the guilt inside me grow.

Was I really worth this much? Worth losing sleep over? Worth risking her life over?

I couldn't fathom why she was doing this. Job or not, she had to have known about the Crowes. About what they do. About how ruthless they are.

She could have been trained for years, been the best at what she did, but no matter, the Crowes always found a way to win.

It was just in their blood.

The money, combined with the bloodlust and need for control, was a dangerous combo.

I pushed myself up slowly, careful not to wake her.

I prayed that this time she would get more than a few hours of sleep. She wouldn't last long without it, and I couldn't imagine facing this alone.

I had to catch the small laugh that threatened to spill from my lips.

How messed up was it?

How messed up was it for me to care about her life? To mourn her even before Russell had a chance to take her down?

I should hate her. I fucking tried to. But it was mutual. I saw the fight in her. It was getting clearer and clearer every day, and I couldn't help the smug giddiness that trickled through me every time I thought of it.

I felt guilty. Awful about what she was going through and the possible outcome.

But I also felt an overwhelming happiness that *finally* someone in my life cared enough about me to protect me from the people who hurt me.

I never thought it possible.

After Russell, I couldn't even fathom getting this far with someone ever again.

Maybe it made it easier that she was just as twisted inside as I was. That she had her secrets, and I had mine. Because she couldn't judge me for them. She wouldn't.

I pushed up from the bed, my feet coming into contact with the cold wooden floors.

I rolled my shoulders, fighting the sleepiness that clung to my bones.

My eyes darted to the living room.

A flash of darkness or something caught my eye. My pulse skittered, and my breathing stopped entirely.

He was here for me.

I shot one glance back at a sleeping Quinn.

I *could* wake her... but that would almost guarantee that she would die with me.

My feet made the decision for me, carrying me out of the room and into the darkened living room.

My eyes scanned the area, searching for whatever it was that called to me, but there was nothing.

A gloved hand covered my mouth as if to stop my scream, but I wouldn't. No matter how much panic ran through my body, I didn't want Quinn to wake up at the sound of it.

This was the least I could do for her.

The body behind me was close. So close I could feel the coldness from the outside seep into my clothing.

His other hand slipped into mine to deliver a small, folded paper.

He pulled away slowly, sending shocks through my system.

"Leave her out of it. If you wan—"

"I'm not here to kill you. He wants to *talk* first," the gruff voice said from behind me.

We both knew Russell didn't want to *talk*. He wanted the USB. He wanted to prove his dominance over me. He wanted to *end* me.

"There will be a car waiting," he said. "*Don't* bring your guard dog with you."

He walked around me, giving me a look at a masked face. I squared my shoulders and tilted my chin up, all but daring him to try something.

It was laughable given how unequal we were at the moment. Him in full tactical gear, weapons strapped to his side. Me in an oversized t-shirt, the only weapon is my blunt nails.

"Get out," I hissed.

I could have sworn I saw the smile in his eyes before he turned and left right out the front door.

QUINN

I'm going to get blacklisted.

I wouldn't even be surprised if my name was next on the list. Or if it had already been given to one of my colleagues.

I had made my decision, and there was no going back after this.

It was stupid. Insane.

It would cost me everything I had built over my lifetime with my organization.

But it would be worth it in the end, wouldn't it?

I blamed my impulsiveness on the lack of sleep, but I couldn't help but feel that instead of it clouding my mind, I had never felt like I could see the end of this so clearly.

It was crazy, but it would work.

It would be because of what they groomed me to be. It would work because never once had they ever expected their perfect little monster to be anything but theirs.

But I have a new owner now.

"How much longer until they give you the okay to leave?" Rolf asked from the other line.

I looked back at Blake, who was sitting on the kitchen counter, eating some peanut butter right out of the container.

Even though her life was in danger, over the last few days, she really shed her anxious skin and learned to love the mundane life we had here. It had been almost a week, and while we got regular food deliveries, we weren't allowed outside.

Her work had told us that they would let us know when it was "safe" for her to leave, but we hadn't heard a peep from them.

I couldn't help but think this was all intentional. They wanted us here, slowly going insane, so that when they finally swooped in to take her, I wouldn't be able to stop them.

But this wasn't the first time I had ever stayed awake this long, and the reminder of the burning cold as I stowed away on a ship sailing toward Russia was alive and well in my mind.

Compared to that, this job was somewhat of a treat. I had everything I needed. *Including her.*

"You know neither of us knows the answer to that," I forced out through clenched teeth. Not only had this been my third call from him since everything happened, but the lack of sleep was starting to get to me.

I had about two more days before it did me in. Until then, I would try to suffice with naps, but nothing longer.

Regardless of how safe Rolf said this place was or the fact that we had a team of service members watching our place, I couldn't chance having any of them coming to take her.

The plan was becoming clearer now. Less like a fever dream and more like an actual way out.

I just needed a big enough distraction.

"Did you learn anything about what she knows?" he pried. "The client is getting antsy."

My eyes shifted back to Blake. She was watching me and could probably hear our conversation, but I didn't care. If anything, I wanted her to hear. Wanted her to know the decision I was making for her.

"You mean about Alec Crowe?" I asked. Blake stiffened as I spoke. The spoon that she had been holding loosely in her hand was now being held tightly. As if ready for a fight. "No. Sorry.

We've mostly been hashing out what happened with her husband. Something I'm sure you're already aware of."

"And did you hear anything about how involved *he* was?"

In all honesty, I probably could have just let Rolf keep talking and ruin it himself. I knew there was something he hadn't been telling me from the start, but the more I learn from Blake, the more convinced I am that this whole thing is some type of setup.

From what it looked like, her husband wanted to enact revenge on her for leaving her. But before he did that, he wanted to do some damage control. But if the USB had already been given to a government agent, why the fuck wasn't he behind bars?

Now that I knew about Russell, the whole job seemed that much more simple, but why was it so hard for him to open his mouth and tell me it himself?

"No," I said with a growl. "Now, if you excuse me. I would like to have just one fucking day where you aren't bothering me."

I hung up just as his angry shout filtered through the phone. I didn't care. There wouldn't be a time after this when he would be able to punish me.

"Is he why you won't sleep?" Blake asked after a moment.

"One of them," I admitted, my eyes sliding toward hers. "Your husband is the other."

Her lips twisted into a scowl. I wanted so badly to close the space between us and kiss her until she never made that face again.

"So you realize he's dangerous now?"

I couldn't help but smile at her tone. It's almost like she had been holding onto the hope that I would be able to take him.

I could.

It was his boss that I was worried about, not him. Russell was but an annoying fly circling a *very* angry boar.

It was the boar that would do the damage. The one I was afraid of.

In all my jobs, I *always* had the element of surprise. My targets wouldn't know what hit them until their lives were drained from them.

But Russell had seen me. Seen my face. My eyes. They were the things that gave me away.

When I was younger, I reveled in the nickname they gave me because of it. *The Sapphire Demon.* Now it was not only embarrassing, but it gave away everything I was trying to hide.

I had thought long and hard about why Russell let himself get shot like he had.

He had to have known. There was no way that the secret service agents had been the only people watching Blake. There were too many, and the ones that flooded her apartment were ones that I had never seen before.

Even after watching her for as long as I did.

Was he there to send a message? There to cause us to go into a panic like this?

"No more dangerous than me, little agent," I said after a moment. "But we are outnumbered here."

Her pout caused my chest to ache. She shouldn't have to worry about this. Shouldn't have to be as scared as she was.

She tried to hide it, but those eyes of hers were so expressive that there was no hiding just how much this all affected her.

The more I thought of it, the more uncomfortable my chest felt. A low headache pounded in my temples, and the world around me began to spin.

It's time to rest before you find yourself incapable of protecting her.

"But I do need to take at least a quick nap." I walked back over to the couch, letting out a sigh as I sank into it. Originally, I thought the couch was janky and uncomfortable, but now it felt like heaven.

Before I knew it, my eyes were fluttering shut.

BLAKE

For the first time, I felt guilt for employing the tactics I used on my husband to get Quinn asleep.

That bastard deserved it, but all Quinn was trying to do was protect me.

My hand gripped the crumbled note in my pocket.

Leave without calling attention and she lives.
9 p.m. service will be dispersed and you can walk freely out the back.
Bring it.

I had replayed the night he showed over and over again. Trying to figure out exactly how he got past the both of us.

If I hadn't woken... what would he have done?

All the doors and windows were locked. I made sure to check after he left, but there was no sign of forced entry.

They got past her. In the short time she took to sleep, they got past her.

Not only did they get past her, but Russell somehow had the power to control the Secret Service as he pleased.

Since when did the Crowe family ever have that power? Is that why he was never taken in, even after all the information I had handed over to the FBI?

I knew corruption and greed had worked their way deep into the systems that were designed to protect, but I never realized just how much people were willing to give to be on the Crowes' good side.

It didn't take long for her snores to echo throughout the room. The medicine was already working through her system. She needed the sleep. It pained me to see how much she was willing to suffer just to make sure I was safe.

For most of my life, there has been no one to protect me. The people who were supposed to, betrayed me in ways I could never forgive them for.

But Quinn?

She wasn't supposed to be protecting me like this. She hadn't outright said it, but I knew her motive for being here.

The USB wasn't hard to find. She could have taken it at any time and finished me. But she hadn't.

Maybe Quinn didn't quite know why she was doing what she was doing as well.

But I understood it all too well. I felt it too.

And because of it, I would end this for the both of us. It was the least I could do.

Because of me, this continued on far too long.

It was already dark outside, so it was easy for me to steal some of her all-black clothing and head out the back. Like he had hinted, there was not a soul outside watching our house.

All the cars and carefully disguised people that lingered in the trees had disappeared, leaving me alone and shivering in the darkness.

He wanted something else. Revenge. Obviously the USB was incriminating, but Russell was a man of wounded pride.

He probably didn't care about what was on there. His boss may have, but not Russell.

I knew what waited for me if I chose to go to him. I had been through it over and over again. He wouldn't kill me at first. He would make me cry out for him. Make me remember why it was a mistake to ever betray him in the first place.

And first, he wanted to *talk*.

So talk we would.

But if he was expecting the little girl that ran away years ago to show up in front of him and just take whatever he was about to dish out, he would be wrong.

Things crunched under my boots as I walked down the path behind the houses. The cold was starting to seep into my bones, but I kept my gaze unwavering, looking for any sign that he may be near.

About a block away from the house we were staying at , there was an all-black SUV waiting for me. The windows were tinted so dark that I couldn't make out anything inside. A man in a suit waited for me and opened the back door for me when I approached.

Another guy rounded the car, seemingly appearing from nowhere, and patted me down. His movements were rough, a bit punishing. In that moment, I was glad I didn't bring a knife with me.

His hand paused when it reached my pocket, the USB and the note feeling like they were burning a hole in my pocket when his eyes narrowed on me.

"We both know what it is," I said. "Take it, and you'll have to explain to your boss why I woke up the entire neighborhood screaming bloody murder."

He watched me for a moment too long before motioning for me to get in the car.

"Mrs. Crowe," the one holding the door greeted as I stepped in. The shock of the name falling from his lips made me freeze.

I bit my tongue to stop from snapping at him. I wanted nothing more than to slam my fist into his face, daring him to say it again until he was bloody and unconscious.

I may not have been the same girl as I was back then, but for my safety, I acted like it.

The man who patted me down slipped in the back and stared at me in warning. The car jerked forward without warning, causing my heart to pound in my chest.

There was no indication of where we were going on the note. If there was, I would have left it for Quinn to come find whatever was left of my body.

Would she burn it like I asked?

I had hope that I would get out of there alive, but I didn't let it consume me like I once had.

Hope was a dangerous, reckless feeling that caused you to act before you thought. When facing people like Russell, a bitter, cold anger was better.

I took in the men around me with the same anger, taking in every single detail.

They were dressed in suits, a flag pinned on their lapels. They both had guns strapped to their hips.

Are they impersonating secret service agents, or are they truly the same type of people I have been working with over the last few years?

They sure looked the part.

They were clean-shaven and barely gave me any second notice, and the car made its way to its destination.

"Since when did the Crowe family hire Secret Service agents?" I asked the one next to me after the silence became unbearable.

This caused a surprise snort to leave him.

"I'm insulted, ma'am," the one driving said. My eyes found his in the rearview mirror. "You don't remember me?"

I took him in. He wasn't remarkable. He was just another white man with brown hair and blue eyes. Someone I would see off the street.

His lips quirked before he lifted his hand, shaking his wrist so his sleeve would fall down just slightly.

My breath caught in my throat when I saw an all too familiar tattoo branded on his arm.

Images of the last time I saw the man played through my mind.

"Cooperate, Mrs. Crowe," he said as he held my head in place, forcing me to look at the woman beat down in front of me.

It was a wife, not much like myself. She was lying on the floor and pleading for the others to stop. Her shaky hand reached up, the diamond on her left hand shining in the dim light.

It too was covered in her blood.

Russell was by her husband, a sick smile spreading across his face as he handed his friend the steel bar.

"Please," I whispered to the man holding me hostage. But it was no use. They wouldn't listen to me.

I flinched so hard when they brought down the metal pipe on her that he lost his grip. I turned to the side, trying to shield my face, but his hands were there, grabbing for me.

He grabbed my chin with one hand, his other across my fore-head, pushing my head back into his chest and making it impossible for me to move.

The tattoos that were branded on all Crowe men were on his wrist, just on the border of my vision.

I locked onto it, unable to look at the slaughter that was happening in front of me.

"Take note," Russell said, his voice echoing throughout the room. "Whoever thinks it's a good idea to run away will receive the same punishment, understood?"

There were a few other women in the room, all of them answering right away... except me.

"Tiffany?"

"Yes," I breathed, forcing my eyes to look back at him.

His face was bloodied, and the smile on his face told me that he would have no qualms about doing this to me as well.

I remembered him. Just like I had committed the faces of every other Crowe man into memory. He had grown up since then. He was a teenager the last time I saw him, but now he was almost unrecognizable.

These weren't Secret Service agents. These were Crowe's men playing dress-up.

I refused to talk for the rest of the way, not that they pushed me. They never much cared for the women tied to the family. If anything, they probably got off on my return just as much as Russell did.

It wasn't long until we arrived at a short pier in the middle of nowhere.

They had taken an uncommonly used route and circled back a few times, my guess was to make sure no one was following.

But it also gave me another hint at what was going to happen to me that night.

They didn't bother to try to cover my eyes or shield me from the knowledge of where we were going.

Because they knew you wouldn't be making it back.

I didn't wait for them to open the car door for me, and I pushed out by myself. The men got out of the car but didn't follow me as I walked away.

Russell was waiting for me at the end of the pier. He was dressed in a dark trench coat and shoes that shone under the single streetlight.

He hadn't changed in the years that separated us. He still had that all-powerful stare. That sadistic looking smile.

But there was something off about him. Something that felt different from all those years ago.

Walking to him once felt like I was walking to my death, but that had changed.

I don't know when it happened or what had caused the shift... but I was ready.

He was terrifying, always had been, but the feelings of helplessness and anxiety that I once had with him lay muted under the anger that now boiled under my skin.

He turned to me with a smile. The same smile that once caused me to relax around him. It made him look kind, but in reality, I knew the thoughts deep in his mind that caused him to smile like that.

I couldn't help but smile back at him. Letting my own sick and twisted thoughts fill my mind.

How many times had I dreamed of meeting him like this to end it all? How many times have I yearned to slam my fist into that cruel face of his?

The shock was obvious on his face. He opened his mouth to say something, but the crunch of gravel caused him to look behind me. I didn't follow his gaze.

He gave them a single nod before I heard the telltale sign of the car driving off. Only then did I look back to note that *both* of the men had left me here with him, alone.

It was a stinging insult. He still viewed me as the incompetent, sheltered woman he had abused. One that could do no harm. One that wouldn't dare to.

"Not afraid to be out here without your men, Russell?" I asked, cocking my head to the side.

"Oh Tiffany," he said with a sigh and shook his head. "You and I both know there is no need for them to see what goes on in our marriage."

I tried not to give in to the fear that his words caused. Unlike the others in the Crowe family, Russell likes to keep his punishment private. Because then, no one would truly know the sick and twisted things he had done to me. Even his fucked-up family had limits.

"What are you doing here?" I asked even though I already knew the answer.

"For you, darling," he said with a light laugh. "I've been waiting *years* to see you again. I can't tell you how much I've missed you."

I stood my ground when he took a step forward, then another.

Let him get close. Let him think of you as weak and unwilling to fight back.

My mind was telling me to run. Telling me to turn right back around and try to make it back up to the main road.

But my legs stayed frozen.

"Did you miss me?" he asked, leaning forward and letting his breath fan across my face.

"You know I didn't," I hissed.

Amusement twinkled in his eyes. "Then let me remind you."

He crushed our lips together, a hand coming up to my throat to keep me in place. I struggled against him, hitting his chest as his tongue pushed past my lips, exploring my mouth.

Russell was a disgusting, sloppy kisser. Each time he kissed me, the same feeling of disgust washed over me. *Each* and *every* time.

Russell didn't care about my pleasure. Didn't care about anything other than his own. He kissed like he wanted to take. Like my body only existed to serve *his* needs and nothing else.

Unable to take it anymore, I bit down on his tongue hard enough for blood to spurt in my mouth.

He pulled away with a cry, stumbling back.

"I'm not here to come back and be your plaything!" I growled. "I'm here to tell you to fuck off—"

White-hot pain exploded from the side of my face. I hadn't prepared for him to move as fast as he did, causing me to totally miss as he swung his arm toward me. The force of the hit caused me to stumble back, barely catching my balance enough to avoid falling off the pier.

I clutched my head, looking back at him with narrowed eyes.

There was a rock in his hand. Larger than the size of a cell phone and covered with blood. When I pulled my hand away from the side of my face, it too was covered in blood.

I couldn't help the laugh that bubbled up in my throat. *Had he planned to kill me while he was fucking me?* I wouldn't put it past him.

"Don't act like that, Tiffany," he warned. "You're testing my temper, and believe me, I have a lot of it built up after the stunt you pulled."

Oh, I'm sure he fucking did. But what he didn't realize was that I did too, but my anger didn't just appear that night. It had been simmering underneath my skin since the moment I was born. Since the moment I realized my parents regretted keeping their little girl. Since they forced me to his side.

My anger has always been there, but until now, it hadn't had the chance to be let out.

"You don't own me anymore," I spat. "And I came here to prove it to you."

"Oh?" he asked with a raised brow. "I think you'll find out soon just how wrong you are."

I took a deep breath, readying myself. It wouldn't be long now. Seconds ticked by, the tense silence between us expanding.

My first hint that it was working was the slight swell of his lips. The skin of his neck, not splattered with blood, had started to turn red.

Then he tried to clear his throat.

"Let's see who wins first," I said with a smile. "Your peanut allergy, or your legs."

This time, I gave into the voice yelling at me to run and turned to bolt back the way I came.

His thundering footsteps against the pier behind me. His heavy breathing filled the air. My heart lodged in my throat. My legs worked faster than ever to get distance between us.

Without the car waiting, it was a straight shot up the bluffs and into the small forest that lined the area. He was tall, meaning he could reach me in fewer strides. But I was faster, and after all the years of training I had for the Secret Service, climbing up those bluffs was almost too easy.

He was fighting against a timer, and knowing Russell, he would most definitely try to kill me before treating his reaction.

I prayed that he would.

I was positive that I would make it. That maybe I would be fast enough so I wouldn't have to face him head-on... until right at the top, his hand grabbed my ankle and yanked.

My fingers dug into the rocks, a sharp pain shooting up my arm.

"Is this what you came for?" he asked, breathless. There was a rasp to his voice that wasn't there before. He was fighting against the inevitable. "A little chase in the woods? Well, I'll get you every single fucking time you cunt."

I turned to him, the crazed smile that I had been keeping bubbled up inside me finally showing up on the surface. Even after all these years, his body reacted to nuts the same. His face was swelling, almost to the point of being unrecognizable.

"No," I said with a laugh. "It's *this*." And with a single, hard kick to the face, Russell's body went flying downward and straight to the rocky cove below.

All these years, I didn't know how I would do it, but I made damn sure to prepare for it. The training, the hiding, all of it prepared me for that moment.

That night would be the last time Russell Crowe *ever* touched me again.

Yes, joining the Secret Service was a way to protect me. But it was also a way to prepare me for that very moment. To break me out of the shell I was forced into. To prepare me to kill.

With ease, I dropped down from the cliffs. Reaching down, my hand brushed across an especially sharp rock.

Russell was still lying on the ground. His eyes were wide and his mouth was flapping open like a fish out of water as he tried to fill his lungs with air.

I stood over him and looked down on him like he had me so many times. But instead of feeling the power that he must have, all I felt was disgust at the squirming creature in front of me.

"Well, I guess I better put you out of your misery, huh?"

Before he could react, I brought the rock down on his head. Again. And again. And again.

With each hit, I imagined everything he put me through. Not just the physical abuse, though I paid him back for each hit. All the shame he put on me. All the disgust.

He made me feel like I was nothing. Like I was disgusting. Like I was unlovable. Like I should have been ashamed of my sexual nature, then used that same hidden desire in me to try and force me to entertain his friends.

I repaid back everything he did to me. Transferring all of those painful memories and disgusting touches back onto him.

I didn't stop even after his body went still. I promised myself that I would let everything out on him, and I did.

The only thing that caused me to stop was the sound of gravel shifting. I looked around me to see if any of his men had come, but the beach was empty.

Looking back at the bloodied and ruined man below me, I felt a strong, sickening rush of satisfaction before the dread crept in.

What did I do?

I pushed myself up and off of him, unable to handle the feeling of him on my skin.

*I just fucking killed a man. Not just that, I **wanted** to.* A laugh left my lips. I had *dreamed* about this moment, but now that it was finally here—

I leaned over, emptying the contents of my stomach onto the beach.

Exhausted, I fell to my knees.

Think Blake. Think. All this time, I had thought of his murder... but never what would happen after.

I could leave. Walk right up the bluffs and down the main road until someone passes by... *but what if it was his men? What if they came back before I could get to safety?*

With shaky hands, I crawled over to him and dug out the cell phone that was hiding in his jacket pocket, dialing the only number I bothered to memorize.

The hoarse voice filled the speaker in seconds, and relief hit me like a tidal wave.

"I need your help."

QUINN

"What do we have *here*?" I asked, unable to keep the excitement from filling my voice.

I don't know what I expected when I showed up to her location, but it sure as hell wasn't a bloodied and feral-looking Blake after she had bludgeoned her ex-husband to death.

When I shined the light over her, she looked more like a wild animal than a human.

I was hardly keeping myself together when I first caught sight of her, but as those startling emerald eyes locked on me, I found it almost impossible to stay at a distance.

"Now normally I charge for something like this, but for you, I'll make an exception."

I turned off the light so she could see it was me and not some random person stumbling upon the crime scene. Normally I wouldn't doubt her abilities to recognize me, but murder does crazy things to a person's psyche.

Not only had I seen it mess up the other assassins at the guild, but I had experienced it firsthand as well.

The panic.

The fear.

The *adrenaline.*

I climbed down from the bluffs, keeping a watchful eye on Blake. Her eyes told me everything I needed to know. She was scared, upset, and looked like she would run at any moment.

I wanted her to.

I wanted her to take off in the other direction while I followed closely behind her, chasing her until I was able to reach her, spin her around, and—

"I didn't think you would come after—"

"You drugged me?" I asked with a laugh. It stung waking up and realizing what had happened. She's either lucky the pills weren't strong enough to do any damage, or she may just be stuck cleaning up this mess all by herself. I was tempted to wait for her in the dark safe house, but my worry for her overrode any anger her actions could have caused. "Should we hash that out now or should we address the dead body first? 'Cause I can assure you that I have some *choice* words about what you did to me."

"Are you mad?" she asked, her voice low.

The moonlight bouncing off the ocean was the only light that we had, but I could clearly see the blood splattered all over her face and clothes. *My clothes.* I couldn't help but think how good she looked in them.

"Furious," I said with a laugh. "But seeing you like this *almost* makes up for it all. Do you know how many times I've dreamed of seeing you covered in blood?" I couldn't stop the groan that fell from my lips. "And knowing it's your shit ex-husband only turns me on even more."

My body was practically vibrating with need for her. I couldn't wait until I had my hands on her. Until I could rub that blood into her skin, dirtying her in ways I only dreamed about.

"You're sick if this is what gets you off," she spat.

I retook another step forward, unable to stop myself. She was playing with fire and I fucking loved it.

"That makes the two of us, baby." I took another step forward. Heat coiled in my belly. My heart fluttered against my rib cage. I needed to get to her. My mouth watered at the thought of being able to taste her again. "Sick in the head. Twisted beyond belief. But you *love* that shit as much as I do."

The shame that crossed her features caused my chest to twist. There was no shame in this. *In us.* We were who we were and even if our souls were filled with darkness, at least we were together in it.

"Let me help you," I said, dropping my voice, trying to calm her. "I'll show you that there's nothing to be ashamed of."

I raised my hand to her. Her eyes looked toward it, but she made no move to take it.

I saw the moment she decided flash across her eyes. The fear in my words set her off, but it was combined with something else. There was a part of her that felt it too. Felt the darkness growing inside her. She was scared, and also...

Excited.

Looks like the little agent wants to play.

She took a single step back.

"You run from me, and you know what I'll do when I catch you, don't you?"

She knew. Her eyes met mine, and there was a moment when her breathing stopped entirely.

She nodded. It was so small I almost missed it. *But I didn't.*

A smile broke across my face that was so large it caused my cheeks to hurt.

"*Run.*"

She wasted no time in turning on her heels and running down the beach. It took me by surprise how fast she was.

She's fucking perfect.

I let her have a few seconds' head start before I chased after her. The sound of my feet hitting the sand caused her to look back at me. Panic flashed across her face before a crazed smile grazed her bloodied lips.

It took me but a few seconds to catch up to her. I reached out to grab the back of her shirt, but the fabric slipped right through my fingers.

That sure as hell got her moving fast. But the rocky beach was only so large, and it wouldn't take long for us to get to the sharp bluffs that encapsulated the area.

But poor little Blake didn't have enough stamina to keep it up for long either. She may have gotten past me the first time, but she wouldn't the second.

The thrill of the chase caused my legs to work faster, my heart to pump harder, my pussy to clench, There was only one thing I could see at the end of this tunnel, and it was Blake writhing under me.

Her legs worked fast, trying to get her petite body as far away from me as she could, but the rocky sand beneath her feet only slowed her down.

"You can do better than that," I called, closing in on her. She spared me a single look back before shooting forward, only for her to trip on her own two feet.

She tried her best to get back up. Pushing herself up with a panicked whine before reaching her arms out, as if attempting to grasp onto something that would save her from my wrath.

But it was impossible. Because I realized in that moment that us ending up on that beach was the true Karma.

The universe was rewarding me. It had put me in Blakes path, not forcing us together, but giving me a chance to make her mine.

And so I did the only thing I knew how to do.

I grabbed the chance with my bloodied, dirtied hands, and unworthy hands, determined to take what I was owed from the universe.

When I was close enough to her, I didn't reach for her, but instead I lunged.

My body slammed into hers, bringing us both to the ground. I turned her around to get a good look at her blood-stained face and body. My tongue darted out to lick my lips.

The image was intoxicating.

I had imagined this once. Having her between my legs,

covered in the blood of my targets, but nothing compared to the actual sight of her under me.

How had I denied myself something like this for so long?

From the moment I saw her on stage, there was a part of me that knew I had to have her. I was stupid to try and stop myself.

Rolf and the agency be damned.

I grabbed her wrists with one hand and forced them over her head. Her breathing was heavy and brushing across my face as I looked down at her. I let my eyes roam her freckled skin, red-tipped nose, and parted pink lips. *No more.* I pinned her lower half down with mine and used my free hand to grab her cheeks, forcing her to look at me.

Her body was shaking against my hold, and tears brimmed her eyes.

"What are you so scared of?" I asked, leaning forward and brushing my lips across hers. "Afraid I'll get back at you for slipping me those drugs? Or maybe it's about the murder of your ex-husband? I have to admit, Blake, he doesn't look too good over there."

More than doesn't look good. That fucker was unrecognizable. She tried to buck me off, but it was useless.

"What are you going to do? The same to me now?" I pulled my hand away from her face and slipped it under the hoodie. She shuddered against my touches, causing a violent burst of lust to rip through me.

Still so responsive.

"It would make this a whole lot easier," I murmured. She let out a gasp when my hand cupped her breast. "But honestly, seeing you go animalistic on him awakened something entirely new in me."

The electric tension that had been rising around us seemed to inflate in that moment. Her heavy breathing became shallow. Her chin jutted out, her lips desperately tried to touch mine. Her bucking changed to something else entirely.

No longer denying ourselves, are we?

"He kissed me," she whispered breathlessly. Red pricked the edges of my sight.

As mutilated as his face was, it suddenly felt like it wasn't enough anymore.

I was so distracted by the need to pummel his corpse that it allowed Blake to lunge forward. Her lips crashed against mine, and I couldn't hold myself back. Especially not when the metallic taste of her blood hit my tongue. I pulled away for a brief moment. Just enough to see her nodding expression.

"I'll make you forget he ever touched you," I vowed and dove back in. I kissed her like I never had before. I kissed her with a voraciousness that I didn't even know I possessed.

Our teeth clanged together, our tongues slipping across each other's like this was the last kiss we would ever get to experience together.

She was lifting her shirt up, bearing her breasts to me before I could do it myself. I broke the kiss to pull a nipple into my mouth, smearing the blood from my face all over her unblemished skin.

The moon was high in the sky, giving me a perfect view of her bloodied body. I trailed my hands down her sides before ripping her pants down past her ass. My hand slipped between her legs, circling her clit in quick circles. Her cunt was so wet and slippery that my mind was begging me for a taste.

So I fucking did.

"Take your pants off," I ordered before biting down on her nipple.

Her cry rang out, though it was drowned out by the sound of the waves crashing against the shore.

When she got her pants off, I positioned myself between her legs, my mouth going straight to her clit while I fit two fingers inside of her.

I had half a mind to try and fist her again. Reveling in the fact that her husband's dead body was just a few feet away. I hoped to

God that his spirit was watching over us as I did things to little Blake's body that he *never* could.

"Harder, Quinn. Fuck me harder!" she cried, and she squirmed under me.

I couldn't fucking deny her. I fit a third finger into her, fucking her at a pace that should have hurt, but all she did was cry and moan my name more. I curled my fingers inside her, watching as her back arched off the sand.

"God, I should be mad at you," I said as I detached myself from her. I licked her wetness off my lips, holding her gaze as I did so. "But I can't bring myself to. Tell me how it felt, baby. Did you like it?"

"Yes," she breathed. "I had been waiting for so—*ah*—long to make him feel like I did. It was like a rush. I couldn't stop myself."

I leaned forward and licked the length of her cunt, over my fingers and all. She shivered against me and tangled her hands in my hair.

"You better come quick, or else we'll be caught."

Her pussy convulsed at that. *She never disappoints.* I vowed to show her my world after this. A world where she didn't have to hide herself anymore.

"Oh, such a bad girl, you want us to get caught, don't you?"

Her hand covered her mouth, muffling her groan.

"No, I—"

"Don't be ashamed with me, baby." I nibbled her clit. "Not with me. Never with me."

Her orgasm caught me off guard. Her hand pulled painfully on my hair as her thighs squeezed my head. I pushed one of her thighs down as I sucked her clit into my mouth, teasing it with my tongue.

Wetness exploded against me, mixing with the blood left on me and turning pink against her skin. I made sure to lick up every single last drop before looking up at her.

Her eyes were wide as she looked up at the moon. Her chest

heaved as she breathed, the metallic balls of her nipple piercings shone against the moonlight.

"Run away with me," I breathed, still between her legs. I hadn't meant to say it. As soon as the words crossed my mind, I tried to push them away. But my mouth had a mind of its own.

"Running away?" she asked with a sigh. "Like in those old movies?"

"The very same," I said, placing a light kiss on her thigh. "We could go wherever you want. Never again having to think about what happened here. Never having our past hand over us. No more nightmares of what's to come. Just me and you, baby."

Her heavy breathing mixed with the crashing waves of the background. Her hands dug into the rocky ground on either side of her. She gave me just enough pause to worry that I had said the wrong thing.

And then...

"Yes," she whispered, her voice barely audible. Warmth burst through me, forcing a smile on my face. I almost couldn't believe it at first.

She said yes. To *me. Yes* to whatever came with our future. *Yes* to throwing away a life she had tried so hard to build.

For me.

I crawled up her body and gave her another burning kiss before pulling away and resting my forehead to hers. It was surreal. I wanted this more than anything. But to actually have her, here and willing to build a life with me?

It was unthinkable.

"It's over," I told her. "After this, we can build any life you want."

I would do anything if it meant giving her the life she deserved.

"You'll help me?" she asked with a tone so sweet that I couldn't help but lean down for another kiss.

"I will do more than help you," I said with a laugh. "Do you trust me?"

She didn't hesitate as she nodded.

"Good. 'Cause I have a plan."

"It's been a minute since I cleaned up by myself," I said with a small laugh.

My heart was pounding in my chest. Sweat collected across my forehead and dripped down my face. Even though the night air was cool, the hike from the small pier where Russell had died to the cliff just across the way was a steep trek.

The woods gave us the cover we needed to move a body, but the ground was rough, and more than once I found myself almost tripping over tree roots.

I stood up, looking down at Russell's body.

His face was still swollen, even in death, but not swollen enough to stop me from prying a single eye out to leave at the scene. Something that Blake seemed a bit queasy about.

I turned to look at the little agent as she sat on the cliff's edge. She had wanted to help, but after the insane trek in the woods, I knew she needed a break.

That and, well... she may have had a darkness in her, but I guessed that right about then she was rethinking her decision to kill him.

"You need to clean up crime scenes often?" she asked, turning around to look at me. There was something in her eyes. I was relieved to see it *wasn't* disgust.

I gave her a nod.

"I have honestly lost count," I admitted. "Since coming back to the States, I have been pushed to my limit. Job after job, trying to rack up clients all while playing house with you."

She cocked her head, a small, teasing smile spreading across her lips.

"*Playing* house?" she echoed. "Something about the way you come on my fingers leads me to believe you indulged a bit too much."

I let out a startled cough, slamming my hand against my chest to try and unlodge whatever feelings that made me react so violently.

I cleared my throat, then leaned down to tighten the knot on Russell's torso. I had ripped his shirt into strips, tied them across his stomach, and intricately knotted them together to keep the rocks in his body.

It wasn't a perfect way to dispose of the body. The tide would cause him to wash up sooner or later, but hopefully it would give us both the time we needed to prepare everything and escape this place.

There would be multiple organizations after us, none of them willing to give us up that easily.

We needed to move carefully and quickly. It would be years until we could breathe without having to constantly look over our shoulders. But it would be worth it.

"Don't act like you weren't begging me to fuck you, little one," I shot back with a grunt as I pulled the material higher around the dead body.

"Oh, I was," she said with a light laugh. "And I won't dare deny it."

Heat rose to my face, and a light burst of satisfaction sparked in my chest.

"You seem comfortable around the dead," I noted, and straightened. The body was ready for dumping.

Blake stood as well, wiping her palms on her pants.

"After marrying him, I learned very quickly that I couldn't let death bother me," she said with a sigh. I could see the painful memories replaying across her vision.

I looked over at her carefully. It was more than death not bothering her...

Stepping forward, I grabbed her wrist, forcing her to meet my eyes.

"Death can hurt," I said slowly. "But his shouldn't. Not to mention you almost killed a man for the senator's wife. I would go so far as saying that maybe a part of you enjoys it."

"You saw that, didn't you?" she said, curiosity burning her eyes. "I wonder what else you've seen?"

Her voice was playful. So much so it caused another burst of heat to run through me. If we weren't on such a tight timeline, I may have had my way with her then and there just to teach her a lesson.

"Not nearly enough," I admitted, my voice lowering. "I want to see every single thought hiding behind those beautiful eyes of yours. I want to listen to the things you never dare tell anyone else. I want to be there as I watch you explore the darkness inside you. The same one that has been clawing at your insides to get out. With me, you never have to hide. *Never.*"

Her eyes widened, and her breath caught in her throat. My hand came to brush her hair, and it was still damp with his blood.

"Let's get this over with and take care of this, hm?" I asked in a whisper.

She held my gaze for a moment longer. *Say what you're thinking. Say it, Blake.*

But her lips paused together, and she looked down at the body instead of responding.

I stepped away and motioned for her to take the feet. Without waiting for her, I braced myself and lifted him by the armpits. He was a heavy fucker, especially with all those rocks in him. Blake and I managed to lift him, and on the count of three, we threw him into the water below.

The sound of the waves crashing against the rocky cliff concealed the slam of his body.

Both of us were breathing heavily as we stood over the cliff and watched as his body sank into the inky blackness of the sea.

The silence was heavy around us, sinking into our bones and reminding us just how much work we still had to do.

"Why did the FBI do nothing about his family?" I asked, unable to keep the question inside me any longer. I looked toward Blake, but she kept her eyes on the water below.

She shrugged, a movement that was supposed to be effortless but felt stiff.

"My guess is they were too powerful," she answered. "Russell and Alec are in deep with different government agencies. It's how they can run around like they do without getting caught."

"Just weapons?" I asked.

"Information, weapons, hits, trafficking..." She listed off the crimes as if she were reading off a grocery list. It stunned me to think how she had survived so long with him in the first place.

I imagined how life was for her back then, how hard it must have been to be by the side of someone like Russell. I had seen men like him throughout my time with the guild.

They were just as ruthless in their marriages as they were in their work lives. If they didn't conform, didn't submit, there would be no telling what they would do.

Yet Blake survived it all and made it out alive.

"Who did you give it to?" I asked.

She stayed silent at this. I didn't want to admit her reluctance to tell me stung. I had just buried her husband. I would kill for her. I just proved it. What else could I have done to get her to trust me?

"Don't trust me yet?" I asked. Her gaze fell to her feet.

The sound of the waves filled the air along with the slight rustle of leaves as the wind filtered through the trees behind us.

"This is... new to me."

"Blackmailing powerful gangs?" I asked, a smile tugging at my lips. Her head snapped up to deliver a burning glare.

"Sorry," I murmured, holding my hands up in defeat.

"Sharing, *you psycho*," she said with a huff, arms crossing around her chest. Warmth burst across my chest. "I've been running and hiding everything for my entire adult life, so forgive me for not knowing how to open up."

I wrapped my arm around her and pulled her close. I greedily inhaled her scent, taking comfort in the fact that she didn't push me away.

"I won't kill him," I vowed, running my hands down her arms in an attempt to warm her against the coldness of the night air. "I just want to talk. You can trust me."

She looked up at me through her lashes.

"You promise?" she asked. "He helped me a lot. Without him, I wouldn't have been able to escape or get a new identity in the first place."

"I promise," I said with my most convincing smile.

Not kill. Rough up, maybe. But for her, I'll make sure not to kill him.

She pulled her lower lip between her teeth, biting it lightly.

"I'll be mad if you kill him," she said after a moment.

"I *won't*," I said with an exasperated sigh. "Not if you ask me not to. Haven't you realized that you have me right under that little thumb of yours?"

She rolled her eyes, but I saw the side that ghosted her lips.

"His name is Agent Jonson," she said. "I ran into him with the senator once, but besides that I haven't—"

Are you fucking kidding me? It took all my strength not to let a string of curse words leave my mouth.

"Please tell me you're joking."

I squeezed my eyes shut, unable to believe what I was just hearing.

What the fuck is with this FBI agent, and why couldn't I get rid of him? The *last* thing I wanted while I was trying to get us to freedom was to get involved with *him* again.

"What?" Blake asked, her voice raising an octave. "You know him?"

"Oh, I know him," I grumbled and looked down at her with a tense smile. "Unfortunately, too well."

She swallowed, the movement of her throat catching my attention. Even through my anger, the lust hadn't died down yet. I wanted nothing more than to lean forward and lick the length of her neck. Maybe even dig my teeth into it.

"Will that be a problem?"

"No," I said, clearing my throat and trying to think of anything but fucking the delicious woman in front of me. "Just... annoying. But I promised you I wouldn't kill him."

Which I almost regret.

But her smile caused my heart to twist. She turned toward me, wrapping her arms around my shoulders.

"What a good listener you are," she teased, her lips brushing across mine.

"Careful," I growled, trailing my hands down her sides. "You're poking a bear, and I think the last thing we need is to get caught because I couldn't keep my hands off you."

She let out a light laugh.

"Just a quickie?" she asked.

I pulled away, sending her a look.

"Who are you right now?" I asked, half joking.

"Someone who's never felt freer," she said and crashed her lips to mine.

I couldn't deny her, not when her hand tangled in my hair and her teeth raked my lower lip. I pulled her to me, not letting myself waste the opportunity.

God, I may have just found my match.

BLAKE

I never felt more at peace than when I helped Quinn throw my husband's body off that cliff. It changed *everything*. There was a weight lifted off my shoulders and shadow of fear and pain that had been following me around disappeared into the ether.

It had been two days after the incident when Quinn and I were released back to my apartment. The threat was gone, they had said. No need to stay hidden out when there were other more important people to protect.

The agencies words, not mine.

But things have changed since we watched his lifeless body crash into the blacked sea. Whatever invisible wall that had been holding us back before was gone. She was around me all the time, and since I didn't have to work until the following week, that was all the time.

But I loved it.

Loved the comfort of feeling her nearby. Loved knowing that no matter what, she was mere minutes away. I had never been able to trust someone in my life like I had with her. Even knowing what she came here to do.

That night, we visited the club for the last time.

It was bittersweet. I had come to terms with myself within the walls of Club Pétale. I owed Ax and Sloan my life because of it. But now I had another life to live.

One with her.

It was crazy to me to think that I was finally able to envision a life with someone. That I was even able to envision a future at all.

But because I owed the club my life, I decided not to leave just yet.

As a last goodbye, I decided to perform in front of the crowd again. I would miss it. Miss the way they would look at me as I writhed in front of them. Miss the power I felt while I had their attention.

But this time she would be there—I *wanted* her there. Wanted her to watch like she once had. Wanted to remember what it felt like to be wanted by her but not be able to touch each other.

Those piercing blue eyes were the first thing I sought out when I entered the stage.

The room was mostly dark, with the lights from the room being the only thing that lit up the masked faces of the patrons. That's another thing I used to love about it. *The anonymity.* Not knowing exactly who was behind those masks as they fucked themselves to my performance.

She was easy to seek out in the crowd. Instead of lingering in the back, she took a seat right in front. Her elbow was on the armrest, her head resting in her hand, a small smirk spreading across her face. Totally and completely at ease with my presence on stage,

She had even been excited when I told her I wanted to perform again. Unlike Bailey, she loved seeing me up there. Loved seeing me take control of my pleasure in a way that worked for me.

What we were about to do was crazy, but I had been living my life hiding and running scared for too long. For the first time, I was going to take control of my life.

This night was special. I was recreating one of my favorite

scenes and one of the first that actually got me into performing live.

I was suspended upright, looking at the crowd head-on. Ropes wrapped around my chest, arms, and legs. My legs were forced open by how Gale had tied them, giving the crowd an unobstructed view of my pussy.

This performance was all about play for Gale. She would get me off as she always did, but most of the time it was experimenting on what could get me off the hardest in a certain amount of time. How many times she could make me squirt in one session. The list went on but at the end of the day it was about one thing: *me*.

And that night it would seem that she wanted to see how far I would go to humiliate myself.

"That's right, my little slut," she cooed. "Try to fuck yourself on it."

I whined as I jerked my hips. She held a large purple dildo at my entrance, teasing me with it as the crowd cheered her on. She encouraged them to participate this time, picking which toys to use on me.

I tried desperately to do as she said, craving the stretch of it, but I failed, earning a disappointed sigh from her.

My entire body was on fire, the slightest touch threatening to set me off.

The feeling of the ropes against my skin, binding me caused my breathing to shallow. It could be such a little, overlooked feeling but after being teased to the point I was, it was almost maddening.

I'm so close. I tried once again to at least rub my wet cunt against it since I couldn't fuck it like how I wanted, but Gale had shifted it at the last second, depriving me the feeling of it rubbing against my swollen clit.

"Do you want some help there, Blake?" she asked.

I nodded wildly. I was beyond desperate for it. And knowing

that Quinn's gaze was on me the entire time made the need please so much stronger.

"Please. Please help me, ma'am—"

She didn't wait for me to finish before she pushed the dildo into me. My breath caught at the stretch of it. I threw my head back, letting out a long moan as she slowly pushed it in, and in, and in.

When she pushed it in as far as she could, she pulled back and slammed it back into me. The action caused my toes to curl and a whine to fall from my mouth. Burst of fire spread through me and ran down my thighs.

More. I wanted to beg, but I couldn't. Not when my orgasm was creeping up on me like a whisper in the wind.

I couldn't sneak it, not without punishment, but in my hazed mind... it was worth it.

"Any other ideas on what we should do to her?" Gale asked the crowd as she fucked me. I jerked my hips along with her movements, unable to stop myself. If you couldn't see or hear what we were doing, people would think she was discussing the weather.

"Her cunt can fit more than that," a voice called. It was Quinn. *Of course*, it was Quinn.

Gale noticed the way I perked up at Quinn's voice and gave me a shit-eating grin.

"If the little slut begs for it, maybe I'll let you come up here and do it yourself."

God. How many times have I fantasized about Quinn coming up here to play with me in front of all these people?

"Please," I gasped. "Please fill me."

Quinn let out a dark chuckle as she stood, her long legs closing the distance between us.

She walked up to the stage with ease, her eyes not once traveling to the people in the crowd who started to murmur about her.

Quinn looked over me as Gale fucked me. Her eyes trailed down to my cunt. I shuddered as her fingers traced my opening as it stretched around the dildo. Her touch scorching my skin.

"She likes you," Gale muttered with a laugh.

"Please," I whispered to her. "Please fuck me, Qu—Riley."

Quinn's eyes flashed at my slip-up.

"Take this one," Gale said, handing Quinn a smaller dildo already covered in lube. "Use your fingers first. Work in tandem with me, and we can stretch her together until she's ready to take it."

Quinn nodded, though she didn't need instruction. She used some of the lube that had dripped off the dildo for her fingers and pushed them into me on Gale's next thrust.

Quinn moved slightly to the side so the crowd could see what she was doing.

"Oh god!" I gasped as the burning sensation of her fingers stretching me spread. When she curled her fingers inside of me, my body jerked in response. I tried to breathe through the onslaught of pleasure and pain she brought me, but it was so intense so quickly that I couldn't do anything but take it.

Fuck. Fuck. Fuck.

My head was spinning. My skin was on fire. My thighs were shaking with the intenseness of the pleasure coursing through me.

"I can't. Too much—"

"We haven't even fit the other one in yet," Quinn said with a laugh. "Already begging for mercy?"

God have mercy. Quinn's words felt like a slap right to the clit.

"Safe word if you need it," Gale reminds me in my ear. I shook my head violently. *No. I couldn't. Not when it felt like this.*

"More," I forced out. Her thumb brushed across my clit, and it was all that I needed to send me into a mind-blowing orgasm.

It was always like this with her, but it was even more intensified by the feeling of all the eyes on me. Because they then knew just how much of a whiney, writhing slut I was for *her*.

"There we go," Quinn said with a throaty chuckle. Her fingers were removed along with the larger dildo, and then slowly, they pushed both of them into me.

"*Yes*," I groaned. "Fuck, fuck, god, yes—"

My moans were cut off by Quinn's fingers rubbing against my clit. My body was so hot all over. Sweat dripped down my back. My nipples hard and begging for attention. The ropes pulled at my skin, reminding me just how bound and useless I was. The shaking in my legs intensified because of what was happening between them.

"That's right," Gale cooed in my ear. "Show everyone what a depraved slut you are. You're going to come again, aren't you?"

"She is," Quinn said. "Look at how fucking soaked her pussy is. Look at how it sucks us in."

I couldn't take it anymore. Not when they started to pull back only to force the dildos right back into me. Not when Quinn's lips came down to suck my nipple into her mouth.

Tears slipped from my eyes, and sobs ripped from my chest.

They were pulling another orgasm from me, slowly and painfully, but I couldn't stop it. They were in complete control of it.

A scream was ripped from me as I came again. Quinn's eyes watched me intently as I came undone, never wavering. It was her steady hand on my clit that guided me through my orgasm. The same hands that had killed so many. The same hands that had pried open my husband and stuffed rocks in him.

They were filthy. Stained with horrors I couldn't even comprehend.

But it made them—and *her*—all that more addicting.

I had faith it was going to happen.

I knew Quinn wouldn't just up and leave me here.

But that didn't stop the nerves from fucking eating me alive.

Nerves up my spine, causing me to continuously look through my shoulder and jump at any small sound. The feeling was all too similar to when I was fleeing for my life for the *first* time.

But this time, I wasn't just running to save myself.

I was running because I had killed a man. Killed *Russell.* And no matter how much I thought about it, I couldn't feel an ounce of guilt.

Sure, I had panicked. xi, I had been scared shitless at what was going to happen to me afterward.

But I was so happy I put him in his fucking place. Paid him back for all the things he had the audacity to do to me. And to watch him humiliate himself as he struggled for air, that was even sweeter than I could have ever imagined.

"Yates," Ryan called, his voice cutting through my thoughts like a razor blade.

My head snapped over to the man. My job that day had been to stand watch in the backyard as the children and mother were chasing after the fireflies.

There was a slight chill in the air, but not enough to seep through the thick suit I wore.

Ryan's gaze shifted from mine to the family, then back to me. His hands clenched at his sides, and there was a nervous quirk to his lips.

Panic shot through me. Even though we had hidden the body and Quinn had assured me it was taken care of, I couldn't help my mind from spiraling.

What if he knew? What if somehow the news broke and my cover was blown?

"Mr. Bennett wants to see you," he said after a moment of silence.

Relief ballooned inside me. *Of course, it was something as simple as that.*

As freeing as it had felt to kill him, there were still so many real-life consequences that were just lurking in the shadows, waiting for one of us to fuck up.

I had been connected to Russell not just through my past

with him, but that fucker had literally shown up at my house while it was being monitored by government agents.

"Oh, that's all?" I asked and rolled my shoulders. "Your expression told me I should worry about it."

He gave me a forced smile.

"Is he not someone you worry about?" he asked with a light shake in his tone.

Ryan, someone who had been a leader in our team and who should have been afraid of *no one,* had shown an awful lot of fear for a mere politician.

One whose campaign still hadn't taken off.

"I protect him," I said, walking toward him. "Not fear him."

I met his gaze strongly. I had so much more I wanted to say. I wanted to tell him to toughen up. To realize that the senator was just a job. One that would be done before he knew it.

Most of all, I wanted to tell him how disappointed I was.

But he wasn't worth the time. Even though I knew soon I'd never see him again, I still couldn't bring myself to let the words slip from my mouth. No matter how bitter they tasted on my tongue.

"He's in his study," he said, his gaze darting to the family and staying there.

I see I'm dismissed.

I walked past him with a huff. Whatever, if he wanted to act like that, then I wouldn't stop him.

The house was toasty as I walked through it. Almost unbearably so. But it was still. All the agents were in their stations and out of sight, the children's voices muffled by the walls.

My footsteps were loud as I made my way toward his office. I paused and I knocked when I got to his door. His gruff command to come in was just audible over the soft music spilling out of his room.

Opening the door, I peeked my head in before stepping in.

Mr. Bennett met me with a smile, his glasses hanging on for dear life at the edge of his nose. Before him there was paperwork sprawled on his desk. His computer was open but pushed to the side.

The room was even warmer than the house, though he wore loose pants and a t-shirt while I had to force myself into the stuffy suit.

"You needed me, sir?" I asked.

"Yes, come in, Tiffany," he said, motioning for me to shut the door, but I left it wide open and walked forward. His gaze traveled back to the door before looking at me with a raised brow.

"Just for some air," I said with a smile. His notice of me not closing the door didn't sit right with me.

"Ah yes," he said and leaned back in his chair. "I just wanted to check in on you. I heard you were in some... trouble?"

"It's taken care of now, sir," I said, trying not to shift under his gaze. "I appreciate you checking in on me."

"Of course," he said, taking his glasses off before placing them on the desk. "Just noticed you were gone, and when they told me about how someone had broken into your house, you can't help but worry, right?"

My blood froze in my veins. No one should have known the details of what happened besides the team that was assigned to me by witness protection and my boss.

"Who told you that?" The words were out of my mouth before I could stop them.

He didn't seem taken aback by the harshness of my words. He just merely smiled and motioned to the door behind me.

"Maybe now you would like to close the door?"

I don't know what it was in that moment that caused my skin to crawl. His gaze remained fixated on my face. The room was well lit, and he stayed seated.

There was nothing in his voice that told me that I should be afraid... but I was.

All my hair stood on end, and the murmurs in the back of my head were telling me to make my escape.

Fuck that. There was no way he could get me into a locked room with him and away from the rest of the people in this house.

The realization of how little agents were stationed in the house and the rest of the family was outside and far out of hearing range only worsened my anxiety.

"My shift is over soon," I said quickly. *And then I'll never have to see you again.* I took a step back, then another. "Let's talk about this next time? It's a long story."

"Ryan won't mind," he said and motioned to the seat in front of him.

"But I will," I said and took another step back. "I have plans, you see."

His hand dropped slowly, along with his smile.

"Am I making you nervous, Tiffany?" he asked. "I'm well-intentioned. I want to know what you're bringing around my family."

His words caused my stomach to sour.

"Nothing, *sir*," I all but hissed. "It's taken care of, and it won't come back."

He gave me a slow nod.

"That's good, next time then."

I nodded and left without being dismissed, feeling his eyes on me the entire way out.

I'm so fucking glad this was my last day.

QUINN

"I should have known you were up to no good when you showed up looking like someone pissed in your coffee," Ugo said, his brown eyes lighting up. A light laugh left his lips when I sent him a glare.

"So are you saying you *don't* have my money?" I asked, crossing my arms over my chest and leaning back against the rickety chair that groaned as I put my weight on it.

The stench of cigars filled the air and clung to the insides of my throat. As if sensing my discomfort, Ugo picked up his cigar and took a big puff of it, blowing the smoke to the side.

I normally wouldn't have done business with someone who annoyed me as much as he had, but I had been desperate to hide the money somewhere before I was shipped off overseas and Ugo was a man who could take a bribe.

It didn't mean he was trustworthy, not in the slightest, but the guild wouldn't want to sully themselves with his slimy reputation so in my mind, that meant it was safe.

I'm beginning to realize just how naïve I had been back then.

One man was at his side, another behind me guarding the door. Both wore suits and looked far too out of place in the dingy club. It was a front of course, like most of the run-down clubs that littered the back alleyways and dark streets of this city.

Loud music filtered from above, the pounding of feet against the floor caused the room to shake. The rhythm matching with my own, panic heartbeat.

No one would hear you if you blew their heads off, a wicked voice purred.

But then I wouldn't get my fucking money, the rational side of my brain barked back.

I was running out of time. Blake and I needed to get out of New York before the body washed up. It had been a miracle we hadn't heard anything yet.

I knew for a fact that his people had found the eye, as it had been eerily quiet around Blake's house for the last few days.

I had guessed that *some* of the people watching her had been from him, but surely it hadn't been so many that more than half of the agents that had normally been watching her disappeared.

At that point, I was having trouble figuring out which agents were with which organization. Many were unmarked, but all of them screamed danger. I just couldn't figure out who was screaming the loudest yet.

"I'm saying I don't have it on me," he said, giving me a slimy smile. "You know things like this take a while to move."

I slammed my fist down on the table, anger running through me. I needed to do this for Blake. Without this money, we would be left with almost nothing.

I had never felt such visceral panic mixed with anger in my laugh.

"You were supposed to keep it to the side for me," I hissed. "If I hear you spent it on drugs, I swear to God—"

I hadn't heard anyone come in, so the moment a hand was placed on my shoulder, I jumped into action. My hand grabbed the wrist, and I shot up, attempting to pull the offender's arm forward and flip him onto the table between us.

But not only was he strong enough to resist my pull, he had

seen it coming. An arm wrapped around my neck, forcing the air out of me. I bucked against the man, viciously trying to claw my way out of his hold.

"Calm," an all-too-familiar voice barked at me. "I said calm, damn it!"

I froze when I heard Rolf's voice. I just jumped straight into action and hadn't taken the time to analyze the hand that grabbed me or take note of the musky smell of his cologne. The same one he had worn for as long as I could remember.

My heart ached when I realized that he was here. It could only mean one thing.

I let go of his hand, and in turn, he let go of his iron grip on my neck. I was frozen as he ordered the others in the room to leave.

He's going to kill me.

Blake will go home tonight, wait for me, and I will never show up.

I didn't know what saddened me more—the fact that I may never see her again or that I couldn't give her the freedom she craved. I wanted so badly to give it to her.

To help her create a life she loved. One where she wouldn't have to look over her shoulder all the time. One where she could love freely and be herself without anyone looking down on her.

I would fight for it.

I would fight him.

I turned around, bracing my hands against the table.

He looked at me with a pity-filled expression. Something I had only seen a few times in my existence.

It hurt to see him look at me like that. Like he cared about what I was going through.

"You were too silent," he said. "That was your first mistake."

"And my second?" I asked, raising a brow at him. My fingers brushed across the back of my pants. I had a knife, but that was all. To remain inconspicuous, I left the heavy-duty stuff at home.

Never thought I'd run into one of my own.

"Getting your money from that bastard," he said with a shake of his head. "It's long gone, Quinn. Now tell me why you need it."

I shook my head, unable to wrap my mind around what was happening. He should be lunging for me, so why was he stepping back with his hands at his sides?

Why wasn't he taking up a fighting position?

"I'm going to kill him," I gambled under my breath.

"Why do you need the money?" he asked again.

I looked him in the eye, thinking of all the possible excuses that I could come up with. I obviously couldn't tell him I was going to bolt, though he probably knew it already or else he wouldn't have graced me with his presence.

This was probably another test of his to see what I would do under the pressure.

"I'm taking a break after this," I said. "The job should be wrapped up in the next few days. I have eyes on the USB, and I just need to finish the target. I'm planning to take the money and buy a house up north. Use the rest to fund my living expenses for the break."

He cocked his head to the side. For a moment, I thought he wouldn't believe me.

My palms started sweating, my heart raced in my chest so loudly that I swear he heard it. I tried to keep my face cold, not letting him see past my mask.

"You didn't get it approved by me," he said after a moment.

"I wasn't going to until I was far enough away that you couldn't threaten to kill me," I said, letting an easy smile cross my face. In the past this type of banter would be easy, but each word that left my mouth caused a dull pain to spread through my chest.

This may very well be the last time I see him.

When he let out an annoyed huff and a light crossed his eyes, I was painfully reminded of what we had been like before I started taking jobs of my own.

It had been hard growing up under the assassin, but he was all I had... and I liked to believe sometimes I was all he had as well.

"I've been working nonstop," I said, adding an annoyed huff. "Come on, you know I deserve a break after this."

He clicked his tongue against his teeth and looked around the room. *Assessing.* What was he seeing? It panicked me not to be able to read him.

"Is there something else you're not telling me, Quinn?" The use of my name almost caused me to spill everything right then and there.

I killed Blake's husband.

I am infatuated with the small agent much more than I ever thought I would be.

*I will run away after this, and you will **never** see me again.*

"She's an abuse survivor," I said, dropping my voice. "She is usually out of my scope. I was wondering why..."

I let my voice trail off.

"You're having second thoughts."

Warning bells rang so loudly that my ears hurt.

"No," I said far too quickly. "Well... a bit. I just want to know why. I don't get it. I know she was married, and he hurt her, but this is not the usual clientele."

He looked down at the floor, his tongue swiping across his teeth.

"The things she has on the USB will destroy someone that is very much a part of your scope," he said. "So instead of taking them out this time—"

"I'm protecting them," I finished for him.

He met my gaze before nodding.

"I'll get it done," I said with a conviction that fooled even myself. "I didn't mean for you to think otherwise."

He gave me another hard look before letting out a sigh that seemed to deflate the tension that had risen in his shoulders and chest.

"Good," he said, motioning for me to follow him. "Because it's not just your ass on the line for this one."

I raised a brow at him.

"Not just mine?" I asked with a light laugh. "Who else? Not you, surely?"

"Me, you, and every other agent I've been on the hook for," he said. "Over a quarter of the guild's best. All decommissioned if you can't finish this."

His admission caused me to pause.

A quarter? Him too?

I was expecting my decommission, sure... but his as well? How could they?

"All for a fucking secret service agent?" I asked.

He sent me a look from over his shoulder.

"Just a secret service agent?" he echoed. "You know the information she has makes her so much more than that."

I didn't get it. I didn't understand how a single person could ever control the guild like that.

"How much power do they have?" I breathed.

He shrugged.

"Power, money, connections, favors," he said with a sigh. "I couldn't tell you."

But they would be—Rolf would be—

"Taking it more seriously now, huh?" he asked with a chuckle. "Good. I'm too young to die. Come on, let's go get the bastard to compensate for your losses, and maybe then you'll find your motivation to end this thing."

I followed behind him, a numb feeling rising in my chest.

I didn't want him to die, nor did I want to be the one responsible for all those agents' deaths. Who in their right mind would even think of that, let alone make it work?

I'm a monster, that much is undeniable, because even as I thought through all the memories Rolf and I had together growing up... I couldn't go back on my promise to Blake.

One day I would prove to him that I could kill the people I cared about... I just didn't know his time would come so soon.

BLAKE

Maybe the darkness had always been inside me, just waiting for someone like Quinn to come in and let it out.

How else would I have been so comfortable killing Russell? How else could I have been so excited when Quinn invited me to her lair?

I had nothing else to call it.

For normal people, houses were a place that started as a shell, but they slowly built into something that was an extension of themselves and their interests. They filled it with furniture they liked, pictures of the people they loved, food that brought them comfort.

But Quinn had none of that.

When she first pushed open the door to give me a look at her almost barren apartment, confusion ran through me.

This... she had to be joking, right?

But when I looked back at her, she just calmly closed and locked the door behind her while giving me a small smile. A smile that seemed almost... *nervous.*

The Quinn I knew wouldn't get nervous, not unless I was in between her legs.

Maybe she was nervous that I would hate it. The thought

caused butterflies to unleash in my stomach and guilt to hang over my head.

Stupid Blake. Of course she'd be nervous. This is her letting you into something. She probably never let anyone in, just like you.

It's hard to imagine how different my life has become since she came into it. Not long ago, I would have never even dared to bring someone home... and now I was making plans to run away with someone I barely knew.

But if I were being honest, I knew her just as well as I knew myself.

Both of us knew what it had been like to be shackled down. To be controlled by someone and forced to be the perfect model of whatever they wanted us to be.

Hers was an assassin, and mine just happened to be a submissive housewife.

"You probably don't have much time to decorate, huh?" I asked and walked into the room. "I mean, with you and all your *jobs.*"

The nervous shell cracked slightly.

"I could use that as an excuse," she said with a shrug. "But in actuality, I just never found the need to. The spaces that we had when I was growing up had to be... sterile, to put it lightly. We could hide things, but more often than not, they would come and find them."

Her dark hair fell over her face, but not enough to hide her blue eyes. Those torn pupils that I had looked at so many times before this stood out in the dim lighting.

Her stance was supposed to be casual. Her hands in her pockets and her weight on one leg... but I noticed the tenseness in her shoulders.

"The people who made you an assassin?" I asked.

There was no use hiding the truth anymore, not when we had come so far. I should have been scared to talk about it. I felt sick to my stomach, but it was as easy as discussing any other job.

She gave me a nod. "Think of it like a really fucked-up boarding school."

I couldn't help the small laugh that fell from my lips.

A fucked-up boarding school. That sounded like it fit her current personality a bit too well.

"You're sure we lost them?" I asked and peered down the small hallway, noticing that there was just a single room.

I can't wait to see what was inside.

I got off my shift not long before, and I was more than excited for this small *excursion.* For over an hour, we drove through the streets of New York, trying to lose my tail. I even made sure to leave my phone at home.

"Positive," she said and motioned me forward, but she didn't step into the space. As if this was her way of giving me free rein into her sad, sterile place of living.

The oddest set of emotions hit me and made me want to sweep her away from this place. I imagined her coming back here, after a day filled with death and destruction, only to be hit in the face with the reminder of her cold, dark life.

"I trust you," I said, walking through the space. The door at the end of the small hallway was calling me, though I made sure to walk around, taking in every spot, no matter how barren. Because even if there was nothing there, *this* was Quinn, and I wanted to know all parts of her.

"Do you now?" she asked, her voice dropping. It was the kind of tone that made the hair stand on the back of my neck. *You shouldn't*, was the unspoken words that hung between us, but I ignored them.

Giving up my charade, I walked back to the only room available. This time, she followed.

Peering in, I noticed a small desk with a monitor and computer. There were files on her desk, though in the darkness I couldn't make out what they said.

What I did notice was the large, multi-panel wall to the right.

Something that looked so out of place that I couldn't help but stare.

Quinn brushed by me, her hand lingering on my back before coming to the wall and pressing a divot that was hidden in one of the panels.

Slowly, the entire panel pushed forward, lowering, until I got a glimpse of the lit-up shelves beneath it. On each of them were small glass jars filled with—*oh*.

Filled with... *eyes*.

If it was anyone else, I may assume this was some type of elaborate prank, but she was far too serious as she looked over me. They would laugh at first, before they got a good look at them, then jerk back probably muttering a string of curses as they retreated.

But not me.

I wasn't *scared*, but there was something else, lingering right below my skin. An emotion I didn't know the name of just yet.

She was silent as we waited for me to take it in.

The eyeballs were in pairs, stored in jars filled with a clear liquid. The shelves she had placed them on all had lights shining up into them, illuminating the eyeballs.

It was grotesque, and it caused goose bumps to rise on my skin and my blood to chill... but it also caused a sense of awe to fill me.

I had never been one of those people fascinated by death, more often than not, I ran from it with my tail between my legs. But the eyeballs?

There was something so hauntingly beautiful about them that I couldn't take my eyes away.

The first thing anyone saw when meeting a person was their eyes. Eyes held emotions. Eyes held hope, fear, love. Seeing them taking out from where they *should* have been and put on display was an almost out of body experience.

I imagined the life they lived. The people they loved.

What had they done to deserve her attention? What life had they lived up until then that caused nothing more to be left of them than their eyes?

I turned my gaze to the many rows of eyes. Some were blue, green, and brown. It would seem that she didn't have much of a preference and there were no indicators as to why she collected *these* ones.

I took a step closer, trying to get a look at the one on the bottom right. There were a few more spots open next to it, so I assumed this was one of the newest.

Quinn shifted and took a few steps back before maneuvering behind me.

Had I... seen these ones before? I tried to concentrate as she got closer to me, but it was hard. All I could sense was her. Her smell. Her warmth. Her gaze on me.

I still hadn't been able to get over how she made me feel, and each moment I spent with her just seemed to exacerbate the issue.

I squinted, taking in the brown eyes again. They were warm, with flecks of darker brown in them.

I knew I had seen them before... but where? The hidden image was deep inside the recesses of my brain, trying to claw its way out.

I cocked my head to the side, trying to figure out where the hell I had seen them before. And it wasn't once. I *knew* these eyes.

"Is the silence something I should be worried about?" Quinn asked from behind me.

Her hands were on my hips as she pulled me back against her chest. Her breath was hot on my neck, reminding me of what we had done our last night at the club.

This had been my suggestion, and now I was facing the consequences.

I didn't know what I expected from an assassin's house... but it sure as hell wasn't a row of eyeballs. Serial killers took their trophies, and even though Quinn was a hired killer, that didn't change the fact that she was just like them.

She took pleasure in it. I noticed it as she was prepping Russell's body for dumping. She *enjoyed* every part of it.

*That should scare me. I **should** be scared.*

"It's Bailey, isn't it?" I breathed, finally recognizing their owner.

I saw images of Bailey's face close to mine, her eyes hooded with desire. It was some of the only times I was able to look at her. Other times, especially when she was angry, I would find myself averting my gaze.

A habit that shamed me as much as it angered me.

There was no doubt about it. It was hers.

I racked my brain to figure out when the last time I saw her was.

The fight. She had come into my dressing room, mad that I had yet again started performing right after figuring out that I had fucked someone she *really* didn't want me to.

She was always doing that, barging into the dressing room or other private quarters just to pick a fight with me. I tried to understand her, but her actions reminded me too much of Russell.

I had tried to call her after, multiple times, but she never picked up. What I had assumed was her ignoring me was now turning into something more sinister. Something that caused something heavy to settle in my stomach.

"Are you scared?" she asked. "Disgusted? *Angry?*"

Angry? Am I? I searched deep within me, into the swirling emotions in my chest... but none of them were anger.

Bailey and I weren't compatible, that much was clear, but I never wished for her death.

It was my fault. The words felt like a stinging slap.

"Guilt," I said, unable to look at her. "Like maybe if I would have brushed her off sooner, you wouldn't have had to do this."

I hated how the words settled on my skin as soon as I spoke to them. Like a disgusting film.

I'm so tired of feeling guilty. So tired of letting the guilt of what I could have or shouldn't have done. It started with Russell, but I wanted it to end here, With Bailey.

"I needed to get her away from you," she said. "I needed you alone and without interruptions, and it didn't look like she was willing to give you up that easily. I didn't have time nor the patience to craft something to break you up."

"I don't know if we would have..." I said, letting my voice trail. As unhappy as I was, I hated the idea of hurting her worse. Hated the idea of breaking her heart. I was much more willing to let myself suffer in an unhappy relationship than to have the hard conversation we needed to have.

"Exactly my point," she said, her hands rubbing patterns in my hips. "It was just part of the job. She and the senator were both issues."

"The senator?" I asked, turning to look at her face.

"There's just so many people around you, watching you," she said. "Before I knew about the witness protection, I thought many of the men were because the senator. But it looks like it was more of a mix. I thought getting rid of him would help, but I was... unsuccessful."

"You tried to get rid of him?" I asked. "How would you even —the arrest!"

I couldn't hold in my gasp. A small, feral smile spread across her face.

"Yes, the arrest, baby," she said with a chuckle. "Though it didn't stick. I should have known given how much fucking money the guy has."

"And influence," I said and turned back toward the eyes.

I probably should have just left it... but I couldn't. There were so many questions flying through my head.

"Did she suffer?" I asked. My imagination was going wild, trying to piece together how Quinn had gotten to her alone. What did she say to her? What had Bailey told her? I wanted to know it all, but at the same time I knew it was a boundary I should cross.

"No," she answered quickly. "Well, not more than any usual death. I didn't exactly have much on hand during. Most of the time I don't try to make them suffer..."

"Unless?" I asked, turning around in her hold so we were facing each other.

"Unless the client asks for it," she said. "Or I'm... angry."

I reached her face, looking for any indication of guilt or self-loathing... but I couldn't find any.

Does this bother me?

No.

I couldn't bring myself to get all that upset about this.

This is what Quinn did. She had grown up this way, groomed to become a killer. This was in her nature and made her the person she was. How could I hate someone who had no choice but to become the person she is now?

"Why?" I asked in a whisper. "Why eyeballs?"

She stiffened and pulled away just slightly before running her fingers across my cheekbone. No, *she was tracing just below my eyes. How many times have I seen that done before?*

"You can tell so much about what a person is feeling from them," she whispered. "Their fear, their arousal, their hatred. You can see it all. It fascinates me."

I looked around the room before spotting the window on the opposite side of the room. I pulled her to it, making her face it.

"What are you—"

"Look at yourself," I said. "Why do you see in your eyes? Is it the same as the others?"

Her gaze locked onto the window, her reflection just visible in the glass. Her eyes narrowed at herself, and it took me only a few seconds to realize that she couldn't make out the emotions deep in her eyes like she could her victims.

Just like what her barren house had told me, Quinn never much cared for herself or took care of how she was feeling or how her life was. Quinn was walking through life, acting like a machine for an organization that cared nothing for her. There had been no one to pull her back to herself and make her critically look at what she was doing.

"I see confidence," I said. "I see strength. I see a woman who has been through hell and back but still manages to find something to live for."

"You can't see that in my eyes," she muttered, a bit of bitterness lacing her tone.

"I can," I said with a smile. "Because I've had the pleasure of watching you, just like you've been watching me."

Her eyes shifted from her reflection to look down at me with a frown. She didn't like to be read like she did others, which made it all the more satisfying when I got it right.

Poor Quinn needed someone to believe in her, and I would be sick to my stomach if I couldn't provide that to someone who had done so much for me.

"Are you ready?" she asked. "There's no going back after this. You still have time to back out."

"Ready to ruin it all?" I asked with a raised eyebrow.

A smile spread across her face. "Not ruin," she said. "Think of this as your rebirthing ceremony."

Quinn

"Are you sure you want to go through with this?" I asked for the umpteenth time as we looked over her apartment.

She stayed still in the middle of her living room, looking over every surface, cataloging just about everything about the apartment.

"Stop asking me that like I'll change my mind," she said, though she didn't bother to look back at me.

My phone vibrated on the table to my right. I glanced at it, taking in the barrage of messages that were blowing up my phone. I grabbed it, looking over the notifications.

All of them were from Rolf, the first being a screenshot of an article.

Warlord's Second In-Command Found Washed-up Off the Shore at Brandford Beach.

Rolf even took the time to highlight the space where it said, "missing eyeballs."

Call me.

I know you have your phone.

If I don't get a call from you in five minutes,
I'm sending people to decommission your ass.

I let out a groan when Rolf's name flashed across my screen.

Blake was by my side in seconds, her eyes widened as she looked down at my screen.

"I feel like I should be worried," she said. "Is that..?"

"My handler," I said, taking a deep breath. "He just found out about what we had done."

She took a startled step back. "Found out?" she asked. "The body was thrown into the fucking ocean. Russell has a million enemies, how does he know it's you?"

I sent her a bitter smile.

"He knows my signature," I said. "It's okay, I knew he would find out."

A semi-lie. I knew he would find out, just not *now*. I had expected Russell's team to try and clean up whatever they could before it leaked to the press, but maybe they had been too slow.

Or maybe it's Karma. But *that* was something I didn't want to believe.

I took a deep breath and accepted the call.

"You killed a fucking warlord's second in command," he growled. "This was *not* a part of your contract. What the fuck came over you?"

"He was hurting my target," I said simply. "And you and I both know the target and her information comes first."

"That's why you were in a fucking safe house!" his voice boomed over the phone, causing my ears to ring. "I had it fucking covered, Quinn. I had people on their way."

"You had people coming to help?" I asked, the thought of him sending backup to keep me and my target safe sent a warmth bursting through me.

He was going to help me?

It hurt. Pain radiated through my chest and traveled up my

throat, sinking it's claws into my flesh and causing everything I wanted to say to get stuck.

"Of course I was coming to fucking help, you idiot," he huffed. "And now you fucked it up! I knew you were up to some shady shit when you were getting that money. Why didn't you tell me?"

Blake leaned closer to hear what he was saying, but I pulled the phone away from my ear and put it on speaker for her.

There was nothing to hide anymore.

"You know why I didn't," I said. *I couldn't.*

There was a bitter chuckle from the other end.

"Because I would have your ass for it," he said. "Tell me honestly, Quinn. What's your plan? This isn't like you."

I bit the inside of my cheek. A part of me wanted to tell him. The child that was still close to him. The child that still looked up to him and thought him to be the most powerful person in the world.

But the assassin who had seen just what he was capable of, knew I couldn't. Knew that if I spilled even the slightest hint of what I was going to do, that his people would be tearing down our door within minutes.

An idea popped into my head. One so perfect that it caused a giddiness to burst in my chest.

Two birds, one stone.

"I'm leaving it behind," I said with confidence. "Everything. After all these years, Rolf, I can't do it anymore."

"No, Quinn, shut up. Don't you dare do what I—"

"Thank you, Rolf. For everything." For the first time, the words felt sincere, and they caused my throat to clench. "I wish we knew each other in different circumstances."

"Quinn, I swear to God. I will send agents to decommission you right now. Don't make me do it."

"Do it," I dared. "Send them, I'll be waiting. You know where to find me."

I hung up and threw my phone to the side to meet Blake's shocked face.

God, I couldn't get over how beautiful she was. Her hair was fluffed up with how many times she ran her hands through it. Her face flushed with panic and her pink lips open, shock spreading across her features.

"Assassins?" she squeaked. "They are sending *assassins* after us?"

She's so fucking cute.

I placed my hand on her hair, ruffling the soft brown locks.

"Yes, but they won't get far," I said. "This will work out for us."

"Work out?" she asked, her voice raising. "Quinn, we were supposed to *sneak* out, *not* start a manhunt!"

"They need to see to believe," I said, pulling her to me. I inhaled her scent greedily, loving the way she felt in my arms. I would do anything for this nervous little agent and I was ready to prove it. "Don't worry. I won't let them hurt you."

She pushed me back with a pout.

"I'm worried about you, not me," she said and dashed for her room.

"Where are you going?" I called, not able to stop the smile from spreading across my lips.

"Packing, so we can get the fuck out of here!"

Despite it all, this is the most fun I've had in ages.

"They'll sure have something to remember you by now," I said, bumping into Blake's side as we looked up at the apartment that was once her home.

I had promised her it would work out and would make damn sure to keep my promise.

People ran all around us, crying and screaming as they evacuated the building. Sirens sounded, filling the air but not loud enough to drown out the cries of the people around us.

I took it in. I hadn't felt an environment with such terror in year.

It was breathtaking.

It caused my skin to heat and my breath to expand in my chest.

It was a perfect cover. So chaotic. So noisy that no one would even glance twice at us, all too worried about saving the people inside and trying to tend to the wounded.

Fires were noisy too. Noisier than I remembered. There was a deep rumbling noise coming from the apartment—the sound of everything inside being burned by the fire. It sounded almost as if we were waking some mythical monster.

Fire licked at the sky, the heat from it was causing the temperature around us to rise significantly. It would soon be unbearable. Not a soul would be able to get near.

Exactly what we needed.

I wondered if it hurt her to see it like this. If it hurt her to leave the life she had carefully built behind. To see all the memories that she had built in that place, burned right before her eyes.

But when I looked down at her and saw the flames reflected back in those emerald eyes of her, I had a feeling that she felt more free in that moment than she had in years.

Because just like me, those memories had been shackling us to the places we were. For me, Rolf and the guild had shackled me to this earth. All the memories of the kills I had completed, all the memories of the kills he had done while I was watching, all of them were like straps wrapped around my shoulders and torso, weighing me down.

If my memories were straps, hers had to be barbed wire, digging into her skin and cutting it open every time she even dared to breathe.

Those memories had made us who we were, but with them, it

was impossible to move forward. Impossible for us to let go and build a life of our own. Not with the weight of them weighing us down.

So we had to get rid of them.

"Do you think they are in there now?" she asked.

I shook my head.

"They would have watched first, tried to catch us when we were distracted. I'm guessing they arrived when the fire started and are taking note as we speak."

Her head tilted to the side, like she wanted to look over her shoulder, but she quickly righted herself and narrowed her eyes on the building in front of us.

"You made sure everyone evacuated before the fire started, right?" she asked, her voice low.

Just like Blake to think of the people surrounding her instead of herself.

I let out a hum, looking back up at the building. Parts of it were already starting to crumble and fall to the ground just a few feet in front of us. Some people ducked for cover and screams filled the air, but we just stayed, reveling in the chaos.

There was power in making the world reflect what you felt on the inside. Cathartic to finally hear the scream outside of your head, to watch as your nightmares took physical shape.

"The alarm was set about seven minutes before the blaze started. Most everyone was already out of their rooms by then and going down the emergency exit," I said. "There were a few stragglers, but I think most of them are out now."

She nodded.

"Will you miss it?" I asked. She wouldn't meet my eyes until the question was out of my mouth.

It made me wonder if she was finally having second thoughts.

She nodded slowly. "It was the first place I had to myself. The first place I had alone. It wasn't anything to write home about, but it was mine."

I knew the feeling all too well. People like Blake and I, we never had a place to ourselves. Never had a place where we could fully take the mask off and just *live*. We were both being watched. Both of us had to adhere to the roles that were assigned to us.

Even more so, in her case, this apartment marked the beginning of her new life.

I vowed to get her an even bigger one. Once this was all over, I would make it so we never had to run again.

I wrapped my arm around her, my hand coming to tug her hood down.

It wouldn't be long before the agents assigned to her would scramble down to try to recover whatever was left in the apartment, maybe hoping that Blake would be pulled out of the rubble.

They were probably freaking out at that very moment, trying to come up with an excuse as to why they allowed their ward's house to be burned to a crisp.

It wasn't their fault, we made sure to layer unwanted clothes and other flammable items doused with gas around to help give the fire a fighting chance.

"But now there is nothing stopping you from getting something bigger, better than before," I said. I could already see it in my head. A beautiful, sparling house overlooking the ocean. One that was ours and ours alone.

A smile played on her lips.

"And who will pay for that now that I'm out of a job?" she asked. The teasing tone in her words caused my chest to warm.

"You know very fucking well I would buy you a Manhattan penthouse if you wanted," I said with a huff.

And I fucking would. I planned to spend every last fucking dime I had on her until she was living like a queen. I planned to make up for every lost moment. Every time she had to go without. I planned to give her the life she never dreamed possible.

She let me pull her through the crowd. More people from the buildings next to ours had shown up, all of them looking up at the fire with a horrified look on their faces.

Just wait till they see what's next.

"One more place," I said. "One more thing to do, and we are out of here."

We only got a few blocks away before the second explosion went off. Blake didn't even falter in her steps as we left the area.

Pain shot up my arm as my hand came into contact with Jonson's face.

He hadn't been expecting the greeting and lost his balance, falling to the floor and looking up at me with a searing look on his face.

"Whoa, whoa," Avery said, her hands coming to my arms and forcing them down to my side. For once *she* was acting like the nice guy? I almost scoffed aloud. "Jonson is here to help us. Let's not go burning this bridge, okay?"

Her tone was warning me that I overstepped, but I didn't care. He was the reason this whole thing started. The reason Russell couldn't leave her alone.

Because of him, Blake had been on the run for far too long. If he had just done his job, he would have never come back.

I threw the USB Blake gave me at him. It was insane how such a small, overlooked object held all the information needed to bring down one of the most dangerous groups in the states.

"Russell and Alec Crowe," I said, my tone deadly. "There is more than enough on them here to open a case against them. So tell me why the fuck they found Tiffany?"

His eyes widened before he shot toward Blake, who had been hidden behind me.

He acted like he didn't know her when he came in. I would have been impressed by his willingness to keep the secret if I hadn't been so angry.

"Tiffany, I am so sorry," he said. I hated how sincere it sounded. "Trust me when I say I tried my best to do what I could with the information."

"Well it wasn't enough, was it?" I asked. "What the fuck happened?"

I wanted to hurt him. Him and anyone else who had put Blake into this position.

She had been through so much and yet after all those years in hiding, she still couldn't have gotten a break?

I didn't even want to think of what would happen if I hadn't shown up when I did.

"I'm not all-powerful," Jonson snapped at me. "Especially back then, I had little pull and worked off of favors. Alec's group is so intertwined with the FBI that every time I tried to get a case going, it would lead nowhere."

If I wasn't so pissed on Blake's behalf, I would have pitied the man.

He may have been able to pull some strings for Avery and Blake, but every single job that I had given him had been a bust.

I mean, how hard was it to frame someone? On top of that, Blake's file had *good* evidence. Evidence that would cause enough swirl to *at least* get a case open.

"So he's been paying people off, is that it?" I asked, my fingers twitching to grip the gun at my side.

"They *owe* him," Jonson spat. "They've *owed* him for years." His gaze shot to Tiffany. "I truly am sorry. I have been trying."

Blake walked a few steps forward, her hand coming to rest on my arm. "It's okay," she whispered. "Without him, I never would have left Russell in the first place."

Avery helped Jonson stand, a small smile on her face. The smile made her look more feral than comforting. He gave her a glare, but it was halfhearted.

Well, it would seem that Avery was getting on the agent's good side.

For a moment, I wished I could be like her. She was so good at putting on a mask that she would get just about anyone to trust her.

I had been able to use some sort of a mask for my jobs, but more often than not, the mask crumbled when I got too angry. *Like now.*

Blake stepped past me, causing my hand to snap out to grab her wrist. She sent me a small smile before tugging her hand out of my hold.

She looked up at Jonson with an even wider smile.

"Thank you, for everything," she said. "I wanted to give this to you—" She bent down to pick up the USB and place it in his hands. "To see if there is anything else you can do."

Her kindness to him caused a bitter jealousy to rise in me. *He had failed on so many levels, so why would she be so nice to him?*

"I can try, but nothing is guaranteed," he said with a frown. "Do you need a newer placement? I could try and get you something further away?"

"She won't need it," I hissed. The way both Avery and Blake looked back at me caused my face to heat.

"We are leaving," she told Jonson. "This is also my goodbye. I apologize for her harshness. It's been a stressful couple of months and well, she doesn't really know how to interact with people."

I don't know how to interact with people?

"I can interact with people just fine," I huffed and crossed my arms over my chest.

"When you're going to kill them," Avery said, her eyes twinkling. "Were you going to tell me too, or were you just gonna disappear on your best friend?"

"We are not friends," I muttered under my breath.

She crossed the space between us to throw her arms around me. The action caused me to stiffen.

I could name the people on one hand that I'd ever let get close enough to touch me like this, and Avery wasn't one of them.

"Good luck," she whispered. "Come visit once in a while, hmm?"

"What are you—"

"There is a seaside town called Port Townsend on the West Coast," she said. "You can thank me after you find what you're looking for."

She pulled away, leaving me stunned. *How the fuck could she read my next move?* No one should have been able to guess it, but her?

"It's not—"

She put a finger to her lips, motioning for me to keep my mouth shut.

"How?" I asked. She gave me a wink.

"That's what friends do, no?"

I couldn't help but smile at her. *Friends, I guess.*

My eyes drifted toward Jonson and Blake, both who were looking at our display with open disbelief.

"Sorry," I said, offering Jonson a strained smile. "I will be indebted to you if you could help out."

He looked down at the USB with a sigh.

"I don't think I'll live through another one of your favors," he said, then turned to Blake. "Good luck out there okay?"

She gave him a tight nod. "I'll try to do well with the life you gave me."

If I didn't know any better, I would say the FBI agent had tears in his eyes.

BLAKE

I s this... what freedom feels like?

Cool air filtered through the windows. The scent of the sea was floating through the car and teasing my nose. The sun overhead caused my skin to heat up and my face to flush.

But goddamn, did it feel good.

I couldn't remember the last time I let myself feel like this. Or the last time I stuck my hand out the window as we were racing down the highway.

The feeling of the salty air coating my skin and the fresh air filling my lungs was addicting.

Low music was playing in the background, and Quinn was humming along to it under her breath.

I cast my gaze toward her, taking in the side of her I had never seen before.

She was wearing a loose tank top, the straps of her sports bra showing through the large armholes. She wore loose black shorts. Her hair was in its normal shaggy mullet, but the side had been touched up by a random barber we found on the drive up.

One hand was gripping the wheel, the other out the window, feeling the wind flow between her fingertips.

I couldn't stop looking at her. Couldn't stop reveling in the fact that we had left everything behind to... do what exactly? To start a new life? To live happily ever after?

Was that even possible for people like us?

It shouldn't be. We were...monsters. Both of us killing people without any hesitation or care for what happened after. There shouldn't be any chance in hell that we deserve a happy life after this.

All my life, I had been taught that people go to hell for even lesser crimes. Crimes they couldn't even help at times.

But for us, we deserved whatever hell we were going to.

She turned to me, a smile already spreading across her lips. The sun shone against her skin and lit up her striking blue eyes. Without warning, she gave me a wink before turning back to the road.

My skin heated immediately.

Maybe if it was with her... hell wouldn't be so bad.

We could build our own little life there, ignoring the demons that threatened our nightmares and caused us to lie awake at night, questioning it all.

"Do you love me?" I asked her.

She seemed startled by this question. Her smile dropped, and her eyes widened. She opened her mouth, but no sound came out. She closed it with a pout before attempting to speak again.

I don't know why I asked that. Why I couldn't have just let us live in the moment.

Because a part of you wants her to say yes. A part of you wants to complete the fantasy and get your happily ever after.

And because there was no one I would rather be loved by more than her. I couldn't imagine a life without her.

Before her, whenever I looked into the future, I would see a dark, blurry image that gave me no idea what was waiting for me at the end of the tunnel.

But with her... I could see a future for us. I could see the time we spent on the beach together, laying on the warm sand and splashing her with water while she glared at me, only to get me back twice as fast.

I could see us getting our own place together, one that looked over the city. One that was small, with only enough space for the two of us, but it would be *ours,* and because of that, it would be perfect.

I could see us traveling the world together. She showed me bits and pieces of her life that no other person had been privy to before.

I wanted it. I wanted it so badly that it hurt.

But I was scared.

Scared of what it meant. Scared because with one wrong move, it would all blow up in our faces and we would have no time to react.

"I have never loved anyone," she admitted. Her face twisted into a grimace. "Maybe my handler once when I was a child, but the type of love you're talking about... I don't know what it feels like, so it's hard to say."

I couldn't help but smile at her words.

"I don't think you would give up your entire world just to give up on killing a target if it was not for love," I said. "Tell me what you feel when you're around me."

"Frustration," she said without missing a beat. This caused my smile to drop.

"Excuse me?" I asked with a shaky laugh.

"Frustration because ever since I saw you, I found myself unable to stay away," she said. "Frustration because I can't be near you without touching you. Frustration because whenever I think about someone who hurt you, all I see is red. Frustration because not once did I try to think of any way out of this except for killing you. Frustration because all I want is to possess you. Make it so I never have to go a day without seeing you again. Make it so you never have to worry about a thing in your fucking life. Frustrating because I feel so powerless to it all."

My heart pounded in my chest. Heat expanded in my chest so

violently it threatened to burst. I swallowed thickly, unable to fight against the barrage of emotions her words evoked in me.

"It may be a little twisted," I said after clearing the knot in my throat. "But I think you *do* love me. In a way. A completely unhealthy way, but..."

"Then I love you," she said, her gaze snapping toward mine. Her face was serious as she looked over at me. So serious, in fact, that it caused my heart to stop. "I love you, Blake."

"You can't just say it like that. You have to mean it," I murmured. My face and the back of my neck were unbearably hot.

"I mean it," she said, a wicked grin spreading across her face. "And you don't have to say it back, *yet*. We will have plenty of time for me to force it out of you as I bend you over the hood of the car and fuck that cunt of yours until you're screaming to the world how much you love me."

Oh my god. I regret ever introducing this type of talk to Quinn. *How is it that for someone so inexperienced, she was able to make my pussy throb with just a few sentences?*

I was suddenly looking forward to whenever we stopped next.

"I knew it," I whispered in awe as I looked out at the ever-expanding ocean in front of us.

The air was even cooler there, hitting my face with each gust of wind and calming the redness the sun had left.

The beach was utterly desolate. We were the only two inhabitants.

The sea was strong, but not like it was that night when it swallowed Russell whole.

Being in front of the sea now was... calming.

I took a deep breath, letting the fresh air fill my lungs.

"Just a small break," she said, sending me a smile. "We will be on the road until late for another two days going west before we can fully rest. There won't be another chance to see the sea for some time."

"No stopping at all?" I asked, turning to face her and walking backward to the ocean. She followed me closely, her eyes darting to and from the ocean as we approached.

"There's a discreet motel between here and where we need to be by tomorrow. I'll stop there for a few hours, but then we have to head out."

I hummed and kicked off my shoes. The rocky floor was slightly warm against my toes, but the cool air chased the warmth away.

"If you go in there, I'm not coming after you," she said, her voice lowering.

I cocked a brow at her and took a big step back, letting the waves brush over my feet. I gasped at the coldness the sea. It was like a shock to my system.

Similar to when my dom used pain when I was so deep in a pleasure filled haze that I couldn't think straight. It caused my head to clear and a smile to play at my lips.

"You scared of the ocean?" I asked.

"No," she shot back, her voice turning dangerous.

I sent her a smile before grabbing her hand and pulling her closer to me.

"Sure, you aren't."

She stopped right before the line of the waves, her face morphing into a deep scowl.

When she didn't come right away, I leaned down, cupping the water in my hand, and threw it at her.

She ground her teeth together, her jaw clenching.

"You think that will make me chase you?" she asked, her voice tense.

"I think it will make you fear the water less," I said and splashed another bit at her. "At least while you're with me."

"I'm not afraid of it," she huffed and took a step closer, but just before the wave hit her foot, she inched away.

I hit her with another bit of water, and this time she didn't think twice about charging in after me.

I couldn't stop the squeal that slipped from my lips at the suddenness of her movements.

I tried to splash water on her as I made my escape, but she was too fast. She used both hands, leaned down, and splashed me straight in the face with water.

I coughed, trying to expel the little bit that got into my mouth. My world spun, and in an instant, I was on my back, water crashing around me. I closed my eyes on impact and squeezed them shut for fear.

Quinn's laugh reached my ears, causing my eyes to spring open.

She was above me, her hair dripping with water. The sun was shining behind her, illuminating her face and that drop-dead gorgeous smile that spread across her face.

I don't know if I've ever seen her smile so widely before. It was breathtaking.

The normal sullen and serious look on her face quite literally melted away, showing a cheek-aching smile paired with laughter that stemmed deep from her chest.

I wanted to commit it to memory. I wanted it to shine bright and force all the bad memories back, so I was just left with this single awe-inspiring moment.

The waves leaked into my clothing bringing sand with it, but I couldn't bring myself to care.

I wrapped my arms around her, pulling her face to mine.

"Maybe I won't be so afraid of it anymore," she murmured against my lips before deepening the kiss.

Her hand slipped into my shirt, the warmness of her skin feeling akin to a burn against the coldness of mine.

I arched into her, needing to feel more of her body against mine. This time was different with her.

Time moves slowly.

Our movements were unhurried.

We took pleasure in each other without fear that it was going to end at any moment.

It was the type of connection and experience that I had yearned for since Russell personally locked the shackles on my ankles.

She freed me.

And no matter how fucked up it was that I was shackling myself to her as soon as I got a taste of freedom, I couldn't bring myself to regret it.

QUINN

She was having a nightmare.

I had shared her bed with her so many times before this, but this was the first time that I'd come across her nightmares.

I stepped closer to the bed, moving my wet hair out of my face.

After her shower I told her to rest first, not wanting her to see how I desperately tried to scrub my skin clean. How I desperately tried to get rid of the scent and the feel of the ocean.

I thought for the most part that I had gotten over my fear of the ocean, but maybe being around her had lowered my guard, and I was able to fully see just how fucked Rolf had made me.

She had to have been so tired to fall asleep so easily. The last few months were a lot for her, I could see it in the way she carried herself. But I had assumed that after we got rid of Russell, paired with her newfound freedom, that she wouldn't be plagued by the trauma of her past life anymore.

Of course, going on the run from the two organizations that controlled our lives would never be easy, but she had *seemed* so happy.

She tossed and turned in the cheap, scratchy sheets of the

motel bed. Her hands clutched them for dear life, and her eyes were strewn shut. The grimace on her face looked painful.

I paused near the bed, the reaching of my hand out to her was automatic. A move that caused me to pause when I realized what I was doing.

I didn't want her to suffer, but I didn't know if it was wise to wake her.

"Get a hold of yourself," I spat at myself.

You can't just leave her to suffer while you watch. Stop hesitating.

I used both of my hands to clasp her shoulders, trying to stop her wild movements.

"Blake," I said in a sharp whisper. "*Blake*, wake up."

She didn't wake up from her sleep until after a good few shakes. Then, her eyes snapped open. Her breathing was ragged as she took in deep gasps of air. Her eyes shot around the room in a panic.

She was looking to run. I could see it in her eyes.

The image reminded me too much of a wild animal caught in a hunter's trap.

"It's me," I whispered, my hands squeezing her shoulders. "It's okay. He's gone, no one can hurt you anymore."

Her hands flailed out to grab me. Her fingernails came into contact with my damp skin. I was wearing a sports bra and shorts, not enough to shield me as she clawed at my skin. She reached out, throwing her arms around me and bringing me close to her. My hands moved to her back, pulling her to me.

"Quinn," she breathed. The sound of my name on her lips was so painful yet so relieving that it caused my heart to clench.

"You're having a nightmare," I said and pulled her away so I could look into her eyes. "We are in a motel, remember? No one will hurt you—"

"I thought they took you," she gasped out.

My heart stopped in my chest. My hands that were rubbing small circles in her back paused.

"What?" I breathed.

"My nightmare," she explained. "They came to get you. They took you from me—I couldn't find you."

Her words were like a punch to the stomach.

I thought that she had been reliving her life at Russell's, that the nightmares that I tried to take her from still plagued her... but she was worried about *me*.

I couldn't quite understand how I felt.

My chest was twisting. My stomach hurt... but there was a joyous feeling threatening to burst at the seams.

She was worried about me.

She hadn't responded to my declaration of love yet, but she didn't need to because her actions and her words already told me everything that I needed to know.

The little agent was just as enamored with me as I was with her.

"Because they're not gonna take me," I said with conviction.

I was confident in my abilities as an assassin. I've traveled the world for most of my life running from people just like the ones that are coming after us now. I knew what we had to do, and I had a plan.

We would travel as far as we could to a remote town where we wouldn't be bothered. We'd stay there for a few weeks before moving on to another one. Each time we moved, we would get farther and farther away from the people who chased us.

It would be hard. We wouldn't be able to live the perfect life, at least not until they gave up.

But at some point, they would realize that I wasn't going to be caught as easily as they wanted. The guild would be pissed. Of course they would want repayment for the botched job, but they weren't going to take away valuable resources from jobs that would guarantee money.

"You don't know that," Blake whispered. Her eyes traveled across my face. Her fingers reached up to trace the line of my nose and cheekbones.

She was committing them to memory.

Just like I had done to her so many times. The dim light of the motel room was just enough so that I could make out her features but also the sparkle of tears in her eyes.

Had she really worried so much about me? Had it hurt her *that* much?

"I'm gonna try my hardest to get us to where we need to go," I promised, hoping she could feel how serious I was. "You trust me, right?"

She gave me a smile.

"If I didn't trust you, I wouldn't be here right now," she said. "You saved my life, in more ways than one."

You saved mine, the words were on the tip of my tongue. I wanted to tell her how dull my life had been before her. How meaningless every single day had been.

How I had longed for something exciting.

Leaving with her meant leaving behind everything that I knew, but in exchange, I got to experience something that I never had before.

"Then trust that I'll get us out of here."

Her eyes shifted to the darkness of the room, avoiding my gaze.

"I just feel so useless," she whispered. "Like all I'm ever good for is running and fucking."

"Well, you *are* good at those things," I said with a chuckle. "But that's not all you're good for. Remember, I am giving up my entire life for you. I could have easily just ended it multiple times and moved on to the next job. But because of you, I have... a *life* now. I'm planning a future for the first time."

Her eyes widen as she looked at me.

"What is our future?"

I leaned down and brushed my lips across hers.

"Whatever you want it to be," I said. "As long as we are together safe and happy, it will be everything I need. I'll get you anything you want, give you the life that you deserve."

"And you?" she asked. "What do you get out of this? Like you said, you're leaving everything, won't you resent me?

"Never," I growled and forced my arms around her. I shifted so I was hovering over her, our skin brushing together.

"To be with you," I said. "That's all I want."

BLAKE

"You're serious?" I whispered as Quinn shoved a spoonful of mashed potatoes in her mouth. "We can really go?"

After another day in the car, we were both ravenous.

I had expected her to mention the nightmare from last night, but she just got in the car and acted as if it never happened.

I was glad because, man, had it been embarrassing.

It had been some time since I had had a nightmare so powerful.

Usually they were images from the past. Traumatic memories that I couldn't run fast enough from.

But last night had been—I repressed a shiver. It felt so *real*. The heartbreak. The pain of watching her being torn away from me.

It only solidified what I had been feeling this whole time.

She raised an eyebrow at me, not bothering to reply until she took a few more bites of her food.

"What kind of girlfriend would I be if I denied you the opportunity to go to the arcade?" she said with a smile.

I looked around the almost empty diner. The sun had set long ago, and normally a place like this would be filled to the brim, but this diner just so happened to be on a long stretch of road in the middle of fucking nowhere.

I was more than just slightly uncomfortable, but Quinn seemed to be at ease.

Just like with the shitty motel we had stayed at the night before. Nothing seemed to bother her here.

Maybe it's because whatever threat of violence, no matter how serious, she was sure that she'd be able to take care of it.

I, on the other hand, still had panic attacks about my dead husband.

No matter how much training I had gone through with the Secret Service, no matter how many times I had faced down bad guys with guns, I still found myself looking over my shoulder at every possible moment.

So while I wanted nothing more than to go to the arcade, there was still a glaring target on our backs.

And after the nightmare, I just couldn't find it in myself to chance it.

"Aren't you afraid they will...?"

She shrugged and leaned back into the booth. "It is unlikely they will come. Especially since the client is dead, there is no rush for your head."

"So it was Russell, are you sure?" I asked.

Russell, the person who had spent years chasing me, had hired Quinn to get what I had stolen from him. She had left out the gruesome details of what he wanted, but I was able to piece it together enough that it caused my blood to boil.

What I didn't understand was *why* he would interfere.

"Pretty positive, at least that's the only person with a motive," she said.

"But then why would he show up?" I asked.

She shrugged. "I think he got pissed that I was not moving fast enough. He called my handler multiple times to try and get things to move along. But well, it would be a lie to say I wasn't trying to prolong the job so I could spend more time with you.

"I would just assume Russell would do it himself," I said, taking a bite of my own meal. "Right after he found me. The idea was that as long as I could stay hidden from him, I would be safe."

Quinn pursed her lips. Obviously, it wasn't sitting right with her either.

"I don't try to get into the minds of my clients," she said after a moment. "A lot of the time, these things are crimes of passion. I just blame it on his impatience."

"Okay," I said, letting my voice trail. "What about the Secret Service, then? Are we not worried about them?"

Her eyes shot around the diner before she leaned forward.

"I am guessing you may have been more of a burden to the team with your little *secret* there than not, am I correct?"

Her words stung, but I couldn't help but nod. They had to put in a lot of time and manpower in order to keep me safe. Me being gone just meant that they would no longer have to bend over backward for me.

"Don't worry, baby," she said and reached out to flick my forehead. I let out an embarrassingly loud yelp and shot her a look. She was trying—and failing—to conceal her smug grin.

"Don't call me that," I grumbled.

She gave me a wicked smile.

"So you like dirty little slut instead?" she asked. "Or maybe princess? Or maybe a combination? How about my dirty little prin—"

"Oh my god, *stop*," I hissed under my breath, but as soon as she shut her mouth, giving me that smile of hers, I couldn't help but return it.

How she had so easily stopped my brain from spiraling into a mess of anxiousness, was something I couldn't help but be grateful for.

She was right, I should just trust her and let her take me where we need to go. I would do my job and be on the lookout for anything that seemed amiss, but besides that, it would do no good to continue to worry about something that hadn't happened.

"Well," she said, standing. "If my little whore wants to meet me in the bathroom for some fun before we leave, I wouldn't mind."

She placed a few twenties on the counter before getting up and leaving toward the restrooms. Of course, I followed her. She disappeared into it, sending me a wink as she shut the door behind her.

Excitement filled me, making me forget all about the anxiety that had been plaguing my mind all day. There was no one around, but there was still something so naughty about fucking her in a random bathroom.

Heat swirled inside me at the thought of it. At the fear of someone hearing us.

As soon as I stepped through the bathroom door, I was jerked to the side. I was met with Quinn's playful eyes as she searched my face, the sound of her locking the bathroom door filling the small space. My heart stuttered in my chest, and heat rose to my face.

She turned us around, her eyes never leaving mine, as she walked me back further into the bathroom. A gasp tore from my throat when my back hit the sink.

"Quickly," she said with a grin. "We *do* need to get on the road again, but I can't deny my little slut what she needs."

My breath hitched. My pussy was already aching, begging for her touch. It had been a few days since we had been able to do anything, and right then, I was feeling just how long it had been since I came.

"And what is it I need?" I asked, lowering my voice.

She didn't answer me. Instead, she turned me around so I was forced to look at myself in the dirty mirror. She was right behind me, a smirk on her face.

She was going to make me watch myself. Something I hadn't done often.

The dirty bathroom should have turned me off, but the image of myself in the mirror as she looked at me with those sinful eyes was enough to make my head spin.

Her hands trailed my torso, pulling up my shirt and baring my breasts to the world. I washed as her fingers trailed my nipples, causing them to harden. It was so much more erotic to see what she did to my body than to just feel it.

My head fell back with a moan as she plucked them.

"My dirty little slut needs to get fucked," she whispered in my ear. Her voice was dark and filled with lust. "Look at yourself. Watch as I fuck you."

I forced my gaze back to the mirror. She pinched my nipples, pulling a moan from me.

Slowly, her hand traveled down my front until it slipped into my pants. Her gaze was locked on mine, watching as her hand descended lower and lower—I gasped when her fingers ran down my folds.

I bucked against her, forcing her fingers to rub against my wet slit. I was unashamedly grinding against her. Pulling out moan after moan from my own mouth. She kept still, watching as I rode her hand, desperately searching for the friction I needed.

Her fingers trailed to my clit, rubbing soft circles in it. Her breathing in my ear combined with the steady plucking of my nipple was enough to drench my underwear.

"God, how long were you squirming in your own wetness?" she asked. She circled my clit harder this time. Once, twice, before slipping two fingers into me.

I needed more. I needed her to throw me across this dirty sink and ram into me like she never had before.

I was shaking with need.

"Since you told me you loved me," I admitted. I wrapped an arm around her neck, using it as leverage to hold myself up. I placed my foot on the pipes below the sink and opened my legs farther for her.

Her eyes widened along with her pupils. Hunger was obvious in them, and it made my body heat even more.

She didn't stop me from meeting her hand as she pumped her fingers inside of me.

The squelch of my wetness against her hand was loud in the room. Our pants mingled together. There was no mistaking what we were doing in here.

I used my free hand to push my pants lower, giving her more room to fuck me.

Delicious pleasure licked at my spine, pushing me to continue my movements against her. She felt so good. It didn't matter what she did to me, I would find pleasure in it all. She played me easily. Like she had completely learned every single tell my body had and used it against me in that very moment.

She brought her fingers up to her mouth, her pink tongue drawing out to wet them before bringing it back to my nipple. The feeling of her now wet fingers rolling my nipple pulled a gasp from me.

My pussy clenched around her, pulling her fingers deeper into me. I was going insane with the need to come. My movements were hurried, and I ground my hips against her, chasing the sweet orgasm that was on the verge of peeking its head out.

"That's what you need to hear?" she asked, fitting a third finger inside of me. I spread my legs for her, needing more. My pussy clenched around her again.

"Yes," I breathed. "Tell me again."

My nails dug into her skin. I watched the mirror version of me. The one with her mouth open, panting and begging for more. I was exposed, arching for her touch. I could just make out the image of my wetness on her fingers as she pumped them inside of me.

"I love you, Blake," she groaned. "I love *you*. I think I did from the moment I laid eyes on you."

Fuck.

I let my hands slip into my pants, rubbing my clit ferociously as she finger-fucked me. So close. I was so close, it was bordering on painful. I was making a mess of my pants and probably calling all staff to the bathrooms with my moans, but *fuck* if I gave two shits about it.

"More."

"I love the darkness inside you," she continued. "I love how fucking ready you are for me. I love seeing just how expressive those eyes of yours are, especially—"

I couldn't contain my whine as my cunt fluttered around her fingers. My orgasm burst through me, causing my body to convulse against her as it destroyed my body.

A few days might not have been long for anyone else, but for me, it had been far too long. All the tension and fear that had acclimated in my body turned into white-hot pleasure as I came, leaving nothing left in my body.

"*Ah,*" she breathed. As if my orgasm was hers as well. "Yes, like that."

I forced myself to look back at the mirror as I rode out the waves, desperate to see what she saw.

She was watching me again, though if I were being honest, I wasn't sure she ever looked away.

A light sheen of sweat covered my body, my face red from the intense orgasm she just pulled from me.

"And most importantly," she whispered, "I love that you love me too."

Her words caused the breath to leave my lungs. I didn't know what to say. Didn't know *how* to say it.

She made it seem *so* easy, but it felt like a tremendous weight to even just *think* the words.

We stayed there for a few more moments, both of us looking into my eyes as I came down.

She was right. Of course she was. There was nothing to hide. We had come this far. *So why was it so fucking hard for me to say?*

The thing that scared me the most was her being taken away from me, that alone just proved everything I felt about her.

So why wasn't my mouth moving?

"Take your time, baby," she said, placing a burning kiss on my throat. "I'll go check to make sure they got our money and pack up. I'll be waiting."

I didn't say anything as she helped me right my clothes before leaving. I was too taken aback by everything that had just happened.

It was true. It had been true.

It wasn't a hard conclusion to come to, but it was... scary.

I didn't think I would ever love. Even when I became more open and started dating back at the club, I never truly thought that I would fall in love, or be loved by someone.

But here it was. As simple and as easy as it was... I loved her.

I let out a laugh.

"I love her," I whispered to myself, a smile spreading across my face. I straightened, looking at myself in the mirror. *I can do this.*

The words seemed heavy, and it was hard to open up to someone... but this was *Quinn.* I had nothing to be afraid of with her.

With a smile, I turned back to the exit, ready to run after her and utter those words that scared me so deeply.

Just as I was about to grab the handle, the doors burst open. Screams filtered in. Bright lights blinded my vision.

I tried to grab onto something—anything—to try and stay upright, but the force of it all caused me to stumble back.

My world turned upside down. My back came into contact with a hard surface. The air was knocked out of my lungs.

I tried to blink away the spots in my vision. Tried to open my mouth to call for Quinn. But nothing worked.

Hands grabbed at me, but they were not the hands I had grown accustomed to. These ones were gloved, and instead of trying to pull me up, I was forced to the ground. The ringing in my ears was loud, but not loud enough to drown out the man's bark.

"Police! You are under arrest for the murder of Russell Crowe!"

BLAKE

T he cell that they had dragged me to was cold and completely empty.

The hard stone bench I sat on caused my ass and back to ache. I sighed as I rolled my shoulders, trying to chase away the discomfort.

The jail itself probably hadn't been updated for thirty-something years. Many of the metal bars in the cells itself had been rusted through, and if you looked carefully, the corners had collected dust. Through all my time working with the Secret Service and helping law enforcement catch those who tried to hurt my assignments, I'd never seen such a jail be so broken.

Not to mention empty.

A burst of panic fluttered in my chest and caused my heart rate to speed up.

I took a deep breath and stood, trying to calm myself down for the umpteenth time that night. I'd lost count of how many hours it had been since I'd been separated from Quinn.

The police station they had taken me to was twenty minutes away from the diner, and I made sure to keep track of the clock on the dash of the police cruiser. But even as I waited for hours on end, I hadn't seen a single sign of Quinn since they threw me in here.

There hadn't even been a second car following us.

I could feel myself on the verge of panicking. My breathing was getting shallower, and the feeling of my emotions billowing out, spreading me thin, pushing at the seams of my being, was beginning to get too much.

Keep it on lock. In and out. In and out.

Besides the single declaration that I was under arrest for killing my husband, there hadn't been much else said to me. They didn't even read me my Miranda rights.

Every time I tried to call for someone, I was met with silence. On the off chance a cop passed by and I yelled for them, they would just yell back at me and tell me to shut up and sit back down.

I was starting to feel like the dream I had with some sort of premonition, warning me that the times I had with Quinn were about to be over.

"Fuck it all!" I growled and kicked at the bars.

"Hey! Keep it down in there!" a faceless guard yelled from down the hall.

His voice bounced off the walls, reminding me just how alone I was in there.

"This isn't right!" I yelled back, letting my anger and frustration get the better of me. "You and I both know that there are ways things like this are handled in this country. We have to keep people like me—"

"I told you to shut up!" he yelled back.

"Why don't you come make me?"

I didn't have it in me to regret what I said even as he stormed down the hallway.

"Listen here, you bitch—"

"You listen here," I spat. As he stepped toward the cell, I took a step back. He fumbled for his keys, angrily trying to find the right one.

This was it. I could find a way out of this. If it was just this one single stupid cop, I could find my way out of this.

"There is a due process to this sort of thing. You can't just *randomly* arrest someone and throw them in a cell without even having a chance to call their lawyer."

He let out a bitter laugh as he finally found one of the keys. "A lawyer? You really think you're gonna get a fucking lawyer here?"

"Clint," another voice said from the end of the hallway. The policemen froze before looking down at the two other policemen that were storming down the hall.

Dammit, I cursed internally. *I could take one stupid cop, I couldn't take three.*

"We'll take it from here," the policeman said, sending a pointed glare at Clint. The other policemen said something and motioned for Clint to open the door. "Clint, you can help me."

He seemed almost as surprised as I was to realize that both of them would be escorting me. It was obvious that there was something going on here. This wasn't a normal arrest, and my fate lies in the hands of these two.

I walked all the way back until my knees hit the stone bench I had been sitting on.

"Come on, let's get this over with," the policeman barked, and they all filtered into my cell.

"*Don't* you touch me," I growled. My protest didn't stop them. They charged.

I tried to run forward, ducking under their hands, but there were too many clawing at me. I may have gotten under the second and the first, but the third was close behind, grabbing my wrists and forcing them behind my back.

"Stay still," one of them growled. The cold metal of the handcuffs fastening around my wrists caused me to jerk against them.

I kicked and fought as they pushed me out of the cell.

"I told you I wanted to call my lawyer," I growled as two policemen escorted me down the hallway.

"For the last time," the cop growled. "Shut the *fuck* up."

It was a short walk from the cells to a dim hallway with marked doors on either side of us. They ranged from one to six, the shine from the metal letters on their door had worn off with age.

When they tried to push me into one, I fought again and attempted to scream, but a hand was placed over my mouth.

"Don't make this harder for yourself," one of them spat in my ear. "I don't know what he wants with you, but once he gets it, he promised that we could do *whatever* we wanted with you."

My blood ran cold.

He? Who the fuck is he?

I wanted to ask, but I couldn't, not as they opened the door and forced me into it.

The room was completely dark as they slammed the door behind me. There was someone else in there. Someone I could feel in the darkness but couldn't quite see yet.

They were waiting, watching in a way that made my skin crawl.

"I want my lawyer," I repeated, my wrists straining against the cuffs as I tried to jerk my arms free.

A huff of laughter came from the darkness causing me to freeze. Light flooded the room as if on cue. I had to blink my eyes a few times to clear the spots, but when I finally did, time stopped.

What the fuck?

"She could have done better at trying to hide you if she really cared," Senator Bennett said as he stood from his seat. He straightened his suit jacket and walked around the table, his dress shoes echoing through the room. "I have some questions that I would like you to answer."

He looked far too dressed to be in a place like this and stood out like a sore thumb.

"Sir?" I asked, taking a startled step back.

What the hell was he doing here? This wasn't him coming to bail me out or something?

I hadn't paid close attention to the map, but I knew we were nowhere near New York.

We had been driving for *days,* sometimes through the night, only to stop for a few hours to get some sleep. There was *no way* he could have gotten so close to me in such a short amount of time.

Not only that... who the fuck was *he* to get involved in something like this? If anyone, I expected my boss to come or someone who had been in charge of the people watching me for my entire time in witness protection... but the senator?

There was no good reason as to why he should be here.

Was *he* the person the policemen were referring to?

"First, I should thank you," he said with a bitter laugh. "Who would have thought you would go as far as to kill Russell? I had tried many times to do it myself, but he always had too many men around him. Maybe I should have hired you instead."

I swallowed thickly. I had so many questions but had no idea which one to start with.

"How?"

He raised a brow at me. "How did I know you killed him or how did I know him? Be concise with your questions, Tiffany. I may be here to get this settled, but I won't indulge you for long."

His harshness caused a wave of nausea to run through me. I've gotten a bad vibe from him for months now... but never in a million years did I ever guess that he would be tied to Russell.

"Both."

He let out a sigh and ran his hands down his suit, chasing away the wrinkles that had formed. He was so casual about something so mind altering that it caused my hackles to rise.

Whoever this man had pretended to be... it was becoming increasingly clear that he was the opposite.

He was dangerous. *Dirty.* He had a lot of money to control whoever he wanted, but how far was he willing to go?

Far enough to try and kill Russell, my brain shot at me.

"Because I had people watching you and the other... I guess

you should be addressing me as your father-in-law," he said, a small smile spreading across his face. "Though, if I'm being honest, I tried everything in my power to make sure that connection would never be made public. And when I found out you were in the Secret Service?" He let out an exaggerated huff. "It was too good a chance to pass up."

I was going to barf. I couldn't believe it, but then, slowly, I started to see the features he and Russell shared.

"You wanted your own son dead?" I asked, horror rooting in my stomach.

"His mother was a whore I paid for a single night," he said with a shrug, as if his words were not as awful as they were. "If I am going to be the next president, I can't have an illegitimate son running out there, assistant to a wannabe warlord no less. Fucking nuisance. You know, people should be glad that I'm cleaning up the trash like this."

"But I—"

"Enough. Next question," he said. "I heard a rumor that you have a very handy USB on you. I need to know where it is and who knows about what you have on there."

Jonson's words hit me like a truck.

Alec's group is so intertwined with the FBI that every time I tried to get a case going, it would lead nowhere.

It was never the FBI that kept putting a stop to this... it was *him*.

The door opened behind me. I whipped around, hoping to God it was Quinn, but instead I found myself face-to-face with Ryan.

All the times I had seen him so scared of the senator now made sense. He was never just a secret service agent.

"You fucking rat!" I hissed at him. His eyes stayed firm on the senator, not even looking in my direction. The dismissal caused anger to shoot through me.

I took a step to the side, not wanting to be in between the two men.

How the fuck am I going to get out of this?

Thoughts whirled around my head. I imagined diving for Ryan's gun. I could take one, maybe two down... but then what?

What about those three that were probably waiting outside for me?

"Do you need assistance, sir?" Ryan asked, his eyes finally looking over at me before darting to the man behind me.

Assistance? Assistance with what?

"Hold her for me."

His hands gripped my arms with enough force to pull a whine from me. He was too fast for me to even think of dodging. I bucked against him, trying to throw him off, but his grip was so tight that I couldn't keep it up for long.

"Ryan? What the fuck—"

The senator gripped my chin, forcing me to look at him. His slimy fingers caused a shiver of disgust to run through me.

"Tell me where it is, and I'll let you out of here alive," he said. A smile spread across his face, showing me a dazzling set of teeth.

Just like Russell, he was a monster with an innocent mask that caused everyone around him to relax. No one could feel the darkness lingering beneath his skin unless you were looking for it. No one could feel just how disgusting his touch could feel unless you knew how much blood the hands were stained with.

How did I not see it before?

"I fucking doubt that," I hissed at him. His grip on my jaw caused the entire lower half of my face to throb with pain. "What do you think you can do, huh? Kill me? If so, you'll never get what you want, and I have no intention of bowing down to shit like *you*."

His nostrils flared, and he jerked back like he had been punched in the face. He pushed my face to the side with a noise of disgust.

"God, I hate your generation," he huffed. "All suicidal idiots from the moment you're born."

"Or maybe it's just that your bastard son made my life so fucking horrible that I have nothing to live for anymore," I spat.

"Not true," Ryan said from behind me. "Your girlfriend is currently getting decommissioned by her handler for failure to complete her job. What if we can put a stop to it?"

The world froze around me. An elephant felt like it was sitting on my chest. *Decommissioned.* I swallowed thickly.

"What does that mean?" I asked, my voice just above a whisper.

"It means they're going to put a bullet in between her eyes and dissolve her body in acid," the senator said with an amused grin. "You know how it is in her world. The less evidence, the better."

"She's not my girlfriend," I said, locking my gaze with him. I willed him to look into my eyes. To see a truth that wasn't there.

"No?" he asked, cocking his head to the side in an exaggerated act of disbelief. "I could have sworn I'd seen footage of the two of you fucking *multiple* times. On top of that, both of you were obviously fleeing—"

"You disgusting son of a bitch—"

"Ah, ah," he said with a laugh. "Let's play nice, huh?"

I gritted my teeth to stop the curses from falling from my mouth.

"How do I know you're telling the truth?" I asked after a while.

"Better than the alternative, isn't it?" he said and motioned for Ryan to leave. "I'll give you an hour to decide. Let's hope she's not dead by then."

QUINN

Searing pain ripped through my body as the bullet embedded itself into my shoulder.

I bit back my scream as I fell to my knees in front of Rolf.

"How the *fuck* did you think this was okay?" Rolf spat at me.

Panic was clear as day in his wide eyes. The heaviness of the men's stares in the back of the room weighed on me.

Was he doing this to humiliate me before he killed me?

I wouldn't put it past him, but what I didn't know was who the *hell* those people were.

At first I thought they were some of ours, but the twisting of Rolf's face as they forced me into the warehouse had me thinking otherwise.

"You're seriously asking me that? You think I'd just sit here and be your puppet for as long as I lived?" I forced out through gritted teeth.

Blake and I were fucked. Plain and simple.

The worst possible outcome had manifested itself. It's like the universe didn't want either of us to leave our old lives behind. Like the universe had been conspiring against us, making it so neither of us would get the freedom we so craved.

I knew the risks from the start, but I had believed too much in myself. Believed that the people we were fighting against were too stupid.

"I gave you everything," he spat. "I gave you a *life*. I gave you the *freedom* to do whatever the fuck you wanted. The only thing you had to do was keep doing jobs for me!"

"The only thing I had to do?" I scoffed at his audacity. "You were going to have me decommissioned... *are* going to have me decommissioned." I gave him a pointed look.

"You know I never wanted to do this," he said, his eyes shifting to the floor.

"You seemed pretty damn sure that *this is* what you wanted to do when you were on the phone with me," I reminded.

"Because you fucked this up for all of *us*," he said in a harsh whisper. "If I would have known that *that* was what you were doing when you were getting the money, I would have tried to talk some fucking sense into you, but look at us now!"

"Look at us?" I asked with a huff. "Look at *you*. You could have let me go. You could have let me walk away. You and I both know it has taken more resources for you to scramble to try and find me. Something I'm sincerely surprised about because I know your record for tracking and it fucking sucks."

He puffed up like he was ready to explode.

"I had help," he said.

"Help from who?" I asked. He shook his head angrily.

"I wouldn't be doing this if the client wasn't so fucking pissed," he grumbled under his breath. "I told you it would be bad for us all if you attempted this."

Confusion and anger swept through me. I leaned to the side, looking back at the men and desperately trying to ignore the pain radiating from the gunshot wound.

He hadn't hit anything vital. *He hadn't hit anything vital.* That had to mean something.

"The client is *dead*," I said, looking back at him. "Don't tell me you *weren't* watching the headlines before they got pulled.

Her husband is gone, and from the looks of it, Alec Crowe won't be coming for her any time soon. He wouldn't care about a lackey enough to come after us."

There was a hunch. A feeling in my gut that turned sour as soon as we walked away from his mangled body. I didn't want to believe it. I wanted to live in the delusion that we had single-handedly killed the person who was making our lives so difficult.

The way his grip on the gun tightened only made me more sure of my feelings.

The people watching us were not a part of our organization. *They were the clients.* So the people that took me and Blake were the same. I watched them, tried to fight them off as they swarmed the diner. But there were just too many of them.

Blake had been loaded up into a cop car, me into an all-black windowless van. The difference in how they treated us gave me a good fucking idea about what our fate was.

Little Blake had too many people who would miss her. Too many secrets in that pretty head of hers that would go to waste.

On the other hand, I was a dangerous loose end that needed to be dealt with.

And who better than Rolf?

Rolf looked back into the warehouse and at the men who were watching us. He had this nervous tic. His hands would twitch whenever his panic was starting to take over his senses.

Just like now.

These weren't our fucking men. Rolf was in the same position as I was, and at the mercy of our client. *Because that had to be who sent them, right?*

The client was pissed, was what he uttered.

In that moment, I saw Rolf in a different light.

Up until now, I had felt like my surrogate father had been slowly betraying me. Had been ready to decommission me as soon as I fucked up and tried to work me over until exhaustion.

But as he turned toward me, his face pinched with stress and a frown marring his face, I could see the weight of the client behind him. I could see just how much he didn't want to do this. See just how much power they had over him.

"Leave me to say my goodbyes. I have things to say that are not for your ears," he ordered them. There was a pause, two of the men looked to the far right at the leader.

He was silent for a moment before he paused and motioned for his men to leave.

"You get three minutes," he said and followed them out.

As soon as they left, Rolf leaned down, his expression taking a turn.

"I need you to listen to me carefully," he said, reaching behind me to undo the ties on my wrists. "There is an exit out back, you need to sprint there. My car is a block away—" He fished out his keys from his pocket and pushed them into my hand. "Tiffany is at the police station two miles down the road. Senator Bennett is probably already—"

"Senator Bennett?" I echoed, grasping the cool metal of his car keys in my palm. My mind was whirling.

"He's the client, Quinn," he said. His crazed movements stopped, and he gave me a look that was so full of sorrow it caused my heart to drop into my stomach. "Listen, Quinn, one last thing..."

"Last thing?" I asked with a disbelieving laugh. "What the hell do you think you are doing?"

"I am *saving* you," he hissed. "I'm sorry for bringing you into this life. It wasn't fair to you."

"You saved me," I said, forcing us both to our feet. "Without you, who knows who they would have sold me to. I was mad you were trying to decommission me, but I always knew without you, I'd be much worse off."

His brows pulled together as his hand cupped my face.

"I didn't save you, Quinn," he said. "I *stole* you. Kidnapped you from your parents because I saw the chance to mold you into something useful for the guild. I'm sorry."

I didn't have time to digest the information before he pulled me into a bone-crushing hug. *Why was everyone giving me hugs as my heart threatened to break?*

"This is me repaying you," he said and pushed me away. He sent me a forced smile and readied his gun. "I know I fucked up, but believe me when I tell you that you became an important part of my life."

I took a shaky step back. I tried to clamp down on the emotional tidal wave that was running through my body and force it into the darkness like I always had. But I couldn't stop the grief from showing on my face.

"Run, Quinn," he whispered and readied his gun.

I turned on my heels, casting one last glance at the man who raised me, and ran out the door and into the cold night.

There was a slight hill on the way back. My lungs burned with the pressure it took deliver air to them. Pain clouded my mind. Deep breathes and the knowledge of Blake waiting for me kept me going.

It took a few more minutes at my pace to find the car, but it was there like he promised. And then, I heard the single gunshot.

"Damn it, Rolf," I hissed, forcing the car door open.

Pain radiates through my mind as I stalk through the police station. Blood was dripping down my arm and to the floor, the sound of the droplets following me as I went.

I tried to block out the pain. Tried to force my brain to focus on the task at hand. I had done it time and time again, but this time panic was infused with the pain.

Calm yourself. Push it away. Think of her.

It wasn't hard, not when the thought of what they could be doing to Blake was taking over my mind. I tried not to focus on Rolf's face when he pushed me toward the exit. Tried not to think of how bad my chest hurt when I heard that single gunshot ring out.

For him, for Blake. I'll make them pay.

The single cop manning their front desk was fast asleep as I approached.

Rage was boiling under my skin so powerfully that I didn't have to even think about what my next steps were.

My footsteps were silent as I crossed the floor, maneuvered around the desk, and grabbed his tie before looping it around his neck and giving it a hard yank. My other hand came to cover his nose and mouth as he struggled.

The jerks of his body sent fresh pain shooting through me. I had to stifle my groan when he gave a particularly powerful jerk.

It took all of two minutes before he slumped into the chair, but I didn't let up for another few until I was sure he was dead. I stole his gun from him, along with his taser.

You would think the senator brought more backup than this.

Just as the thought passed through my head, a figure stepped in the room. They froze, allowing me enough time to use the taser on him. His body jerked, his scream got caught in his throat as he convulsed.

His body fell to the ground in seconds. I tied the dead man's tie tight against the trigger, knowing that he would be dead before I came back.

I wanted them to hurt. I wanted to hear them scream for taking what was mine.

But I also needed to reel myself in enough to get her back.

I thought of her face as she was taken out of the diner. How blood trailed down her neck, the head wound from a few days ago reopening.

How dare they?

I walked the hallway, peering into every room I could find.

All of them were empty. I paused when the sound of voices hit my ears. I walked slowly toward it, noting that it came from an interrogation room.

"One more chance." Senator Bennett's voice came from the closed room. "I'll call it off right now. Just tell me where the USB is."

Shit. I gripped the gun in my hand tightly. *What would they do when they realized we didn't have it anymore?*

"I need it to be written," Blake said. "I need to be assured that she won't die."

The senator let out a hard laugh. "Really, this is what you choose to waste time on?"

There was no answer.

"Go get a paper or something."

There was a shuffling, and the door was pushed open. I barely had time to step away, the metal of the door brushing across my skin.

A secret service agent looked me in the eyes, his hand already going to his gun.

But mine was faster.

The sound of the shot echoed throughout the hallway. All light left the man's eyes, and he fell to the ground at my feet, his blood coating my front. Without him in the way, I saw Blake sitting there, her hands behind her back, and Senator Bennett on the other side of the table, leaning forward with a devilish smile spreading across his face.

"So happy you can join us," he said. "Why don't you—"

Blake stood, bringing her arms from behind her, only one of the cuffs hanging on her wrist. The other was bruised and swollen, but she used both of them to grip the back of his hair and slam his face into the metal table.

Fucking deadly and beautiful.

I have never fallen more in love with someone than I did when I saw the look of joy on her face and the sound of his bones cracking filling the air.

How could I have been so lucky?

He let out a groan and pushed himself up, only for me to cross the room, put my hand on Blake's, and shove his face back down into the counter.

His body went limp, but I didn't care. All I cared about in that moment was seeing Blake's face.

"I'm sorry I'm late," I whispered, taking in her bruised and bloodied face.

I would pay back the rest of the guards in kind whenever I found them.

Her eyes fell to my bloodied shoulder, and she let out a gasp.

"Quinn, you're shot!"

I grabbed her hand to stop it from coming down on the wound. She just had to have gone and ruined her dominant hand, huh?

Another reason to make the man below me hurt.

"And you broke your hand," I said, lifting it up for her to see.

"Fractured, maybe," she said, giving me a smile that caused my chest to lighten.

"Let's get out of here," I said and stepped away from the unconscious man.

"Where are you taking me?" she asked.

"*Home.*" I wanted to live in the moment as we smiled at each other. I wanted to swoop her in my arms and kiss her pain away, but the telltale signs of men walking down the hall stirred me.

"After this," I added with my hand on my gun. Her eyes locked onto the dead agent blocking the doorway, a smile spreading across her face.

"Mind if I help?" she asked, the most wicked, sexiest grin crossing her face.

I had never been more turned on in my life.

"Fuck ya you can help," I said and pulled her close to deliver a quick, but burning kiss to her mouth. "I love you."

"I love you more," she whispered against me before diving to the dead agent and stealing his gun.

I was almost too stunned by her words to move. Heat traveled up my face.

She said she loved—

My thoughts were interrupted by her shooting down the hallway.

"Come on, lover girl, you promised me a home."

I couldn't help but laugh.

That I did. And I would deliver. It didn't matter if it was only two police men out there, or twenty I would make damn sure that she got the happy ending she deserved.

Epilogue
Four Months Later

Hands grabbed me. Forcing me to the ground. Pain radiated through my entire left side.

Their laughs echoed through my head. Taunting me.

I tried to break out of their hold, but I couldn't. Just like then, I was powerless.

I opened my mouth to scream but no words came out.

Please stop. Please, let me go. Words I had said over and over again, but they fell on deaf ears.

Please. Please—

I sat up with a painful gasp.

Sweat poured down my face, the covers pooling at my hips. My eyes darted around the room, trying their hardest to find any of the devils that may have followed me out of the dream and into the real world.

But there was none.

Instead, I was met with light-colored wood. Splashes of blue wallpaper. And the sound of waves crashing somewhere in the distance.

Quiet.

I let myself revel in it, just like Quinn had taught me. To listen to the world Letting it remind me that I was no longer in danger.

I took a deep breath. The not-so-stale scent of Quinn filled my senses.

Knowing that she was somewhere near helped the panic die down just enough for me to swing my legs over the bed, my feet coming into contact with the cold floors.

I could feel her here. Her presence was unmistakable.

I followed the hallway out onto the living room. White couches with blue blankets

and splashes of yellow hit me, but there was no gloomy assassin waiting for me.

Then I saw a movement right outside the window.

A smile pricked at my lips.

I walked out onto the porch and of course, Quinn was there. She spread out lazily on the outdoor couch, a coffee in her hands, mine set aside on the small side table next to her.

She met me with a smile, her dark hair falling messily over her face.

Just like every morning in the remote beach town, I felt my breath caught. Every time I saw her, I still couldn't believe how lucky I was to find her. How lucky I was to have been able to create a life of my own with her.

"You should have woken me," I said, sitting next to her, making sure I could lean against her heated skin.

She handed me my coffee before placing a kiss on my messy bedhead.

"It's an important day," she reminded a smile in her tone. "I wanted to make sure you got enough rest."

I leaned into her, delivering a kiss to her throat. She let out a breathy sigh.

"And you?" I asked letting my tongue tease her skin. "Are you *nervous*?"

She let out a laugh that caused my skin to heat.

"*Excited*," she whispered. "And a bit turned on to see you covered in blood again."

Images of *that night* flashed through my mind. How she rubbed the blood into my skin. Her tongue traced patterns in my thigh.

"They are there, right?" I asked, nervousness creeping up on me. I squeezed the ceramic mug the warm liquid inside doing nothing to calm my racing heart.

"Yep," she said, taking a sip of her coffee. "Exactly where they said they were."

"*All* of them?" I asked.

Quinn delivered a kiss to the top of my head.

"All six," she confirmed.

Relief and excitement ran through me. *This was my chance.*

Before settling down at the cottage, I thought that I would be able to leave my life behind. I thought that maybe after killing my husband, I would be able to forget the life that I lived with him... but instead, it showed up in the weirdest way.

I still had the nightmares every once in a while, but now instead of the fear... I felt guilt. Because each painful memory from that time may have been in *my* past, but I wasn't the only person forced to those monster's side.

Maybe it was because, for the first time in my life, I had an expansive future in front of me. One that I could do anything with. One that had a person next to me who would stop at nothing to make my dreams a reality.

No matter how bloody they were.

"Thank you," I said, pulling away from her to send her a grateful smile.

"Anything for you, baby," she said, her voice dropping into a low murmur. "I'll be there the entire time, watching, and making sure no one stands in your way."

I'm such a lucky girl to have the perfect, murderous girlfriend willing to put her life on the line for me.

"I love you," I whispered, and just like every other time her eyes widened and a light brush of blush covered her cheeks. This was the only time *I* could render her speechless and I drank in every moment of it.

At first, I hadn't been able to say it, but now that I delivered the lines more often than her, it was her turn to be caught off guard by them.

"And I you, little agent," she said. "More than I ever thought possible."

I let us sit in the warmth of our conversation. Committing that moment to memory. The smell of the sea. The feeling of her skin against mine. The look of her hair splayed out messily around her face.

Because of her, I would finally see the end of this.

"Three men, just outside the dining hall." Quinn's voice came in a low whisper from the communicator set up between us. "You're clear."

I took a deep breath as I turned the corner of the dimly lit house the Crowe's called their home base. It was large enough to keep the entirety of his main men as well as their wives and a few small children.

Many of the men were meeting for dinner, the women were banished until they needed them for their entertainment later.

This plan had taken months to figure out and weeks in just waiting for the right time. A time when all the men were preoccupied while the women were all in one place, the kids away from the house.

"Jonson has the children," Quinn said. "We are all set to proceed."

A weight lifted from my shoulders.

Three children, one barely a year old. They would no doubt become the casualties if we were not careful.

I knew the place like the back of my hand. After years of violently weaving through the same place, it was easy to find the "preparation room" they gave to the wives.

I listened to their murmured voices from the outside, my heartbeat thrumming in my ear.

"Going in," I whispered to Quinn.

When I heard one I recognized, I quickly pushed into the room.

Small gaps met my ears when I slipped in.

I turned to the group, pulling my face mask down so they could identify me, but paused when I realized that I only recognized *two* of the women I had been with all those years ago.

Amy and Lauren. Both were standing huddled together as if I had just interrupted their plan. The other four were sitting on the couches at the back of the room, staring at me with wide eyes.

"It's Tiffany," I whispered. Amy was the first to break out of her stupor and step forward.

"No," she breathed. "I thought he killed you!"

Lauren pushed past her, running at me with her arms wide. When our bodies collided, guilt exploded in me.

These girls had to suffer through the consequences of me leaving. Not only that but even after all the years I was gone, they *still* remembered me.

They remembered while I had the privilege to forget.

"You have to get out of here," Amy said, pulling Lauren from me. "You were lucky to get away last time. This time you won—"

"You're coming with me," I said quickly and looked back to the women huddled at the back of the room. "*All* of you. I have friends helping. Securing the children. All that's needed is for you to follow me."

Fear, plain as day, flashed across Lauren's face.

"No," she whispered, horror feeling her tone. "You don't know what they would do to us if they found out. To my baby."

My heart ached for her. I had been there. I had been paralyzed by my own fear and unable to move on until it was literally life or death.

"I have everything ready for you," I said. "I will protect *all* of them. You don't need to fear them."

"Hurry it up," Quinn ordered through the communicator.

I looked around the room, spotting the back window that was opened slightly.

They didn't even have locks this time around.

"Out the window," I said and pushed them to it. "Quickly. I will explain once we leave the house but please—" I pulled Amy back, looking her in the eyes. "*Please* trust me."

Amy swallowed thickly, before looking toward the other girls.

"Looks like our plans have been moved up," she said, a sly smile spreading across her face. "Get your shit."

That was all they needed to spring into action. Lauren and the others darted toward the small corners of the room, lifting pots and pulling up the cushions. Each of them found a small, well-hidden bag full of what I could only assume were bare necessities for their escape.

"You were already planning?" I breathed, awe filling me.

Amy gave me a look.

"For years," she admitted giving me a look. "You think I was just waiting here for a knight in shining armor to rescue me?" I floundered for a response and she elbowed me lightly. "You do look pretty good for my knight though."

The door burst open, causing the girls to pause.

"I knew you bitches were up to no good," a man's voice said from behind me.

I turned, grabbing the gun from the holster on the back of my pants and aiming toward him.

But I had been too slow. He charged, hitting the gun out of my hand and knocking me to the ground with one push.

"Run! The window!" I commanded the girls.

I recognized the man. One from many years ago, though before he was but a foot soldier.

I didn't want to know what he did to get promoted.

I readied myself to attack only to see Quinn come up from behind him, her face clouded in shadows. Her blue eyes were in stark contrast to the rest of her and made her look like some sort of demon hiding behind him.

In one, smooth movement she dragged a shiny dagger across his throat and pushed him to the ground. Only then did I get a good look at her blood-splattered face.

She pulled down her face make, exposing her wicked grin to the world.

I shouldn't have been so turned on by her covered in blood... but I was.

Everything about her at that moment just reminded me how hard I fell for her in the first place.

"I told you I had your back, baby," she said and leaned down with her hand out.

I couldn't help but return her smile as she pulled me up.

"I never doubted you for a second," I said and turned back to the women. "Now let's get a move on. Just beyond those walls awaits a new life."

The same life I took my force. The same one that led me to Quinn.

And the one that I never trade for anything... no matter how sick and twisted we may have turned out.

BONUS EPILOGUE
BLAKE

It was surreal, seeing the club I once loved towering over me again.

When we had left, I had thought for sure I would never see it again, but Quinn still had some surprises up her sleeve.

"I can't believe you," I whispered sending her a smile.

She looked down at me, a smile playing on her lips. The top half of her face was covered by a mask, but her piercing blue eyes shone through, the broken pupils making it clear who she was.

Her hair fell around her face in light waves, longer than the last time we were here. Instead of wearing a suit, she wore a tight silk top that hugged her chest and laid neatly over her slacks.

I couldn't believe it. After being on the run for so long, I could finally get this part of my life back.

"We're not moving back," she said. "Too many prying eyes for that. But we can stop by every once in a while."

Even just that caused my heart to soar. To be able to come back to just visit was far more than I could ever ask for.

"Am I performing tonight?" I asked as she leads us into the house.

The guards at the door nod to us as we enter and instead of

the usual hostess coming to meet us, Sloan is there in all her might.

My heart twists at the sight of her. Her silver hair slicked back. Her maskless face gave me an unobstructed view of her pierced face. Pale skin with intricate black tattoos traveled up her neck and diapered into her button up.

She welcomes me with open arms. Quinn is the one who pushed me into them.

Sloan's hugs have always been warm, but that night they were especially so. Tears threatened to spill and an explosion of emotion ran through my chest.

"I missed you, Blake," Sloan said. "The club hasn't been the same without you."

"I missed you too," I said pulling away and looking up at her with a smile. "Sorry, I disappeared suddenly. I changed my number and—"

"No need to explain," Sloan said her hand coming to ruffle my hair. "Riley went ahead and let us know ahead of time."

I looked back to Quinn, shocked.

"When did you do that?" I asked. A smirk spread across her features.

"Right before we left," she said. "Couldn't have anyone get too worried about us now could we?"

"Speaking of which, you can tell me how the honeymoon was as I show you to our room for the night," Sloan said, pulling us further into the club.

Honeymoon?

I sent a look back and Quinn only to catch her wicked smirk.

"Blake Riley has a nice ring to it, doesn't it?" Quinn commented.

Sloan let out a laugh. "Now I *know* the story was fake. Blake would never take such a ridiculous name."

My face flamed.

"It's kinda nice," I mumbled under my breath.

I couldn't help but let my eyes linger around the club as Sloan let us through. People were so happy. Enjoying each other and having fun. I could feed off this energy for years it felt like.

I hadn't even noticed we had made it to the room until Sloan stopped at a door I'd never seen before.

"Ready to see our new addition?" she asked with a smirk.

"Should I be nervous?" I asked leaning back into Quinn for support. Her hands found their home and my hips, her lips near my ear.

"You'll enjoy this little agent," she whispered.

Sloan pushed open the door causing my breath to catch.

They had created a big, shared room. Blacks and reds were splashed around but the biggest sunken leather couch I had ever seen.

And it wasn't empty.

Ax was right in the middle, a drink in hand. Her honey hair brushed her collarbones. The paleness of her skin caused her honey eyes to shine that much brighter. She looked up to meet us as we walked in.

On her lap lay Nyx's head, her face flushed and her hair spread all around the couch. She was dressed in a tight dress that was pushed up to her hips and between her legs was Lillian on her knees, curly hair pulled back into a bun, and face in her pussy. She was dressed in a similar dress to Nyx, though hers was a deep blue, complimenting her taupe skin. The back had been pushed up, no doubt by Sloan at some point, and showed her bare ass.

She didn't pause her efforts as we came in, but Sloan let out a breathy chuckle.

"Keeping our girls entertained, Ax?" Sloan called and ushered us in before shutting the door behind her.

"They couldn't keep their hands to themselves," Ax said, her tone hard. "They were too excited about our guest."

Normally the tone would scare me, but there was something in it that caused my body to heat.

Just the thought of me made them like that?

"Fashionably late, Quinn?" called a voice from our right. I didn't have time to prepare myself as a body brushed against us.

I turned my head to see Avery wrapping her arms around us, her face pushing against Quinn's.

"You don't care for rules do you?" she hissed but I noticed she didn't push her away.

"Nope," she said with a light laugh. "Blake, have you met Willow? She and I have this thing we want to try tonight and I —"

"Let's not get too excited," Ax called from the couch, her sharp tone causing all chatter to cease. "Continue," she told Lillian as she paused to look up at her. Ax's hand pushed Nyx's top down her fingers teasing her erect nipples.

Heat flared through me as Nyx's moans filled the room.

Yes. This was what I had been waiting for.

"Right, right," Avery said and pulled away from us. She pushed her wavy blonde hair out of her face and gave us an apologetic smile. "Willow is running late but she will—*Ah.*"

The change in Avery's tone caused us all to look back at the opening door. Willow I assumed, I believe I saw her once, slipped in, and closed the door behind her. Her long auburn hair cascaded down her back, even longer than the short pleather skirt she wore. On top was nothing but a see-through bralette.

"You look positively fuckable tonight," Avery cooed, closing the space between them. Avery forced her hand between Willow's thighs causing her to gasp before pulling out a wet bullet vibrator. "You got my present."

Sloan cleared her throat.

"Rules, yes?" she said stepping away from the group. "Ground rules, hard stops, and then we can commence with welcoming our favorite plaything back into the club."

Favorite plaything. Quinn's hands were warm as they traveled my sides.

"For you my little agent," she whispered. "Get excited."

Hands, mouths, all of them dancing over my skin and lighting me on fire.

I threw my head back, unable to keep the groan inside me.

"Oh she likes it," Nyx said with a light laugh.

"I've never been much of a top," Lillian said, her mouth by my ear and her hands coming around to pinch my nipples. "But there's something so sweet about how you react to our touches."

"Coming in." That was all the announcement I had before Sloan put a long red wand, right on my thigh. The click of the button was drowned out from my yelp as an electric shot went through me.

I jerked against them, unable to control my reaction. A mouth was on my nipple before I could bring myself back together. Then Lillian's hands were on my face, pulling my lips to hers.

My head was swimming with pleasure.

I could hear Avery and Willow to the side of me. Both had the chance to join when comfortable, but first, they were watching.

I didn't mind, if anything the extra eyes only fueled me.

Ax was in front of me, enjoying as her partner explored my body. Sloan and Lillian tagged teamed me, one teasing while the other delivered the pain.

And Quinn, she wasn't far. To my left, her eyes never leaving my body.

I could feel the weight of them on me, taking in as I was ravished by everyone.

This was the best welcome I could ever receive.

I locked eyes with said devil as Lillian was ravishing my mouth and Sloan delivered another stinging bolt of electricity straight to my cunt.

I almost keeled over from the shock of it but then Nyx's fingers were right over my clit rubbing away the pain.

Sloan delivered another shock to my nipple. When she pulled away Nyx pulled it into her mouth.

Lillian's tongue danced with mine. Her hand gripping my face so I could do nothing but kneel there, in the middle of the room, and take it.

"Come on ladies, lovely Willow finally decided she wants to play," Avery's voice said from above. Lillian pulled away, our spit following her and making her let out a light sigh.

"Quinn's taking my spot beautiful," Sloan said and delivered a kiss to the side of my face. "Shall I give her the wand?"

My eyes glanced to Lillian. Her lip was pulled between her teeth and there was a hooded look in her eyes as she watched Sloan.

"I think Lillian wants a turn," I said.

"Nyx," Ax called.

The group in front of me dispersed and we all watched as Ax patted her lap.

Nyx needed no other message to get her to run over and spread herself across Ax's legs.

"I'm spoiling you," Ax said, her hand diving between Nyx's legs. Nyx melted into her and spread her legs, giving me an unobstructed view of her pussy as Ax pushed two fingers into her.

Willow was pushed down on her knees in front of me, her eyes wide and her tanned skin flushed. Avery's hand was tangled in her hair and caused pain to flash across Willow's face.

God. The image went straight to my cunt. I was dripping from all the teasing.

"Willow has never done something like this before," Avery said. "So I'm thinking we can start slow. Quinn come fuck your little agent while I make her watch."

"Don't order me around you psychopath," Quinn muttered, her voice from close behind me. Avery's bright blue eyes flashed playfully.

When I met Willow's eyes I could tell we both had the same thought going on in our mind.

They're going to kill each other.

Avery kneeled down behind Willow, pushing up her skirt and putting her hands between her thighs. I couldn't make out what she was doing, but her little mewls from Willow's mouth gave me an idea.

"Are you having fun," Quinn whispered to me, her hands traveling my sides.

My body heat intensified and I couldn't help but shudder as her mouth came to leave an open, wet kiss on the side of my throat.

She was kneeling behind me, just like Avery, but when one hand disappeared only to reappear with a vibrator at my clit on high, I let out a panicked moan.

Willow's eyes widened at my noises.

"God you're clenching me so tight," Avery said with a laugh. "Does seeing poor little Blake tied up and fucked really turn you on that much?"

Avery continued fucking her, but inched Willow forward, almost as if egging her on to touch me.

My hands were still bound so I was unable to reach for her.

"Come on, no need to be shy," Avery said and used her free hand to guide Willow's to the vibrator in between my legs. "She's our toy to play with tonight."

"Not yours," Quinn spat out, obviously toward Avery.

The blonde-haired girl only let out a laugh. Willow took their distraction to take the vibrator from Quinn and push it harder into my clit.

"Oh f-fuck," I moaned, my breath catching in my throat.

My eyes traveled to Avery, she was taller than the both of us and even on her knees easily towered over both me and Willow. And she was staring right at Quinn.

"Someone's possessive," Avery sang.

Quinn's now free hand snapped forward to grab Avery's shirt, her back pushing into mine and pushing Willow and I closer. The small redhead let out a gasp.

I took a moment to search her face. To see if she liked what she was doing to me.

"Higher," I choked out.

A beautiful flush covered her face and with a few clicks the intensity soared.

I struggled against my impending orgasm, barely able to focus as my partner and Avery talked in muttered tones.

"You won't," Avery dared. "Even now you're neglecting your toy just to growl at me like a territorial dog."

"Not a toy," Quinn grunted and surprised me by pushing a dildo into my sopping cunt.

I couldn't hold in my gasp. She was fucking me with such ferocity that I couldn't stay still. I crumpled head-first into Willow.

"I can't," I choked out.

But Willow didn't respond, instead, she also let out a choked moan.

"That's more like it," Avery teased. "Let's see who can make them come first huh?"

"I'll win," Quinn grunted.

The competitiveness shouldn't have been such a turn-on as it was but it lit a completely different fire in me.

Willow and I were completely at their whims. No longer bothering to hide our reactions as they fucked us.

"Let's level the playing field, shall we?" Avery said with a chuckle and pushed Willow forward. "Sharing is caring."

The toy was tilted slightly and Willow's hips pushed forward so her cunt was also directly on the large bulbous head.

She was leaning into me, shaking against me as the vibrators tore through us.

Fuck. I was coming. So fast and powerful that I couldn't even let out a warning cry.

But the thing was... Willow wasn't far after.

Neither of us finished before Quinn growled, "Again."

"Shit, fuck, Avery I—" Willow's sentence ended on a whine.

We were sweaty, bodied sticking together and at the mercy of the two people behind us.

I was allowed one more orgasm before Sloan broke through my haze.

"Just fucking kiss already won't you?"

Both Willow and I perked up at just the right time to see a wicked grin spread across Avery's face.

"I'll fucking slit your throat in your sleep," Quinn threatened.

"You know just what to say to get me wet," Avery teased back. Her hand shot forward, tangling in Quinn's hair before Willow and I both watched as their faces collided.

The move caused us to squeeze even tighter together but they were tall enough that we could peer up to see their kiss.

Well... a sort of kiss. It was more like a fight than a kiss with teeth clashing together.

"Fuck I'm coming," Willow cried, pushing her head into my chest.

The image of Avery and Quinn kissing did something to me. Enough to push me closer to an orgasm but there was just one thing missing.

"No one's paying attention to our guest," Sloan said from the side. Quinn froze as Sloan's arms slithered between Willow and I to roll my nipples between her fingers.

"At least I can multitask," Avery said, pulling away from Quinn. "Her hand had kept a steady rhythm between Willow's thighs while it took that reminder for Quinn to push the dildo in and out of my cunt again.

No matter, I was basking in the attention. They were watching. They were touching. Everything was perfect, but the one thing missing...

I leaned my head back, meeting Quinn's gaze.

"I fucking love you," I said through my pants.

"And I love you, my spoiled little agent," she said with a smirk before leaning down to capture my lips in hers. Not only could I taste Avery on her, but Willow as well.

Club Pétale was a once-in-a-lifetime experience. It meant the world to me.

It was the first place I could be myself. The first place I could explore what I wanted without any shame and without fear.

The people here accepted me, *loved* me... and I loved them.

I had left the club with no idea that one day I would return to it. But one thing that I knew was this: No matter what, the club would be there for whoever is in need.

I just couldn't wait to see what the future of the club brought next. Maybe in time, I could be a part of it again too.

But until then, I would enjoy that night, filled with pleasure and the company of people who made me who I was and protected me when I needed them the most.

Thank you, Club Pétale.

THE END

Want more Club Pétale?

Check out my kickstarter for all new special editions!
Set to launch next sping!

Click here to get notified when the project goes live!

Continue the fun!

Ax & Nyx

Ex Bf's Mom

Lillian x Sloan

Step Sisters

Avery x Willow

Stalker "Student"

Quinn x Blake

Assassin x Target

Check out the entire series here!

Want exclusive NSFW art?

For NSFW DFM art (and other series) join my Patreon!
I also update my novellas on there every other week and they are the FIRST to get
ARCS of all my newest releases!

Check it out here or go to https://www.patreon.com/ellemaebooks

ACKNOWLEDGMENTS

I don't even know where to begin...

Club Pétale has been such an instrumental part of my career and a series I have loved deeply. I truly feel changed after being able to write these characters.

I used to joke that it was just "wlw smut" but it's honestly so much more than that. To me, and to you.

So thank you to my reader. Thank you to the characters. And thank you to anyone who has ever given my writing a chance.

About the Author

Eden Emory is a contemporary spicy pen name for Elle Mae. This pen name will mostly focus on spicy dark wlw romance that pushes the boundaries and incorporates troupes normally seen in f/m romance.

Eden Emory was born out of a want for more. More spice, more wlw, and even more smutty vibes with little to no plot.

Loved this book? Please leave a review!

For more behind the scene content, sign up for my newsletter at https://view.flodesk.com/pages/61722d0874d564fa09f4021b

𝕏 x.com/mae_books

instagram.com/edenrosebooks

goodreads.com/ellemae

Made in United States
Troutdale, OR
04/23/2024

19398258R00206